Castles
IN THE
Sand

Dallas White,
Book One

SUSAN RODGERS

This book is an independent part of the Drifters universe.
Join the *Drifters* family by signing up at **www.susanrodgersauthor.com**.
As a welcome gift I'll send you a free bonus/deleted chapter from book
one of the *Drifters* series, *A Song For Josh*.

Happy reading!

Contents

Prologue

*B*y the time Dallas White was delivered in a black SUV to the backstage area of his Seattle concert, a steady stream of folks were picking their way through spattered raindrops over the graveled VIP lot toward the metal fences of the main gate.

Double time, longish sandy-blond hair bouncing, Dallas hopped up the metal steps into his designated RV and pulled a cold beer out of the fridge. Twisting off the bottle cap, with a bent elbow and a pronounced snap of a thumb and forefinger he sent it flying through the narrow kitchen. The cap spun its way across the floor and skittered to a definitive stop against the closed screen door. Making a mental note to pick it up later, Dallas watched it settle before he whipped around, strode to the far end of the RV, and dropped his athletic body down into a cushioned easy chair.

After guzzling back a first satisfying taste of the cool, crisp brew, he fixed a wary eye on the gray outdoors and watched his fans pile in. A tinted window perfect for spying spanned the camper's width. Dallas had an advantage over his fans—he could see out, but they couldn't see in.

One gal caught his eye—a redheaded woman. Maybe thirty-five, her plump country girl apple cheeks were pinked up with joy. Fingers twined through her guy's larger ones, she was swinging his hand as they strolled along. Her man was an average sort, slightly rotund in the belly as if he enjoyed his woman's apple pies a little too often, *likely with dollops of whipped cream or ice cream overtop,* Dallas caught himself thinking, recalling that his mother's home cooked meals on the distant Alberta ranch he grew up on were always punctuated with hefty desserts. The guy outside was jolly, and apparently funny. His plump redhead had to stop to adjust a camp chair slung over her shoulder, she was laughing so hard.

Dallas slumped deep into his chair and tried to quell a growing nausea. A second long pull on his beer did nothing to help. He was trembling, too. A few short hours ago a light tremor had started his body quaking from the inside out. It was as if a big hand had reached inside, twisted his gut, and given him a good shake. He felt like one of those bobble headed dolls people put on their car dashboards—out of control, at the mercy of everyone's staring eyes, left to shiver and vibrate.

Today his stomach hurt worse than most days. Less than two hours ago a big ole needle got scratched across his record, its high-pitched *zzziiippp* putting the brakes on Dallas' desire to stay on the music biz treadmill, to keep fighting the good fight. The needle was dropped by Deborah, Dallas' fiancée—*well, ex-fiancée now*, Dallas told himself, taking another hard look outside the tinted window of the RV. Two young girls were now outside joining the VIP lineup, their denim cutoffs so short that Dallas averted his eyes. Disgusted with the girls for choosing outfits for his show that concerned him, he was also deeply sorry for being the magnet that highlighted their sleazy choices in the first place. *They're too young for Daisy Dukes*, he thought. The admonishment was accompanied by an inward growl. *You're showing your age, old man.*

Dallas switched to a new track. A track his own age. *Deborah. Now there's a woman who can wear short denim cutoffs to a country music show. Old enough to know what kind of trouble they can get her into, and mature enough to handle it.* Dallas' mind strayed to what Deb usually wore above the shorts…*a plaid shirt, unbuttoned and tied above her navel…*

Not that Dallas' favorite shirt of Deborah's, her red one, was tied over her tight abs two hours ago. In fact it was the first thing Dallas' eyes had picked out in the dim light of his hotel room after returning from a scheduled rendezvous with local media. It was on the floor, a rumpled mess.

At first Dallas' eyes had brightened. *Ahhh, Deborah and her games, always ready to strip down and greet me from the bed, sometimes under the covers, most times on top.* She was a vixen, that one, all curvy southern grace, seemingly uncomplicated and always ready for a little fun.

"Or a lot of fun," he muttered in wry remembrance.

So down to earth was Deborah that apparently it had been nothing for her to casually invite a friend over for a romp on the bed this morning. Dallas' good friend Cole, in fact. In Dallas' hotel room. While Dallas was otherwise occupied.

The explicit sounds of their betrayal had caught Dallas off guard two seconds after he eyed Deb's shirt on his floor. Even now he couldn't shake her moans or Coles' grunts. Dallas' brain had immediately detonated into a fractured fire engine red; his ripped body exploded into instant motion. Cole's prized heritage Gibson guitar was reclining against an antique sofa. The sofa survived. The guitar did not. It ended up in pieces, some in Dallas' now ex-friend's butt.

Deborah's private security, a young muscled Asian man stationed outside Dallas' hotel room door, had vaulted inside and rescued Deborah. Cole, who Dallas always figured for a wuss when it came to real action, wasn't in need of rescue. He didn't even bother grabbing his jeans when he leapt over the sofa on his way out. To the startled amusement of another singer on tonight's bill, a rookie gal who caught the unscripted action while waiting for the elevator, Dallas threw the remains of the guitar into the hallway behind Cole's retreating ass. A mess of strings and tainted wood, the Gibson came to rest up against the wall, its music eternally silenced, its songs forever lost.

Afterward, the closer Dallas got to the concert grounds the more the angry red in his brain morphed into a vintage claret red, then into a sort of light cranberry red, and then into a more sorrowful mushed-up strawberry kind of red. Now, in the RV, it was a pale, drained red.

And it was quickly becoming a defeated little girl pink.

A long drag on the beer bottle, and Dallas wiped his plaid shirtsleeve across his mouth. Sucking in small breaths, panting almost as he pressed a thumb and forefinger to the outer edges of his eyes, he didn't move his gaze from the window. His eyes latched onto a family just beyond the dusty metal gate that divided the backstage area from the concertgoers. A mom, a dad, a young son, a small daughter. Clinging to her mother's hand, the girl was playfully stomping her mini cowboy boots in the dirt, showering gravel up into the air like fireworks.

3

The way Dallas' stomach clenched at the sight of the little family was far, far worse than the disemboweling wrought by Deborah's deception. It was just on the other end of the spectrum of hurt, that's all.

Like a plague, a deep sadness settled in Dallas' tired soul. He thumped the beer bottle down hard on a nearby table, which protested his frustration with a small shudder.

"Old man," he growled at himself, jumping up and grabbing another beer. "You're on the back side of forty now. You may as well wipe that empty dream off your slate. You gave up the only family you ever had years ago, when you traded in life on your dad's ranch for music. What'd that get you? Huh? Lonely. That's what."

He pictured his mom and dad back in Cochrane, Alberta. Today was Sunday. They'd be gathering the clan for dinner—Dallas' brother, sister, their sprouting youngsters, their forever loves. Not for the first time in recent years, Dallas' heart hurt at the simplicity of it all, of what he was missing while he chased his crazy music dream.

A hard knock startled him. The sharp hammer of boots hurrying up metal steps followed it. A door opened and closed; a hollow echo across the RV's floor announced the presence of Dallas' manager, Phil. Dallas had to turn away so the wiry, wise guy wouldn't notice the moist brightness of his eyes.

"Deborah said it was nothin', Dal," Phil tried to tell him casually, smacking his lips nervously. "A tequila fling, that's all. You know what she's like. She don't just sing country, she lives it."

"I damn sure do know what she's like," Dallas grumbled, twisting off the new beer's cap and flinging it into a dark corner of the fancy motorhome. "Take the damn ballad off tonight's set list."

"Can't do it, Dallas." Phil settled his butt against a countertop. "Your fans paid big bucks to hear you sing the ballad with Deborah."

"Give 'em a damn refund, Phil."

"Sure. I'll just do that. A few mil ought to do the trick."

"I can afford it."

"Your career can't. You need Deborah."

"Thanks for that."

He didn't need the crusty recap. Sure, Dallas' last album wasn't performing as expected. He knew it, but other than a niggling grudge that he ought to do something about it, it wasn't bothering him. There was no heart in that album. There was no soul. Dallas lost both of those somewhere between caring and carelessness—more on the carelessness side these days, after his twenty-year career at the top of the country music charts.

"Do your vocal warm-up," Phil ordered, swinging around and slapping the counter while storming toward the door. "Take the emotion out of tonight, Dallas. This is business."

Mmpphh, Dallas fumed. *No problem.* "You never damn fail to remind me, ya heartless bastard."

Toeing his chair around so it faced away from the window, he watched his buddy tap a 'so-long' finger to the worn fedora Dallas was fairly certain Phil glued to his balding head in the hopes that it could reverse or at least stall the passing years. Phil disappeared down the steps, and Dallas was alone with his dark thoughts again until a bubbly assistant stage manager summoned him to the spotlight.

Even the usual adrenaline rush Dallas usually got from the opening rhythm of the rolling bass and pumping percussion failed to inject life into tonight's set. At the end, the sultry, apologetic Deborah slinked on stage to numbing applause, slicking back her red hair with the nervous slim fingers of one traitorous hand as she moved. Watching her slither toward him, Dallas averted his gaze from her face and instead focused on the embroidered snakeskin boots he bought her back when they first hooked up. Looking into those deceitful, rueful eyes was not an option.

The second she was close enough, Deborah covered her microphone and bent toward Dallas. Recoiling as he half-assed listened, Dallas wondered why her syrupy, sugary Georgia whine hadn't grated on his nerves before. He used to find it sexy, especially the way Deborah drew out her vowels in bed while he pleasured her. His favorite was, "Oh, Gaaaawwwddd, Daaahllll..."

Repeated many times over, of course.

Finding her in bed with Cole had unleashed a few "Oh, Gawds," too. But they were more the begging kind, volubly tossed at Dallas while he was throwing his things into a large duffel bag. He'd tuned Deborah out by the

5

time he pitched her bra and panties into the hallway, where they landed in recalcitrant repose on the splintered guitar.

Damn, Dallas thought now, on stage. *I'm gonna see this woman in Cole's arms forever.* The god-awful image was ingrained on his brain—that gorgeous body moving over Cole instead of over himself, Deborah's toned back slicked with sweat while, underneath her, rugged Cole groaned with pleasure.

"Dallas, honey," Deborah entreated, disregarding the thunderous adoration of the thousands of fans spread out before them on the concert grounds. Under the unforgiving hot glare of lights, her limber body no longer Dallas' alone, she whined into his ear, "It was just a bit of fun. Ask Cole. It meant nothing. I love you."

The residual anger vanished. In its place a familiar, acute loneliness settled in.

Like a cancer, loneliness had gnawed its loathsome way into Dallas' heart. It had developed over a lifetime of playing on random, merciless stages, singing meaningless songs that had less and less depth each year, songs that became nothing more than products meant to bring in unseemly wealth. The tumor expanded until the moment Dallas yanked open his hotel room door and settled his eyes on the twosome in his bed. Like a stick of dynamite it exploded then, leaving a deep, dark hole in his soul, rendering him completely bereft and lost.

Tonight's concert was the gray leftover lifeless bits of that cancer; it was a fractured, lonely blur of emotionless lyrics and false smiles.

The ballad was meant to be the climax of the concert. Encores were slated for afterward, but when the guys in the band swept back onto the stage after a brief break, Dallas wasn't with them. By the time Phil realized his talent was not interested in singing any more tonight, Dallas was on his way to the airport.

Scrunched down in the back seat of the hired SUV, he pulled the brim of a cowboy hat down low over his long face, and put a permanent kind of leaving on his mind.

Soft white candlelight flickered in the wine glass Cassie held aloft in front of a framed photo. The muted light lent a gentle reflection to the image she was studying, giving it a wavy effect. Inside the wine glass, a mellow Merlot rippled lightly in echo.

Standing on tiptoe, swaying slightly, Cassie leaned toward the picture. "Eddie…"

Her husband's name was like melted chocolate on her lips; she licked both the top and bottom lip after she mouthed it as if the simple act of recalling the soul behind the image could make Eddie real again. Could let her taste him again.

He was a fireman. At least—he once was. Eddie, frozen at his fireman best in a dark dress uniform decorated with shiny brass buttons, peered out at Cassie from behind the glass of the picture frame. Fastened neatly over his broad chest, the candlelit ornate buttons lent Eddie a ghostly glow and gave him an ethereal, mystical presence.

Tipping the wine toward him, Cassie teetered, but she held Eddie's confident, quiet gaze, relishing the sparkle of light forever settled in his dark, loving eyes—a tiny pinprick in each pupil, effectually giving life to a well loved man, and the dignity of solemn remembrance to a cherished union.

"Oops!" Her flailing hand groped for something sturdy to hold on to. Cassie's small fingers tightened and whitened on the edge of a shelf; her petite shoulders slumped. Still, she didn't lose Eddie's steady gaze. To look away would be like letting go. To look away would be admitting defeat.

Classical music—Beethoven, this evening—soaked the elegant living room. It tumbled into the dark corners and drifted across the few phantom cobwebs wafting unnoticed from the ceiling. The composer's historic angst swirled and stirred, reverberating in wavelike swells throughout the house. It was inevitable; Cassie always buried herself in music when she was lost in Eddie, in their beautiful long ago love.

Cassie let her weary eyes close over. Their jade intelligence was dimmed tonight, rendering them a watery, pale aqua. Tipping her head back, she raised her slender arms in a welcoming gesture, inviting the grand, restorative music inside her spirit. She could take all of it in this way; she could breathe in the exquisite strings and thumping timpani in the false hope that together they would have the power to fuel her next breath and restore her worn heart.

A subdued voice called to her from the nearby stairwell. "Mom?"

A child's hand, the small hand of a mussed-up blond eight-year-old boy, gripped the worn mahogany newel post at the base of the stairs, rooting the child's small body to its smooth surface. Like Cassie, the boy who belonged to the hand sometimes thought he might rise up and float away.

Cassie didn't answer right away. Captivated and entranced by the soothing wine, the flickering candlelight, the overpowering music and the soaking wet memories, she had to work hard to cajole her mind into returning her to the present—to a reality she cared little for.

"It's okay, Ry," she finally assured the boy—her son—her voice thin and weak. "It's Dad's day. I'm just saying hello."

The overbearing orchestral music was crushing Ry. He eased down onto a stair and watched his mother depress a manicured nail on the remote control's volume, nudging Beethoven's genius up louder and louder so that the windows rattled and the house shook. Overwhelming, daunting, it resonated in Ry's body like thunder, which frightened him because he understood thunder on a deep, dark level.

When he was six, his no-nonsense Aunt Caroline had explained thunder to him, and what it meant to their tiny family. What she said was that mighty percussions had rolled in the sky each day Ry's dad was in Alberta fighting the god-awful fire that eventually took him, a deeply loved husband and father, away from them. In Ry's mind the thunder was stuck to the harsh splinters of lightning that Caroline said started the fire in the first place, and even though the rains eventually came and soaked Ry's dad, the outpouring of water was not enough to save him.

Long dead Beethoven was taking over the house. The crescendos seemed to be escalating.

The music boomed.

Ry shuddered.

"Go to bed," Cassie demanded without looking at him.

Ry was only too glad to obey his mother, to escape the heavy music. To escape the dark loneliness he saw drenching his mother's half-lidded eyes with pain.

Upstairs, Ry sat on the edge of his bed and bent over. He tried to be strong, but he couldn't help himself. Huge choking gasps snuck out; he hugged his belly tight to try to stop them from coming. Sometimes this dark heritage house felt like a tomb.

Below, his mother lowered her dog-tired body down onto a stiff Victorian sofa. Crossing her ankles, she tipped back her delicate wine glass and let the last of the warm Merlot slip down her throat into the nothingness that had consumed her from the time she got word of her handsome, rugged husband's death. She leaned back and let the music surround her; let it go through her until she was less than nothing. Until she was a speck on the ceiling, a dust mote in a corner, a sliver of light…where once she radiated gold.

Momentarily the wine glass slipped from her hand and smashed into bits on the hardwood floor. But Cassie didn't blink. She was used to things that shattered—love, for one, and life overall.

Drifting into sleep, she smiled. Eddie's strong, trusted, loving hand wrapped itself securely around her small fingers. In a make-believe Technicolor dream world—in a different dimension, maybe—they strolled lazily down a sun kissed Prince Edward Island beach. Her husband's soul was warm, inviting. Cassie angled her head against his familiar neck, against Eddie's red-bandana'd black curls, and breathed in the musky maleness of him. Commingling in the sea-salt air floating around them, dancing around them like glittery fairy dust, was love. Behind them, to the rhythm of contented splashes—wavelets happily rippling their way to shore—Eddie's larger feet and Cassie's petite toes left impressions in the sand, evidence that they were there. That at one time Cassie—and Eddie—existed together in life.

When Cassie awoke hours later, the melancholy white light from earlier was gone. The candle no longer flickered. It was still as a statue now, its wick black and withered, wax drips beaded down its sides like teardrops. Cassie's hand was empty; her graceful neck was cricked and sore. Raising a hand to rub it, she couldn't stop a silent droplet from floating down one pale cheek.

The only good thing, she thought, forcing her stiff knees to bend so she could rise, *is that Ry never really knew his father. A fatherless child since he was two, Ry can't possibly be buried under the burdensome pain of loss the way I am.*

Upstairs, Ry dreamed of the families he knew from school—dutiful dads who took their kids to hockey, and moms who smiled a lot when they bent to hug their children.

At three a.m. he woke with a start and began to tremble. Visions of tall trees consumed by fire, accompanied by the low rumble of thunder, were suddenly overloading his frayed, taut-as-wire senses.

He turned his nose into his pillow so if his mom checked on him she wouldn't see that he was crying.

Chapter One

*T*he first thing Dallas noticed about the kid was his hair. It was unavoidable. Long layers cascaded down the boy's face, almost hiding him from view, as if the waterfall of beach-bleached sunshine-blond could protect him from the world.

The second thing Dallas picked up on was the studious, committed way the kid went down the line of frozen slushie flavors. The boy, who Dallas figured for about eight, tipped the black handle forward just a little underneath each colored bin of frozen ice. A little grape, a drop of strawberry, a pinch of lime, a squeeze of lemon. Either the boy was just having fun, or he simply couldn't decide which flavor he liked the best.

The third thing Dallas couldn't help locking his eyes on was the boy's mother. Hovering nervously above her fit, tanned boy—who Dallas heard her call Ry—she was clearly confused as to why he would want to mess up a perfectly good summer slushie by melding all of those rich, tangy flavors together into one mushy mess. Evidently mother and child were polarized opposites. Plainly they were operating on completely different wavelengths.

Dallas felt Ry's wide, pale eyes land on him at about the time the kid took his first sip of the sugary ice drink. But it took Dallas a moment to look over. First he had to force himself to unlock his gaze from the woman who apparently belonged to Ry. Petite and slender, her wispy buttery silk tresses were pulled back in a ponytail and fastened with an oval pewter Celtic clip with a small cross at its center. Judging by the way she was sighing and brushing nervous fingers over her sweaty forehead, she seemed at a loss as to how to communicate with her son who, at this point, had yet to speak in words at all.

The woman drifted to the wooden counter of the small camp store and paid for her son's drink, then turned to go, but paused when her searching green eyes rested on Dallas.

Damn, they recognize me, he muttered under his breath, caught in the crossfire of the woman's curious scrutiny and her son's steady study. Reaching up to yank the brim of a worn Blue Jays ball cap down lower over his forehead, Dallas strode forward, but not before identifying something in the kid's stare first, something that unsettled him, and that, Dallas was sorry to see, was also reflected in the dim light of the mother's moist eyes.

Sadness. It was sadness he saw there, a deep angst and longing that haunted the child and mother the way ghosts supposedly hover in white mists over graveyards. Recoiling just slightly, Dallas was stunned to feel a wave of energy pass over him. The brief ripple was pain; Dallas knew the reason he understood this was because he recognized it in himself.

Dallas' sadness was seeded in the curse of loneliness. It was only a few short days earlier that he had stormed off the Seattle country music concert stage and jetted home to Toronto. There, he packed a few necessities and ripped a torn grease-stained cloth tarp off an old pickup truck. The truck was the very same beat-up blue pickup he'd driven across the prairies to Toronto years ago when he first met with Sony executives in the hopes of generating some buzz about his music.

Back then, when the stubble on his cheeks was new, in the days when his brother Dale called him 'scarecrow skinny,' Dallas was only too glad to park the ancient truck and salute it goodbye. He'd taken his advance from Sony and marched on down to the Ford dealership. The first car he bought was a candy apple red Mustang. The second, only six months later, was a silver Porsche. Now a dozen sports cars were neatly lined up side by side in the large garage at his Toronto mansion. In a nearby hanger were three airplanes. Parked at a private airfield was a Learjet, shiny white and striped with gold.

That troubled morning just a few short days ago when Dallas stood in his garage eyeing his collection of muscle cars, all his heart wanted was the old pickup. Dusty blue, blemished by patches of rust above the wheel wells and now pockmarked with Prince Edward Island's ubiquitous red dirt, it hadn't let Dallas down. It sprang to life with just one twist of the key.

Dallas had puttered the old blue truck slowly out of the large garage and focused a hurt, angry stare at an orange-pink line threading its way low across the horizon. Making a hasty decision that somehow just felt right, he pointed his trusty companion toward the eastern sunrise.

"Hell, I'll drive off the damn continent if I have to," he'd grunted at the time.

Two days and twenty-one hours of driving later, a large billboard planted in the New Brunswick soil greeted him.

Prince Edward Island...the Gentle Island, it proclaimed. Underneath the corny slogan was a photo of a happy family digging around a sandy beach, building a sandcastle, a perfect one with tall towers and a low wall over a sea green moat. *An idyllic paradise,* the sign seemed to proclaim. *P.E.I. is a laid back place; it promises a warm, beckoning indigo sky and miles of white sand perfect for sublime bare-toed sandy strolls.*

Dallas hardly knew what he was doing when he swung a hard right off a highway rotary and nosed the truck toward Canada's red-cliffed island with its endless leafy potato fields and homey patchwork landscape. It felt like his soul was doing the driving, and not his brain at all. As if Dallas' soul knew something his mind did not.

One fifteen-minute bridge drive later, and he'd found himself sighing in relief. His shoulders curved inward with the sheer reprieve earned by running his tires over island roads. Instantly, the small paradise felt distant and safe.

Sourcing out a place to stay was easy; Dallas had stopped at a small gas station and asked about lodging. "Somewhere by a windswept shore," he'd said off the cuff, casually resting an elbow on a worn wooden counter.

Maybe because of the old pickup, a kindly older man pointed him to Castle Beach, a campground on the island's north shore that catered to all sorts of folks, including seniors in large RVs, families, and young couples in tents. The park was large, set between the picturesque cobalt blue of the Darnley Basin and the sometimes ferocious, roiling waves of the Gulf of St. Lawrence. It boasted enough amenities to serve Dallas' simple needs— a cozy, rustic camp store, a tennis court, laundry facilities. He'd chosen a solitary site bordered by trees; it overlooked a white sand beach. Dallas could have easily afforded a cottage rental; heck, he could have bought himself a magnificent home on the water. But he'd brushed those notions away as quickly as he later snuffed out an annoying mosquito that buzzed around his ears while he was trying to sleep.

"No more," he'd said. "No more luxury, no more false friendships, no more random, faceless women, no more alcoholic binges, and no more ridiculous wealth." Nope, Dallas White was seeking anonymity and seclusion. He wanted no more association with things that hurt.

Which brought him back to his current problem. The pretty woman in the short pink floral sundress was looking at him funny—a little humorous glint was dancing over her eyes. *Maybe because,* Dallas thought, *I'm staring.* Sure enough, the kid, Ry—with his untamed surfer locks and big, sad eyes— was striking enough to warrant a long look. Ry's mother—well, one peek into that soft, tortured, jaded soul and Dallas' knees had instantly buckled.

The woman touched her son's back and they left, the boy with his mixed-up slushie and the mom with empty arms. After a confused moment to collect his wits, Dallas White, International Country Music Superstar, wandered up to the counter, set down his few groceries, dropped a pile of random change into the outstretched palm of a willowy brunette's hand, and bought himself a hot fudge sundae.

Cassie's heart was racing when she shut the door of the camp store behind her. Did she recognize the country star in the store? Hell, no! Cassie Keough was a sophisticated woman schooled in the classics when it came to music. Mozart, Bach, Beethoven, those were her pals on the nights when dumping Merlot into her gullet and disappearing into a dulled sleep was the only remedy capable of washing away hard memories, and to sink the acute pain of loss she'd suffered since the day the parish priest had stepped timidly over her flagstone walk and tapped on her door.

His gentle proclamation on that dark day was replayed over and over in a continuous loop in Cassie's brain. "Eddie is gone, Cassie. I'm sorry."

Eddie disappeared from her life back then; Eddie and nine other fire-fighters he toiled alongside back when the Alberta forests were singed with black, when the rabbits and deer and bears and snakes fled for cover while humans fought a valiant fight. But they'd lost, the humans did, at least that small group of firefighters lost. Overtaken by a vicious wind that suddenly turned on them without remorse, they died huddled together—praying, Cassie knew, because that was Eddie's way. Her husband infused his life with laughter and joy, in faith and prayer, in love and kindness. An outdoorsy guy who craved adventure, Eddie was Prince Edward Island born and bred, although they were living in Halifax at the time, in the province of Nova Scotia where Cassie still lived, if you could call her day-to-day functions actually 'living.'

Each day she went to work at the local performing arts theater and managed the administrative operations the same way she had since before Eddie left her to raise their two-year-old son on her own. Budgets, grant applications, tedious board meetings and attempts to book successful shows filled the wearying days of Cassie's life. In linen shifts and heels, she went about her days with a quiet grace and a humble generosity, surviving mostly on yoga and Greek yogurt while carrying out the necessary duties to raise a child. But really, when all was said and done, she was living on the outside looking in.

For some reason, this year was tougher than most. It was as if the more time that crept by after Eddie's passing—six years now—the harder it was to go on. Early June, the anniversary of the Alberta fire tragedy, was always a time to be feared, to dread. Every year when June third rolled around Cassie let the intolerable day pass without nourishment, barely without acknowledgement, almost without thought. She stayed in bed and listened for the quiet footsteps of her sister, knowing that Caroline would have the day in hand. Cassie's tall, dependable older sister would feed Ry, would get him to school, would carry him off to soccer after school, would get him fed again and back home to bed while Cassie slept the hard memories away.

This year, though, June third's pain turned into a two-day retreat.

On day two, quiet Ry had finally picked up his mother's phone and texted his Aunt Caroline. *Mom won't get up.*

Those four words. They may as well have read *Mom's in crisis.* Caroline showed up with lattes and fresh baked raspberry ricotta muffins. In no uncertain terms she told Cassie to put her record on a new loop.

And that was that. Cassie could either stay forever in the sanctified calm of her sea-blue bedroom, or get out of bed and put one foot in front of the other. Try to carry on. Do more than just survive. Thrive.

Easier said than done.

Cassie started by taking the summer off work. Stress leave. *PTSD. Call it what you want,* she told the theater's board of directors. Ry had gotten through the school year, but he was a silent partner in his education. Private and watchful, Cassie's son was heading down the same path as his mother, one of retreat and caution. Something had to give. Something had to change. She couldn't save Eddie. But she had to try to save her son.

There was money to spend. Insurance money—a nice chunk. No day went by without Cassie's mind always, always, always drifting off to a world with Eddie still in it. His happy smile, his winning kindness, his warm big-heartedness. What mattered to Eddie most? His beloved island, that's what. Cassie's tousle-haired, muscular husband was a pansy when it came to the land of the bright red mud. Give him falling stars and dreamy sunsets and hand-in-hand walks down the beach, followed by shared glasses of Merlot or Pinio Grigio in front of a roaring fire. Laughter encased Eddie wherever they were, whether they were entertaining neighbors at their harmless campfire, or wandering down the beach greeting the many dogs that always rushed over to say hello. Eddie was Cassie's rock, her strength, her hope. And some-times, he was her voice.

She'd gone out that very day after her sister's visit and bought a 35-foot Montana fifth-wheel trailer, a tough new silver Ford truck to pull it, and a tiny bandeau-topped polka dot bikini to wear on the beach. A floating body board for Ry and a campsite at Castle Beach in Darnley, Prince Edward Island, that's what Cassie wanted, and that's what she got. The bottom of a gently sloped hill overlooking Eddie's favorite kayaking spot, the spar-kling Darnley Basin, was where she planted the luxury trailer for the sum-mer. Cassie enlisted help to get it set up. There were a few hiccups, like learning how to empty the toilet tank, to figure out along the way, but they were settling in, she and her son. They didn't talk much, still, but they were getting by.

By the time they ran into the roguish guy with the wistful, faraway gaze, they'd been at the campground a week. Ry was already tanned and rosy-cheeked from days on the beach and from spirited, vigorous bike rides around the park.

Cassie, to her credit, was getting out of bed. Every day. That was a start. As long as there were no...unseen complications...they would get through the summer just fine, with Eddie's rugged, loving face in every cloud, and his spirited essence in every nighttime star.

But...complications. What was that back there in the camp store, that... feeling? The tingling that shot up Cassie's legs was completely unsettling. When she looked into the soft, lonesome eyes of the unkempt-looking man in the torn-up jeans, his strong arms cradling three cans of beans and a carton of milk, she almost crumbled. What was it about his chiseled jaw and muscular, tanned forearms that set her heart on fire, that sent a wave of desire cresting through her? Simply by meeting his wistful gaze, Cassie was rendered mute. Was it the dusty brown boots, the firm set of his mouth, the three-day beard? It was like his eyes sent a shockwave from his soul to hers, like he was grasping for her, for a connection of sorts. The result was an immediate sizzling surge of energy that shot up Cassie's spine and, somehow, jumpstarted her heart. It hurt to feel it. The raw longing brought Eddie back, in crippling waves and with an aching need.

"Some powerful essence," Cassie considered under her breath as she steered Ry toward his bike. She swung a strong leg over her own brand new ride. "Some aura."

Starting to pedal, she had to lean over the handlebars and fight for control. She was suddenly feeling physically sick.

What hurt even more was spying a nearby father joking with his small son. Scooping up his child and tossing him onto his shoulders like a bag of flour, the guy's eyes were lit up with a hearty joy. The boy was whimpering; the curly-haired youngster had apparently just fallen and skinned a knee.

"You'll never make a good Tarzan," the dad teased, easing his son's tears with good-natured jest. "Ya gotta be tough to be Tarzan."

"You gotta be tough to simply survive," Cassie whispered inwardly, steering carefully past the duo. She hung her head when she saw Ry's gaze linger on the father and son. With a proudly raised chin he turned his head away, one hand grasping his bike handle, the other balancing the colorful slushie. "You gotta be tough to live," Cassie added, sobering further.

They pedaled off toward their big Montana on the luxury side of the campground.

Behind them, Dallas White, incognito country music hero, stepped out onto the wooden verandah of the small camp store, and watched them go.

Chapter Two

"Like this," the visual artist hired by the campground to teach the craft of sandcastle building instructed Ry as they worked intently, brows furrowed in concentration. "Slide and swipe. Slide and swipe. But keep it wet, add lots of water, because dry sand will just crumble on you."

They were on their knees by a big pile of sand that the artist, a friendly forty-something man with kind eyes, had dug up and prepared for Cassie and Ry. Similar piles were scattered over the beach within a hundred foot radius. Yellow buckets dotted the sand; curved handles of small spades—blades thrust into the sand near the piles—reached for the sky.

The warm 'beach day' was wrapping up with an evening of sandcastle building that started just as the sun began its slow, liquid descent into the Gulf, saluting the day and succumbing to night by spreading its golden warmth across the sky in gauzy pink-orange hues. The rich aroma of mouthwatering steaks and burgers being grilled on private lots in the campground above and beyond wafted enticingly over the groups of families working in small huddles on the beach. Fantasy towers and stairs and moats were being molded under their capable hands while, not so far from the sandy toes of the builders, lace-tipped waves crested over and over each other in noble, endless quests to get to shore.

Curious, Dallas watched the goings-on from an undisturbed, unnoticed vantage point. A wooden boardwalk led up from the beach to the camping area. To the left of that ramp (from the beach's perspective), a small deck used as a viewing area was the perfect place to sit in silent wonder and meditate on one's place in the world. The platform, which technically rested on a sand dune, was a new favorite spot for Dallas. He had lowered himself onto a movable high stained-spruce platform used as a table on Saturday evenings when Castle Beach staff served steaming plates of mussels to campers, and was peering down at the beach from between sharp blades of tall saw grass. Always, the surf whispered its secrets to him, and this serene, idyllic evening was no exception. *There is more. Life is not about the accumulation of wealth. It's about making every moment count. It's about connection. It's about reciprocated desire and...*

A needle skipped over his record. "What the hell?" Dallas muttered, lowering his dog-eared boots to the built-in bench below, and toeing a blade of the saw-sharp grass around. "Desire?" But he knew where the thought was coming from. Universe, be damned. It was Dallas' thing, this sudden desire, not the universe's. And it had shit all to do with that lying, cheating Deborah. Shoving up a sleeve of his gray Henley, nervously repeating the action on the other arm, Dallas flexed a forearm and considered the thought further.

On the beach below, Ry and his enigmatic blonde mother were kneeling side-by-side working on their pile of sand. At least one of the two had relaxed into the beach vibe enough to show up in an oversized hoodie and bare feet, but it wasn't Ry's mom. Another pretty sundress—this one with yellow flowers on a pale cream background—adorned her slim figure. A post-swim ribbon was carefully tied around what seemed to be a usual sleek ponytail. Everyone around her was barefoot, but her toes were tucked into sandals or flip-flops, Dallas couldn't quite tell which, since the dainty feet he'd observed at the camp store were pointed slightly away from him. It seemed to him that she was afraid to let herself go, to let her skin absorb the healing sun-warmed sand. As if she couldn't quite let herself be rooted to the earth.

Stealing a glance down at his booted feet, Dallas grimaced. His usual jeans flared overtop, tight on his well-muscled thighs but loose and scraggly overtop the worn boots. A few dangling threads were also present, screaming up at him that he was a redneck with or without a trusty guitar and forlorn lyrics at his disposal. He thought he looked good, regardless, because most of the women he saw on the beach or passed during his morning walks around the campground stared at him. To be fair, Dallas had to wonder whether the lingering had more to do with his noticeably 'not beachy' attire than him actually rocking his jeans and boots. He sure as hell hoped the ladies weren't wondering why, underneath his customary ball cap, he looked familiar.

"She's pretty as a picture," he mumbled now at the sight of Ry's mom working in quiet companionship next to her son on their castle. Settling one forearm on his thigh, Dallas raised the other hand to scratch at itchy whiskers. Dark sunglasses hid his eyes from the world; hid those thoughtful baby blues his fans had come to love through skillfully lit close-ups in his music videos. He tipped the glasses farther up his nose in the hopes that somehow they would more fully illuminate this lovely porcelain-skinned woman for him.

Rarely did a woman captivate him like this. Usually Dallas went for the tight, skimpy denim shorts types, the ones with the clingy tank tops and visible 'touch-me' breasts (which he did, often, at least before Deborah he did, heck they were handed to him on beer-stained platters). Sex with those women was always satisfying on a physical level, earth shattering even, sometimes, but Dallas' soul was left empty and wanting after such rendezvous. Even the women with smarts and generous layers of kindness didn't warm his bed the way he needed them to. And with each passing nameless, faceless romp, the hole in his heart had grown deeper.

Hence the reach for Deborah, whose external warmth somehow compensated, at least for a time, what she lacked in soul warmth. Old high school friends had nice homes in the suburbs now, three kids on average, and attractive wives who drove their kids to hockey and figure skating in standard SUVs. They vacationed in February without the kids in the Dominican or in Cuba, and took the whole family to Disneyland in April. Dallas was usually on the road or in the studio while his friends lived their normal lives. He could go to Cuba or to the Dominican any damned time he wanted, but who would he take now that Deborah was gone? His wily snakeskin-booted manager, Phil? Yeah, beers on the beach with Phil…random sex with voluptuous dark-skinned women…it was fun in the 'nouveau rich' days. Now the thought was just plain nauseating.

Dallas straightened. The petite woman…she was sitting back on her haunches now, swiping loose hair away from her face, and she seemed resigned. Even from up here, seventy feet away, Dallas could see that about her. She was watching a nearby family laugh their way through a castle build.

Ry was watching them too. What the two seemed to see as an incomplete-ness of their own little family was weighing heavy on both of them. Sucking in a breath, Dallas crunched on his bottom lip when, with one mighty swoop, the woman raked her arm through a tower she'd just built and sent a heavy load of sand flying back to the beach.

Considering his attire, which he decided would have to become beachier and less cowboy-ey tomorrow, Dallas hoisted himself upright and sauntered off the deck and down the wooden ramp. His boots clicked heavily on the wood and he almost slipped on loose sand as he stepped downward, but he grabbed the rail, locked his eyes on Ry and his mother, and forced himself to move forward. Sand shuffed up from underneath his feet when he hit the beach. It was like trudging through mud, a slow slog. Nervous, wishing he was bare feet so he could dig his toes in the sand, he fingered a large engraved silver belt buckle that lay low over his tight abs, a souvenir earned from some country music award show. Reaching the big sand pile that Ry was focused on shaping into turrets with a low fenced-in moat at its base, Dallas dropped onto his knees and reached out a timorous hand. Slowly, he pushed some sand backward with both hands and started to form a new tower.

"Like this?" he asked Ry quietly, forcing his eyes to remain on the ther-apeutic, repetitive movements of his guitar-callused fingers as they dug around the sand, shaping and reshaping. A waft of some delicate perfume fell on the light evening breeze toward him, tumbling and turning and tossing in its invisible current, kindling a magical fairy spell, igniting Dallas' senses so that he almost lost focus. He wanted to sink back to stare at its source.

The boy's small voice brought him back to reality. "You need to add a lot of water, the guy said." Demonstrating, Ry shoved his boyish fingers into a bucket of waterlogged thick beach sand and pulled out a handful. The gooey mess dripped between his fingers while Ry applied it to his own wobbly work.

"Ah, I see," Dallas acknowledged with a slight nod.

Reflecting on the kid's voice, Dallas was surprised to find it low, raspy, as if it was rarely used. The simple words made Ry seem older than his years. Wiser. Life hardened.

Before Dallas followed Ry's example and added watery sand to his own tower, he finally let his gaze flicker up to the boy's mother. He couldn't help himself; he needed a closer look at those pink cheeks and soft lips. At the sun-honeyed skin and melancholy green eyes. At the taut, toned back he yearned to graze a finger over.

She was watching him. Studying him—Dallas—who was squatting down beside her son in dirty cowboy clothes that made no sense on the beach, who was staring at her from behind dark sunglasses, cowardly hiding his curiosity and resigned fear of what she already meant to him.

Ry's mom was like a mother bird guarding her baby—ready to strike, it seemed, judging by the way those silent, kissable lips were turning down at the corners. But then—a hint of a smile lifted one side of one lip. It sent rainbows of joy and promise to Dallas' aching, lonely soul.

He grinned back, and got to work building their castle.

The thing about this mysterious man that is really getting to me, Cassie thought as she watched the guy work alongside Ry—who was actually speaking to the man, actually *speaking* for a change, spouting directions taught to him by the hired instructor—*is his hands. He has a working man's hands,* she mused as she watched him dig in the sand. *Strong, capable hands with lean fingers, and his forearms, too, they are something.* His arms were easy to spy on beneath the soft cotton three-button Henley. Cassie figured rightly the shirt must be annoying him because he kept shoving his sleeves up toward his elbows.

His solid arms taunted her, almost begged her to touch him. The desire to slip a finger or two up under the cotton just above the silver buckle at the stranger's waist was overwhelming. The thought of actually laying a palm there, flat against his stomach so she could feel the heat of him, could soak up the energy behind those tight abs, caused Cassie to emit an inadvertent gasp that she hoped the guy didn't hear, and which she glossed over with an arrogant head toss.

I wonder what he does for a living. Carpenter, maybe? Roofer? She had to refrain from reaching out and drawing a finger along the muscles that rippled as he moved.

23

One thing was for sure. The guy was overdressed for the beach. But his old boots and faded jeans were sexy as hell.

The tiny smile she sent across Ry's blond head toward the stranger was meant to address that, the fact that he was wearing jeans and boots while most folks around him sported comfy shorts and rumpled T-shirts.

Cassie leaned back so she could sneak peeks at the guy behind Ry's back. Their helper was working avidly next to her son now, so her covert looks became less guarded and more open. It didn't cross her mind that he could read her, could feel her interested peeks scanning his body, could sense her eyes drifting up and down his wrinkled shirt and eventually lingering on the large silver buckle.

The not-so-secret looks ignited every isolated pore on Dallas' skin. He fidgeted, but kept working.

Cassie's wandering eyes roved upward. What she saw were rather wild layers of sandy-blond hair sneaking out from underneath Dallas' ball cap, dusting his shoulders, almost. The hair was straight for the most part, the loose bits blowing gently around in the slight island breeze. A bit darker in places, his hair gave him a depth that made Cassie think maybe he was more than just a simple country hick. That aspect of him was still there—the rural feel—Cassie was sure of that. No way was this hard man a city boy. No way did those solid forearms and that firm chest spend days in a crowded paper-strewn office, unless he spent hours in a gym before or after. She pictured him on a tractor, roaming a wide, lush green field.

I need to see your eyes again, she breathed, haphazardly molding sand again. *I need to feel…*

Stopping herself from pondering the guy further, Cassie roughly grabbed a fistful of sand and started to place it on a new tower. But she wanted the stranger to take his sunglasses off. She wanted to see if what she felt at the camp store was real or just…wishful thinking.

One more last peek. The guy needed a shave. Yet the way his newish whiskers were sitting upon his jaw gave him a raw, edgy aura. Rustic, that was it. This guy was rustic; he had an old-world feel, an old soul dynamic. An old soul worn-out wisdom.

He is wise, she mused. For a moment, she almost collapsed with the simple need that washed over her. *Oh God, I miss the manliness of unshaved whiskers and piles of messy T-shirts in my laundry. God, I miss the feel of rough skin on my arms, on my face, on my…*

She stopped again and drew her arm away from the tower she was forming beneath her graceful fingers. A sudden unexpected urge to cry filtered up through her body. Abruptly, Cassie sat back and made a move to stand.

But then a hand reached across in front of Ry; it was a strong hand made of all things male. It radiated strength and heat. Before Cassie knew what was happening, the fingers of that hand wrapped around hers and drew her back to the castle that she, Ry and this redneck stranger were building together. A small squeeze encouraged her while, at the same time, electric desire consumed her.

A second gasp escaped from between Cassie's lips, louder this time—audible, no doubt—just before a name offered itself to her, and made him real.

She had to ask him to repeat it. The request came out stuttery and small. "Wh-what did you s-say?"

"Dal," he told her, one corner of a full lip easing upward, his eyes searching hers for acceptance. "My name is Dal."

It was as if he was telling her not to be afraid. As if he was begging her not to run.

"C-Cassie," she managed in bewildered response. Between them Ry wrinkled his nose and raised his eyebrows in one big question mark.

"Let me help you," Dal offered, leaning close enough so that Cassie had to close her eyes and breathe him in, that musky, manly, sweaty scent of him. She couldn't help herself. Dal placed her fingers back on her castle tower. He drew them downward, then let go and molded the sand there for a few seconds before Ry pushed the water bucket closer.

"Thanks, buddy," Dallas said casually to Ry.

Cassie was astounded. She watched her son award this stranger—Dal, what an odd name—a smile wide enough to crack his jaw.

"My name's Ry," she heard her little guy say. A closer look and Cassie noted that Ry's eyes were alight, beaming. Reflected in them she saw the cherished sunset start to take hold. It was breathtaking but it belonged to Eddie, she told herself, and she lifted her face to the source, to the western bank of silvery pink-lined clouds, to the peace and hope and faith and memories she knew she would find there.

After a slow exhale later, Cassie turned back to their castle and smiled fully, enough so that Dallas could see the tips of perfect white teeth, and she began to build.

Chapter Three

*C*assie and Ry did not lay eyes on Dallas again until another sun was setting over the Gulf. This time was as unexpected as the man's gentle, quiet help on the beach the evening before. And this time, they heard him first.

Just before they put each day to rest, they'd gotten in the habit of finishing up the dishes and riding up the slope to the store on their bikes for ice cream, which Cassie and Ry always ate while seated on wide brown benches in front of the Laundromat. Spooning the creamy treat out of Styrofoam dishes was only half the fun. Most of the entertainment came from other campers—kids followed by harried parents were always running in and out of a large fenced-in playground just below the brown wooden building where Cassie and Ry sat. On the second floor above them, a bustling café had folks jogging up and down a set of outside stairs. Behind the laundry area, in the same building, an activity space used for karaoke, kids' crafts, and a novel form of bingo played with chocolate bars was always hopping.

Apart from the beach on hot days, this was the most populated area of the campground in the evenings. The benches were perfect to discreetly people-watch from.

To dream from. To remember from.

Once Ry's usual cookie dough flurry was in his tummy and Cassie's hot fudge sundae was spooned up—the last little bit of chocolate always scraped off the side of the dish and licked off the spoon—they always got back on their bikes and cruised the quaint dusty lanes of their summer neighborhood. Fueled by the intoxicating smell of wood smoke and the cheery sound of laughing children (and the odd snipe from an exhausted parent) they rode, pedals ticking with pleasure underneath their toes, muscles straining, eyes landing on each solitary treed campsite so they could inconspicuously spy on families as they passed.

Contained within the parameters of each semi-private site were whole worlds to discover, to wonder about. Most campers in this part of the park were transients, not seasonals like Cassie and Ry who, in their big luxury fifth-wheel trailer with its separate living room, fireplace and big screen television, were set up for a long term stay. Along these rustic lanes were folks taking a week or two off work, spending their hard earned dollars relaxing in Prince Edward Island's gentle sun kissed embrace in tents or in pop-up campers. Tonight these salt-of-the-earth people were rocking their babies in front of metal-surround fire pits, lulled, by the mellow chirp of crickets and the dreamy chorus of night birds, into sleepy peace. Occasionally Cassie and Ry overheard tired parents tossing cautious warnings to sprouting youngsters—*Don't stuff melted marshmallows into your mouth before the hot centers cool.* Or, *No running near the fire!*

Biking at an easy pace, Cassie followed her son up and down the dusty roads. Each announced itself with a quaint road sign—Keel Lane, Pier Lane, Jetty Lane…

Near the beach they took a hard right and started to cruise down Atlantic Drive. Instantly, their ears perked up. Music…at first Cassie thought it was coming from a radio, but no…someone was playing a guitar. Clearly, Cassie and Ry heard chords, mellow ones…forlorn ones in a minor key being played at a slow waltz tempo, accented with occasional fingerpicking…so pretty…so…unexpected.

Somewhere down the dead end lane, experienced fingers were being drawn slowly over the finely tuned strings of a guitar. A sad, dusky voice was there too, conjoined in sweet perfection with the music, although the lyrics were being sung too softly, too far away, for Ry and Cassie to make out their meaning.

The melancholy melody floated down the narrow lane. The musician, whether he or she intended to or not, was also releasing his or her gift into the far reaches of the endless ocean. First, though, the music had to pass over Atlantic Drive and then over the sandy beach below the lonely dunes that bordered this secluded part of the park. Perhaps the sad song was meant for the enjoyment of the seagulls alone, and not for human ears. It had a very personal feel, yet to Cassie it somehow seemed universal for its power to speak for what her heart was feeling. The tune—its comforting strings, the dusky voice, its empty hollow lilt—reached Cassie's ears on the same invisible current that carried all the usual campground smells, like heady wood smoke, spiced meat on the grill, the cozy vibe of leafy trees. The composition, however casually written and performed, was as much alive as the natural environment that encompassed it.

A lithe chipmunk caught Cassie's attention by dancing across a nearby exposed tree root. Slowing her bike so she could have a closer look, Cassie was amused at the way the little guy stood on his haunches and peeked up at her. From her perspective, the creature's posture felt like a scolding stance.

"What? Does the music mean something to you, little fella?" she asked it with a light giggle before it zipped back off into the woods. The small critter almost seemed to toss a reprimand back over its furry shoulder as it scurried away. "Uh-huh," pondered Cassie. "Wise guy. What was that look supposed to mean? Are you telling me to pay attention?" She squinted into the semi-darkness of the brush but the chipmunk had disappeared. "Huh," she mumbled, picking up her pedaling pace so the bike wouldn't wobble and stall. "Either that or you're simply annoyed." The bike cricked its way down the lane. "Us campers are cramping your style, huh?"

Music, she sighed, cruising closer toward the soft strumming of the guitar. *Ahhhh.* Her spirit started to melt, to heal. Like the chipmunk, she was at the mercy of the lovely, rich chords surrounding her. She let them embrace her, let them float within her.

Ry took off, his soul perking up at the unexpected pleasure of hearing a guitar being played in the light dusk of a perfect evening. He was only too happy to focus on something other than the families with dads as well as moms all hunkered around their campfires, reminding him of what he was missing.

"Hold up!" Cassie called to him in warning. Castle Beach was a busy, full campground in early July. Sometimes small children wandered the lanes haphazardly, unwatched, leaving the perimeters of their campsites while their parents tended to other kids or to meal prep or dishes, and at other times cyclists like Ry and Cassie forgot to adhere to simple precautions like staying on one side of the road.

"Watch where you're going, Ry," Cassie added unnecessarily. Atlantic Drive was a quiet, more secluded area of the campground. The surface of the short lane was really two threadbare red dirt trails separated by a higher mound of sparse rough grass and the odd rogue wildflower, which suited it perfectly, leading as it did to almost another world entirely. The babble of children and gentle reprimands from parents receded. Barking dogs were off in the distance now. Only the slow strumming of the guitar and a husky, sad voice remained.

On the left were about a half-dozen lots populated by tents and tent trailers. On the right were similar sites, with two almost unnoticeable lots hidden in amongst the trees. One was deep enough in the woods so as to have its own trail, which Cassie had earlier wisely cautioned Ry never to take, since it seemed an obvious invasion of privacy. The second, betwixt and between that hidden, lonely site and the more visible lots before it, was where the mournful guitar strumming was coming from. This sheltered site, to the right of Atlantic Drive, was far enough down the dusty trail to have an unimpeded, unhindered view of the ocean. No tents blocked the stunning view. One only had to look beyond the sand dune that led down to the beach.

Ry got there first. Drawing up behind him, using a combination of her foot sliding on the ground and a squeeze on the handbrake to slide her bike to a halt, Cassie knew right away that the guitar player was the helpful cowboy from the sandcastle building. It was evident in Ry's expression, in the way his eyes shone and his shoulders were suddenly raised in high alert, that there was something special about this music and the person—the man—playing it.

"Ohhh," Cassie whispered quietly when she spotted Dal perched comfortably on the top of a picnic table with a scratched up Gibson acoustic in his arms. Facing the ocean, he was evidently entertaining swooping seagulls and an odd assortment of bumblebees and mosquitos while sitting there, in jeans again but barefoot this time. The ragged ball cap still covered his longish hair. A plaid shirt draped out over his hips, unbuttoned, Cassie realized with a jump when she dared a peek behind the guitar Dal was resting on his knees. She took a jarring breath at the startling sight of the man's broad chest. Of his...touchable...broad chest.

And...no sunglasses this time.

Dal looked up when he heard the crunch of tires draw to a halt. After a last haunting phrase on the guitar, he let the music fade off into the cooling evening. At the same time, his eyes latched themselves into Cassie's. Forcing a smile to cover up his surprise, he relaxed his arms around his trusted friend, his guitar, his...wall. "Well, hello," he started.

Ry swung a leg away from his bike and let it fall to the earth with a rather ungracious clang.

"Ry!" Cassie admonished, uncertainty tingeing her voice which, to Dal, sounded like a church bell pealing over his soul, healing and refreshing his broken spirit. "He might not want company. You shouldn't wander onto peoples' campsites without being invited."

"It's okay," Dal assured her as Ry, eyes wide and excited, approached the picnic table. "Do you like music?" he asked his young beach friend.

"Depends on the music," Ry answered with a grin. "I don't like what my mom listens to." Tentative, he reached out a finger and drew it down over the guitar's body.

Inquisitively, Dal raised an eyebrow and focused a sparkling gaze back on Cassie who, he was almost relieved to see, was stepping off her bike and laying it on the ground too, albeit much more carefully than her son did. He winked at her but aimed a question at Ry. "And what does your mom listen to?" Dal's heart picked up its pace but somehow he knew the answer before it met his hopeful ears.

"Classical crap. Like...that Beethoven guy." Ry snickered up at Dal who, he just knew, was playing anything but Beethoven on the guitar.

Dal's spirits sank. *Strike one.* But he was willing to play this game to see how far it could go. "Beethoven's got a few things going for him," he told Ry. Nearby, Cassie rocked back on a heel and folded her arms across her chest.

"What do you play?" Ry was bouncing.

"Umm...." Working his jaw, Dallas tried to sort out how to respond. If she listened to classical, Cassie would not likely know him, but it was a gamble.

As far as he knew, Dallas White was a household name. He took a chance. "Mostly country," he said with a confidence he really, truly, didn't feel.

"Coo-ool." The word was spoken with a hushed reverence that instantly raised Dallas' chosen profession back up in his jaded eyes.

Cassie was frowning. She braced her arms tighter around her small body and petulantly switched her weight to her other sandal. Tonight she was wearing denim shorts and a light body-hugging gray hoodie. Dallas was relieved to see her letting her hair down a little, for once. Sort of. It dangled sleepily underneath a girly pink bike helmet. His nervous grin faded at her soldierly stance, however, and at the sour way she scanned his small camp-site—tiny tent and rusted out pickup included.

"Ry, come back to your bike," she ordered her son. "I'm sure Dal doesn't want to be disturbed."

"But, Mom…" Twisting around, Ry accented his protest with a pissed off foot stomp and a death ray glare.

"Ry." Her word was stone. Ry stormed his way forlornly back to his bike. Cassie forced her eyes up to Dal, who was still sitting on the wooden table-top holding his guitar tightly on his lap as if by letting it go he would expose a vulnerable part of himself.

"It's okay," Dal tried. "He's a nice kid. He seems interested in the guitar."

"I am," Ry insisted loudly with a stubborn pout. "I want to learn how to play."

It was almost an outburst. In fact, in Ry Keough's quiet world, the ada-mant demand kinda was just that. Cassie was astounded. "Ry!" she exclaimed, silencing this new wild boy at once.

She aimed her focus back at Dal, who seemed as shocked at the way she spoke to Ry as Cassie was at Ry for voicing, rather exuberantly, his surprise request.

"I could teach him," the guitar-playing outlaw offered.

There. That did it. Dal was throwing a lifeline out into the big wide world, to Cassie, and Cassie and Dal both knew it. Dallas needed it—the connec-tion, the purpose, and the touchstone to this elegant, perhaps untouchable woman. Cassie needed it because, well, Ry needed it. But what would it mean for them? For all of them?

Oh, Lord, Cassie thought, curling her petite hands into fists at her sides and swallowing uncomfortably. *I can't let Ry get close to this man. I can't…*

Her solemn gaze drifted up Dal's hard body and landed *kerplunk* in the middle of his intense heartfelt, soulful eyes.

Under her scrutiny, Dal wriggled. Something gave in his soul, and he blinked and looked away. He was a wealthy man, yet somehow he felt the woman standing in front of him with the moody stare was completely out of his league. Words escaped his lips before he had time to even consider what they meant. "If it's money you're concerned about," he glanced around at his old pickup, and at the small orange and gray dome tent he'd purchased in the nearby small city of Summerside, "I don't need it. I'm happy to teach Ry just for fun."

"Humph. You look like you need it." *Oh, shit. What was that old sign in my grandmother's house? 'Be sure brain is engaged before putting mouth into gear.'*

In front of Cassie, Dal bristled while Ry sulked and kicked his bike tires. *I should come clean,* Dallas thought. *I should tell this stuck-up little princess just who I really am.*

Considering that, Dallas realized that by giving himself up he would likely lose the anonymity he craved and was enjoying, as well as…

He gazed over Cassie's yoga-toned shoulders at the expansive soothing blue of the ocean before him, just beyond the lane, the dune and the beach. Without really wasting much thought on the subject, he knew he was breathing easier here on this small island—he was slowly learning to relax, to let go of the wild world he left behind when he cursed that stage in Seattle and hightailed it for Toronto on his private jet.

Dallas set his guitar aside. Cassie inhaled slowly when she saw him tenderly, lovingly, touch the guitar with those fingers, those callused man-fingers that she knew, she just knew, would sizzle on her body if she ever let him get that close…

She shivered.

He noticed, and frowned at her. "Your kid can't go wrong with music, Cassie," he told her. "Everyone needs a passion."

"A place to hide, you mean." Drawing her shoulders up proudly, Cassie challenged him to disagree.

But he didn't. "Damn straight," he whispered, while she immediately crumbled.

Biting her bottom lip, Cassie fidgeted with the zipper on her hoodie and shrugged. "Maybe it's what you're hiding from that's making me think twice about letting you, a stranger, spend time alone with my son."

"You can stay too. You can be here while we work." *Please. Although… I must be off my rocker.*

He wasn't giving her any reason to flee. Cassie froze. Almost unbidden, quiet words crept out from between her pursed lips. "I…I suppose in that case it would be okay."

From behind, she heard Ry suck in a breath. He bounded in front of her and grabbed her forearms. Tears stung her eyes when she saw light replacing the usual sadness with joy. "Mom, really? Sweet! Thank you! Thank you so much!" After a quick hug, Ry leapt back over to Dal, who thrust out a friendly hand for a shake. Cursing what she must look like with her bike helmet on, and needing something new to do with her hands, Cassie reached behind her head to grab and re-elasticize her low ponytail just below the helmet.

"Gentleman's agreement," Dal said with a righteous wink to Ry as Cassie tried to regain control of her emotions. "I'm not doing this just to kill time. I'm agreeing to teach you as long as you take it seriously. Which means you gotta practice, kid. I want to see you work at it."

"But I'm paying you," Cassie tossed in with a desperate need to take control. She waved a hand around Dal's rustic site. "Suck up your pride and accept it."

"I can pay him, Mom," Ry pledged, turning back around to his mother. A serious promise danced over his face now, a rainbow passing by after the storm of the last many years. Of a father he barely remembered. Of a mother who Ry still occasionally heard crying herself to sleep.

"What?" Cassie fixed her now serious son in a confused, wide-eyed gaze. "How?"

"I'll teach him to build sandcastles. I practiced today while you were sleeping on the beach."

"Ah. Oh. Okay, if that's what he wants…" A genuine wisp of a smile flitted across Cassie's pink cheeks.

"That'd be just fine." Dal hopped off the sturdy picnic table and extended a careful hand to his female visitor, who he felt might flee before he could offer a time to start teaching her son the ins and outs of country music. Before he could really reach her.

She hesitated before taking the strong fingers in hers, but when she did, Cassie shivered for the second time in a few short minutes. Closing her eyes, she sighed and let the big hand warm hers, let her new acquaintance offer comfort whether or not that was even his intention.

When she looked at him again, Dal was exhaling with an uneasy low *pffft*. He licked his lips nervously and blinked back at her.

Oh, baby, Cassie breathed to herself as Ry stepped behind Dal to greedily eye the Gibson. *You're scared too.*

Suddenly she wanted to know everything there was to know about this man, about the hurts that drove him alone to this secluded part of the world, about the music he drew from those beautiful, callused fingertips, about the pains that wounded his soul.

Crumpling into his arms was not an option, not here, not now, but as Cassie pedaled away from Dal she let herself dare to dream that someday, somehow, maybe it would be possible to melt into his body, to let him hold her and send her own deep ache far, far away over the distant horizon where it would no longer have the power to sink her to her knees.

And it was then, as the kaleidoscope sunset poured its liquid pink-gold into the cool, soothing ocean that Cassie realized things were changing. It occurred to her that because of the evening bike ride down the dusty lane, she was now more curious about the lonely man with the guitar, than she was sad about Eddie.

Chapter Four

*D*allas was just putting the finishing touches on positioning a tarp for rain cover over his tent—he'd run into the nearby town of Kensington for it earlier (along with a number of other supplies he'd learned the hard way that he needed)—when Ry and Cassie wandered onto his site early the next evening. Held aloft in one of Cassie's petite hands was a recyclable tray into which was inserted four red cardboard cups with white cornstarch lids. Dal gave a final pull on one of the tarp's corner tie-downs, ratcheted it firmly closed, wiped his hands on his faded jeans, and strode over to Cassie, who fidgeted timidly and pointed to the tray.

"Chai tea for me, chocolate milk for Ry, and for you?" Adjusting her stance and taking a deep breath, she stated in a voice she hoped sounded plain and unaffected, "I got both. Coffee and tea, I mean. Because I don't have a clue what you like." She couldn't help herself. The last bit was streaked with a thinly disguised hint of high-pitched accusation.

"Thank God for the Castle Café." Ignoring her slight jibe, Dallas added kindly, "It's saved my life a few times. Cinnamon roll breakfasts." He nodded at the tray. "Coffee. Please and thank you."

"Did you get wet last night?" Heavy rain showers had started soaking the campground just after midnight and hadn't let up until dawn's pink hug butted in and put the run to the misty gray clouds. This Cassie knew because she had lain awake most of the night trying to ignore the urge to hop on her bike and pedal down to Dal's small campsite, unzip the door of his tent, tiptoe inside, and cuddle up with him. The idea of those strong arms holding her in a gentle embrace all night long just seemed so…soothing…so…right.

Now, back in his physical company, she had to focus on taking even yoga breaths—in, out, in, out—to keep from blurting out a thousand questions, starting with 'so what's your favorite color?'

I'll bet it's blue, she told herself. *Blue like the sky in late afternoon, deep and intense, or like the ocean on a hot day when the waves are just hushed whispers. Or…light blue like your eyes in their dreamy, piercing sort of way, as if they can see right through me, to my soul, to all that loneliness I buried inside the day my husband forgot to say goodbye.*

"Mom!"

Startled, Cassie jumped and focused a fierce glare at her petulant son. With both arms crossed over his chest, Ry was facing her, but his probing, impatient eyes were on Dallas, who chuckled and toed the ground with a leather flip-flop so new it was distinctly out of place against the roughly clipped wild grass and the drifting wave of dandelions that spotted his camp-site all the way from the dusty lane to the dense tree line.

"Uh…sorry, did you say tea?" Dallas reaching forward and thoughtfully taking the tray from her hands made recovering from tuning out easier for Cassie. She let go with a downward flourish that ended in a nervous wipe of sweaty palms on her thighs.

Setting their drinks on the picnic table, Dallas averted his amused grin by scanning for the hot drink meant for him. Spotting a white lid marked with a C, he wriggled the cup out of its comfy recess. A small paper bag was crumpled up in the center of the tray. Dallas dug noisily around inside it. With two fingers he casually hauled out a creamer, gave it a gentle toss to rearrange his fingers around it, pulled back the paper top, and dumped it into his hot drink. At the same time, he answered Cassie's original question.

"You asked me if I got wet last night. Put it this way—a lot of things have improved over the years but somehow tents are as unpleasantly damp now as they were when I was a kid. At least this one is, when subjected to monsoons passing over Darnley."

He glanced toward the new tarp, which was stretched taut over the top of the dome tent, secured tightly now at each corner. An almost blinding late-day light was dancing on the shiny tarp, which irked Dallas because it felt like nature was rather succinctly giving him the finger after gifting him a restless, uncomfortable night. As if the world was reminding him just who—or what—was in control, via a wet night of tossing and turning followed by an almost annoying day of dazzling heat and dancing sunbeams. He quelled the childlike urge to stick his tongue out at the outwardly unconcerned sun while, in the trees bordering his campsite, his still damp sleeping bag and pillows were hanging mercilessly from branches, drying ghostlike in the day's lingering warmth.

Giving his coffee a stir, Dallas moved to the fire pit where he dropped the wooden stir stick before pivoting back around to face his visitors. "I took the tent down and put another two tarps underneath it, too. And I now have a full queen-sized air mattress to cushion my sleeping bag and keep my aching body off the hard ground. I'm not gittin' any younger. It's requiring more effort to unlock the cricks and cracks in these old bones in the dewy mornings."

For the second time in a few short minutes, Cassie zoned out. Last night's dreams of this man's touch on her skin were doing her in now that she was in his actual company. *I'm doomed.* Deflating, she sighed and stepped forward to accept a cup marked CT that, Dal assumed as he watched her take it from his hand, stood for chai tea.

"Thank you. So…" Letting her thoughts drift away, Cassie couldn't suppress a cute smile at the sight of a new clothesline, which stretched beyond two trees at the back of Dal's campsite, backdropped by the sleeping bag and pillows in the trees, which were too heavy for the small line. Only two items hung from the new rope—a small blue towel and blue swimming trunks. *Aha,* she mused. *I was right. You like the color blue.* The pickup truck was the first clue, the towel and trunks the clinchers.

She considered asking about where she should sit while Ry had his guitar lesson, but she cornered right instead. Dallas read her first thought anyway, and jumped toward a full-sized camp chair as she spoke. He settled the chair close to the metal-surround fire pit that was already set with newspaper, kindling and wood, but not yet lit. Cassie's words were pure innocence. She blurted out, "If you want a bigger beach towel, I've got lots."

To Dallas the offer was a reminder of just how unprepared he was for this weird detour from the world's largest stages. After a quick glance to the small towel on the line—barely big enough to dry his chest with, much less his entire body—he deposited his coffee on the picnic table, slouched back over to the fire pit, and mumbled back, "I'll add a beach towel to my list." Crouching by the laid out skeleton of a campfire, he set to work trying to light the damn thing. It took five tries and a few muffled curses, since a light breeze kept putting the flame out each time Dallas touched a match to paper.

Watching him, Cassie turned an ankle over and winked at Ry. "I don't suppose a proper lighter would be on that list."

"Geez, Mom." Even at his young age Ry could sense the slight antagonistic, supercharged energy between his mom and the man he didn't want to piss off. This guy had a magnetic energy that Ry was compelled to seek out. He had access to things that Ry wanted and needed that he couldn't even begin to process, starting with a kind of music that, with only one small bit of exposure, somehow felt manly and real to Ry as opposed to the stuffy, weighty classical stuff his mother insisted on listening to. Uncertain just how this was going to go down, he held his breath, his eyes darting back and forth between the unpredictable mother he knew and the seemingly self-possessed guitar teacher he wanted to know.

Dallas stood, his knees crunching when he turned his back to the fire pit and narrowed his eyes at Cassie. "I'd ask if you want to try but as you can see, it's lit now." He forced himself to suppress the snarky additive, *Princess.*

"Mmmm, I see, but you mighta wanted to use dry paper and kindling." Sure enough, the fire was smoking enough to signal campers on the other side of Prince Edward Island.

Frowning, Dallas shifted his weight to his other leg. He tapped the small box of matches against a thigh. Opening his mouth to speak, he changed his mind, touched the back of the camp chair as a sort of signal to Cassie, and marched back over to the picnic table to retrieve the coffee she'd brought him.

Cassie hunkered up her shoulders and giggled her way to the chair. Dropping her chai tea in a mesh cup holder built into the arm, she leaned forward and picked up a thick stick her new friend apparently used for poking at his fires. Expertly, she messed the wood around until the fire was more flame than smoke. *I was married to a firefighter,* she reminded herself, trying not to really look at the flames. Just being this near to a fire made her tremble.

But somehow her pride was at risk here in front of this bewildering man, so she shoved away the awful memories that haunted her.

"Your mom's good at this." Dallas took a good hard look at his new pupil.

Eyebrows furrowed in confusion, Ry was watching his mother work the flames. Sparks spit every which way after Cassie rumbled through a nearby stack of wood, found a split she thought was drier than the others, and tossed it cross-ways into the pit. "My dad was a fireman," Ry disclosed to Dal. Then to his mother he bit off, "I thought you said we could never have campfires anymore."

Pausing, Cassie dangled another split in midair. "This one's his. Not ours."

A piece of the puzzle. Dallas considered why Cassie wouldn't let her son enjoy campfires in a place where nightly fires were such a necessary part of the summer ritual that drivers on the way down the Lower Darnley Road in the evenings caught homey wafts of the woodsy scent before they even laid eyes on the thick white haze. There was so much smoke in the air on warm starry nights that it hovered over the campground in seamless patchy tufts the way clouds drift aimlessly over the earth.

Summoning up his courage, Dallas jumped in. "Look, kid, I've got stuff to make those things y'all like to make over fires—"

The sentence remained unfinished because Ry raised his head, sucked in a breath and gave Dal a look that almost stopped Dallas' heart, it was so filled with desperation, surprise and yearning. Like a kid finding the latest video game under the tree on Christmas morning. *For me? Really?*

Cassie's glare, though, almost skidded Dallas' heart to a halt for a different reason. Her look was more of the *you bastard, he's mine; you should have asked first* variety.

"It's just a few marshmallows and graham wafers," Dallas mumbled to her in a sort of half-assed attempt at apologizing. "For after our lesson. If he works hard."

"And chocolate?" Ry beamed hopefully. He grabbed the zipper on his orange hoodie and zipped it up and down, up and down, until a reprimanding look from his mother silenced the nervous action.

A wide grin bloomed across Dallas' face. Screw Her Highness. This kid was easy to please. Unable to help himself, Dal reached out and tousled the long-layered messy beach hair. "Of course. I grabbed a kit up at the camp store. We'll eat until we're sick."

"I didn't bring my son here to load him up on sugar." The bitter, anxious voice from the wilderness was enough to crack the joy in two, like the split wood for the fire. *Whomp.* Just like that.

But it was two against one now. There was no destroying the newfound friendship blossoming between this wayfaring man and the sad kid at his side.

"C'mon, Ry. Let's get to work." Bending over the picnic table, Dallas started snapping open the gold clasps on the Gibson case. Inside, the treasured guitar patiently waited for his magic touch.

Ry touched the side of the weathered case. He fingered the many faded stickers that announced a lifetime of playing music in strange towns and cities; that proclaimed a long and successful career in country music. "You've been to a lot of places."

At the fire pit, where she was sipping chai tea and nervously fuming, jabbing the poker stick here and there as she worked up the fire, Cassie straightened and went on high alert.

A pink flush swept across Dallas' cheeks. He shot a guarded look in her direction.

"Some two-bit redneck bar singer," he heard her mutter. "Lovely."

High-handed society girl, he decreed to himself so as not to upset his new student. *Music snob. Well, you're missing out, girl. Country music's the heartbeat of America. You scared I'm gonna corrupt your kid? Let me toss in some beer and whiskey.*

But when their eyes met, his pale blues a little hurt and her intelligent greens guarded and scared, the energy that caught and danced between them had the power to fizzle out the fears that both Cassie and Dallas held dear, that had them trembling with the unknown.

Interesting, Cassie considered as she studied him. *His eyes are sad like that liquid blue of the ocean at night when the sun goes down, when it looks shiny like a mirror. Only without the light, without the orange-pink hue the sun leaves there as it melts into the water, as it disappears.* She wondered what happened to his light. She wondered where it went. Who—or what—stole it away.

Funny, Dal thought, blinking away the need to defend his music, his essence, to the elegant woman who completely unsettled him. *Her eyes are like the trees behind my campsite, the softwoods with their spiked fronds that, when you touch them, are actually as soft as clouds.* He wondered if she, too, was soft to the touch.

Ry's next question threw him. It jarred Dallas back to reality. "How long you staying here? At Castle Beach?"

Perking up, Cassie bent an ear to listen.

"Hmm?" Dallas' eyes darted back to the kid at his side. "Uh...a few weeks. I'm not sure."

"We're seasonal," Ry piped up with newfound confidence. "We're here for the whole summer."

"You're in a trailer, then." *Duh,* Dal chided himself. *Of course they are.* Glancing back at Cassie, he furrowed his brow. *Did she curl her hair? For me?* He flushed again and twisted around, plunking his butt on the top of the picnic table so he could start tuning the guitar and avoid looking at Cassie altogether.

Eyes locked on the experienced fingers, Ry and Cassie were spellbound, for different reasons. Cassie sank deeper into her camp chair and sighed wistfully. Ry practically bounced.

"A big trailer." Ry pointed southwest. "On the other side of the camp-ground. It's brand new."

"Overlooking the Darnley Basin," Cassie added. To Dallas' relieved sur-prise, her words emerged soft and almost tender, for once.

Dallas shrugged, twisted his head, and looked over at her again. "I admit I never really considered how long I'd stay."

She gave the fire a poke. Sparks cracked again and, like beacons, rose up into the fresh evening air. "You don't look to me like you considered much."

"The camping thing was last minute, yeah. But so far it's all good." Dallas caught Ry's eye. "Kid, look, tuning's the most important part of playing. You always gotta keep your guitar in tune or else there's not much sense in pick-ing out a song cause it'll sound like horseshit."

Cassie recoiled.

Dallas noticed. "Oops," he managed, shooting his student a quick grin. "I shoulda said it won't sound so good. Sorry, kid."

Ry lit up and grinned back. Cassie groaned. Already the two had their own secret bond. A secret, silent language that consisted of shining eyes and happy smiles meant only for each other.

She wanted in.

"You need anything, I likely have it." It was a shot in the dark. Cassie refocused on the woodpile near Dal's campfire pit. She half stood and picked out a few more good pieces she could tell he'd bought from the pile for sale by the security gate at the campground's entrance. They sizzled when she laid them, pyramid style, a little more carefully than the first few, against the already burning wood. "I stocked up pretty good."

Dallas fixed his gaze on her. He watched her swallow and avert her eyes from the fire as the flames crept upward. A sick feeling clawed its way into his belly. *Another time,* he thought. *I'll ask about that another time.* He nodded at Ry. "How about I make you a trade?"

Cassie tensed. "For what? You have something besides lessons to trade?"

"I wanted to run this by your mom first," Dal said to his eager student who, he realized with a growing sense of happiness and pride, was anxious to get his hands on the guitar, "but I may as well just throw it out there. This guitar's kinda big for a kid to be learnin' on. I'd like to get you working on a smaller one. Besides, you need one to practice on. I can get you one if it's okay with your mom."

"Really? Mom!" Ry's wail was infused with joy but laced with fear. His mother would never go for this.

Cassie was silent. Flecks of fear settled more deeply into the jade eyes Dallas was finding equally captivating and fretful. "Students need to play along with their teachers, Cassie," he offered quietly. "Look, I make my living as a musician. I've got so many old guitars buried here and there that I've simply lost count. Let me give the kid something to learn on." Raising a hand, Dal raked his long fingers absently through the blond layers Cassie ached to touch. To run her own fingers through.

"Why don't we see how he likes it, first of all?" She sat back in her chair and wondered again who this man was and what he was doing here, hiding in this small lot overlooking an endless cold ocean where, now, seagulls chattered and played. "If you think he's picking it up, and if Ry's still keen after a few tries, I can buy him a guitar."

Ry was still. Watchful. Afraid to speak in case his words might burst this coveted, tenuous relationship, he waited.

Dallas' voice was gentle and encouraging. He recognized the need for caution with this pretty woman's apparently already bruised heart. With her need for control in a new situation that of course felt daunting and likely fleeting. "Fair enough. Let's see how the next few days go. We'll talk then." But he poked away a reminder to call his manager, Phil, the next day and have him send his assistant over to the house in Toronto, or to a music store, maybe. He'd find a guitar somewhere, a mini, one of those new parlor guitars the youngsters were playing these days, and he'd have it sent down anyway, and he'd give it to Ry with, if it eased Cassie's mind, a promise that it would just be on loan. For now.

Cassie seemed to have lost her spark of fight. Oddly, on some subconscious level, Dallas sensed it had something to do with the fire. It was almost as if the higher the flames got, the lower her spirits sank. Her voice now was defeated and subdued.

"How long did you say you were staying?" she asked. "I'm not sure how much Ry's going to learn in a week or two anyway."

Is that hope I'm hearing? Amongst that...desolation? "I might stay the summer." Dallas handed the guitar to Ry and helped place it in his arms. "I suppose it will all depend." He said this last part without looking at her. Instead it made more sense to place his own hope in the eyes of the excited boy before him. Resting his strong forearms on his thighs, Dallas grinned at Ry. He wanted to grab a photo but decided against it. Taking pictures of another person's kid was not an option, not until a certain amount of trust was built between he and Cassie. *We'll get there,* he thought. *One chord at a time.*

"You gotta stay for a while." Ry was adamant. "We have castles to build. Castle Beach is famous for its sandcastles and ours has to be the best. There's a contest."

Castles, thought Cassie. *Fairy tales. Happily-ever-afters. Castles of sand that the tide will just wash away, like the one Eddie and I built all those years ago. Where, once, a prince and princess lived until nature wiped us off the face of the earth. Where magic happened before one big wave crashed our party.*

"We'll build ourselves some castles, Ry. Some good ones. You'll see."

Fondly, Dallas adjusted the guitar in Ry's arms and placed the boy's left hand up the frets to where his first chord would be fingered.

From his left, he heard Cassie whisper. The pain in her voice was such a far cry from the perky snaps he'd heard from her earlier that Dallas found himself startled and confused. "You two go ahead and build your castles," she said. "How about I just watch?"

Ry frowned.

Dallas sent Cassie a look that he hoped was warm and understanding. She suddenly seemed to be close to tears. If he could have, he would have taken her hand and caressed those perfect, noble fingers. "We'll need your touch on the towers," he suggested carefully.

She smoothed her sundress on her lap and looked away. "I'm better at walls." A moment later she caught his eye again and said, "I'm not so good at building castles, Dal. Especially ones built of sand. They tend to just come crashing down on me."

His kindness, mingled with a gentle tenderness, almost brought her to her knees. "How about Ry and I don't let that happen?" he proposed. "We'll take pictures. Our castles will be ours forever."

"We get a lot of rain and wind here in this part of Canada. You're from Ontario." Cassie waved her chai tea toward Dal's blue pickup. The license plate on the front bumper clearly gave away at least a small part of who he was, of where he was from. "Your tent will never hold up all summer."

"Then I'll buy me another one." His grin was hopeful. Infectious.

"It's that easy, is it?"

"D'ya ever notice the waves, Cassie?" he tried. "How on some nights you can't pick out just one? When it's windy they all break together. Their sound gets all mushed up in each other when they crest and break on their way to shore. I think we can learn a lot from waves."

"Learn what?" she harrumphed in return. "That they get lost in each other? That they lose their uniqueness when it's windy?"

"No. That they become one when it's windy. That when it storms they're not alone."

A quiet hesitation preceded Cassie's next words. They emerged in the most honest whisper she dared. "You're on the run. Everything but your guitar and your truck is new. What do you know about depending on someone? On sharing strength in storms? Looks to me like you walked out on someone. On a family, maybe."

"Of sorts," he answered roughly. "But it's not like you think."

Their final look was as long and as layered as Dal's wrangy, oh-so-touchable hair. As restless and curious as Cassie's aversion to the flames she'd built up herself.

Lowering his shoulders, Dallas fixed a rueful half-smile on his student. On the child that seemed as desperate for connection as his mother but who, as yet, wasn't as scarred by his own life. Just by hers, apparently.

"Ry, this is G," Dal started, taking in a breath. He started to teach by positioning Ry's small fingers on the strings. "G is your friend. It's the easiest chord to learn and it's in a lotta songs. G will never let you down."

"Hello, G." Hesitating, Ry looked at Dallas for the encouragement and faith he knew he would find there, before he swept his right hand down over the strings in his first strum ever. "Welcome to my life."

Even Cassie couldn't avoid the small upturn of her lips at the sweet, playful innocence of that simple, welcoming statement, spoken from between the small pink lips of her fatherless child at the very first moment music became Ry's refuge and safe harbor.

Dallas smiled too, but for him it was in remembrance, in gratitude, for music had been his haven for many years, and never more so than in these last few weeks away from the hectic world of stardom. Now, upon sharing his gift with this young boy and his wistful mother, his talent for music was taking on a whole new meaning. Imbued with the past, suddenly it was giving him hope for the future.

Chapter Five

"Phil, my reception's crap down here. Make it quick, will ya?"

An impatient *hmmph* uttered in Ontario landed instantly in Prince Edward Island, loud and abrupt enough to make Dallas pull the phone away from his ear and wrinkle his nose at it, as if the phone was the annoyed party instead of Dallas' long time manager and buddy.

"Liar," Phil growled, his voice eerily suspended until Dallas sighed and brought the phone back to his ear. "I called the campground's office. They said the reception at your site is fine."

"Whatever," Dallas grumbled in response. "Maybe I have better things to do than sit around taking your abuse."

"You do. You need to be up here rehearsing for all of those summer music festivals you walked out on."

"Tell them I'm having vocal surgery, and pay out the contracts."

"Dallas, you owe me and your band and your fans an explanation. What in God's name possessed you to bail out of the busiest season you've had in years? And don't blame that little minx Deborah, because she's never been more than a bed warmer to you anyway, has she? Not really. Bless her heart for hoping for more from Mister 'My-shit-don't-stink-and-neither-do-my-millions.' It shouldn't have come as a surprise to you that she crossed the fence."

Deborah. Now there was a quandary. Occasionally Dallas did feel a twinge of sadness at hanging her out to dry by walking out in the midst of their dual tour, despite what she did to accelerate his leaving. He almost felt bad for leading her on, as she often accused him. Her infectious sense of humor had often dispelled the gray moods that haunted him these last few years, and her body—well, there wasn't a twenty-something vixen on the shoulders of some hunky boyfriend in the front row of Dallas' concerts that could compete with raven-haired Deborah's voluptuous figure. And her agility in bed? Sex with Deb, as much as it left Dal empty and dull when their playtime was over, sometimes catapulted him out of his body to the ceiling where he stayed suspended while he climaxed. Nope, there wasn't a damn thing wrong with Deborah except maybe that she didn't, all things considered, really need him. He wondered if she'd hooked up permanently with Cole. She certainly didn't need Dallas anymore; she was high up the country music ranks now, and rising higher, on his friend's back. *Or on hers.*

Dallas tried to force a chuckle as the knot in his stomach eased a little.

No, the issue wasn't so much Deborah. If anything, what she did to him, as much as it did hurt, had proved to be the catalyst that got him walking, which Dallas long knew he had needed to do anyway. The real issue forcing Dallas from the stage was himself.

He considered what to tell Phil. How do you explain gut-wrenching loneliness to the guy who built your career, who was responsible for putting cash in your bank account and stardom in your arms? Phil was more of the 'get-over-it' type. As in 'suck it up, what the hell gives you the right to be sad' type.

In the end Dallas went with, "Exhaustion. I'm burnt out, buddy."

Standing at the perimeter of his rugged campsite, one hand on his hip, staring out over the ocean as he said the words which, in Dallas' opinion, were not an outright lie, he focused on a lone fishing boat plowing through the boisterous Gulf in search of lobster traps to empty. A neighbor had filled Dallas in on the quaint boats with their forward cabins, long, low back decks designed for lifting traps in and out of the water, and their usual grunting chug-chugs. This morning Dallas and the guy, John, who planted his large camper on the same campsite overlooking the cliff every year (just down the cliff from Dallas toward the main part of Castle Beach Campground), had counted twelve lobster boats charging through the waves, some closer to the beach than others. Now, with Phil on the phone reminding Dallas that he was needed in a world that constantly drained him, Dal felt about as trapped as the coveted seafood. He was a bottom-dwelling lobster who'd clawed himself into a trap but who was helpless to get himself back out.

"Look, the media's clueing in that something's really wrong here, Dallas. I got you out of Phoenix and Vegas and I'm not telling you what it cost me, you ass, pride notwithstanding, but let me just put it this way. Rest up and keep your voice in shape. Unless you're on your deathbed—and you better not be, or you woulda told me—you woulda told me, right, Dal? The next few shows will sue us up the yin-yang if you don't put your stupid mug on their stages this summer."

An exasperated *ppffftt* escaped Dallas lips. "I'm not dying, Phil." *I just feel like I am.*

"Then call me in a few days. Or every day if you need to. All right, Dallas?"

"Fine. But hey, Phil, can you do me a favor?"

Ten minutes later, after he ordered a new mini guitar via Phil (who stuttered and stammered 'why' but who was completely ignored) and half heard Phil's list of 'be carefuls,' Dallas decided to walk off his frustration and anxiety by heading up the gentle slope toward the main part of the campground. Maybe, just maybe, he would take a stroll around the newer bay side where most of the luxury trailers were nestled in lots overlooking the sparkling, crystalline Darnley Basin. He decided to grab an ice cream on the way, and was almost at the camp store when he spotted Ry alone on a nearby faded green shuffleboard strip, desolately pushing heavy discs around with a long two-pronged stick. It was a hot, pristine, cloudless day, around four in the afternoon, and it was apparent by Ry's pink cheeks that he had likely been down on the beach for a while earlier. His hair had that salty beach look—straggly, windswept and wild. Dallas, too, was feeling rather like a beach bum. Unaccustomed to shorts and flip-flops, he constantly fingered the button at his waist as if he was reaching for the ubiquitous silver buckle he usually wore on his wide leather belt with faded jeans. Now, though, he raised an eyebrow and wandered over to Ry, whose face lit up when he saw his new—and at this point, only—campground friend.

"Whatcha up to, buddy?" Dallas inquired, trying to keep his voice light, but searching the immediate vicinity for Cassie.

"Staying away from the trailer. Mom's taking a nap." Using the stick, Ry gave a red disc a half-hearted push. It faltered to a stop a few feet away.

"Oh." Disappointed, Dallas tossed in another question, this one a little more pointed. "She sick?"

"Nope. Not more than usual, anyway."

"Oh. Geez, ah—your mom's, um, usually sick?" *Oh, shit. That might explain a few things.*

Grasping the shuffleboard stick with both small hands, Ry leaned heavily on it. His big, wide eyes sought out the concerned kindness in the grownup he desperately wanted to trust. "She gets sad sometimes and needs to sleep it off. My aunt says to let her be." Earnestly shifting his weight, Ry added, "Wanna play shuffleboard with me?"

Sad. Huh. Pondering the 'whys' of that simple truth, Dallas chewed on one corner of his lip. Cocking his head, he studied Ry's solemn face. Cassie's issues would have to wait. Right now it seemed her kid, like a cat left alone too long, was in need of a good scratching. "I'll play but if I beat you I'm walking you over to the store and you're buying me an ice cream, okay?" Dallas nodded at a damp fiver clutched in Ry's sweaty fingers.

Relieved for the company, Ry grinned and pocketed the bill so he could better hold and aim the shuffleboard stick. "I was gonna get ice cream now but it can wait. I've been practicing," he added in his low, weighty, serious eight-year-old voice.

"Oh." Toeing a black disc to behind the white start line painted on the narrow board at their feet, Dallas playfully grabbed Ry's shoulder and tousled his hair before thrusting a fist against his own chest. "Bummer." Half bent over, he feigned a mortal wound. "You're killing me, kid. I guess I'll be the one buying the ice cream."

Wriggling away, Ry dashed over to a wooden rack. Grabbing a stick like the one he was using, he thrust it out to Dallas, who took it and held it horizontal to the ground like a pool cue.

"Goofball," Ry laughed. Rolling his eyes he said, as Dallas lowered the stick to hold it properly upright with one end resting on the ground, "Not shuffleboard. Guitar. I've been practicing guitar." He beamed proudly up at Dallas. "I can play G and D now without that weird dull sound. Mom says they sound crystal clear. Do you miss your guitar?"

Dallas straightened. He'd loaned Ry his old guitar overnight. "Well, kid, that's something. High five!" Raising a hand, he cheered when Ry slapped his small palm against Dallas' bigger one. "One small step at a time. Soon you'll be playing in the big leagues." His stomach twisted at the thought… all those nameless faces staring out at him, the younger set who often froze at his shows because they dressed to show off their bodies instead of for the weather, the wealthy patrons who wanted nothing more than to grab selfies to say they'd met him, the concert promoters who treated him like nothing more than corporate product. "And no. I kind of don't miss it."

They started their game with Ry lining up four red discs on one side of the start line. Dallas followed suit with the rest of the black ones. Ry positioned his stick behind one disc—two prongs nestled the disc perfectly— then he gave the disc, via the stick, a hard shove. It flew over the scoring area and zoomed off the far end of the board.

"You don't know your own strength, Ry," Dallas teased. Following suit, he frowned and *hmmphed* when his disc flew off the right edge. Groaning as Ry jumped up and down with boyhood glee, Dallas made a mental note to ask Cassie about the wisdom of letting her son roam the campground alone. Not that Ry was likely in any danger, but did she really know that? About him, for that matter, or about anyone out here?

Focusing on the game, Ry drew back his stick and let another disc fly. This one slid over the playing surface and landed in a triangle marked with a painted white numeric ten.

"Ha! I'm gonna school you," Ry said to his new friend. He jumped up and down again, which made his hair bounce. Dallas liked the look. It was something to see the boy genuinely happy. Ry's eyes were lit up; it was like one of those garden solar lights had settled inside him, inside his soul. Energized by the sun, or by the simple joy of having a buddy for company, it was giving off a bright, steady glow.

Too bad he's stuck with an old guy like me, crossed Dallas' mind while he set up his next shot.

What he failed to consider was that Ry was thinking the same thing about him, only he had reversed it.

Too bad he's stuck with a kid like me.

Cassie awoke to a dog's sharp bark and a baby's mournful cry. For a few moments during the gray fog between sleep and wakefulness, she thought she was back in Halifax, in the architecturally eclectic southern end of the city in the dark but cozy Edwardian home she once shared with Eddie. When Ry was an infant and Eddie was still alive to warm her heart and shelter her soul.

Memory jarred her back to reality with a stab and a twist, with a serrated dagger dipped in poison. Reflecting on why she felt disoriented and misplaced in time, Cassie realized that she'd dreamt of Eddie. In the depth of sleep he was walking beside her on the beach murmuring words of comfort and hope, the setting sun lighting his face with a peaceful, transcendent golden-orange hue as he stepped barefoot over the wet sand lining the water's edge. His words were lost in murky fog; they were buried in the thick walled layers that divided Cassie's painful wakeful state from the sweet perfection of the dreamland stroll on the beach. Reaching for the blissful dream, desperate to reconnect with her husband, to pull him back to her, Cassie wept when it hit her that Eddie's feet had not left footprints in the sand.

Burying her face in her pillow, she let out a mournful cry. It had been a while since Eddie visited her in a dream. "Why now?" she begged the universe. "Do you think I'm going to forget you, Eddie? I won't. I swear. I could never forget you."

Eddie had been a tall, solid man, youthful and vigorous, and never happier than on the day their son was born. Rugged and handsome, with a strong jaw and thick dark curly hair that Cassie always had to gently urge him to get cut every six weeks so it wouldn't grow into a wild and woolly mess, he was her rock. He was her everything. He was kind, and generous with his time. Eddie shoveled the older guy's driveway next door when the man was stranded at work during snowstorms.

"He's got to be able to park his car in the driveway when he gets home," Eddie used to say. Or he'd cut the guy's grass in the summer, and even go so far as to use the weed trimmer around the foundation of the man's home. This after mowing and trimming his own lawn. "It takes me less than an hour to do our small lawn," Eddie would say as he tied a red bandana around his curls to hold them back in the wind. "It's no biggie."

Now, Cassie had to count to ten and focus on the tapping of the wind-blown blind in the Montana's small bedroom in order to get her mounting anxiety under control before it took her down a dark road. The king-sized bed dwarfed her; the bed was too big for one small body.

Once she felt she could breathe normally again, she eased over onto her side and hugged a pillow to her chest. There were two ways she could look at the brief dreamtime in Eddie's company. One, appreciate it for what it was—a gift. Short and sweet, yes, but still—a gift.

"I felt his hand in mine," she breathed, remembering. "I smelled the salt tang of the ocean, I saw the sea breeze blow through his hair." His presence was so overpowering, he was so real in the dream, that Cassie had to convince herself that she was alone here in this large trailer, in this campground, with a son her husband would no longer know, since Ry was only two when Eddie died.

The other way to look at the time with Eddie was as a curse. As if his appearance was meant to wound, to hurt, so that upon waking Cassie wouldn't be able to cope. So that she would sink into that desperate state again, the one where only sleep felt safe, because that was the place where Eddie might be found once again.

But—Ry. Always it was her son that motivated Cassie into action, that got her moving. Where was he now? She'd sent him to the store with a five-dollar bill, but that was...

She glanced at the digital display on the clock at her side.

"Oh, no," she moaned. The clock read six-thirty. Cassie'd laid down for her nap at three.

Pushing her husband from her consciousness on a wing and a prayer, because it was a helluva lot easier to bury his memory than to relive the pain of loss again on a conscious level, Cassie slipped out of bed and into a long soft cotton sundress that flowed over her ankles. Tie-dyed horizontal stripes circled it, in different primary colors that decorated a white background. Moving quickly now, peeking out of the small windows to see if Ry was maybe outside on the picnic table, or lounging on one of the deck chairs, she poked her toes into jeweled sandals and fingered a new gold clip to ponytail her beach-mussed hair. One thing about living at the beach, ponytails were not only accepted, sometimes they were a downright must.

Eyeing the big silver Ford truck, Cassie considered grabbing the keys and running it around the campground in search of Ry, but in the end she closed the trailer door behind her, locked it, and trudged up the small slope on two feet and a heartbeat. There was an arcade on the bay side, at the top of the slope, but Ry's five bucks would be long gone if he'd decided to duck in there. Perhaps he was watching some other kid play a game. Perhaps he'd made a friend? Beyond the low wooden building that housed the arcade was the Lower Darnley Road, which separated the campground into what was known as the new, or bay, side, and the older, treed part, where the main beach was found down another slight slope beyond the lanes of private campsites. Directly beyond the road, before the old section filtered off into campsites, was the main collection of buildings that included the camp store and laundry facilities.

Cassie ducked into the arcade first. No signs of Ry, and the young teen attending the building hadn't seen him. Half-running, chiding herself the entire way because no mother should leave her eight year old unattended in a busy campground like Castle Beach while she sleeps away a debilitating loneliness, Cassie hoofed it across the wooden boardwalk that connected the old and new sections of Castle Beach.

The day was blistering hot even now as the shadows lengthened and campers back from the beach fired up their barbecues. Around her, Cassie hyper-noticed things as she moved, like the man and woman walking their dogs toward her on the now gravel path, two on leashes and three wandering alongside, all different breeds, big and small. Dramatically different, in fact. They were a made-up family since the breeds were so varied. Cassie had to force herself to stop staring.

A made-up family. Could she do that? Could she meet someone new and start again? Would a man take Ry under his wing and treat him like his own son? Even the thought felt wrong somehow. Traitorous. Dream-Eddie floated back to her, accompanied by the blissful nirvana state of simply being by his side again. *I don't want anyone else,* Cassie wailed to herself, her sandals slipping and crunching in the thick gravel as she hurried along. *I just want what I had.*

You're living in the past, her sister would say.

It's time to move on, her mother would admonish.

As if they understood. As if Cassie was a schoolchild who'd lost a puppy. As if she was even capable of forward motion when it came to finding someone new. As if she was capable of letting Eddie go.

Glancing up, Cassie saw Ry. Seated on the wooden bench outside the Laundromat behind the store, he was eating what appeared to be an ice cream sundae instead of drinking his usual slushie or inhaling a cookie-dough flurry. And he was with Dal.

Relief outweighed anger, but Cassie took her frustration at herself out on her son. "Ry, you were supposed to come straight back to the camper." Averting her narrowed gaze from Dal, Cassie crossed her arms and slid to a stop directly in front of her happy, suntanned child.

Digging in a pocket, Ry withdrew his hand and held out a fisted palm. "Here's your money back, Mom. I beat Dal at shuffleboard so he had to buy the ice cream."

Cassie's shoulders sagged. Sighing, she bit her bottom lip and let her gaze drift over to Dal. Instantly, remorse flitted across her face. He was regarding her with a not-unfriendly stony silence that, somehow, was infused with sorrow. *What'd you tell him?* Cassie silently wondered of her son.

"I fell asleep," she said simply by way of both explanation and apology. "The hot sun at the beach today…it did me in. Entirely."

"Um-hum." Dal spooned up the last of his sundae, looked over at Ry's to see that he still had a way to go on his, although it was rapidly becoming a soupy hot fudge mess in the heat, and he got up and dropped his Styrofoam dish and plastic spoon in the nearest garbage. Returning, he settled by Cassie, choosing to stand instead of taking his seat on the wooden bench again.

A thought occurred to Cassie. "Do you have kids, Dal?"

She thought she saw sadness in his eyes, but if it was there it was fleeting. Dal recovered quickly. "Nope. Not even a dog. Or a gerbil, for that matter."

"So…Dal just takes care of Dal," she sniped without meaning to. If anyone deserved sniping at right now, Cassie knew it should be herself.

"And your boy, apparently," he responded quietly, with a furtive glance at Ry to see if he caught on. Ry didn't. Instead, he jumped up to question a little girl of about six about a tiny puppy she was cradling in her arms. Dallas heard him ask what the puppy's name was.

"Look, I'm sorry," Cassie managed with sincere regret. "I didn't mean to sleep for so long. Ry usually knows to come straight back."

Dallas raised his arms in a truce. Palms out and elbows bent, he took a step backward. "Look, I'm the last person to be judging here, Cassie. I'm not a parent so I don't have any experience in this area, but I can't help but think that a kid his age ought not to be running around a busy campground on his own. Even for ice cream. I mean, I gotta ask you, how well do you even know me? I just played shuffleboard with your kid for two hours. I could have convinced him to come down to my campsite for another lesson on the guitar. He would have come."

Sorry for causing alarm, Dallas exhaled slowly and touched Cassie's elbow. She was tearing up now, and was swiping at the corners of her eyes with curled-up knuckles. "Aw, heck, Cassie," he said. "Don't go getting all emotional on me. I'm not dangerous."

She tossed her ponytail and drew up her shoulders. To Dallas, Cassie was small but feisty, a formidable warrior when she wanted to be. "Aren't you?" she fired back at him.

"Touché," he said softly, effectively erasing Eddie from Cassie's mind for at least the next five minutes as she recovered her senses from the corners of the campground to where they'd disappeared. Touching her cheek lightly, long enough for Cassie to close her eyes and hold back a wince, he set them on a safer path. "I don't know a lot about kids, but I do know we ought to feed that shuffleboard swindler of yours something more than just ice cream for dinner. It's almost campfire time."

She opened her eyes. "Um...we?"

Dallas shrugged and smiled. "Why not?" Holding out an arm to Cassie, his smile grew wider when she took it.

Abandoning the puppy, Ry lit up like a Christmas tree and bounced along behind them as they started to saunter down the road toward Dallas' campsite.

"You like steak, kid?" Dallas asked, tossing the question over his shoulder.

"I do," Ry answered honestly, with a hop and a skip behind his mom. "But she won't eat red meat."

"Do you have tofu?" Cassie's eyes were shining now, and not from sorrow or frustration. She laughed when Dal froze.

"Maybe they have some at the store," he stuttered, starting to walk backward to retrace his steps.

"As if. Goof. I'm joking. I'll eat whatever you have."

"Steak, mom?" Ry's eyes were wide. Scooting up beside her, he slipped his hand in hers. Cassie was suddenly too choked up to do more than nod.

Dallas bent and whispered in Cassie's ear. "I've got chicken," he grinned, starting to walk forward again. "Later we can grab my guitar from your trailer, Ry," he added. "Another day, another lesson, okay kid?"

Oh, God, Cassie sighed, because as far as she was concerned Dal's warm breath in her ear was not quite enough sensation on her body on this gorgeous summer evening. She wanted—needed—more. Suddenly it struck Cassie funny that her new friend was now walking alongside her on the same side where Eddie was not all that long ago, in the dream. The sun was still rather high in the sky on this early July day, and it imprinted a happy light in Dal's blue eyes.

Or maybe it was simple joy Cassie spotted there when she dared to look, a joy that she too was feeling now, much to her surprise. It was coming from an easy unexpected companionship, and from the hope that friendship might grow from that the way all good friendships grow, with love and faith, and with a sincere, wholesome trust.

Chapter Six

"*R*y, pass me the ruler, will you?"

After his new young friend handed him a plastic see-through ruler, Dallas playfully poked him with it. They played a little game of good-natured touch-tag until the frown on Cassie's lips at the amount of beach sand flying around alerted Dallas to her disapproval. But after their barbecue last night, he was starting to understand her a little better. Underneath Cassie's slight down-turned lips today was a wisp of a smile; happy flecks danced across those aqua-jade eyes. Ry had become an animated kid these last few days, and that, Dallas guessed, was lightening some of the cumbersome load on Cassie's petite shoulders.

With a mischievous glint and a wink, Dallas flicked the end of the ruler at her. Like some delicate fairy blessing, a tiny spray of white beach sand arced through the air and dusted her arm.

Ducking her face shyly, Cassie's cheeks pinked up. With a quick flick of her wrist, she took the ruler from him. This little game amused the heck out of her, mostly because it brought her right back to elementary school play fights when boys were first starting to realize girls were different. "Either you use this for carving out a set of stairs on that pile of sand," she warned with a light sparkle, "or I confiscate it and you don't get it back til later."

His quickly raised eyebrows and rascally grin crested Cassie's already flushed cheeks with instant magenta highlights. "Oh, Lordy," she breathed inwardly so Ry, who flanked Dallas' other side, couldn't hear or read into what Cassie felt Dal was communicating to her. But she got the message loud and clear.

Last night, sparks were flying, and not just from the campfire Cassie built. Too many times, at least in Cassie's humble opinion, Dal's warm fingers rested on her arm, or his needy gaze smoldered in her eyes just a little too long. The campground last night was humid and sticky. While the evening stars popped out above, shining silently in regal benediction on the unsuspecting campers below, things had heated up even more, ending with an almost unbearable need to shatter the longing between Cassie and Dallas with a final, explosive touch.

But it couldn't be, not...yet.

They'd practiced on the guitar first, Dal and Ry. Cassie had walked up to the Montana and retrieved the guitar while the boys did the supper dishes. Later, while Ry had patiently turned marshmallows, toasting them over the fiery embers to a cautious uniform brown perfection, Dallas' and Cassie's intense smoky eyes shyly scrutinized each other across the bits of glowing ash rising up from the fire. Theirs wasn't necessarily entirely a sexual passion, at least not all of the time. Instead what they were feeling was more of a base human need to just connect, to let the sizzle sparking between them land in a place that could unite the two on a deeper level than on the rudimentary, yet complicated, playing field Ry's presence engendered.

More than once Cassie found herself wanting to lay her fingers over Dal's when he touched her. At one point he offered up a square of chocolate to place under the marshmallow Ry had toasted Cassie for her own s'more. At the same time he lifted his second hand and rested his fingers, for the briefest second, on her bare shoulder. Letting her eyes close over, she'd almost moaned at the sweet pleasure of it, at the sheer helplessness produced by the erotic energy that crackled from his body into hers by a simple stroke of his finger. Dallas could do that to her, briefly; he had that power, as if his touches were ashes rising from the fire, red-hot bits that sparked off the burning wood, died, and disappeared into the night.

Ry's watching, wondering eyes peeking up at them from over his roasting stick last night were hopeful and naïve, too much so for Cassie to risk more, to risk touching Dal back, to see if her skin on his had the same effect. Surrendering to the man was not an option, not with Ry's openhearted longing for acceptance and friendship clearly revealing a want that sliced just as deep.

The boy had an innocence that brought the two adults together in a natural need to protect him, to keep him safe from the big, bad world. For Cassie, once the mother in her clicked back in, the desire that seeded itself in her heart the instant she first got lost in Dal's pale eyes was trumped. Partly it was an excuse. She craved her own safe haven as far as her new friend was concerned. The man's power over her was disconcerting. The fingers he brushed against her shoulder may as well have been embers lifted from the fire— their heat had a depth and breadth that somehow ricocheted deep into her body, leaving invisible burns that Cassie knew would scar if she let them, if she didn't put the fire out. Yet she wished every finger led to a kiss, led to his moist lips trailing across her shoulder and up her neck; to his hands roaming fully over her body with free rein to land at will wherever the man had the desire to place them. The only way she had of knowing that Dal was having similar urges, to explore her yoga-toned body with kisses and touches that had no parameters, was by his growing silences, which were interrupted only by quiet responses to Ry's bubbly requests for help with the gooey s'mores. The silences deepened as the evening lengthened and were overtaken by the excruciating touches. Only occasionally did Dal accent them with his husky voice and questioning eyes.

Near eleven, Cassie had wriggled in her camp chair and grudgingly cued her sleepy son that it was time to go. She started packing up what was left of the s'mores kit. Standing, Dallas sucked on a lip and watched her.

She almost begged him to let them stay, to let them end their perfect night in his company. Ry could sleep in a made-up bed in the back of Dal's truck, maybe, under the stars, the night was warm enough…Cassie would unzip the flap of the nearby tent and end the night on her back—in Dal's arms, captive. She would welcome his erogenous touches with moans she wouldn't hold back, and with half-lidded eyes, and with lips that would beg for more until, like healing from grief, a perfect pink dawn would break over them.

But…Ry.

Trembling, Cassie had politely thanked Dal for a good time, for barbecuing chicken just for her, and for what she felt were genuine kindnesses—and patience—with her son. Ry thanked him too, wiped his eyes with a knuckled fist, and stumbled toward the red dirt lane bordering Dallas' campsite.

Cassie struggled against Dal's strong essence and the urge to stay. Wisdom and caution forced her to put one small sandaled foot in front of the other, to leave his powerful presence one step at a time.

Near the edge of the campsite a new grief overtook her, but this one was more about the possibility of loss in the face of already having lost, about walking away from a man she ached to know. It was about the need to suck the marrow out of life, or what was left of it—to heck with society and its conventions. To heck with fear and to heck with worrying about what a man like Dal, seemingly a bar singer with very little means, could possibly offer her in terms of some kind of accepted middle class security.

Wheeling back around, she'd held her breath and searched his eyes.

Dal's eyes were moist and shiny—he looked about ready to cry. He, too, was a prisoner of their instant, disarming connection. She'd caught him off guard by suddenly turning back around. Cassie's knees weakened at the sorrow she spied in the way he stood with one knee bent and his weight on the opposite leg. Her heart plummeted. So much for a surge of bravery. The guy had secrets, that wasn't a stretch. A wife? Children? A newly broken heart?

"Dal," she breathed, asking all of those things without really saying anything at all.

Her quiet bell-peal voice saying his name that way, infused with ache, was the sweetest music Dallas decided he'd ever heard, and he'd heard plenty in his abundant lifetime. Infused with longing, Cassie had spoken his name to him with a tenderness Dallas didn't expect to hear from between those perfect pink lips tonight, from that small mouth. An almost desperate sadness was communicated to him in that one three-letter word.

Beyond Cassie's small frame was an endless, seemingly limitless ocean, just beyond the red dirt lane, bordered by a thick green nautical rope designed to protect campers from venturing too close to the sand dunes leading to the beach. The rope, faded by the hot sun, was suddenly a big ole stop sign, a wall separating Cassie and Dallas from the type of freedom the boundless ocean represented.

In order to get to it, to that freedom, to live the lives of liberty both desperately wanted, they would have to metaphorically climb over the rope.

Cassie took the first step. She moved back toward Dal, who breathed in softly before holding up two fingers. Slowly, slowly, slowly he pressed the callused tips of those fingers against Cassie's mouth. A tiny gasp escaped her lips and her eyes closed over; her lips parted just the tiniest bit when he did that, when he touched her that way. Sighing, tipping her face shyly downward to the black abyss between her feet, she dropped both hands to his hips.

"Cassie," he whispered, sensing that her wary movement was the same fear that was ruthlessly taking over his already breaking heart.

A low rustling sound tuned him in deeper to her nerves—Cassie's foot was moving back and forth. She was toeing some small gravel rocks around and around. Calming her, reassuring her, Dallas laid almost the whole heel of his palm low against her cheek and allowed his thumb to brush that sweet spot just above Cassie's chin, below her lips.

Leaning slightly into him, she lifted a hand, covered his fingers with hers, and inhaled deeply.

His T-shirt was a soft, brushed cotton; it smelled of comfort—cozy wood smoke mingling with barely-there sweat. The maleness of his simple presence quieted Cassie, and brought Eddie back for a shooting-star kind of moment to remind her that she was glimpsing perfection in these few sacred minutes with Dal. In her mind a star was arcing across the sky as surely as her heart was beating. Stepping away from Dal would break the enchanting spell. Love is possible; that's what Eddie was gifting her now by popping into Cassie's mind this way. He was offering up a sacred memory that was once theirs, and theirs alone. Walking away from Dal would shatter the fairytale-like glow. Leaving him behind, ending this amazing evening to drag her tired body back to her lonely camper, would flood Cassie's mind with a cluster of unwanted thoughts, of the harder, painful memories that came with loving Eddie, of having to let him go.

Breaking the spell would be overwhelming; it felt like all the stars would chime in at once, in a chorus, and try to talk to her, send her messages and warnings, to inject harsh realities into this new surreal aura encircling Cassie and Dal that it somehow seemed Eddie was trying to endorse.

Walking away from Dal would be like disappearing back into nothingness, into the overwhelming life without purpose and joy that Cassie had become accustomed to living. Her shooting star would fizzle out, its flawless glory banished to the place where all perfect memories go, hopelessly dark and beyond the scope of touch and time.

"You're a good mom, Cassie," Dallas told her in that brusque, dusky voice he used when life got too big and possibilities seemed impossible. The raw longing in his tone had brought Cassie tumbling back to him, back to a lingering few moments of budding star-crossed love where she was his and he was hers. "Ry's a lucky kid."

"I shouldn't have…today…I don't…" Frustrated, scared, she'd found herself at a complete and utter loss of words and, for that matter, the ability to speak in full sentences.

"I would never hurt him. He's safe with me."

And me? Am I, she wondered, opening her anguished jade eyes, which were pale and wanting now in the moon-washed semi-darkness. Looking up, she finally met his tender gaze.

Dal took her solidly in his arms then, just for a few seconds, holding her under the watchful, protective crescent moon whose far-reaching moonbeams were not imprisoned by the rope boundary, and which therefore reached the calm, cool ocean just beyond. The moon was projecting a watery, hopeful shadowy white now, a fluid faraway warmth that blended easily into the cool embrace of the welcoming Gulf.

There was no kiss from Dal tonight, there was just this loving hug, a safe set of strong arms around Cassie's shoulders, a gentle pull to him, and a reckless, earnest whisper in the hollow of her neck.

"Let me walk you home," he begged. "Please."

Cassie swore the request was accompanied by a low moan as Dal pressed her body to him, but she wasn't sure. *Maybe the moan came from me,* she'd instantly thought, with an almost embarrassed panic that surpassed the urge to hold on to him forever, for dear life, even. There was just something about being held by this man, about being safely enclosed in his embrace, that made her want to just let go, to cry, to scream, to wail, even. To finally grieve Eddie. The arms of this man, for whatever reason, carried no threat. Dal's aura was mixed-up and lonely, sad and wistful, but at times it was also happy and joyous, especially in Ry's young company.

By no means was the man angry or mean.

The liquescent moon dipped behind a cloud, leaving a dramatic smoky Halloween trail high in the sky. It was time to let go. But as they untangled their arms from around each other, Cassie shook her head slowly from side to side and fixed a solemn gaze on the man she ached to take home to love.

"Not tonight," she breathed back to him, instantly sorry for holding back because her spirit sank even further at bringing the evening's magic to a final, crashing halt. And because the sorrow in Dal's lonely eyes was acute.

He studied her before responding. "Okay, Cassie. I understand."

No, you don't. You don't understand.

"Dal, I…Ry and I, we'll be fine. It's not that far. I need—I mean, I like—the walk."

"You're the independent type, huh?" he'd teased. At her unsure frown, he'd added quickly, "Tomorrow, then." He looked so hopeful with his long sandy-blond hair peeking out from under the ubiquitous baseball cap that Cassie couldn't suppress a tiny smile, which quickly upended her nervous reaction to his 'independent' comment. Reaching up, she removed Dal's ball cap, flipped it around and tugged it down so the brim was at the back, covering his kissable, musky neck. Bending forward, she pressed her lips to his fuzzy cheek.

"I'll see you on the beach," she'd assured him softly. "I'll bring sandwiches for my two hardworking sandcastle sculptors. I hope you like tomato."

"Tomato's fine." Sighing, Dal let go.

Like a spirit, Cassie drifted out of his fingers. After a moment she twisted around to face Ry's small body down the lane, and she faded off into the night.

Shoving his hands in his pockets, Dallas had watched her float away. Quickened light thuds over the dirt told him she was jogging a little to catch up to her son, whose tired head was down and whose feet were barely dragging over the loose dirt.

Dallas was a man completely unaccustomed to being turned down. Ever. It confused the hell out of him, yet at the same time Cassie's cautious choice built seeds of respect that he took inside his heart and treasured. Starting to step backward, he moved slowly. Dallas wanted the last possible glimpse of this elegant gal and her quiet son on this starry, magical summer's eve.

Cassie flipped back around again just as Dallas was considering running after her and begging her to stay. Under the faint moon, she was barely there. An illusion, maybe. A dream. He could barely see her.

She hollered something at him. It jarred him, her voice loud again in the blackness like that, as if the dream had ended and all that remained was a blanched reality, leaving behind a mythical glow. He had to ask her to repeat what she said. When she did, her words brought a grin to Dallas' face and lightened the heaviness crushing his heart. He'd see her again. And maybe… just maybe…

"Do you like mayonnaise?" she was asking. "On your sandwich! Do you like mayo?" The inquiry came to Dallas from beyond, from somewhere in the darkness. Its simplistic absurdity brought him light.

"I have so much to learn about you," he grinned inwardly before calling out, "Yep. I'm a mayo man. Hey—do you?"

Giggling, she whispered loudly back, aware now that at least some of the hardy campers around her were already tucked in for the night and likely unimpressed with her hollering. "I'm making the sandwiches. You don't need to know whether or not I like mayonnaise."

"Oh, yes I do," he chuckled under his breath into the night. "I need to know everything about those pouty lips and those small hands and that sweet face." Aloud, he called instead, "See you on the beach tomorrow!"

She raised a hand to wave goodnight.

Seconds later, Dallas could no longer hear the slow shuffle of Ry's and Cassie's feet. Grabbing a last piece of wood from the ground near the fire pit, he'd dropped it into the smoldering embers, plucked himself a beer out of the cooler behind the tent, dropped into a camp chair, leaned heavily back, sighed into the stars until sleep overtook him, and finally surrendered.

Now, on the beach, Cassie moved to hand the ruler back to Dallas, but she gripped it for a few suspended moments when he reached out for it because he wrapped his fingers around hers and held on tight. She lost herself in the heady feel of his skin on hers and the needy look he was clearly telegraphing in her direction.

"Clouds are moving in," he told her, jolting her back from some wistful dream-state when he found his voice. She let go of the ruler. Lifting it, he leaned forward to start carving out a tiny set of curved stairs in the sand, but before Dallas made the first sandy cut he paused and nodded toward a wall of gray that was, indeed, moving atop them. A monumental dark cloud, Hindenburg-like in its rounded edges and power to block out the sun, was in the middle of the threatening pack. "S'gonna rain." Bringing the ruler down carefully, Dallas cut a precise five-inch long riser and step out of the sand of the castle before him. He followed his cut and swipe movement by carving another stair just below the first.

As if the clouds could hear him, the sand around the three started to darken in haphazard spatters. Cassie angled a palm against her forehead and peered out from underneath it at the blackening sky. "And that ends our beach day." Sitting on her haunches, she was watching the boys work. A shiny green travel mug was in the lowered hand. This she brought to her lips now with a practiced solemnity as she studied the darkest cloud. The cup's lid was soon a bubbly spattering of pearlescent raindrops.

"The sky is really something out here, isn't it, Dal?" she stated with a solemnity that nature's ever-shifting power deserved. "It's like I've never noticed it before. Running from home to the office to the grocery store… is it always this incredible? Like…it's always changing. The blue is never the same, sometimes it's light and sometimes it's got this crazy saturated depth to it…the clouds are puffy, they're sharp-edged, then the next day they're all soft and fuzzy at the edges, or all thin and wispy, and you can see through them. Mare's tails, my grandmother called them. Even the sunsets…"

Meeting Dal's content, glad eyes, she blushed and tried to memorize the adorable tiny laugh lines emanating out from the corners while he listened. "The sunsets," she said again, "are all unique. Sometimes they're this glowing orange with layers of color and little peek holes of light that are always moving, evolving. Sometimes they're pink. But they light up the sky with an entire spectrum of gray and white and yellow and orange and purple. Like oblong rainbows that make the red cliffs of this beguiling island shimmer before they dissolve into the ocean."

"Maybe you just don't look up often enough." The statement was delivered with a hint of humor, but its simple veracity was humbling. Dallas had to admit to himself that in the last few years he sure as hell hadn't looked anywhere but down either.

Every day it seemed they were teaching each other how to live again. The infectious smile now blossoming across Cassie's rosebud cheeks confirmed that Dallas' off-the-cuff truth had hit its mark. The words had surprised Dallas every bit as much as they enlightened Cassie.

With a grin to Ry who, with a green plastic shovel balanced easily in one small set of fingers, was staring up at the sky in wonder, Dal let the insightful declaration soak in further. Leveraging his hard body upright, he wiped sand off the plaid shorts he'd taken to wearing to the beach and that, to his surprise, felt like a comfy pair of boxers. They rode a little low over the hips, and were a tad baggy over his butt, as if he wasn't sure what size to buy. A green T-shirt, tight around the chest, showed off muscled arms and a dark blue band tattoo in some mythical Celtic rope design, inked around Dallas' right bicep.

Aching to touch it, to run her fingers around the faded art and learn what the tat meant to him, Cassie studied it before letting her eyes drift up to meet his once again. Dal allowed a small half-smile and reached down to help her rise.

Ry shoved his shovel into the sand. "It's just a little rain!" he complained. "We won't melt."

Streak lightning lit up the sky. Cassie screeched. Her tea spilt over the small hole in the travel mug when she jumped, and Dal's right arm slipped around her waist to steady her. Ry watched in optimistic, thinly disguised glee.

"You okay?" Dallas asked Cassie, looking like a tiger ready to pounce. Not on her, though, on the beach gear at their feet. At her slow yoga inhale and ensuing quick nod, he mobilized his body into action and started tossing sandcastle-building tools—the ruler, buckets, plastic knives and forks— into a large black and white zebra-striped waterproof bag. A hearty roll of thunder changed Ry's mind real quick; he ran for the ocean with dirty buckets that he dipped three times each before dumping the water out to clean them off. Cassie grabbed the beach blanket, rolled it and shoved it into a large yellow faux-something-or-other carryall where it nestled up next to a bag of low-salt rippled chips, three large beach towels, and a Tupperware container Cassie'd used to travel the tomato sandwiches.

Another crack had her screaming, the heels of both palms flat over her ears.

Ry was laughing. "Mom, stop!"

"Let's go, Ry!" Dal called. Hooking an arm through Cassie's, he grabbed the bulging striped bag and headed for the ramped boardwalk.

All three hightailed it up the wooden ramp. At the top they cornered to the left, ran down Atlantic Drive, and vaulted into the cab of Dallas' old blue pickup. Settling in the middle, Ry was in good-natured hysterics. On his right side, Cassie dropped the yellow bag at her feet and tried to wring out her now-soaked locks. Over the Gulf, lightning was now crackling in steady rips. Hunkering down lower into her seat, Cassie gave up on her sopping wet hair, gulped, and squeezed her eyes tightly shut. Momentarily an arm snaked its way around Ry's shoulders and a hand wiped a wet strand of hair off Cassie's cheek. Forcing open her eyes, she bit her bottom lip and looked gratefully over at Dallas.

He was soaked, endearingly so, his T-shirt clinging to his chest, and neither wished for a first kiss more than at that moment, with Ry safely between them bubbling over at the excitement of the flash storm.

Cassie accepted Dal's simple touch instead, and forced the fear in the pit of her stomach far, far away. They waited out the storm in the truck, Cassie trying to hold her trembling at bay so she could sip on her tea while Ry and Dal talked thunder and lightning. Her curiosity was peaked when Ry asked Dal about his most frightening storm experience. Something about Dal's expression changed while he pondered how to answer; he turned to the window at his left and sucked in a breath.

"On a stage one time," he told them, his back now a barrier between the present and the past, his eyes lost to the dripping window and to the sodden memory.

Another mammoth crack rocked the sky and roared over the earth below. The truck shook. In the Gulf, the waves rolled viciously and crashed over each other in frenetic delight. The usually composed and unruffled water was suddenly a wild animal released from captivity, fiercely bucking in triumph and exhilaration.

"Where?" Ry wasn't going to let this one go, but Cassie touched his arm.

"Sweetheart," she warned him. Already she could read the troubled man sitting quietly behind the shabby, dirt-stained wheel. There was a sadness in his voice again, one that frightened her, that alerted Cassie to a life that, for all its musical insulation, seemed to have left a trail of hurt as surely as the pouring rain was now leaving puddles in the back of Dal's ratty old truck. "I don't think he wants to talk about it."

At that, Dallas rotated back around and captured her in his gaze. Instantly Cassie instinctively knew there was a lot he wanted—or maybe needed—to talk about. But again, a desperate fear was as much a wall between them as the nautical rope bordering Dal's campsite from the ocean, and as much a wall as the invisible crackling between the flashes of lightning and the inevitable thunder rumbling outside their safe haven.

"It was in Nashville," he admitted quietly, drawing a finger down a rivulet of water that was leaking down the inside of the passenger side window just past Cassie's shoulder. "The organizers had to stop the show."

"An outdoor show?" Ry was like a new puppy that didn't know when to stop jumping on people, or nipping at their heels. Still, his inquisitive nature today was rare and therefore welcome. Also, bonus—Cassie was grateful because it meant she didn't have to ask the questions. She flushed when Ry added, "Like at the North Shore Music Festival? That big country music concert everybody's talking about?"

Dallas' eyes flickered down to the sopping wet locks of the blond surfer boy sitting alert and bouncing between he and Cassie. Cassie, Dal was deathly aware, had gone silent at this singular clue to his past. "Yeah. Like that." The pale eyes flicked back up to Cassie. *Ask me,* he seemed to be saying. Begging.

But she couldn't. No, to Cassie, as much as she wanted to know, this was a key to a door she wasn't yet ready to unlock. A slow shake of her head, barely there, signified that this was a barricade she was not yet ready to scale.

Dallas' shoulders slumped.

"Holy cow! Musta been some big show."

Dal's response was mumbled. Looking away from Cassie, he sighed. "Sure was. I've done a few of those."

Who are you? Cassie shrank lower in her seat. *What happened to you? Why are you here?*

Another splintering crack split the sky in two. Like a call and answer riff in a smartly composed tune, streak lightning immediately followed and then, more of the relentless thunder. The storm was about five miles over the Gulf now, close enough to scare the bejeesus out of all three of the stalwart watchers. Rain on the windshield splattered vehemently and then dripped down like tears, making it almost impossible to see the incredible heat and light display playing out before them.

Dallas poked a few long fingers around under the seat and held up a set of keys on a worn black leather keychain. Shoving a key into the ignition, he gave it a twist and, without going so far as to start the engine, he flipped on the windshield wipers. At the same time the radio roared to life.

A quick thump of a knuckle on a button, and Dallas immediately changed the station.

Ry poked a small finger back on the auto tuner a few times until he found the station Dal switched off. "Country," he announced proudly.

Cassie couldn't help herself. Catching Dal's eye, she sniggered under her breath, calling on grace and good manners to try to hide the majority of her amusement. "Redneck," she winked.

A low grunt, and Dallas randomly poked another button. "No," he said simply, in a tone that both Cassie and Ry knew was meant to be listened to. Both of them quickly sobered.

Jann Arden's soothing voice filled the old cab. Ry's lips curved downward. "But you play country."

"I play it. Don't mean I listen to it, kid." Trying to ease the sudden tension, Dallas gave Ry a finger-flick on the cheek. Ry yelped, which gave Dal an excuse to avoid Cassie's curious eyes altogether.

The storm was moving on, the slick gray clouds being pushed along by forces bigger than its watchers.

"What about my lesson?" piped up Ry, grabbing Dal's arm behind him, bringing it around his shoulders and giving it a happy hug.

At least the kid's got a short attention span, mused Dallas with a wry twist of his lips. Reaching over to ruffle Ry's hair with his left hand, he fought against the hard memories he thought he left behind in Seattle, and forced the light back into his eyes. At the same time, he pushed away a small shudder.

Leaning her right elbow on the window ledge, Cassie waded carefully in. "We'll do it up in the Montana, Ry." With a nervous look to Dal, she added, "If that's okay with your instructor. How about I make us some pasta while you work, boys?"

"Uh…I guess that'd be fine." Dal's voice was raspy now, drained, even. He removed his right arm completely from around Ry's shoulders and put his left hand on the door handle. "Let me grab my guitar. We'll drive up, okay? The big rain's letting up but the drizzle looks like it's here to stay." A look to the sky confirmed his suspicion. The clouds were more of an even gray now. No more big thunderheads loomed, but nor were blue skies apparent. The lane in front of the campsite was filled with eerie red-mud puddles, connected by fast-trickling streams—the legacy of the flash storm. Walking in this Prince Edward Island mud would be messy for a while yet.

At Cassie's and Ry's feet were the beach bags. While Dallas ducked out of the cab and into his tent for the guitar, praying that his new tarp was keeping his rustic sleeping space dry, Cassie reached for the bag of rippled chips. She and Ry munched quietly while they waited for Dal. He seemed to be taking a long time, and Cassie wondered idly if he'd stepped around the back of the tent to take a leak, as Eddie used to do, albeit Eddie only did it in the middle of the night and not in the broad light of day, and certainly not in the rain.

Inside the tent, which was a four-person sleeper high enough to stand up straight in, Dallas was quickly, privately, checking his phone for messages. One glared up at him. It was a simple text from Phil that read *You're costing us a bloody fortune. Say yes to the North Shore Festival. You're twenty minutes away, damn it!!!*

Phil rarely took the time to use punctuation in his texts. Three exclamation marks said more than the message in its entirety.

Dallas grimaced, tossed the phone on the thick log cabin patterned quilt he'd picked up at a craft shop during a cruise to quaint Victoria-by-the-Sea on the south side of the island one afternoon, and pulled down his shorts. He grabbed jeans from a messy folded pile in his duffel bag and pulled them up over his hips. Zipping up, he did up the belt that was still looped through the jeans and made a frustrated face, because the jeans were still giving off little wafts of last night's wood smoke. Hopping toward the half-zipped door for a peek into the truck cab, he yanked on one boot and then the other. This messy P.E.I. rain called for the old standby cowboy boots. Jeans, flip-flops and thick island mud just didn't jibe, in Dallas' cowboy opinion. Besides, he was about to spend time in Cassie's fancy fifth-wheel. He needed to look like the guy that women drooled over at his shows, however fake Dallas felt that guy was.

Hell, it ain't the music they want, he growled, picturing the half-dressed young twenty-somethings at the Seattle show, hell, at all of his big outdoor shows. Sure, the girls knew the lyrics, every word in fact, which he paused to consider, but when all was said and done Dallas knew damn well all they really wanted was to catch his eye. Every single one of them. They all needed the affirmation he, because of his stature as a country icon, could give them. The songs were just the reason to be there.

He'd have to come clean to Cassie if he wanted her to take him seriously. Strange thing, though, a part of Dallas felt that if she didn't like him for who he appeared to be, which was a half-assed singer with few funds at his disposal, then what was the point? If she clued in to his true identity, either via him telling her or via her simply figuring it out, she wouldn't be any different than the rest of the star struck women jostling for front row position when he was on stage. The only thing that might set Cassie aside was, perhaps, her seeming lack of interest in—even sheer aversion to—his chosen genre of music. That and, of course, whatever dark secrets she was obviously holding close to her own heart.

A short time later, when they rolled up to Cassie's brand spanking new luxury 'glamper,' Cassie watched Dal for signs of discomfort. *Give it up,* she chided herself. *This is not the 1950's. A woman can accumulate more than a man.* Still, she couldn't help but wonder what her mother and sister would make of her dating—*are we dating?*—a man so obviously short on funds as Dal. She chided herself for the second time. *I'm not dating him, damn it!*

Cassie's shiny new Montana was cozily nestled into a premium campsite with full amenities—water, sewer, electric—overlooking the restful Darnley Basin, a relatively shallow body of water really only large enough to cruise a small sailboat around in for a few hours. The Basin fed out into the Gulf via a narrow manmade channel excavated to accommodate fishing boats while also providing a speedy passageway to more tumultuous waters for adventurous entertainment watercraft, such as jet skis and small motorboats. These were usually launched from nearby Malpeque Harbor, which was just off the Basin on the northwest side, where the fishing boats tied up. Occasionally even the odd dory motored through the channel, usually towing an inflatable raft or sometimes even a water skier.

Castle Beach had a right to boast of stunning sunsets; viewed from Cassie's site, they were surreal. The skies were already clearing after the storm. In a few hours the violet-pink warmth emanating from the lowering sun would be magical, spreading its prism'd love slowly through the dissipating cottony clouds. Now, though, as the motley damp crew pulled up next to the dazzling silver Ford truck, the evening's enchantment was still no more than a hint and a promise. Before day's end, there was more to learn about each other; there were truths to unearth and old hurts to discover.

Starting with…well, Cassie's almost apologetic air couldn't hide the fact that her new truck was stunning. The big rig sparkled in the newish golden light as, on the Ford, the dispersing raindrops from the storm intermingled with spots of peekaboo sunshine, leaving the truck's high-waxed finish glistening in waves of diaphanous bubbled perfection.

Not lost on Cassie were Dal's serious eyes when he let his gaze ponder the truck and what it likely meant to Cassie. The gentle, intense study he gave it—and then the Montana, in turn—was not wide-eyed and wondrous, or even remotely envious, as far as she could tell. Instead, Dallas, who unbeknownst to Cassie had long ago scoped out her site based on Ry's description a few days ago—and had also found it via Ry's neon green swimming trunks and one of Cassie's bikinis, which were strung on a clothesline stretched across the back of the camper—simply gave it a scan before eventually averting his eyes. He touched the truck, and let his fingers trail across its passenger side door, not in any way admiring it, it seemed, but instead computing its value and purpose to a small woman like Cassie.

She swallowed. "I needed it to haul the camper," she told him.

"You hauled this yourself?" He may have hid exactly what he was feeling about the shiny Ford, but Dallas was less than expert at disguising his awe and surprise at Cassie's ability and apparent fearlessness in hauling a thirty-three-and-a-half foot camper all the way from Halifax to Castle Beach—a four-hour drive, he calculated roughly.

Drawing up her petite frame, she raised her chin. For good measure, she tossed in a smug wrinkled nose. "Yes, well, women can be trained to do almost anything."

"Imagine." That tiny playful glint Cassie was growing to look forward to seeing—accompanied sometimes (if Dal smiled the right way) by two sweet dimples at the corners of his mouth—appeared.

Cassie relaxed. Holding out a hand which Dal gratefully took, she shyly led the way up a step to the small one-level wooden deck she'd had built by a local carpenter. Crossing the deck, she approached three metal steps that would bring them up into the big summer camper. Ry was already waiting inside, the guitar case—which had sat between his knees on the short ride up from Dal's site by the beach—propped up between his arms.

"Geez, you two are slow," Ry admonished, stepping sideways to let his mother and Dal into the trailer. His eyes blinked down to their linked fingers. Pressing his lips together and squinting slightly, Ry didn't comment on what he saw pass between his mother and his sandcastle and guitar friend, but neither Cassie nor Dallas missed a beat. They let their fingers disentangle themselves the second Ry's eyebrows twisted as he tried to sort out just what all this tenderness he was seeing pass between them meant and how it would filter down to him.

"Ry, why don't you show Dal around the camper?" Cassie suggested, partly to distract him and partly to buy herself some time to compose herself. Talking to Ry about her feelings for their new friend was going to be a priority. Too bad she was so confused herself about just what the man was coming to mean to her. It was hard enough to explain this new reality to herself, and they had yet to even kiss...

Kiss. *Omigod.* A thrill zipped up her legs and landed in her heart. Just touching Dal's fingers was electric. Touching her lips to his stubbly cheek last night when she left his campfire was over-the-top erotic. "It's just sex," she scolded herself. "I crave a man's touch. I can't let this man's powerful aura disarm me. I need to consider Ry..."

But, watching Dal with Ry, Cassie had to ball her hands into fists and squeeze. At the same time she tipped her face up to the trailer's low ceiling, closed her eyes, and said a silent prayer, the main gist of which was *please let me remain in control of this situation. Don't let me fall into his arms just because he's…*

She was going to add *here,* but it was more than that, and Cassie knew it. Ry was practically jumping around the camper, leaping from one thing to another, his agile body and surfer locks bouncing, and Dal was sporting a smile so wide it lit up more than just those beautiful eyes that took Cassie's breath away every time they were aimed in her direction, which they were—often.

"And this is a fireplace, and it actually works, and we have surround sound so music sounds Ah-Maaa-Zing in here, and this here's where I sleep, my mom has the actual bedroom but this here's a camper so I just close this curtain thing…"

Ry demonstrated, pulling a white accordion-type curtain across the divider between the living room area and the tiny kitchen. Cassie cocked her head when she heard him say, "So this comes out into a bed, see? It's pretty comfy. Want to try it?"

Groaning slightly, Cassie considered the look on Dal's face if she asked him the same question. *Oh, here's where I sleep, it's pretty comfy. Want to try it?* "You're a wreck, girl," she admonished herself, tossing her usually sleek but now seriously rain-frizzed blonde hair as new unbidden thoughts and a random selection of, um, tingly sensations, accompanied them.

The curtain was withdrawn. At the far end, where Dal's flushed cheeks telegraphed that he was likely thinking the same things Cassie was, Ry was pointing out two blue swivel wingback style chairs that framed a large back window. He showed Dal how the chairs could be maneuvered into easy chairs with footrests, then he bounded up and landed with a bounce on the couch. Three slides in the fancy camper remained out all summer—these were partitions that, with the push of a button, extended out beyond the main body of the trailer in order to create more space. One was in the living room where, next to a fireplace and entertainment unit, more space was needed to accommodate a desk and a chair. The second was in the kitchen where a small island in the center created an easy workspace to feed two hungry fellas. The bedroom had the final slide—and a king-sized bed. A full shower and tons of storage made the fifth-wheel camper large and eminently long-term livable.

As Cassie got to work slicing veggies for pasta, and as the guys settled on the couch with the guitar, she thought it was odd that Dal didn't in any way seem awed at the extravagant 'glamper.' He almost seemed to know his way around. Even the fireplace didn't faze him, as it had her mother and sister when she toured them through it while it was still on the lot in Halifax. Dal was as cool as a cucumber, albeit he always seemed rather put together. Just…sad. Maybe this kind of luxury bothered him—she wasn't sure. If it did, he kept his thoughts well hidden. *You'd rock at poker,* she breezed while she chopped.

Watching Dal with Ry when she set down her knife to put some water on to boil, Cassie eyed his worn cowboy boots. She'd chide him over those later, when she knew him well enough to say *take 'em off, Cowboy.* But then again…maybe he'd prefer to make love with his boots on…

She laughed. That could be a lyric in a country song. *Maybe it already is…*

Country music. Cassie hoped Dal would graduate Ry at some point to other musical styles. Country was just so much, well, beer and pickup trucks and cheating partners and back roads. Dirt covered back roads, in fact. Not her style at all, as Ry had so eloquently voiced. She peeked up beyond her long, feminine lashes and watched as Dal easily corrected Ry's small fingers on a chord.

"C's a tough one to play," he was saying. Ry frowned and groaned in frustration. "You need to be patient. You have small hands, kid. You'll grow into this. You'll grow."

After he said it, Dallas seemed to sense Cassie's eyes on him. Looking over, he treated her to a sweet smile meant just for her and for this perfect moment. But then he absently scanned the living area in a casual kind of way, before he intended to go back to Ry. His gaze landed on a framed photograph tucked into the entertainment unit. Instantly, Cassie knew what it was because Dal's expression changed. It morphed from a contented sort of joy to a curious, almost hurt squint as he tried to bring the man in the photo into clearer focus. A second look to Cassie, this one guarded and quizzical, cemented her conjecture.

Eddie, in his oversized fireman's jacket and hat. This one taken a few months before he passed away—an action shot snapped in the brush by a friend with an iPhone. Eddie with a wide grin, dirty mud-grimed cheeks, and a twinkle in his wise eyes that Cassie desperately missed.

She paused, a hand suspended over a green pepper on the cutting board. Ry, who was waiting for Dal to answer a question for him, followed his teacher's unguarded stare.

"That's my dad," Ry said lightly, drawing his right hand over the strings. The C note emerged dull and numb, the way both Cassie and Dal were suddenly feeling, Cassie because Eddie was, and always would be, her one and only, and Dal had no business being here, really, he shouldn't be here because Eddie ought to be; and Dallas because it was plainly obvious from both Ry's dad's jubilant expression and Cassie's sudden freeze-up that the guy was, well, a much-loved normal working class kinda husband and dad. A saint, even, the way Cassie seemed to be swiping at moisture in her eyes with the back of a hand at the moment.

Ry forged ahead. "He died when I was two. He was famous."

Dal swallowed. *He died. Jesus. Cassie...* "Famous? Famous how?"

"Oh, Jesus." The quiet exclamation from Cassie—almost an echo of Dallas' silent curse—was her signal to Ry to stop, to 'just not go there.' But he did. Her quiet son voiced the tragedy that disarmed Cassie every time she thought about it, every time someone asked her if she was married or what her husband did. Like a mammoth roar, its own kind of thunder, it crumpled her to hear it, especially when mouthed to a man whose touch she craved, about a man whose touch she once had, by a boy who, to Cassie, somehow seemed caught between the two. Like a toy to be passed back and forth between two worlds, the old and the new.

Dallas' eyes were on her when Ry said it. Standing there with her own damp eyes shut and her head bowed, with wispy tendrils of her drying sodden hair stuck to her cheeks like trails of golden tears, Cassie could feel those tender pale baby blues searching her, studying her. Even before her real tears fell like the rain that had finally stopped its light patter patter patter against the trailer in that cozy sort of way rain falls on campers parked in glorious splendor overlooking crystalline paradises bordered by white sand dunes and picturesque red sandstone cliffs.

"He died in a famous fire. Him and a bunch of other guys he worked with."

"Oh geez, Ry. I'm so, so sorry." Dal sucked in a breath and looked back at Ry, astonished at the cavalier, nonchalant way the boy delivered the news of the soul-crashing tragedy. At the way he made it real again to the world—to his mother—just by simply voicing it. Nervously flipping a hand up to the brim of his ball cap, Dallas gave it a subconcious yank and darted his head back around to Cassie.

Letting her eyelids flicker open, across the small space she met Dal's worried gaze. There was a resignation in her faded jade eyes; it escaped outward from the depths of Cassie's soul but it wasn't the peaceful kind. It was more like the defeated kind.

Dallas knew it well. He sighed, leaned his hands on his thighs, and unbuckled his body and stood. "Back in a sec, kid. Work on that C chord."

Approaching Cassie in the kitchen only took him a few steps. Dallas stopped across from her on the other side of the small kitchen island and used a thumb to tenderly wipe one of the rogue strands of hair off her cheek.

Her lips parted and the cute bottom lip trembled. "I don't want to talk about it," she whispered, at the same time burying, in the solemn love she found in his eyes, her need to someday tell him.

"Someday we will. Talk about it, I mean."

Dal's assurance was set in stone, Cassie could tell. He knew—he just *knew*—they would someday get to a point where they could talk about the serious stuff. That knowledge alone was enough to weaken Cassie's knees, to almost send her into a complete tailspin. Six years now she had buried the pain, that deep, disemboweling pain that hurt too much to recall, to acknowledge, to voice. She refused to discuss Eddie with anyone, not with her mother, not with her sister, and certainly not with the child who lived every one of his days with the silent fear of an unmentionable loss.

Now, looking into the caring eyes of this obviously down-on-his-luck musician who seemed far beneath what Cassie felt was her station in life, suddenly she wanted to blurt it out, to let it go. She ached to release the debilitating truths of Eddie's passing into the warmth and love she found in those sensitive, understanding eyes; into that beautiful soul she instinctively felt could take it; onto the shoulders of a man whose large, compassionate fingers so carefully guided her son's small hands on the strings of an instrument that could provide a release for Ry's hurts for life.

Those very same fingers were touching Cassie now with a tenderness born of complete and utter love.

The wetness in her eyes was spilling over even more now. Cassie was afraid she was going to completely let go in front of Dal and her son. That was a no-no. She did her mourning in private, or so she thought. Trembling, she moved away from Dal and stumbled up the three stairs into the bedroom, calling behind her, "I just need to change into something dry."

With an almost exaggerated forced *shuffttt,* she closed the door behind her.

Watching her go, Dallas wanted to reach for her, to offer comfort. But eight-year-old eyes were watching him. No numb sounding C chords had followed Dallas into the kitchen. Ry was not going to be a silent observer while Cassie and Dal sorted out what they were beginning to mean to each other. Ry was going to be an active—even through his silence—participant in this friendship or partnership or whatever the heck it was.

Turning back to him, Dallas threw his arms out to the sides. "You know what we need? We need that other guitar so I can play along with you. That's what we need. I hope your mother's cool with that."

Phil had called earlier. He would be bringing a brand new Gibson— a mini child sized guitar designed for small fingers—to Castle Beach when he came for a visit sometime in the next few days.

"Who cares what she thinks?" was Ry's cheeky response. He flipped his head; a rogue blond layer cascaded itself away from his eyes and landed in a whole other place on his head. "It'll be my guitar."

"You eight going on eighteen?" Dallas forced a laugh. With one last wistful glance toward the closed door to the bedroom, he dropped down again beside his eager student.

"Nope. She just doesn't much care most of the time. She lets me do what I want."

The admission threw Dallas for the second time in a few short minutes. He had to compose himself before answering. A hasty, shallow cough did the trick. "I suppose, Ry," he said afterward, "that it hasn't been easy for either of you. Losing your dad."

Ry stared at his fingers on the wooden guitar fret and shrugged his shoulders. With the wisdom of a life-scarred child he said, with frankness far beyond his years, "He may have been my dad, but I don't really remember him. To me he's just a picture." He whipped back around to Dal, who saw a child whose whole body screamed that he *wished* he remembered his father. "But to my mom he was everything."

"She remembers him." Dallas spoke in a subdued tone, the words infused with the reverence they deserved.

"Sometimes she remembers him too much. You know? Like…when she sleeps a lot. That's when I know she's really remembering him."

"He was a good guy, your dad." Dallas couldn't resist. This subject was dear, a real clue to the woman whose sad eyes mystified and intrigued him.

"He was a fireman." And that was that. Ry may as well have said his dad had saved the world. The admiration for the father he never knew was filled with enough awe to grant Eddie the wings of an angel. As if by virtue of being a fireman, Ry's dad was superhuman. A true hero.

And what am I, thought Dallas. *A man who stands on a stage in front of drunk and high groupies and plays guitar. Who sings songs about love that, I gotta admit, I know shit-all about.*

No way would Cassie want him. No way could Dallas White, country singer, compare to the man staring at him now from some frozen moment in time when Cassie had a husband and their future was carved in stone.

His spirits were sinking lower when the door to the bedroom finally opened and Cassie emerged in jeans and a v-necked T-shirt. She'd swept her hair back into its usual silky ponytail, which was brushed back now to its flawless shining self, exhibiting no frizz from the earlier rainstorm.

At the same time, Ry played a clean, perfect C chord. "I did it!" he hollered.

Dallas had to tear his eyes away from the woman now back in the kitchen with her hair in the fresh ponytail and her eyes puffy and damp from a good cry. "You sure did, little buddy. It sounded just fine," he stated softly. "It was a perfect C."

A perfect family. The picture was complete now, although Dallas had yet to know the fireman's name. In his mind's eye he just saw a father, a mother, and a baby boy. Maybe there was even a dog back then. Who really knew? *Will I someday really know?*

He had no way of knowing that Cassie, who'd turned her back to him to dump a box of rotini in the pot of boiling water, was thinking about the perfect family too. But her cry in the bedroom had pushed Eddie from her mind the same way the earlier rainstorm had sent red mud down Atlantic Drive in fast-moving rivulets. Cassie's vision of the perfect family now included a sexy man in strategically faded jeans, a green T-shirt that hugged his broad chest, and muddy cowboy boots that, in any other lifetime, would sure as hell not be on his feet in her camper's living room.

She smiled.

And went back to slicing a green pepper.

Chapter Seven

"It's mystical," Dallas said to Cassie later. They were sitting by the fire, humbled by the tiny specks of starlight peeking through the curtain of black hovering over the Darnley Basin. The summer storm was a distant memory; the monsoon-like clouds were startling tourists in some other part of Prince Edward Island now, leaving the Darnley skies crystal clear.

Cassie had taught the fellas how to make spider dogs—poke a stick through the longitudinal center of a hot dog, slit the ends crossways like an X, and roast the hot dog until the ends flare out and it resembles a spider. Voila. They capped those off with the usual s'mores made, as always, with roasted, melted marshmallows and a square of chocolate tucked neatly between two graham wafer crackers. Now Ry was asleep in the Montana, curled up on his bed with a small white Dalmatian Beanie Baby at his side—his only pet since Cassie didn't have the energy to get him a real dog. A homemade quilt (a gift from his father's mother at his birth) snuggled him up to his waist on this warm summer's eve.

Tonight the white moon with its shadowed craters flared brightly to the south, hanging above Cassie and Dallas like a partially inflated bubble. It seemed suspended in the sky from some invisible filament; like a Christmas ball, its festive grandeur added a distinct enchantment to the almost holy feel of the dreamlike evening.

Cassie was finding Dal easy to be around. Bonus, Dal was good-natured and relaxed in Ry's company. Ry, usually a quiet kid who took things in and analyzed them before he spoke, who liked to assess a situation and get the lay of the land before offering an opinion, was turning out to be effusive and confident around his new buddy. It was as if the man's appearance in their lives was somehow balancing the inequality between Cassie and her son, or at least bridging the break in communication that Ry intuitively understood had to do with his mom missing his dad. Dal was safe, supportive and patient in helping Ry figure out the best places to position his fingers on the guitar frets and, as Cassie was beginning to see, that quiet serenity transferred to the way Dal approached other areas of his life. Like Ry, the man was also a watcher, the kind of guy who assessed situations before jumping to hasty conclusions and speaking quickly and impatiently.

Now, after pushing a square of leftover chocolate between her lips, Cassie recrossed her ankles and took a breath. "So…no kids, huh? Not even a gerbil to tie you down, you said." The remark was uttered as casually as Cassie could manage while she chewed. Tonight seemed like as good an opportunity as any to gain more insight into the guy who had captured her imagination, who was sinking tenterhooks into her heart. She'd have to be cautious, though; it wasn't a stretch to assume that something in Dal's likely recent history had sent him running to his hiding place on the sandy cliff overlooking the campground's peaceful beach.

"Nope." The answer was simple and direct although Cassie was learning to read Dal's moods and the meanings beneath his responses the same way a researcher looks for the missing parts of a photograph by conjecturing on what's outside the frame. "I guess you could say I always thought I had a lot of time," Dal added, poking at the fire with a stick. "I made some bad choices in my life." He gave a piece of hardwood a calculated shove. It landed sideways, shocking a split underneath. Like angry dragons, they sparked and hissed at each other. Glancing sideways at Cassie, Dallas, who was leaning forward in a camp chair with both forearms resting on his thighs, added hopefully, "I'm hoping it's not too late to make a few things right."

The sparks drifting upward from the fire pit may as well have been in Cassie's soul. She almost moaned with the want and the need she saw in Dal's eyes when he fixed his expressive gaze on her. Firelight and moonlight and stars and now sparks—all were doing an optimistic dance in his usually solemn, pale eyes. Shadows, lit and carved by the orange hue from the fire, added a mysterious Hitchcock-like drama to Dal's stubbled jaw and cheeks.

An overriding sadness remained; it played tug-of-war with the hope flickering in Dal's blue eyes, pulling it down with grappling hooks as if it was trying to sink the good stuff beneath the surface.

Dallas saw comprehension pass over Cassie's pretty face in the way she tilted her head just slightly and allowed a tiny reflective smile to flicker across the sensuous pink lips he ached to set his tongue upon so he could taste the sweetness of her. So he could soak her in and maybe, just maybe, offer solace for her heavy loss.

Cassie shifted in her camp chair and watched, in the misty reflection of Dal's pensive eyes, a few more flickering sparks ascend upward. She was lost in that place, in the aura and essence of him. He had captured her as surely as a P.E.I. fisherman catches lobster or mussels and was now, with his soulful eyes, pulling her up from the depths so she could breathe in the invigorating salt air that would make her whole again. Dal had power—enough, at least, to put out the angry fire that started burning the day Eddie left Cassie to raise a child on her own.

She needed to respond to Dal. The way he was looking at her now— watching, studying, wondering—was an extension of the small touches during dinner. The small graces that, when strung together, made for one big expressive overture that screamed *I like you. A lot.* Cassie had washed the dishes; Dal dried while Ry put them away. And occasionally their fingers touched, sending their pulses into overdrive and tingling their nerves with anticipation. Now, in this surreal place, lit by twinkling stars and a promising ornamental moon, the night was coming to a head. The kindnesses, the gestures, the everlasting patience with Ry, the electric touches, the aching eyes—they were all one big question mark.

Cassie started them down an easy road.

She pointed to the fire. "Eddie loved fire. He was that guy at the campground who always built up huge flames, even on the windy nights. We went through a lot of wood back in the days when we used to tent here." Almost as an afterthought she said, trying to keep longing from coloring the elegant voice Dallas found so captivating, "We could never make s'mores until the end of the night. He had to get the blazing fire thing out of his system first, and let the flames settle into coals. Usually our s'mores were burnt because by then Eddie'd enjoyed a little too much of the Captain, or wine if he was in a more relaxed mood, and I was almost always finishing up the last of my own wine. We lost more gooey marshmallows than we ate, put it that way."

Dallas considered what to say. Finally he simply voiced the sorrow in his heart. "I'm sorry for your loss, Cassie. I really, truly am."

Staring hard into the center of their campfire, Cassie allowed herself to consider how fire—something that fascinated her easygoing, happy husband so much—could have turned on Eddie the way the Alberta forest fire did. Something about Dal's warmth next to her, his calm presence, gave her the courage to look deeper. To feel.

"I push him aside," she admitted. "That's what I do most of the time. It's like he tries to get through, to make me think about him, but most of the time I can't do it. I still can't go there, I still can't let him in. It hurts too much."

"But when you do, when you let him in, you sink into sleep."

Spoken out loud in a reverential tone swollen with new love, the quiet acknowledgement almost brought Cassie to tears. Hanging her head, she nodded. "I'm not proud of myself, Dal. It's not like I forget about Ry, it's more like I just can't deal. There's nothing in me for him. To give him. I switch to empty. I get drained." Letting herself peek back into Dal's tender eyes, Cassie almost melted. She was like the sugary marshmallow Ry'd tossed into the flames earlier to see what the fire would do to it. She shuddered at the memory.

"The fire, Dal," she whispered. "Sitting here in front of it, trying not to think about it and what it did to my husband…" A small sob escaped from some forgotten place in Cassie's chest. Rallying, she continued. "It's this living thing, fire is. It consumes, you know? Whatever's in its path."

Describing fire's power was not enough. Bringing her hands together, Cassie pressed her palms hard against each other and gave them a hard outward twist. "There's no mercy there. There's just an unforgiving power with a mandate to destroy. Yet Eddie loved fire. To him it was majestic and beautiful, this living thing that he could build or tear down, whichever he saw fit."

"And it destroyed him."

Cassie drew a hand upward as a tiny tear trickled down her cheek.

Hopelessly lost in the past, and fearful of the future, she pressed the hand against her chest. "It destroyed *us*."

"Mostly you."

From Dallas' lips to Cassie's ears, the spoken truth was a final opening. It wasn't just an acknowledgement of Cassie's pain—it was also an invitation into a soul with the power to heal. Because, Cassie knew, that soul understood on an empathetic level. That soul had suffered too.

"Yes," she breathed.

"I know about fire," Dallas murmured, holding her gaze, reaching out and soaking up the trickling tear with his thumb. "I know about power that feeds on small things like twigs at first, then goes for bigger branches and before you know it consumes an entire tree. I know about power that's unstoppable, that destroys everything in order to get what it wants."

Watching him, Cassie hardly dared breathe. There was something about this place, about this magical healing Prince Edward Island shoreline sanctuary that was enabling a kind of divine release. That could set hard truths free.

Encouraged by Cassie's honesty and by the celestial environ and the now settling fire, Dallas went on. "I got swept up in it too, Cassie. But I'm done now. I took a step back. I know how powerful that kind of fire can be. I walked away."

"I wish to heck Eddie had walked away."

"Sweetheart, Cassie...I don't know what to say to that. I wish to hell your husband had walked away too, before...before it was too late. I would walk away from you and Ry if it meant I could give him back to you. But Cas... giving him back to you is not something I can do. And I gotta tell you. A tiny, selfish part of me is damn glad I won't have to. I'm sorry."

He was still brushing her cheek, the thumb moving against her skin, igniting a passion that had long since sparked and was now almost its own full-blown blaze. There was a slight breeze off the water, enough to stir up the embers just the smallest bit, and it gently sifted its way through Cassie's hair. As usual Dallas was half-buried under the Jays cap, his sensitive eyes large and somber under the brim. Strands of hair wafted around his face, framing the three-day beard he kept to help hide his true identity.

"I'm sorry too," Cassie managed, shoving down a brief flash of anger at herself for stepping out on Eddie this way. For caving, for admitting that this man with her now, seated in front of the only kind of fire she felt a person should ever have to bear witness to, was worth risking Eddie for. Even if it was only Eddie's memory she would have to let go of, to bury.

There was a brief, suspended pause then, and it lingered between Cassie and Dallas until they either had to move forward, or retreat with some kind of awkward grace. Neither knew who should make that decision. The uncertainty was disabling.

An instant bubble formed, consuming them, soaking both with a thousand thoughts and a gazillion possibilities. In the forefront was the unspoken notion that once the magic of this island paradise faded and stark reality set in, a future together was unlikely. If Dallas and Cassie chose to grab the brass ring that the mystical night, aided by long-buried truths and honest utterings, was handing them, it would just be for the 'now.' It would be a frame or two of time, snatched from the starlit sky for the briefest of moments. Would tomorrow be right? Would the next day be right? What would happen at summer's end?

Even at this early juncture it was clearly apparent that Cassie and Dallas were from different worlds. Castle Beach was an illusion. It was a place to hide—an enchanted, dreamlike respite. Like the ubiquitous fairy-tale castles on its white sandy beach, prey to weather and water, its healing power was as fleeting as the tide.

"I want this," Cassie said, allowing her bubble to quietly dissipate into the cooling, moist air. The fire before them was only embers and ashes now, glowing red and seemingly harmless. The fire in her heart and body was raging. "Oh, god I want this." She closed her eyes.

"Cassie…" It was the husky Dal voice now, the cherished, tender voice Cassie was imprisoned by for its capacity to say so much more than just the word or words it embraced; for its ability to wrap her in love and safety.

Dallas' bubble of objections and questions and cautions and reasons 'why not' burst for a second too, disappearing into the ether to mingle with the big dipper overhead the second he nudged forward in his camp chair and touched the tip of his tongue to the barely parted center of Cassie's soft mouth.

A small probe first, just to get the taste and feel of her...a moan from her that elicited an equal gruff need from him...

Dallas ran his tongue lightly, slowly, around Cassie's pink lips, careful not to frighten her lest she panic and run; careful to hold her delicate chin in his fingers and see that she was in this quickly building ecstasy with him, before he relaxed enough to taste her more with tiny nibbles and a long, sweet caress of his tongue on her body.

Brushes down Cassie's elegant neck were next. Dallas' hair tickled her when he cupped her cheek and pressed his mouth more firmly to her skin, aware as he moved down to a hollow in her shoulder he'd been coveting—been wanting to cover with kisses—that she was crumbling under him, that her body was giving in and her soul was not far behind.

The heat ignited by the sweet, gentle intimacy in their kisses frightened Dallas. In truth it frightened them both with its intensity and with its warm, honeyed waves of pleasure, but when the scales were tipped the new heat scared Dallas more.

This moment grabbed from time—fisted from the air and set before them—was spurred on by Cassie's acknowledgement of her biggest hurts. So she was glowing a little more brightly under the hallowed moon and its own vague mysteries, under its shadows and luminosity. But years of insecurity and distrust wrought by fame meant that Dallas wasn't yet ready to fully release his hurts, the hurts that brought him here to this sacred place, to this lovely, tragic woman and her quiet, watchful, musically talented son.

The stakes are higher for me selfishly crossed Dallas' mind. He paused in laying on the lovely kisses that had Cassie arching her head back and moaning, begging almost, for more...

For more of Dal's flesh against hers, for more of his need to consume her, want her, soothe her.

The pause was brief, but Cassie felt it. *Please, baby, no,* she moaned inwardly, eyes closed and heart racing.

Dallas' ball cap, nudged awry by the kisses, was falling off anyway. Dal moved away so he could resettle it.

Sitting back, his breaths came unevenly, raggedly, saturated with want and an almost desperate longing for connection. *This isn't fair to her,* he considered. *She is too needy; she isn't like those nameless, faceless women that sprawl across my sheets in the unwitting sunrises after my shows. Cassie deserves to know what she is getting into.*

At this point Dallas had to admit to himself that *he* didn't even know what he was getting into anymore. If Phil had his way, there would still be shows this summer. Heck, if Phil had his way there would be a few good decades more of shows. If Dallas had his way...well, he really didn't know what he wanted. On the grand scale of Castle Beach's healing vibes, he was stuck somewhere at the base of one of those omnipresent castles on the beach.

Cassie's confused, wounded voice drew him back to the present. "Are you married, is that it? Is that why you stopped? Is that why you look so scared?"

Turning his head away from her, Dallas absently scratched the stubble on his chin. "No, Cassie," he said honestly, "I've never been married, I swear. I just...there are things I need to sort out. That's all."

"With a woman." A light mist spread over Cassie's eyes.

Panicking suddenly, Dallas was momentarily afraid that the dampness in Cassie's eyes would spill over. Yet he already knew enough about her to ascertain that she was proud, that she would not release a well of tears in front of him. He glanced down at her fingers. She was clutching the arms of the camp chair, ready to leverage herself up and bolt.

"Cassie, I want this," he admitted, pleading. "I want you and I want Ry. It scares the hell outta me to know how much, how...bad..."

"Sex?" she dared. "Is it sex you want? Because maybe that's enough for me too." Cassie wanted to add *you bastard,* but she forced her lips tightly together instead. Hell if she was going to give him the pleasure of seeing her completely lose control.

"Hell, yeah," he grinned sadly, a new wet sheen settling over his pale eyes as well. But the way he said it was lighthearted, as lighthearted as they could get here, now, and it did what Dallas hoped it would. It eased the hard atmospheric gray stone pressing down on them. "Don't you?"

"Oh, baby," she murmured in return. "I think you know I want that. As scared as I am." Her small smile eased things just a little more. Enough.

Sighing, Dallas took her hand. "A friend of mine is coming down in a couple of days, Cassie," he said.

She sucked in a breath and sat back.

Instantly, Dallas realized his mistake. "No," he jumped in quickly, before she could cut and run. "Not a woman. And no I am not gay. It's just a friend, Cassie, a good friend, a guy I've known for years. I trust him."

A quizzical look passed over her face. "You need to ask your friend about me? You can't decide on your own?"

Softening, Dallas smiled sadly at the adorable way her lips puckered slightly. "It's not that, Cassie." He groped for the words. "Look, I didn't expect to come here and be blown over by a woman I can't take my eyes off of, and by a big-eyed soulful kid who I swear to God I'm starting to wish was my own."

A glimmer of light reappeared in Cassie's eyes.

Dallas continued. "I don't know what I thought would happen when I got here, except that I knew I had to be alone for a while to figure things out. Career things, not personal things, although they're kind of mixed up in each other," he added quickly when the spark of light in the eyes he was buried in suddenly disappeared. Lowering his voice, Dallas tried to speak in a steady, reassuring tone, but it wasn't lost on Cassie that he'd let go of her hand and was wringing his own big paws together and staring at the fire as he talked, his words emerging scarred and blistered. "It's not fair to you," he was saying. "To bring you into my mixed-up world. At least not until I can sort out a few things."

"You need some time." Cassie rose. Dallas looked up at her, his heart sinking like an anchor when he recognized the *F-you* in the way she was staring down at him. "Dal, I guess I'm impressed that you aren't telling me this after jumping into bed with me. But at the same time…look, I know you're the kind of man women should stay away from. I knew it the second I first saw you, wandering around the store confused as heck, wearing jeans and cowboy boots on a blistering hot day. And on the beach, later. And then when I saw your tent…"

Dallas stood abruptly, effectively silencing her.

Pursing her lips, Cassie cocked her head, crossed her arms, and waited.

"Cassie," he started, "don't you tell me that you're judging me based on my tent and my rusted old pickup. You're better than that. I know you are. And somehow, despite this behemoth fancy camper and shiny silver truck you towed it with, I think you don't really give a shit about material things. I know you've learned the hard way what's really important in life. And it ain't *stuff*."

"You're right, Dal. You are. I mean that." Uncrossing her arms, Cassie shifted her weight onto one foot and leaned down toward a plastic table so she could grab the half empty box of graham wafer crackers. She stuffed the remaining last bit of chocolate into it, closed the box top, and knuckled the marshmallows in the other hand before she stood tall and proudly faced him again. "To be honest, I don't need anything. Material or otherwise. Especially," she pointed the bag of marshmallows at him, and they caught in the moonlight and eerily judged him with their white skin and gooey hope, "a man facing a midlife crisis at, what, forty? Who appears to have spent his life rambling around in seedy bars and boozing his way into poverty. Who, you're right, already means more to me than the sum of all those rusty parts. But who, you're also right, appears to be wise enough to know that when a man is lost he needs to find himself before he lets a single mom and her son in. I just wish you had considered that before you agreed to teach Ry guitar. Because," she pointed the bag at herself, "I'm tough enough. I'm not that into you that I can't let go. But my son? Ry? He's just a kid, Dal. He's a kid desperate for a dad. You let him get close to you when you knew you were gonna run. When you knew you had nothing to give. And that just sucks."

Moving to go, she was yanked to a stop by Dallas' grasp on her bicep. Cassie swiped away a tear with the back of her hand before she turned around to face him again.

"I have a lot to give, Cassie. And by that I mean I have a big heart, and there's room in it for both of you. I knew the first time I looked at you that you would have some kind of power over me. I gotta tell you, it scares the hell out of me. I have no intention of walking away from you and Ry, and I don't intend to hurt either of you. But we need to go slow here. You'll understand one day. I promise you. I don't want to blindside you. You need to know what you're dealing with when it comes to me, and I need to figure out how to tell you."

Cassie sighed. "Am I that scary, Dal, that you can't be honest with me now? I gave you my soul. Do you know how hard it is for me to even have a fire? To look into a fire?"

A choking feeling in his throat made Dallas' voice emerge thin and wary. Drawing up his courage, wiping sweaty, nervous hands on his jeans, he said, "I do, Cassie. I really do. And I think that's why I'm so scared. Because I feel like I can read you, like I know what that mind of yours is thinking. And don't think I don't know that you're scared too. Of course you are. I mean, I know what I must look like to you. But it's not what you think. I'm not as messed up as I come across, I swear. I just needed a little distance from my usual world, that's all. And you and I need to take it slow until I can figure things out. I'm not that guy who will take a woman like you to bed and walk away. Not a woman like you," he added softly.

Something flickered in his eyes, and Cassie shot him a look that clearly read *I want to trust you.* But she snorted lightly, spun around on her heel, and marched toward the screen door of the Montana. Her flip-flops flapped on the small deck when she stepped up onto it. Over her shoulder she tossed, "Put the fire out, will you?" It was followed by an acerbic, sallow, "Oops, I guess you already have."

His earnest appeal followed her. "Look, I'll see you on the beach tomorrow. We'll talk then, okay Cassie? Maybe I can, I dunno..." Lifting the ball cap, Dallas rifled a hand through his layered hair and replaced the cap with a hard yank down over his eyes, "Illuminate you a little bit. Okay? Cassie? Ry and I have to work on our towers tomorrow, on our sandcastle."

But she was inside and had the door shut behind her before Dallas could even lift the nearby watering can to douse the embers.

"Damn," he muttered, wheeling around to deal with the fire. As it steamed to submission with an eerie, loud *hissss,* he angled his head back and stared up at the stars. Four jets had passed recently, leaving foamy white trails behind them. All four smoky wisps were parallel and fading, just like the hope that Dallas could somehow figure out his confused life and build some kind of future with the pretty blonde who was likely inside right now shedding tears she was too proud to let loose in his presence.

When Dallas started the old blue pickup a few minutes later, it protested but came to life as he knew it would. Dallas trusted it to carry him back up the slight slope toward the gate to the older part of the campground where his tent was nestled amongst the trees; where whispering wavelets would rock him to sleep; and where nobody could reach him to lay judgment on his decision to step away from the speeding chaos his life had become.

Only he could, and would, do that tonight—lay that kind of judgment against himself. He would be even harder on himself for messing up with Cassie.

In his heart Dallas instinctively knew that in order to sort out the disorder of his life, he needed to unlock some serious shit. And Cassie, he was beginning to understand, might have the only key.

Chapter Eight

*I*n the morning, which dawned clear and sunny, Dallas emerged from his tent alongside the first greetings of the robins and chickadees. The harsh chattering of an angry squirrel that may as well have been in the tent with him, it was so close, had made a good alarm clock. Grumbling, rubbing his back and stretching in the freshness of the early salt breeze, his toes damp from the dew, for the first time since coming to P.E.I. Dallas wondered why the hell he had traded in the king-sized specialty European mattress he'd had flown to his Toronto home a few years ago for a cheap air mattress. It all seemed so clear a few short weeks ago—escape for a while and rest. Now life was as muddy as the puddles drying up on the red dirt lane in front of his campsite. No longer was a brief vacay an uncomplicated time to heal. Life had tossed a sad woman and a sweet kid into the mix. What Dallas originally called his 'considerate deception' toward Cassie—hiding his true identity—was suddenly a serious omission. And his feelings for her were as confusing as heck.

After wolfing down two eggs and a chunk of bacon he fried in a cast iron pan over an open campfire (*so lip smacking good cooked that way, with the eggs bubbling in the bacon fat,* he decided) Dallas stood with his hands on his hips and faced his trusty old pickup.

"A cruise around the island, that's what I need. That'll clear my head."

Ten minutes later, just after passing through the gated entrance to the campground, Dallas turned left on the Lower Darnley Road. Instantly he did a double take. The physical pain of leaving his Castle Beach island sanctuary was startling, debilitating, and unexpected. Realizing that a good chunk of that came from leaving Cassie and Ry behind was equally excruciating.

Biting his lip and forcing his booted foot down on the gas pedal just about did him in. But Dallas held forth, sucked up his courage with a forced swallow, and trundled up the Lower Darnley Road.

Cassie hadn't slept a wink, so after a seven a.m. pee she climbed back under the covers and stuffed foamy bright orange earplugs in her ears, telling herself she would be no good for Ry that day if she didn't grab some *zzzzzzs*. In reality, even though she couldn't admit it to herself, the truth was she was sinking into a low-spirited day—the kind that only made sense if she muffled her pain by stuffing her face into her pillow. It was only in bed—unobserved, alone—that Cassie had the freedom to sink into dreams with Eddie. Sometimes he got so close she could smell his aftershave; spicy, vibrant clouds of it had followed him in invisible trails back when he used to walk the earth.

Around ten Ry finally stored up his courage and tiptoed up the three stairs into the fifth-wheel's main bedroom. His mother was sleeping on her side, both arms wrapped around a pillow, her hair spread out around her face like the silk of the corn they'd husked and eaten for dinner the other day.

"Mom?" he asked in a whisper, his stomach tightening and his fists curling. Pressing his boy-sized hands into his belly, he inhaled slowly and stared at the prone figure of the woman who was supposed to take care of him, who was supposed to make his breakfast and who had promised to take him to the beach later.

She didn't budge. She didn't even groan and send him away.

Scrunching up his nose, Ry backed out of the small space and went into the kitchen area. Retrieving a bowl from a cupboard, he dumped a load of Captain Crunch cereal into it, topped it up with milk and a spoonful of sugar, and sat cross-legged on the couch Dal had helped him pull out into a bed the night before. While he ate, Ry tried to focus on a favorite minion DVD. After a while he got frustrated and turned the movie off. There was still no movement from his mother's room, not even the muffled springs of her rolling over.

It was sunny outside and getting darn hot inside. Switching out his pj's for swimming trunks and a T-shirt, Ry brushed his teeth and left the camper.

Echoing Dallas' stance a few hours earlier, he put his hands on his hips and stared at his bike. With a last, lingering look toward the Montana's bedroom, Ry pulled out the bike and hopped on.

"I'll just go for a short ride," he told himself. "She'll prob'ly be up when I get back."

Near a set of large blue metal waste watch bins on the opposite treed side of the park, Ry slid to a halt. He propped his bike up on its kickstand and dug a basketball out of a rack attached to a pole with a net at the top. He bounced the ball around for a while, shooting at the basket and, when he went after his ball, sending longing looks to the assorted families wandering up and down the nearby lane on their way to the café, the store, or the playground.

A quarter hour later a redheaded boy a few years older than Ry approached.

"Uh, est-ce que...uh, I play too?" the boy asked in faltering English. "Levi." He pointed to himself before making a grand gesture toward the beach. "My family camp down that way. My sister, she only want to follow boys around." A hand flew out in the direction of the main buildings, just above the basketball net. "My fadder, he work. Need Internet, you know. Café have Internet."

Ry bounced the ball over to him. "Is your mom here?" It seemed too good to be true, that the boy, like Ry, might only have one parent.

"She read by our tent." Levi made a drinking gesture. "My fadder bring her coffee already." He laughed. "She like her coffee in the morning, my mudder. At night she like wine."

Ry forced a small smile through his lips. The ache in his belly lessened.

Levi was an easy companion who liked to talk. Ry found himself a little in awe of the kid, who said he was from the Canadian province of Quebec and who spoke with a significantly clipped French accent.

They shot baskets for a while, got bored, and eventually moved to the fenced-in playground. There, Levi's good-natured, persuasive encouragement engendered a few new recruits and soon Ry was having a blast playing color tag around the slides and swings. A constant fretting over his mother slipped away, the lonely sadness replaced with friends and fun.

Near noon, Levi tossed out an invitation. "Come to beach wit us, we got boards." He threw in an invite for barbecued hot dogs.

Ry's stomach was growling. Uninvited, his mom slid back into his mind. He frowned, annoyed that he was more worried about her than she seemed worried about him. "Okay," he agreed, a new confidence from a few hours of playing with this kid bolstering his courage. "I just have to go back to my camper to check on, um, with my mom first."

Ten minutes later, after half-heartedly scanning all the adults he passed for signs of Dal, Ry quietly closed the trailer door on his still sleeping mother and, a towel tossed lazily around his shoulders, started biking through the lanes of campers and tents on the treed side of the campground. Halfway down the third short lane he found Levi watching for him. The boy held out a hot dog bun and introduced his parents, who were nice enough, Ry thought, but pretty casual overall since they didn't ask about his mother or anything. He soon figured out that their capacity to speak English was almost non-existent. Translating started to frustrate Levi so eventually the adults just smiled at Ry and let the boys be.

On the beach a half hour later, Ry dropped his towel on the sand, grabbed a blue kid-sized body board Levi offered him, and followed his older, taller friend out into the ocean. It was blistering hot; the beach was jam packed with campers, almost all with colorful umbrellas marking their spots. Camp chairs sprayed out under the umbrellas. Shoved into the sand in semi-circle formations, in most cases they faced the water, although some were turned so that their owners could stretch out in the sun's direct path and tan in sleepy peace.

Leaning on the boards, the kids dug into the waves, hollering with glee when breakers crashed over them. Yesterday's storm had left its legacy—significant waves with a force strong enough to easily push swimmers around. The boys drifted sideways a few times, often losing their footing and relying on the boards for stability, but Levi's mother was watching them—she called them back more than once. Dripping and happy, they listened, taking frequent breaks to run back to the family's cooler for fruit juice drinks, popcorn and apple slices.

Mid-afternoon they played in the sand for a good hour; once they dried off, Levi's mother sprayed both boys with sunscreen, tut-tutting at both of them in French, concerned that their skin was pinking up just a little too much under the summer sun. Ry had no clue what she was tut-tutting about but he didn't care. It felt good to have a mom care for him. Comfortably pudgy, Levi's mom had nice eyes and a ready smile. Ry thought her dark hair was beautiful, the way she wore it all frizzy and loose around her face like a child. The father was okay—redheaded like Levi. Once he even put his beer down and cheerily tossed a Nerf football around in the water with the boys.

Levi's older sister, braided and petulant, seemed to be the only person concerned about Ry's appearance on the beach without a parent. "Where your mudder and fadder?" she asked in her French-accented English.

"Sleeping," Ry answered half-honestly, pushing a pang of worry away. He was completely unwilling to talk about his messed-up family. Heck, this was so much fun, hanging with a real, proper family. His mother wasn't going anywhere and he didn't feel like crashing his mood by being the recipient of sympathetic looks about the father he barely remembered. Nah, Ry preferred the complete family he'd attached himself to over the half one that seemed to sometimes forget he was alive.

Late in the afternoon the French campers packed up their things and left. Ry sucked up his pride and told them his mother was set up down the beach near the sandstone cliffs with friends by then. He even pointed out a woman in a pink bikini who happened to casually look his way and wave to someone beyond Ry. The Quebec family bought his story.

"You go to chocolate bar bingo?" Levi hollered, dragging his board behind him on his way to the boardwalk ramp. The board left a watery trail in the hot sand.

"Yep!" Ry called back, sauntering down the beach toward the woman he told Levi was his mother. Chocolate bar bingo—bingo played with chocolate bars as winnings—was a staple Monday and Thursday nights at Castle Beach. Played in and outside the rec hall near the main gate, the fee to play was a chocolate bar that would go into the winnings. Ry had often wanted to play but always found himself sitting on his bike watching families play instead. His mother told him she wasn't into chocolate so the bingo didn't make a lot of sense to her. Ry didn't know that the real reason she didn't want to play was that she found it hard to sit amongst families. The memory of her own lost dreams gutted her.

Now, Ry spotted a couple of kids he and Levi had chummed around with at the playground that morning. Noticing that Levi and his family were now up the ramp and out of sight, he dropped his towel back on the sand and made a beeline toward them. These kids, like Levi, were older and taller. They'd made their way to a sandbar. The water where they were ducking and diving in the waves was only up to their knees, with the exception of when the waves crashed over them. Then, it was over their heads.

With a relieved grin that he had made more than one new friend today, Ry stepped into the water.

Dallas was just pulling back into his campsite when Ry made the decision to enter the water for what he told himself was his last swim of the day. The day, for Dallas, had been lonely as hell. He'd cruised around the north coast to Cavendish, Prince Edward Island's National Park, an area famous for the Anne of Green Gables House, and populated by a gazillion tourists. The overall Cavendish stretch was only a few miles long, was a bit hilly, and was lined with beach stores, cozy family restaurants, cabins, campsites, small amusement parks and a golf course. Dal found himself a Tim Horton's coffee shop about midway through the area, grabbed a large coffee with cream and kept on cruising. At two p.m. he stopped for a dip at Brackley Beach, a white sand beach further east than Cavendish, dried off, and prepared to head back to Darnley. Stuffing a roadside dairy bar burger into his mouth, he ate while he cruised, halting once to take a call from Phil, who announced that he would be on the island in two days.

"Good," Dallas had mumbled, swigging back a chocolate milkshake to wash down his burger. Picturing Cassie and Ry on the beach, a wave of pleasure washed over him and he decided to join them. No doubt they'd be there cooling off in this insane heat, which Dallas suffered through a thousand times over because his old truck's only air conditioning was the hot outdoor air blowing in through his windows.

Sweat trickled down his back the whole damn day. He was yanging pretty good for a swim when he finally pulled to a stop next to his orange and gray tent.

With a sigh, Dallas hopped out of the truck. He stepped over the dirt lane and glanced down at the beach. It was late afternoon now but the beach was still full of people, dotted with umbrellas and colorful bathing suits and towels and, he noted with a lick of his lips, lots of beverage toting coolers.

He was just about to turn to head toward his tent and throw on his trunks when he scanned the water and spotted Ry's neon green trunks. A quick glance back to the sandy beach revealed no sign of Cassie. Squinting, Dal thought maybe she was just hard to find amongst all those people, behind all those umbrellas and camp chairs.

"What are you up to, Ry?" Dal wondered, watching the boy struggle to make his way through the big waves toward a group of kids further out in the water. A quick pulse started in Dallas' gut. "I'm too damn attached to this kid," he muttered. "He's not my business."

But Ry had quickly become imbued in Dallas' soul, whether or not Dallas himself really acknowledged and accepted it. And right now the kid was alone in the water, charging his way through powerful waves much bigger than his small body. Watching, squinting to see better, Dallas recoiled when a big breaker crashed over the kid. For a few terrifying, precious seconds, Ry disappeared from sight. Dallas' entire body went taut; blood started to pound in his ears.

Ry appeared again, flailing in the heavy surf, struggling for a foothold. Another hasty scan of the beach and Dallas couldn't see a damn soul who seemed alert to the boy's increasing peril.

"Well, shit," Dallas bit off, recrossing the dusty lane at a quick trot and reaching back into his truck for his still damp swim trunks. He ducked into his tent for a super fast change from the sweaty jeans and boots he'd worn during his drive. Skipping flip-flops and a towel altogether he took off running, a damp blue T-shirt clinging to his overheated chest and the usual Jays cap lying forgotten on the passenger seat of the truck where Dal had abandoned it earlier. A narrow path over the dune in front of Dallas' site led down to the beach. He lunged over it. Skidding down the sand on the beach side, Dallas told himself that Ry was likely fine. That Cassie had to be somewhere nearby and, even if she wasn't, somebody must be keeping an eye out for the kid. Parents on the beach were always watching each other's kids; it was a kind of unspoken Castle Beach code.

But no…Ry was in serious trouble now. Unmistakably. According to the way the blond head kept sinking under the large waves, it was crystal clear. From his own fairly newbie ocean experience, Dallas figured Ry hadn't counted on the waves increasing the depth of water as much as they did between sandbars, nor would the boy have considered just how much power these waves carried when they hit a person. Between the mighty undertow and the formidable grasp of the crashing waves, on post-storm days like this when they were constantly being battered by waves, swimmers easily lost their footing and often their breath.

Bursting through the assembled sunbathers, kicking up sand as he ran, Dallas hightailed it into the water. The kid wouldn't have to be Ry—Dallas would have gone in the water after whoever was in trouble. From the high vantage point of his campsite overlooking the beach, Dallas had a bird's eye view that the sunbathers below didn't have. But because it was Ry, Dallas was in high gear. Barreling into the surf, he launched his strong body toward the child who, he realized as he scanned the water, had gone under again.

"Damn it!" Dallas shouted, panicked. "Ry!"

Ahead, he spotted a floundering arm reaching for the sky. A small face tipped up too, hair plastered to a cheek, open mouth choking, gasping for a saltwater-free breath.

By the time Dallas got to Ry and scooped him safely up into his arms, other beachgoers had taken notice, some because Dallas had just about knocked over their umbrellas when he ran past them into the water, and some because they finally realized a kid was in trouble. A few of them vaulted off their comfy camp chairs and watched in a kind of scared, hushed alarm.

None of those people were Cassie.

Ry wrapped his arms and legs around Dal, around the strong body of the man he had grown to love and trust over the last few weeks. Burying his face in Dal's neck, he coughed up water, his body fiercely taut, the relentless hammering of his heart giving him away—telling Dal, whose big hand was on Ry's back, that he was still deathly afraid. Big swallows of air eventually gave way to irregular, choking sobs.

Trembling, at first Dallas was more relieved than pissed, but it didn't take long for his fear to transmute to anger. He wasn't sure whom he was most angry with—the kid clinging to him like a baby monkey to its mother, or the kid's mother.

Dallas, too, was struggling to regain his breath. Over Ry's shoulder he spat out a mouthful of salt water, ignoring the sprays the waves were still christening him with while he struggled back toward the sand to bring this sacred rescue mission to fruition. More than once while reaching for Ry, Dallas had lost his footing on the stormy, sandy bottom, and a few briny mouthfuls of ocean water had found their way inside his lungs.

Grabbing a handful of soaking wet hair, Dallas shoved Ry's head back. Coughing, choking, he stared into the small, scared face.

Ry squeezed his eyes shut. Sobbing, he tried to bury his embarrassment and fear in the strong shoulder he so desperately needed.

"You okay, Ry?!" Dallas cried over the roaring surf. "You okay? Where's your mother? Where's your mom, damn it?" Finally breaking free of the water, stepping over wet sand on the shore, it hit Dallas that people were staring. He panicked. "Oh, Jesus," he cursed, and ducked his nose into Ry's tangled hair. Being recognized was not an option. Disregarding any offers of assistance, he forged through the few anxious people privy to the rescue. As discreetly as he could, he glanced around for Cassie, circling and turning while Ry quaked in his arms.

There was no sign of her. Dallas headed up the narrow path that led to his campsite. There, he deposited Ry on the top of the picnic table, but he had to pry the kid off his body. Swiping an arm across his nose, Dallas placed that hand on his hip afterward and gave Ry a good look to make sure he was, indeed, okay. Again he asked where Cassie was.

Curling his legs up into his arms, Ry finally looked up at his new buddy. "Still sleeping, I guess," he confessed, eyes wide, his heart finally starting to slow down.

"What?" Aghast, Dallas added, "She went for a nap and left you on the beach?"

"Noooo." A hiccupy sob snuck out. Ry hunkered up his shoulders. He shook his head. "She didn't get up today."

A string of curses turned the air blue. Gathering his senses, Dallas was about to apologize when Ry's accusing tone stopped him cold.

"You were supposed to come too. We were going to work on our castle today, remember? On the doors and windows. Today was 'practice our doors and windows on the towers' day.'" A new round of sobs cemented the heartache of abandonment and loss that Ry had been feeling all day.

Dallas was completely thrown. Not once did he consider that, by backing out of his previously planned day with Ry and Cassie, would he be leaving Ry at the mercy of a depressed and lonely mother. He was floored.

"Oh Jesus, Ry," he managed, sucking in a jagged breath at the sudden fear that charged over his body and sliced his heart like a dagger at the idea of what might have happened out there in the water. "I'm sorry, kid. I'm so, so sorry. But Ry, I can't imagine you are allowed in the water without your mother there to keep an eye on you."

"It was hot. It was so hot, Dal! And I had a family for most of the day, I made a friend and I had his family, but they were done and they went up to their campsite for supper. They didn't take me with them. I was hoping they'd take me with them!"

It was true. Ry's eyes were as sorrowful as Dallas felt his own were all that long day. Dallas' mood was so low that he'd driven almost mindlessly along the gorgeous Prince Edward Island roads, so completely tuned out that he missed most of the beauty the island had to offer, like the island's renowned patchwork canola, striking in an almost neon yellow vibrancy; and potato plants just starting to really take off, their leafy greenness spreading like comfy blankets over acres and acres of roadside farmland.

"Well, kid," Dallas offered, lifting a bare foot and resting it on the bench seat of the picnic table, "you scared the shit out of me. And out of yourself too, I think. I'm damned sorry you were alone out there. And now I think we need to get you back to your mother. I hope she's on the move, because she's about to be jarred awake if she isn't. Ry, your mom's had a rough time, but kid, you're too young to be left alone the way she leaves you. This can't happen again. Okay?"

A slow nod was Ry's teary answer. He lowered his legs over the side of the table so they hung there all little boy skinny. Dallas cringed sadly when he saw him grab the edge of the table with both hands and clutch it til his small knuckles whitened.

"C'mere kid," Dallas said quietly, wrapping his big arms around the bony shoulders. "You're safe, Ry. You're safe now and you're not alone. You got me on your side now. You and your mom. You got me."

"Forever?" came a low whisper from somewhere in Dallas' neck, from under his own long wet hair that dripped in comfort over someone else's kid.

"Oh, kid." A heavy sigh preceded Dallas' next remark. "I wish. But you know, sometimes these things are complicated. Life is complicated." Pushing Ry away from his shoulder, he swiped wet hair away from his forehead. Dallas smiled, not a big one, but the corners of his lips turned up a wee bit. "But just so you know, Ry, I hope so. Forever, I mean. Although I have to say that I'm about to give your mom a bit of a talking to. I hope you don't mind. There are a few things that pretty stubborn head needs to hear. And I'm the one to say them. That okay with you?"

"You can't get mad at her for sleeping, Dal." Ry shook his head slowly from side to side. His still dripping hair was puddling his sorrows on the table. "She sleeps because she's sad about my dad."

And if she'd lost you today too? I guess she'd just disappear. Dallas cringed. "You know, Ry, it's okay for your mom to be sad. People can get real sad. But there's help out there for sad people. In the big old world. To help them be a little less sad. Sometimes we just need to give people like your mom a reason to go get that help."

"She has a reason." Ry's sobs had settled into more of the occasional heavy sigh. "She has you now. I saw her smile a lot at you last night."

"Oh, kid." Dallas had to force his voice to remain calm. This kid was wise beyond his years. Sometimes he broke things down into the simplest common denominator. "I'm glad I can make her smile. And you know something? I'm gonna try harder to get her to smile more, okay? Come on. Let me just change into something dry and we'll go up to see your mom."

"I left my towel on the beach. I need to go get my towel or she'll be mad."

"We'll get it. Give me a sec, Ry. Stay put." Dallas was about to duck into the tent when Ry's voice stopped him.

"I was really scared, Dal." The small shoulders were shaking again. But then the chin came up. Ry looked to the side, where Dallas was trying to disguise the wet mist suddenly covering his own eyes. "I'm glad you're here."

"You know something, Ry?" Dallas' voice was low and husky. "I'm glad *you're* here."

At that, Dallas left Ry sitting on the table to dry off in the sun while he changed into shorts and a dry T-shirt. Relief settled over him. Smiling, he pushed his feet into flip-flops and retrieved his ball cap from the truck to pull down over his eyes. Just before he turned back to Ry he said again, softly, and only to himself, "I'm really glad you're here."

Chapter Nine

*T*he Montana's outside door was closed, and the purple petunias Cassie always moved behind her wooden windscreen at night to protect their fragile petals from the sometimes unforgivable wind were still there, hunkered next to each other in wilted defeat instead of brightening up the small deck the way they usually did during the daytime.

Not good signs for a kid hoping his mother was awake, barbecuing him a burger. Or for a man hoping the woman he was becoming seriously attached to was functioning on a level he considered healthy.

"Wait out here, Ry." Deliberately taking the metal steps in light hops so as not to alarm the boy, Dallas tried the Montana's handle. The door swung open. Dallas went to close it but paused at the sight of the forlorn child standing before him in dirty flip-flops they'd retrieved from the beach with Ry's towel. Ry was disconsolate, judging by the droopy lips and sunken shoulders.

Dallas mustered up a small smile and pointed toward his pickup. "My phone's under the seat. My niece put Tap-Tap-Muppets on it. Cop a squat on the picnic table and work on your musical reflexes."

He waited until Ry turned toward the truck before he stepped into the trailer and closed just the screen door behind him.

Inside, the kitchen was in order. The only signs of food or drink being consumed were Ry's dishes from his long ago breakfast, staunchly guarded by a cereal box. The door to Cassie's bedroom was closed.

"Not the way I had hoped to get into your bedroom for the first time," Dallas grumbled. In truth, the fear and worry roiling around in the pit of his stomach outweighed any nerves associated with this unplanned visit.

Twisting the knob to the right, he gave the door a careful shove and padded into the semi-darkness.

It took Dallas' eyes a few seconds to adjust. When they did, he was relieved to spy the gentle rise and fall of Cassie's chest. She lay on one side of the big bed, hugging a pillow. She didn't budge. Sleep, Dal knew, was her escape. Sacred time with Eddie, no doubt. Waking her would hurt her, would destroy whatever lovely world she was hiding in. For a few minutes Dal just stood and watched her sleep. She was enchanting in sleep, cheeks pink and lashes long and feminine like tiny curtains protecting Cassie from the outside world. The lips Dallas had finally tasted—that with remembrance caused a stir in his heart—were slightly parted, drawing in even breaths that Dallas took to mean Cassie was deeply resting.

As pretty as she was, he couldn't understand how she could float away like that so deeply...how she could just shut Ry off and on, as if at will she could pretend he didn't exist at all.

He felt a little like a voyeur seeing her this way, without giving her due time to dress or brush her hair. Cassie was sleeping in a light camisole on this hot day, with one sheet pulled up to her waist. Creamy in color, it fell over her petite body in graceful waves, covering the parts of her Dal ached to see and touch with Cassie's loving participation. It had risen and bunched just below her breasts as she slept. Bare skin, tanned from Cassie's bikini days on the beach, peeked out at Dal. *Touchable* bare skin. He had to stifle the urge to reach out; even worse, the top strap, thin to begin with, had slipped off her shoulder and was resting against a yoga-toned bicep.

Luscious, that's what you are, Dallas decided as his eyes pored over the rest of the sweet body. Slim legs that ended in toenails painted an elegant light pink, hair that he knew smelled like beach and sand, long piano-playing fingers, that was Cassie.

Dallas wanted to lie down next to her, he wanted to pull her close and tell her everything would be okay. But reality set in and he figured she'd scream if he startled her and she found him in her bed; hell, she might scream anyway to find him standing there staring down at her, telegraphing a wistful desire and the simple need to care for her, a woman who life had hurt in such a sudden, terrible way.

He had to look away.

The room was small. The bed took up most of the space, across the width of the trailer. A mirrored closet on the far side, the kind that slides across when jeans and shirts need retrieval, bordered it. A built-in chest of drawers a few feet off the foot of the bed left just enough of a passageway between it and the bed to get through. Dallas could stand tall in here, but that was no surprise to him, he'd often lived in similar campers when on tour or at various concert venues.

Taking a step back, he grabbed the door and knocked lightly. On the bed, Cassie stirred. Moving back through the door, Dallas gave it a harder rap.

"Mmmphh?" Cassie was awake now, but Dallas could tell she wasn't quite sure what world she was in. He decided to give her a reason to come back to consciousness quickly.

"Cassie, get up," he demanded.

Her eyes widened. She half sat up, pulling the sheet up over her breasts as she blinked up at him. Again, Dallas had to look away. Swallowing, he gathered his wits and tightened his fingers around the doorknob to keep himself from vaulting onto the bed and pressing that small body to him in some misguided thought that by holding her and sharing his energy she would be okay.

That they would be okay.

"Cassie," he said instead in a guarded kind of way, unsure of how she would take it. "I just hauled your kid out of the ocean. He was going under. In fact..." The emotion of the last forty-five minutes was catching up to Dallas. With a strangled sound, he turned his head away and tried to summon up the rest of the words. She was staring at him, disbelief and shame crisscrossing her pretty face while Dallas tried to explain just how bad this was, to find her in bed and her child in the water. At five p.m., nonetheless. "In fact," he repeated, stronger now, "he *was* under."

"What?" The shock of finding Dal in her bedroom was embarrassing and, on many levels, appalling, not the least because Cassie'd been there all day neglecting her son and wallowing in self-pity. But hearing that Ry had gone into the ocean and required rescue far outweighed the shame that oscillated its way into Cassie's brain and that quivered up her body. Vaulting up, she launched herself at Dal with no regard for her state of half-dress.

He averted his eyes, but not before he discerned that the silky cami was partly see-through. Blocking Cassie's way at the door, Dallas grabbed her arm. His voice husky and his body trembling, he barked, "He's fine. Ry's fine. He's outside." A nearby chair was layered in clothes; a soft gray hoodie was on the top. Grabbing it, Dallas wrapped it around Cassie's diminutive shoulders.

Stepping back from him, she wrapped it around her body and fell backward on the bed, but not before peeking outside the small window to see her son on the picnic table, long blond layers falling over his face, fingers poking unhappily at an iPhone.

"It's dinnertime here on this planet, Cassie." Dallas was taking no prisoners. This woman needed a friggin' good wake-up call, and today she was getting it.

Her answer was a raised chin and a chilly stare. "What time we eat is none of your damn business."

Unable to help himself, Dallas let his voice rise. A quaking hand pointed a finger at her. "What part of what I just said to you didn't compute? Cassie, Ry is not a strong swimmer! Even if he was, he would not have been able to get himself safely out of the ocean today, but then again you wouldn't know how crazy the breakers are down on the beach because you haven't been down there. Judging by the look of you, you haven't been anywhere today!"

"Dal, Ry can take care of himself. He knows sometimes I need to take a day! I'll talk to him, he knows not to go in the water by himself."

"No eight-year-old kid should be left alone while his grieving mother 'takes a day,' Cassie."

Jumping up, she gave him a shove. "I'm not grieving! I did that a long time ago."

"Bullshit! You shoved the pain aside and buried it. That's why it still steamrolls you. You've never grieved that man! I don't even think you've accepted that he's actually gone. Because if you have, Cassie, you would wrap your arms around that lonely little boy of yours and never let him out of your sight!"

"Seriously? This from a man who lives in a tent, who can't even bring himself to talk about what's haunting him? You have no right to be telling me what I do and do not feel, Dal. Because apparently you can't feel at all!"

The last bit was delivered in a rising crescendo that caused even greater agony for the kid outside on the picnic table who was losing at Tap-Tap-Muppets. Ry couldn't focus. All he could see in his mind's eye was salt spray and great thrusting waves of water, sucking him down and taking his feet out from under him. Closing his eyes, Ry tried to focus on the steady, powerful hands of the man who delivered him from that fear and who, now, was trying to appeal to Ry's mother to actually take care of him.

There was one other person Ry knew loved him and worried over him. Sobbing, he shut down the Muppets App and opened the phone screen on Dal's iPhone. Ry had long ago memorized his mother's sister's phone number. Caroline had insisted, in case…well, just in case.

He dialed.

Inside, the fight hit its climax.

"I feel, Cassie!" Dal shoved a finger in his own hard chest. "I feel more than you know. I bleed all over the whole damn world, that's how I *feel*!" *In song,* he wanted to add. *In lyrics and in music.* But Dallas could not bring himself, even in the heat of battle, to go there. It hit him like one of the waves that crashed over him when he rescued Ry earlier that he was no different from this tragic woman hunched up on the bed in front of him. He just hid in music—and in tents—while she buried herself in sleep and in dreams.

From outside, a small boy's sobs alerted the adults inside the camper to the fact that Ry could hear them. Just as Cassie rose and tried to walk past Dal, Ry's voice drifted on the breeze into the bedroom of the luxury Montana.

"Aunt Caroline," he was saying between gasps of great, gulping sorrow, "please come. Please come get me. I want to go home with you. I don't want to take care of her anymore."

"Oh, Jesus," Cassie moaned. "I suck."

Sighing, Dallas eased his tired body down next to her. One arm stretched up and landed around Cassie's hunched shoulders. "Sweetheart," he started, "I'm no better than you are. In my books, you've done okay. Ry's an amazing kid. All I've been is selfish."

"He thinks he's taking care of me." Lifting her fragile hands up, Cassie placed them over her face. Shoving the heels of both palms in her eyes, she winced when her body started to shake. Burying her face in Dal's chest,

Cassie released this new pain into his heart. At the same time, he wrapped his second arm around her, hiding his own hurts in Cassie's messy golden hair.

A few minutes later, they heard the door to the camper open and close. A shadow blocked the doorway to the bedroom. Dallas and Cassie looked up, and Cassie opened her arms.

Taking in his mother in Dal's arms, Ry backed up. "I'll make us some hot dogs," he announced, raising his shoulders proudly. "And salad. Okay, Dal? Do you like salad?"

At Dal's humbled nod, Ry went off to rustle up supper. Speechless, Dallas grinned crookedly at Cassie, who grabbed a handful of his T-shirt and used it to wipe her eyes.

"He's making that salad for you, Dal. Contrary to how bad this looks on my part, Ry's never made a meal for me in his life. He's trying to impress you."

Recovering his voice, Dallas chuckled. "Hot dogs and salad. Sounds like heaven to me, Cassie. He's quite the kid."

She gave him a light shove. "Go out there before he tries to light the barbecue on his own. I need a shower."

Sniffing her hair, running it through his fingers, Dallas couldn't let her admission pass. "You're telling me," he teased.

Laughing, Cassie stood and pulled him upright. Leaning forward, she treated him to a tender kiss on the lips. "Don't read more into that than you want to, Dal," she said softly afterwards. "It's just a simple thanks. For today. For Ry. For everything."

One corner of his lip stretched up, and Dallas lit up. "For the record, Cassie, you can kiss me all you want to. I'm not calling a halt to us, whatever 'us' is at this point. And one day you'll understand me and my crazy life a little better. But for now, let's just have our hot dogs and salad and cherish that cool kid of yours. Okay?"

"You got it." A last, longer kiss, and regretfully they parted, although Cassie's cheeks flamed pink at the longing look and raised eyebrows Dallas gave the big bed.

"Later, tiger," she breathed, forcibly turning him toward the door.

Dallas was too red to answer. Shaking his head, he closed the door behind him just as Ry squeaked open the lid of the barbecue.

Chapter Ten

*A*nxiously *tut-tutting* before she even had her Beamer's door open, with a flurry of *I told you so's* Cassie's sister Caroline landed at Castle Beach promptly at noon the next day. With a designer Michael Kors bag hooked over one arm and a Gucci suitcase dangling from the other hand, she stepped up into the camper and took in the small space with pursed lips and blatantly undisguised concern.

"And you're planning to live here for the remainder of the summer? Cassie, darling, I love you dearly, but where am I supposed to sleep?" she preened. Caroline's insensitivity masked a caring heart; unfortunately, most people couldn't see past the baubles she blended into her exterior persona.

Cassie was Caroline's live-action Barbie from the moment Cassie was born. Three years between them, she was a deeply adored toy and the constant object of Caroline's attention.

Sadly, in the last six years Caroline wore her worry the way she dangled her fancy bags—in a parade of color according to Cassie's levels of pain. Yellow for the good days, shades of blue for sorrow's grip, pink on the more hopeful days, the ones when Cassie shoved excuses aside and actually attended family gatherings. Today's Michael Kors was black but it was spotted with white dots, as if Caroline was optimistic that the good could get through and her sister would rise above the troubles tethering her to the earth the way thick, briny lines of rope held Prince Edward Island's ubiquitous lobster traps in place.

Ry launched himself forward and took Caroline's suitcase. Struggling with it, he dragged it to the front of the small sofa that opened up to become his sleeping nest. Brushing his palms together in satisfaction, he grinned up at her. "You can have my bed," he proclaimed happily, eyes alight. The world just felt safer when he was not alone with his fragile mother.

"B-but…" Caroline stammered, waving a hand uselessly in the air in the general direction of the sofa.

"Relax, Caroline," Cassie smirked. "Ry says it's quite comfortable. It opens into a daybed. Ry can help me put up the tent for him." Tearing her eyes away from her sister's pristine white linen shift dress to glance at her son, she tossed out, "Maybe your new friend Levi will come up for a night with you?"

"What about Dal, Mom?" Ry asked hopefully. "Can I go ask him instead?" Cassie gave him a funny look.

Caroline hauled off her heels one at a time, rubbing each foot as she did so. She dropped each shoe smack dab in front of the trailer's door. In all her innocent glory, she piped up, "Who's Dal? I'm glad to see you're making friends here, Ry."

"Dal's my guitar teacher. And," Ry added with a tinge of uncertainty, "he's more Mom's friend than mine."

"Oh?" Caroline's newly waxed brows rose up in identical arcs. "Curious."

"Later," Cassie warned her, before speaking to Ry. "We'll ask Levi. We'll probably see him on the beach. I can talk to his mother to see if it's okay."

Ry frowned. "She won't understand you. She doesn't speak very good English."

"Then Levi can translate. Caroline, have you had lunch? How's our boho-chic mother? Has Des taken you to lunch with the Premier yet or did you skip over him and brunch with the glitzy Ottawa folk instead?"

And with that final punctuation steering the conversation in a direction that didn't put her pulse on overdrive, Cassie whipped open the fridge door and rumbled around for gluten-free sandwich fixings to suit her picky guest.

Caroline, too, made her home in Halifax, although instead of going for a character heritage vibe like her sister, she and her husband Des parked their always shiny, always new vehicles in a pretentious subdivision just outside the city. Des was an M.P., a Member of Parliament. Breaking free from a career as a high profile lawyer to serve the people, he wasn't home a lot, but Caroline was cool with that. She soaked up their public lifestyle the way her pampered skin soaked up expensive body creams, by hanging on his arm at a myriad of coveted social events when he was home, in essence serving his career as well or better than he did when it came to hearing problems and offering solutions. If anything, the only downside to Caroline in terms of Des' career was that she liked to spend what he made. That being said, she had a marketing business of her own in which she was busy, busy, busy, so Cassie appreciated the little unplanned vacay Caroline was taking now, despite the fact that it was in response to Ry's desperate call yesterday.

"He said you slept all day again," Caroline stated matter-of-factly on the beach later, with only a hint of what was truly an all-consuming worry for her baby sister sneaking through her artificially steady voice. She spoke from a colorful low beach chair. The women had relaxed their bodies into chairs they'd placed side-by-side facing the water. Snugged comfortably into the sand, their goal was sun tanning although they had the option of being shaded by a dainty pale pink and white flower-shaped umbrella that Ry had patiently anchored in place with piles of sand and a few carefully chosen sandstone rocks.

After his cheerful, "The wind won't get this sucker now," and Cassie's surprised admonishment at his redneck language, Cassie and Caroline had quite succinctly placed their chairs mostly in the sun and their cooler bag with its clear plastic pitcher of sangria in the shade.

"Priorities," Caroline had mouthed to Cassie, smiley-eyed and winking.

Happy to be together, the sisters were staring languidly out at the ocean, which today was settled and calm, an almost perfect flat peaceful blue. Like twinkling bells, harmless barely-there lace-crested waves were making their way to shore, one after the other in a never-ending parade of contentment. In the ladies' hands as they stared over the oasis, content and mesmerized, were see-through blue plastic wine glasses brimming with fruit—strawberries, raspberries and orange bits, and a sprinkle of blueberries—that Cassie had plucked from the Montana's freezer. Just a few moments ago she'd also filled both glasses to the rim with the sweet wine spritzer.

Taking an easy sip, Cassie locked her eyes on Ry's wiry body as she considered how to respond to her sister's thinly disguised worry. Caroline's presence had Cassie's son bubbling over with joy, as if he'd exhaled from the bottom of his soul and unloaded all of his worry and loneliness onto her pseudo-aristocratic shoulders. At this very moment he was in the water with his young French friend. The boys were cruising the nearby coast on child-sized body boards. Riding the soothing wavelets close to shore, the boys had tucked the boards under their small bodies, chests down, so they could paddle around and look through the water for crawly things on the ocean's bottom. When Levi's sister jogged over to peer down at their latest find, Cassie laughed aloud at the girl's happy scream.

"Must be a crab," she explained to Caroline, who visibly cringed and wrinkled up her pink toes.

"And you like it here, why?" Caroline asked, dipping recently manicured fingers into a bag of salty pretzels Cassie held out to her.

Cornering right, Cassie sighed and stated, "Because it's peaceful. It's healing."

"It's a good place to hide in old memories, Cassie. I'm not so sure about this healing shtick you're feeding me."

"Healing. Hmm." Thoughtful, Cassie recalled last night's campfire with Dal. Just before they put the fire out at about two in the morning, a falling star had zipped overhead, sweeping through the sky in a graceful curve as if someone had orchestrated its sparkle with a willowy wave of a finger. At the time, with Ry in bed asleep, Cassie and Dal were holding hands, avoiding the topic skidding over their hearts demanding airtime. In theory it seemed easier that way; at least they were still spending time in each other's company, but in truth it hurt more. Now, recalling the ache to climb into the arms of the man who still remained such a mystery, Cassie hung her head. Temporarily forgotten, her beachy wine glass slanted toward the sand.

She'd pointed out the falling star to Dal. "Life goes by that quickly," she'd told him, humbled at the great expanse of stars overhead and the mysteries locked within them, within her friend's soul. "People we love come and go that quickly. Poof. Gone. Just like that."

It was the first time all evening that Dal took her hand. He'd leaned forward and whispered the first clue about the pain manacled around his body. "That star is me, Cassie. I'm that falling star."

Startled, she almost sobbed her answer. "Why?"

He shook his head. "Would it be enough right now to tell you that I was on a speeding train? And that the only way to get off was to jump off? To leave?"

"Did you do something illegal, Dal? Did you hurt somebody?"

"No." The word was a half-truth. But Dal was not overly concerned about Deborah. The little vixen had already found a new ticket to the fast track. "I just couldn't breathe anymore. I needed to breathe, Cassie. It wasn't like I did anything. I was doing the same stuff I always did."

And that was that. He hadn't offered more and Cassie hadn't pushed him. Something about the way he had looked at her, the stars glistening in those sweet, pale eyes, encouraged trust from Cassie. Trust that he would talk when he was ready. He did kiss her when they finally parted, and there was nothing tentative about it. When Dal's lips touched hers, and one big hand caressed the back of her neck when he pulled her to him, the other pressing her waist so their bodies could ignite, Cassie had melted. Willingly, she hooked both thumbs over his belt—(he'd run home when the night cooled, and pulled on jeans and boots—now, she moaned at the memory of the simple roguish look of him, which was enough to make her want the man fully and completely)—and sighed into his body, into the passion he urged from her. Again it was Dal who pulled away, but Cassie intuitively felt that he did not want to.

"When you're ready," she'd whispered into those searching eyes, "I'll be here for you, Dal. If I learned anything when Eddie died, I learned that moments like this are too few and far between to let slip away. I want you, baby. I know I have work to do, to deserve you. I'll try. I swear."

"You don't know me well enough to know if I'm worth the effort, Cassie," he'd breathed back to her, a quiet desperation washing over the strong jaw and fuzzy cheeks.

"Funny," she'd smiled, tilting her head to one side in that cute way of hers that Dallas adored, "I feel like I've known you forever."

Now, on the beach, Cassie shivered with delight at the way Dal had responded to that. The tenderness in his eyes softened even more, if that was even possible. Although, as she snuggled into her pillow after his old truck chugged off down the lane, Cassie had gone over their entire evening together and got stuck on a new thought—*What if he's hesitating because he knows I'm such a wreck?* The notion was sobering, and if she hadn't been dozey from a few glasses of Pinot Grigio, she would have likely tossed and turned until dawn, worrying about it.

Unable to help herself, she glanced around the beach for signs of the tell-tale white and green plaid swim trunks Dal wore most days. Over lunch at the camper, Ry had spilled the beans to Caroline about him, that the man lived in a tent and was kind of 'scraggly looking.'

Caroline had instantly paled. In her mind, the last thing her delicate sister needed was a sex-starved hobo with bedroom eyes.

"Is he here?" Caroline took a ladylike pull on her sangria and tucked her toes deeper into the sand.

"Who? Um…nope. I'm sure he'll be down later." Swerving right, Cassie took a new tack. "Caroline, I'm doing okay. Really. I'm sorry about yesterday. Ten steps forward, one back, that's all. Sometimes the dreams are so nice… they can seem so real sometimes—"

"That you don't want to wake up," Caroline cut in. "I understand, Cassie, I do. And I suppose being here where you and Eddie used to share sunsets only brings the memories back in pure, sweet Technicolor. But honey…Ry told me he got caught in the waves. Your friend pulled him out. Honey… Ry was really scared."

A gentle touch alerted Cassie to her sister's deep concern. Peeking over at her, she frowned. The worry Caroline was sending her way was laid bare. No more 'chill-it's-all-good-we're-getting-by' sister.

"I learned my lesson, sis. I'll be okay."

"I'm sure you did, honey. Until the next time."

"You make it sound like I'm an alcoholic or something!" Exasperated, Cassie adjusted her bum in the low chair. *Ohhh…maybe he's a recovering addict…he is a musician, after all…*

"I suppose those lovely dreams starring Eddie can be a kind of addiction? Who wouldn't want to go there, to be with someone they love again, even if it's not real?"

"Caroline…Eddie is as real to me now as he ever was. In my dreams I can feel his skin on mine. I can see him and I can even smell him, like… that aftershave he always wore that trailed after him like a shadow. I smell

117

that as well as I ever did! But it wasn't just Eddie that set me off yesterday, that sank me."

"Oh?"

"No, um…" *Might as well get this over with. She'll figure it out anyway, the second I lay eyes on Dal…* "No, Caroline, look. Ry's right about Dal, he's become a good friend. But…" A low choke was Cassie's way of struggling for words. Finally she said, "I've grown quite fond of him. The way he is with Ry, so patient, so natural. And he's just got this aura about him. It may as well be some kind of potion, it's so powerful. He's a musician; he's got this natural gift for music that just sinks me. His voice is dusky, like a—"

"Stop. Cassie, just stop." A hand held high between them put the brakes on Cassie's introduction to her beach bum hobo.

"Sorry," she mumbled, slumping low into her chair and taking a sip of the fruity sangria, which had turned her glass a weird blue-pink. "I guess I was rambling."

Pragmatic, realistic Caroline took the reins. "He sounds like a great guy. Really. It's obvious Ry adores him. But he's living in a tent for the summer? What do you know about this guy?"

"Ha. That he's living in a tent for the summer." Amused at her own capacity for having such a deep attraction to a man she hardly knew, beyond nothing more than an instinct that said he was special, Cassie allowed a small chuckle to brighten her spirits. "But I don't care. There's something about Dal that I can't resist, Caroline, and it's not just that he is one helluva male specimen in jeans and boots. He's a mystery, I admit, and I know he's running from something but I've also grown to trust him. I have yet to sleep with him, by the way." She shook her glass at her sister, whose deeply furrowed brow was a clear sign that Cassie needed to put the brakes on defending her new man. Cassie shrugged. "But—if he'd wanted to get in my pants, I have news for you, dear sister. I would not have stopped him."

"So you need sex. What red-blooded woman doesn't? Hell, Cassie, have your fun if you need to, but draw the line at getting emotionally involved. At least until you know more about your redneck hero." Caroline pointed to the ocean, to the area where Ry and Levi were joyfully paddling in on a small wavelet. "For your baby boy's sake."

"He's not a baby," Cassie pouted.

"Ry needs a mother who doesn't take mental health days to dream about sex with some guy she doesn't know from Adam!"

"I didn't—I…Oh, for God's sake, Caroline. I admit that Dal and I reached a kind of impasse and that's what set me off, that…that…need for someone. For…him. Which got me sad about Eddie. It was wrong. I'm good now." Changing her tone, she ramped her pitch up a notch and casually tossed in, "So, how's Des? Life in the public eye getting him down at all?"

Effectively ending the conversation would not have worked if a shadow hadn't stolen Caroline's sun. She was just about to open her mouth to protest Cassie's rapid right turn when the sexy main topic of their conversation dropped a towel down next to Cassie.

Dallas thrust out a hand, but not before he pushed his ball cap down lower over his eyes first. "Dal," he said quietly, having decided that this obviously well kept woman was, like her pretty sister, in no way a country music fan.

"Oh. Oh!" Straightening, Caroline leaned forward to offer Dal a set of refined porcelain fingers. But she couldn't help stuttering, which, to Cassie, was pure vengeful delight. "Oh, Jesus, Cassie, this is…this is your new friend?"

A smile tickled Cassie's lips. Smug, she leaned over on one arm toward Dal, and exuded a joyous warmth Caroline had not once seen in the six years since Eddie's passing. "Well, Dal," Cassie announced brightly. "Congratulations. I rarely see my society sister lose her composure. Look at that! She's lost for words."

Letting go of Caroline's hand, Dallas shifted his weight. Caroline caught something in his eyes that Cassie didn't see. It was a spark of fear. Sucking in a breath, Caroline held his gaze until Dallas muttered something about welcoming her to the island and going for a swim, before he turned away to drop his ball cap on his towel. From the water Ry waved an excited hand at Dal, who raised an arm in greeting and jogged off toward him with a hollered, "S'water warm today, Ry?"

When he was out of earshot, Caroline oozed warmth and surprise as she watched him wade out to Ry and Levi. Both boys howled with glee when Dal dove right in without giving his body time to adjust to the shocking coolness of the Gulf.

Caroline's eyes widened at the ripple of muscles on the man's lightly bronzed, tanned back. "Jesus, girl," she managed. "I see the issue here. He's damn precious. And he likes you? That's something!" Trying to regain her composure, she struggled for something to say to cover up the way the unspoken angst in Dal's eyes unnerved her. She'd just met the guy and already he was a confusing quandary.

Laughing, Cassie lightly slapped her sister's knee. "He's downright adorable. And he's every bit as nice as he is good looking."

"Something about him is vaguely familiar, Cassie." Truly, there was something recognizable about the guy that Caroline couldn't quite put a finger on. So many public events with her government husband…M.P. life was so demanding…was it something in Halifax? Had she seen him at some event? Squinting, Caroline tried to focus on her sister's new friend more clearly as he splashed about with the two boys. "Where is he from?"

"Toronto. I know that much. But I get the sense that he doesn't spend a lot of time there. I think he hops around the bar scene, maybe down in the States and across Canada. I'm not sure. He's done some outdoor festivals too. He said something about lightning closing down some show."

"One step away from riding the rails like old Stompin' Tom, huh?" At Cassie's downturned lips, Caroline added easily, "Oh, lighten up, Cas. He sure is cute. Those dimples…I wonder where I know him from…" The thought drifted off.

When Dallas came in from the water twenty minutes later, he instantly propped the ball cap back on his head and adjusted it to shade his sexy bad boy looks before he turned back around to the ladies. Caroline raised an eyebrow. Laying out his towel beside Cassie's chair, Dal sat for a few minutes and chatted idly until Ry came dripping in from the water with Levi at his side and grabbed the toy bag full of sandcastle building tools.

"We have to practice, Dal," he insisted. To Levi and Caroline he explained, "We get lessons on Tuesday nights from a guy who can even carve angels out of sand. He's the coolest! We're building a huge castle for the campground's contest, and it has to be perfect."

"S'cuse me," Dal grinned shyly to the ladies, using his hands to push his muscular body up from the towel. "I'm being called into service."

A self-satisfied beam settled across Cassie's eyes. "Told you," she said to Caroline, who finished off her third drink with a loud slurp and tossed the plastic cup into the sand at her feet. "He's damned near flawless."

"Don't kid yourself," Caroline snorted as, ten feet from the water's edge, Dallas grabbed a large sand shovel out of the zebra striped bag and started piling loose sand into a small mountain. "Nobody's flawless."

But by the end of the afternoon, when white clouds started to roll over the beach, before they gathered up their things for a trip to a nearby seafood restaurant for dinner, Caroline had to consider that Dal sure seemed damned close to flawless. It wasn't the muscles rippling on his back as he worked, nor was it the strong jawline and intelligent way he communicated so much more than she figured words could ever say that led her to think so. Instead it was Dal's obvious care and compassion for Caroline's nephew, and by extension to Ry's friend Levi, who Dal took under his wing and good-naturedly coached on the skillful art of sand-castle crafting.

Before they finished the castle under the shade of the cottony-soft clouds, themselves some kind of mystic art as they floated dreamily above them, Dal had a whole group of youngsters at his heels, all yanging for a hand in building and decorating the castle. He and Ry taught them—and in the end, a few curious parents too—to 'swipe and slide' the towers, to utilize sand retrieved from a watery sand-filled bucket to form balls between their palms to use as the basis for minarets on the tower tops, and to carve village houses within the castle walls using bendy plastic rulers.

A group splintered off and molded a Volkswagen Beetle—complete with wheels and wheel rims—next to the castle. The day was so close to perfect that Cassie later swore it would have burst if she pricked it with a pin.

Just before packing up to leave the beach, Cassie and Caroline wandered down to the ocean for a final swim (a tentative wade up to her knees, in Caroline's case). On the way back to their chairs they stopped for a peek at the sandy creations.

"You have fans," Caroline said to Dallas, crossing her arms in hesitant approval.

Blanching uncomfortably, Dal darted a glance at Cassie, who was bending down near Ry a few feet away and so hadn't heard the comment. He stuttered back a low, "Wh-what?"

"The kids." Caroline twisted her head to study him closely. "All these rug rats. They worship you. They're learning a lot from you."

He visibly relaxed. "You got that backwards. I'm learning a lot from them." Starting to back away, he added, "There's something to be said for the innocence of childhood."

"You can say that again." Caroline's voice was lowered now. She gestured toward her sister. "And there's something to be said for the innocence of my sister."

Dal stopped moving. Cocking his head, he stared her down. "Is that a warning?"

Caroline shrugged. "Call it whatever the hell you want. Just don't hurt her. Or my nephew."

"Ah. You got that backwards too, Caroline." Dal looked like a little boy standing there, the damp plaid trunks sagging almost to his knees and the long blond hair sticking out from underneath the dirty cap in an unruly mess. The slumped shoulders, bronzed now to perfection and glistening with sweat, were downright touchable.

Caroline was a happily married woman, or so she told herself on the lonely days when her husband was in demand by so many others, but she still had to resist the urge to reach out and lay a palm flat on this man's sun-warmed chest. *You need healing too,* she mused sadly, wondering how a man like Dal, with obvious secrets, and sorrow hanging over him like the billowing clouds now shading the beach, could possibly be good for Cassie and Ry.

Dallas watched awareness bloom across Caroline's features like a rose that had just been watered. Carefully he told her, "It's *my* heart that's at risk here." A sad smile at Ry's back, at the happy child now bouncing like a joyful puppy as he showed his mother the intricate crevices and smartly molded windows and doors of the day's work, illuminated Caroline further. If Dal lost, he'd lose more than just Cassie. He'd also lose the amazing kid now showing his mother how to grab a handful of wet sand and drip it onto a pile, more at the bottom and less at the top, to create trees around their castle.

Caroline angled her head at Dallas. Inquisitively, she narrowed her eyes. "I do know you from somewhere, Dal. I just haven't figured out from where. But I have to tell you, it's where I know you from that you're hiding from my sister, isn't it?"

Gripping the ball cap brim between his fingers, Dal almost crumbled as he lifted it, swiped back his hair in one quick movement, and shoved it back onto his head. The whole time, he credited himself for not looking away from those piercing, curious eyes. They were similar to Cassie's, Caroline's eyes, but instead of giving off a wounded vibe, Caroline's were sharp and protective. Wary. Almost brutally confident.

She had a post-script to add. "I will figure it out, Dal. If that's even your real name. And if you're hiding something that will hurt either one of those two people who, you should know, are as dear to me as anyone in this crazy world, then I suggest you pack your bags and find another set of trees to piss under. Preferably in southeast Asia."

Circling one bare foot around so she could take her sensitive skin back up to her chair for one last pass of sunscreen, Caroline stopped when Dal's husky voice stopped her. "Caroline…"

She turned. Waited.

He bent down and grabbed a shiny half clamshell. Studied it and played with it for a moment before turning and pitching it onto a nearby pile of sand. Looked back at her. "If you figure it out," he said, the words emerging pitchy and uncertain, "don't tell her. Please. Let me. Let me tell her."

"What?" His words were an admission. But…of what, exactly? Caroline struggled for a reply that would sound coherent and strong. But still… Jesus. Cassie was right. This was the kind of man a woman wanted—no, needed—to wrap her arms around. To comfort. To…hold.

"I just mean that it will confuse her," Dallas added carefully. "I know it will. It has to come from me, so I can explain. Please, Caroline."

Mystified, Caroline could only nod. After a moment, with those pale eyes digging deeper into hers with genuine apprehension and, well, hope, she spun around so quickly that Cassie looked up.

What Cassie saw was a very confused anxiety in her sister's usually steely, proud posture. "Huh," she wondered, and sat back on her haunches just beside and behind her son.

Dal moved then, and Cassie glanced up to see him fix a lonely gaze on her. It only lasted a second or two before he strode to the water for a last swim to cool the sudden anxiety threatening to overtake the afternoon's—for the most part—jubilant mood.

"What'd you two say to each other?" Cassie muttered inwardly, raising her hands to brush her palms together and wipe off the sand. Ry twisted around and grabbed her wrist, which effectively got her attention and steered Cassie back toward the castle—now almost a whole, perfect village. Studying the miniature buildings and trees, she sighed. "Who lives inside your hallowed walls? A family? A mom, a dad, three kids? Oh, a puppy and two cats too, I bet," she half-smiled.

Not far away, in the cool Atlantic, stroking hard to dispense the sorrow welling in his spirit, Dallas gulped for air as a new desperation overtook him. The afternoon with Ry, joking around with the kids and pushing the truths of who he was and what was expected of him far beneath the surface of the sandy beach, was about as sweet a day as he had ever had. He'd even gone so far as to flip the ball cap around so that the brim wasn't in his eyes while he worked, he was so confident nobody recognized him. Hell, not one of these ordinary souls would ever expect to find a star like him on their local beach. Why would they make any assumptions that he was anyone other than a guy from Ontario enjoying a serene summer day like the rest of them? No one asked questions and no one gave a sweet shit. Today they were all just normal folks enjoying a respite from busy lives. Today they would go take showers, barbecue burgers or run down to Cavendish for an easy dinner, and they would end the day by making s'mores over benign, smoky campfires before cuddling their children and tucking them into sleeping bags. Could life ever possibly get any better?

Almost choking on the false reality of the blissful day, Dallas realized he had not felt lonely until the moment Caroline called him on his true self. On who and what he really was, and on what he was hiding from Cassie.

Dallas reached a sandbar in a few strong strokes. Planting his feet on the sandy bottom, he faced the distant horizon, placed both hands on his hips, and pleaded into the salty depths of the endless ocean.

"Please," he begged the universe. "Please." Falling to his knees, he swiped water over his face, christening the desperate plea with a baptism of hope, praying that nobody could see him for what he was—weak, the world's puppet, a lost man on a wild ride that had long ago stolen him from himself.

Chapter Eleven

*P*hil arrived in a flurry of curses and contracts. Didn't bother Dallas, who was cool and welcoming regardless of Phil's ornery mood. Because, dangling from Phil's hand when he left his rented cottage on the bay side of Castle Beach to seek out his artist's campsite, was a small guitar case. And in it was the guitar he'd promised to bring Dallas, for Ry.

Dallas grinned when he took the case from Phil's grip. Immediately he placed it on the picnic table and opened it. Lightly running a finger along the polished wood of the expensive instrument inside, he spoke over his shoulder to his manager. "Phil, you've outdone yourself. Ry will love this—his small fingers will love this. The kid'll learn much quicker."

"And the kid's mother'll turn somersaults. You gonna sign it?" The grimace on Phil's face was not becoming. The wiry man had once upon a time smoked a shit ton of cigarettes, among other things, which left his teeth a dirty, soiled nicotine-yellow. Clutching the brim of the fedora on his head, he gave it a nervous yank.

Dallas picked up the guitar and strummed a few chords. "Nope," he said quietly, referencing the comment about somersaults. He added, "She's not what you think, Phil." Turning, settling his butt next to the case on the picnic tabletop, he started to tune the special instrument.

To Phil, it was an ominous sign. The guitar was tiny, diminished, out of place in this famous singer's arms. Watching Dallas fidget with the tuning pegs set Phil's stained teeth on edge. "I'm sure she's keeping your bed real warm, Dal. Cold island nights and all, right? Do you sing her to sleep, buddy?"

Dallas spoke in a subdued tone, with the reverence the costly guitar and his burgeoning relationship with both Cassie and Ry deserved. "She's better than that, Phil," he said. "You're wrong. She won't be happy about me giving her kid a guitar. She's the independent type. But," he said mostly for his own benefit, as if to reassure himself, "she won't know its value. I'll talk her into it." In his heart he truly doubted Cassie would ever take to the gift, but he felt he could warm her up to it, if just for Ry's sake. Dal's guitar was adult-sized. This mini was suited to kid-sized chords.

"Whatever," grumbled Phil. "Got a bar in your beach hideout, Dallas?" He bit the question off in a long practiced cautious manner. Phil had learned the hard way that pissing off his star would only serve to delay the inevitable man-to-man chat they had to have. "Let's grab a drink so we can get your midlife crisis sorted out." Accenting the request with a succinct snap of a finger up to the brim of his fedora, he resisted the urge to pull the hat down over his eyes. When he lowered his hand, he stuck it in his back jeans pocket instead. "You've only got me for twenty-four hours," he ragged, puffing up his chest and almost whistling through a sharp, nervous inhale. "Let's git 'er done. I'm jetting off to L.A. tomorrow to hold the hands of spoiled pansy artists who actually want to work."

Grimacing at Phil's impatience, Dallas fingerpicked a few pretty sequences on Ry's new guitar. The generous, full sound was so pleasing he closed his eyes and concentrated on the music instead of on his manager's shifting feet. Phil wheeled around to glower at the sparkling water of the Gulf spread out before him, scowling at what Dallas considered the ultimate simple, unspoiled, natural view. Dallas had long ago learned that music was the key to easing a racing pulse and the kind of binding, twisting anxiety that tangled his guts up in knots. Playing it or listening to it, it didn't matter to him. Didn't have to be his music, in fact he usually preferred that it wasn't. Other songwriters wrote beautiful melodies too, some much more complex and unique than what Dallas wrote. The way he saw it, you couldn't learn and grow as a songwriter and performer without exposing yourself to the work of others, regardless of the genre.

A low harrumph alerted him to Phil's disapproval of, well, everything. Ignoring him, Dallas riffed a few solid tunes out on the guitar before he tenderly laid the gift back in its plush blue bed. After closing the lid, a pleased grin lit up his face. He snapped the gold clasps of the guitar case closed and paused to reflect on what it would mean to Ry.

He spoke to Phil without looking at him. Instead, Dallas tossed the words over a shoulder. "Been a long time since I saw that kinda light in a guitar player's eyes, Phil." Silence greeted the serious proclamation. Raising his head, Dallas watched Phil swing back around to face him.

"What's the kid know, three chords?" Phil asked, roughly putting both hands on his hips and throwing his weight onto one leg. The acerbic accusation did a poor job of keeping Dallas' rising frustration on the down low, but he managed to stay cool enough for Phil to half-confidently toss in a cocky, "G, D, and what, A? That hardly makes the kid a musician, Dal."

His manager was trying to make a point, but Dallas skirted over it with a light shrug. "And C. He nailed tough old C in minutes. On my big Gibson. Ry's a natural. And Phil? I mean it. This boy's hungry to play. He hasn't been beat to a pulp by the business. For this kid, picking out chords is joyful. There's joy in finding the perfect sound."

Waving an arm around the simple camp, unable to stifle a weird chuckle at the ludicrous sight of his superstar's boxers drying on a clothesline strung between trees, Phil snapped off, "So what you're trying to tell me is that you've lost the joy, is that it, Dallas? We're running a business here, bud. You and me." He shoved a finger in Dallas' chest and then pointed back at himself. "You. And me. We decided that when we started out. We wanted to go to the top and we did, by working our asses off to get there. Your music became nothing more than a brand a long time ago. It's a product, Dal, a product that did a damn good job of lining that cool garage of yours with sports cars, I might add."

Scanning the small site, Phil's searching eyes landed on the flaking rust lining the wheel wells of his artist's truck. When his steely gaze darted back up to Dallas, Phil was cringing. "You even have air con in that relic?"

"I've got all the air conditioning I need." Holding his arms out to the sides, Dallas turned a slow circle and deeply filled his lungs with fresh island air. Someone at a campsite beyond the trees was poking at a fire. The heady, homey smell of wood smoke wafted toward the men on the southeast breeze, stirring tingling memories of the recent fires Dallas had shared with Cassie, including the equally enticing fires of desire that inched up his body with every shared kiss.

He dropped his arms. "I haven't lost the joy of playing music," he said sharply to Phil, steering them back to the overriding issue necessitating his manager's visit. At the same time, Dallas tried to move his thoughts away from a profound longing for Cassie's easy company...

...Away from a longing for Cassie, body and soul, from that sweet smile he ached to taste, that porcelain skin he wanted to linger over all night long, soon, his kisses landing in places on her body that even now made him tremble and half-turn away from Phil, lest his friend comprehend what Dallas was powerless to hide.

And what was he hiding? That part of the reason for staying so long in Prince Edward Island was because a woman—one who didn't know him at all in terms of his status in the music world big leagues—intrigued him far beyond distraction, to the point where Dallas was desperate to know her, to really know her, to touch her and taste her. To...simply hold her.

He longed to help heal Cassie's hurts, the ones she tried so bravely to put forth as if they were no more than holiday decorations taken out once or twice a year, used for a short time, and then neatly tucked away.

"So why'd you run then, Dal?" Phil was asking—or prodding, more like. Dallas tuned back in. Noticing, Phil took a chance and pushed a little harder. "Why'd you walk out after the Seattle show? That night was as good as any I've ever seen you play. I don't get it."

"What, not waiting for the bar, Phil? We're going there right now, are we? To the heavy stuff?" Stepping over to the back of his tent, Dallas brushed some leaves and a twig off the white lid of a Coleman cooler before he lifted it. With one hand he pulled out two locally brewed ales he'd purchased from the small, quaint liquor store in Cavendish the day he went on his lonesome drive. "Here," he said, twisting the cap off one and handing it to Phil. "Cop a squat and we'll talk. It's either this or a drive. This campground's a family park. No bar."

Settling back on the top of the picnic table so he could peer out over the dunes and lock his nervous gaze on a distant fishing boat plying through the waves, Dallas maneuvered the cap off his own brew. Phil grunted and said, as he leveraged his wiry body next to his artist and nudged his butt comfortably into place, "Family campground, huh? That confuses me even more. Why the hell would you want to stay in a place overrun by whiny kids and exhausted parents?"

"Call it a compromise." Dallas took a long pull on his cool drink, then swiped his hand down the bottle to wipe water from it. It was a hot summer day—he wiped the cool moisture onto his opposite forearm and mopped his forehead the same way afterwards. "Ice melts in the cooler," he mumbled to Phil. "Remind me to get more later."

"You must be missing your minions." Grunting, Phil lifted his beer, resorting to trying the local brew. To his surprise, it was smooth and refreshing. Over the years he had become more accustomed to exotic scotch than to what he considered redneck booze.

"I don't. I don't miss the constant attention." Dallas was watching the fishing boat bob up and down in the easy waves. He went on. "I don't miss the false smiles and the lack of sincerity in every conversation. I don't miss the $ 800 dinners that people laud on me before they send me back to lonely hotel rooms where I punch the remote and see hungry little kids staring up at me, praying for a night out of the rain. I don't miss those things."

Phil tried to urge patience into his voice, but it was tough. All he could see when he looked at Dallas now was dollar-like symbols prefaced by a whopping big red minus sign. "We've always supported charities, Dallas. You've always given back. I don't see how stepping away from a lifestyle that entertains people, that's allowed you to give back as generously as you do, is solving anything. If it's not the music…" Drifting off, he thought about waiting for Dallas to fill in the blanks but he couldn't stop himself from adding, "I know one thing you miss. Deborah, huh? You're running from Deborah." Idly, he scratched at a brand new mosquito bite on his hand. "I'm sorry she messed you over."

Dallas picked at the label of his beer bottle before answering. To Phil, it seemed Dal needed the idle motion to stall the conversation while he figured out what to say, but to Dallas, the nervous movement was to cover up the heavy emotion that swept over him like an icy wave at the mention of his ex. Even just hearing her name spoken aloud by someone who knew her as well as Phil did raised a lot of shit Dallas was not yet comfortable talking about, to anyone, really. He sure as hell hadn't shared that old relationship with Cassie yet. Cassie, whom, he instinctively felt, would somehow understand. She'd probably be able to put a reasonable perspective on the whole Deborah thing, on why she did what she did back in Seattle and how damn much it hurt. Hell, Cassie'd likely be able to put some perspective on his whole f'd up life that would make sense. *If she can handle the truth of who I am, that is.*

But Phil…well, he had been along for the country music ride pretty much from the time Dallas rode into Sony Music in Toronto in the old blue pickup. He was as much a friend Dallas had as anyone, and that wasn't saying much at the top of the ivory tower where the air was thin, and where so-called friends were no more than hangers-on wanting to hitch a free ride to the big time.

"Phil, look." Edging deeper into the conversation on a whim and a prayer that his buddy would take off his manager hat and try to understand, and not push him further than he was ready to go, Dallas tried to explain. "Seattle was just the last straw. Too many cities, too many shows, too many people sucking up to me and treating me like I'm made of gold. Too much booze, too many women. Not just Deb."

He raised his bottle in a half-assed salute and went for it. "Too many young women, in particular, dressing in shorts so short you could tell if their waxes originated from Brazil, if you know what I'm saying. Wearing tops borrowed from Daisy Duke, you know?" Touching his chest, he drew a curve to illustrate his next point. "Girls who are still teenagers in a lot of cases, showing off their bodies hoping to get attention, in the rain, in the freezing cold, drunk or stoned or both. It just got to me, it…gets to me. The older I get, the more disturbing I find it. The more false. Like…I want to grab these girls and shake them, and tell them to get a grip, to have some self-respect. That someone like me can't help them learn to love themselves."

Phil cocked an ear and interjected. "What do you mean someone like you? The star you or the man you?"

Dallas grimaced and took a big swig. "Ha. You do get it. I'm two different people. No, look Phil, even if I loved them, me, the real me, just one of them—and I mean love, not sleep with—it's not gonna help them love themselves. And it's obvious to me, it's so damn obvious, that it's the same

131

problem with all of those kinds of girls—and there are hundreds of them, thousands, they're all the same, I see them at every show. For whatever reason, they just don't love themselves. They're there, in the front row of every show, trying to catch my eye so I can give them something they can't give themselves. And yet…"

With a long, slow exhale, Dallas prepared to give Phil the coup-de-grace he knew the man was waiting for. To his credit, Phil remained silent and waited.

Staring at his beer, watching the bubbles inside the bottle foam up and burst, Dallas spoke quietly. "And yet, the loneliness I see in their eyes…it's in me too. Phil…" Imploring him to understand, Dallas looked up at his friend. "Phil, I want the same thing they do. And it's not what Deborah wants. At least not yet, and maybe not ever. She can live with that part of herself, apparently. But I'm like those young girls—I'm doing the same damn thing they are. I'm standing up there on stage trying to be some crazy version of what these girls think is sexy, playing tunes that sometimes don't even make sense to me, hoping against hope that someday I'll look into just one set of eyes and feel understood. Like one of those girls will see the real me, instead of just some jacked-up country singer paraded out in front of them with some stylist's version of what I need to dress like in order to fit into some cool image. Phil—I used to hope that would happen some day, that I'd meet a gal backstage or at some charity function who would look at me that way, like I was the real Dallas White and not the made-up one. But the more shows that go by, the more years that pass, I realize they'll never see me that way. I thought Deborah could, at least at first, but…the women I've met, they're all either buried in their own lost dreams and lack of self-respect or they're trying to get their hooks into me like Deb did so they can coast to the top and enjoy the ride. It's become easier just to go along for the ride myself than it's been to find someone who sees me for me."

Phil paused before responding. Then he dove in. "You've never had any problem with those kinds of women before, Dallas. You've had many lustful starry nights along the way, and I'm guessing some very willing mind-blowing young bodies to take away the ache. Your videos are filled with them."

Sliding off the table, Dallas turned a circle before answering. When he did, he faced his friend directly. "I'm not a hypocrite, Phil, if that's what you're saying. At first it was fun, it was part of the game. It was a thrill to be someone who was treated as a male fantasy, if that's what you want to call it. But over the years it started to grate on me. It started to leave a sour taste in my mouth, you know? I know you know this, I know you saw it coming."

Phil raised his arms and absently nipped the brim of the fedora with a thumb and forefinger. "I suppose at some point I did, Dal. I wouldn't still be with you if you weren't the kind of man who occasionally showed his scruples. Who is always a gentleman in public, who treats women respectfully for the most part, Deborah notwithstanding, and by that I mean the day you left. But even so, I have to ask why now? Was it just Deb that sent you running to this hick place?"

"Sitting on the tour bus looking out at the people coming in through the gate, that's what happened. It was raining, remember?"

"It's always raining in Seattle," Phil guffawed. "Designer umbrellas are part of the city's cache."

Stepping backward as emotion caught up to him, Dallas almost tripped over the rough ground. Phil would have snapped off a wisecrack at the stumble in this rustic place if the conversation were less heated and less necessary. As it was, he was too damn humbled at his artist's openness, at Dallas' need to empty his soul and mind of what troubled him, to lessen the man's hurts by cracking some lame joke.

Dallas looked like a little boy, a small child backdropped by an immense ocean as he clutched his beer and spoke from his heart. "The girls were the same, regardless. Most with no self-respect, with cleavage that left nothing to the imagination and bodies that, no matter how many I consumed, could never fill the ache that came from seeing past them to the couples in love. It hit me that Deborah was as much a stranger to me as anyone. That the love I had for her was missing something. I was a chalk outline with no substance, just going through the motions. That's what happened."

"Love?" Phil's brain was misfiring. "Really? Since when did you care about love, Dallas? Is it even real? The Dallas I know was handling the wild Deborah just fine. You two seemed great together."

As he said it, Phil had a wink for Dallas, though. Dallas almost took the bait. Raising his head and opening his mouth to retort back at what he considered his friend's insensitive remark, he ended up half-grinning instead, with a tiny smile and a beacon of light in his intelligent, wise eyes. Shaking his head, he laughed and tipped his bottle back once again. He turned toward the water and his eyes lit upon the fishing boat bobbing on the waves, far beyond a swimmer's reach in the dangerous Gulf. *Hope you fellas have good women waiting for you at home tonight,* he mused. *Hope there will be hot biscuits like my momma used to make, and steaming bowls of chicken soup alongside. And maybe a few sweet rolls in the hay afterward.*

"Love, huh?" Phil, too, tipped his bottle back, and he even licked his lips with satisfaction at the refreshing craft beer his artist had quite capably sourced in little ole P.E.I. "I don't suppose there was any sincerity to those love ballads that got all of those pretty young fillies to your shows in the first place, Dal." Locking his eyes on the distant boat, Phil licked his lips again. *Succulent fresh lobster right off the boat, that'll be on the menu tonight,* he decided. *With Dallas by my side, hopefully in a better mood and ready to travel.* There had to be one perk to this small island. The beer was a pleasant surprise, yet Phil knew the real prize was the seafood, fresh enough to curl his toes with glee and make his socks roll up and down in anticipation.

Relaxing his shoulders, Phil pointed the tip of his bottle at Dallas, who turned back to him when he started to speak. "Dal, don't think I don't know what loneliness feels like. I gave up a chance at something real too when I took you out on the road. And I know how hard it is for you to trust anybody. I think we've both learned that the hard way. Dallas, songs like the ones you write, that are wistful and filled with longing, or the ones that tell the rest of us what love ought to be like, well—Dal—they're not based in any kind of reality. At least not the reality I know. You singers, and Hollywood, you've created this imperfect notion of what love ought to be. Seriously. Do you think maybe you're looking for something that doesn't even exist?"

Cassie. Once again the sad jade eyes wisped gently into Dallas' consciousness. That faraway look she got sometimes, like when they were strolling quietly down the beach the other night, into the magic golden hour orange-pink light of the setting sun…the way she slept so gracefully, so lost in dreams of the man she lost that she couldn't even manage to raise herself to care for her son...the way she stared at the benign fires they roasted marshmallows over at night, almost choking sometimes on the unreality of how something so perfect, so safe, designed to entertain campers, could have stolen the man she loved away from her...Ry, the pensive beach-blond child of a union that, indeed, may not have always showcased the parts of a romance selected for a Hollywood final cut but which still seemed pretty damned perfect, if one judged by the sorrow in Cassie's eyes...

"N-no," Dallas said, his voice lowered, the affirmation accompanied by a barely there nod. "It exists. I know it."

Unsure where Dallas' mind had whisked him off to, Phil wrinkled his brow and watched as his musician tightened his grip on the beer bottle clasped between his fingers. At the same time, Dallas tipped his chin down and fixed a meditative gaze on the toes of his cowboy boots, which, as usual, peeked out from underneath frayed hems of strategically faded jeans. A cascade of long hair almost blocked him from Phil's studious view.

"You sayin' this from experience, Dal?" Phil asked cautiously. "Or just because of all those lovers you happen to see on date night at your concerts? That's not reality, bud. That's just a night away from the kids. The fights start the second those couples get home. Or in the parking lot when they realize they've got two hours of bumper tag to play first before they even reach the highway."

"I'm sorry if that's your experience, Phil," Dallas tried, hoping to somehow explain to this man why staying here in this barebones campsite was a must, at least until...at least until Dallas knew whether what he saw in Cassie—an ability to love a man fully and completely—was something that could somehow be gifted onto him.

Because I can love her back. The same way. I can love a woman that way too.

He added, for both his benefit and for Phil's, "Call it wishful thinking if you want, Phil. Or call it my gut. Intuition." Lowering his head and staring at the ground this time as he moved back toward the picnic table, Dallas took a seat again next to Phil. Once again fixing the fishing boat in his hopeful gaze, he watched it start to nose its way back through cresting waves to safe harbor with an easy putt-putt-putt.

"Whatever it is, I've seen it," he said simply. "I've felt it. I...feel it. It's real.

And Phil?" Turning to contemplate his friend straight on, he added brusquely, "I want it. And it's not Deborah who's going to give it to me. She hurt me, Phil, but only because she wasn't who I needed her to be."

"Well, shit." A long, last drink, and Phil set his bottle on the table with a hard thump. Wiping his hands on his jeans, he jumped up, giving Dallas' elbow a hard yank as he did so, almost knocking the bottle out of Dallas' hand. "On that note, I have a feeling we have a helluva lot more to discuss. But first..."

Disappearing into his rented car for a moment, Phil reappeared with a vinyl LP in a cardboard jacket in his hand. He met Dallas' somber, curious eyes before handing it to him.

"Deborah's apology. She knows something's missing, Dal. She's willing to work with you to find it."

"Like hell." Dallas had nothing more than that to grunt out loud, but he was awed and touched when he turned the LP over and saw a glittery gold *I'm sorry* scrawled across it in Deb's open, cursive handwriting.

"Good relationships take work, Dallas. They get harder once the honeymoon period passes. She wants to make things right."

Striding to his tent, ripping open the zipper, Dallas tossed the LP on the quilt covering his airbed. The LP was a limited release single of the famous ballad he and Deborah had written together, with the instrumental version on the B-side. Holding it in his hand brought back memories Dallas didn't want—a 'come hither' body, what he considered false magic in Deborah's moist eyes when they recorded the single, catching Deborah in bed—in Dallas' hotel room, as if he was meant to catch her, to see that someone else desired her—with a singer Dallas once considered a good friend.

Phil's gentle voice brought him back to the present. To the sweet, careless sea breeze, to white seagulls announcing what freedom truly meant by dipping, swooping and soaring joyfully over the white-capped ocean, to a woman close by who also understood loss.

"Come on, boy," Phil said, placing a caring hand on Dallas' hunched shoulder. "You can have all the love you want. I hope you get it. I truly do. But I hope that love's got room for the singer in you too." Lightening the suddenly heavy load Dallas was carrying was suddenly a priority. Phil knew him well enough to discern the depth of Dal's longing, the gravity of his need. It scared him. Inhaling, his voice came out a little higher than usual as he added nervously, "As for me, right now I want me some of that fresh seafood those boys out there on the water are about to unload. Let's chase some down while you consider how to anchor that tent of yours against the wind. Cuz if the wind comes up, that bag of beans is gonna need some extra bracing while you're playing down in the States next week."

At the dismay crossing Dallas' tanned face, he said, with a smile he hoped looked more sincere and playful than concerned, "What? You think I never went camping when I was a pot-smoking youngster? I had a life before I met you, you big dumbass. I slept me plenty in soaking wet sleeping bags. I anchored me plenty a tent. Let's go."

Turning away from Dallas, Phil set his lips in a straight line and fixed a stony eye on the pristine view spread out before him. Allowing himself to see what his buddy saw was easier after their soul-deep chat. But somehow, he had a feeling the real view Dallas preferred—the one that was keeping his artist here in this godforsaken place—had to do with curvy hips and pouty lips.

They were doing dinner together tonight, and the new gal's sister was coming along to keep things cool and to even things out. Soon Phil could sit back and read Dal's new woman from a safe perspective. He already felt he knew what he would see—a gold digging vixen no better than Deborah. At least Deborah had talent. At least she had a purpose in Dal's life beyond sucking his bank account dry. At least the woman could sing. And she sure as hell could sell records.

That evening, after dropping Ry off to hang with Levi and his parents, Cassie and Caroline scooted by in Caroline's BMW to pick the men up for dinner. Phil was dumbfounded when, as the sleek sedan bumped down the red-dirt lane toward them, Dallas grabbed his arm, hemmed and hawed, and finally mumbled after Phil's impatient *What? Just spit it out!* "She doesn't know who I am. She thinks I play for beer. Don't spill it, Phil. Let me tell her when I'm ready. Please."

An air of quiet desperation accompanied the request. Phil stuttered back a reply just as Caroline cursed her way over a large bump onto Dallas' campsite. "You f-ing serious, Dal? You couldn't have told me this earlier?" At his friend's despairing nod, Phil agreed. With one condition. "I don't let it slip, you play the shows next week. Deal?"

One superstar eye roll later, and Phil had the answer for which he'd flown to the land of the bright red mud in the first place. With a warm, happy smile, he swung around to the ladies, quickly discerning that the soulful, sad, quiet one in the passenger seat—a surprisingly un-vixen like, sweet girl—was the one who'd stolen Dallas' vulnerable heart. After a moment to digest that unexpected development, Phil called out, "Ladies! A pleasure to meet both of you. Lobster on the menu tonight, is it? Do you eat that unbearable sickly green stuff in the middle or just the claws?"

Winking back at Dallas, whose genuine nerves were flooring Phil, and who had paled to a sickly green himself, Phil pulled the handle, opened the back door of the luxury car, and waved Dallas in.

A brief, nervous smile to Cassie, and Dallas obliged.

Muttering and mumbling, Caroline tried to turn the car around in the narrow dead end lane. In the end, after everyone hollered at her for almost plowing the car into the green rope bordering the sand dune, she gave up the driver's seat to the calm, engaging, helpful Phil. Being the bossy control type, Caroline shushed Cassie out of her seat on the passenger side so she could dictate instructions to Phil. Blushing, Cassie slid into the back beside Dallas, who immediately took her fingers in his and lifted them to his lips for a gentle kiss.

"You okay?" she whispered to him while, in the front seat, Caroline and Phil launched into an ornery loud-mouthed dialogue about how best to turn the car. "You look a little pale."

It's gonna come out, he was thinking. *It has to.*

Already in these early days Cassie was nurturing Dallas, brushing her thumb over his and tumbling into his eyes to land in his soul where he had no hope of ever disentangling her. There were deep feelings here in the backseat of Caroline's Beamer, an electric need for a more enduring, deeper touch that was driven by a need to understand, to connect, to be understood. And those needs were being gently feathered by a tender facility that Cassie had for simply listening; for offering Dallas everything he had told Phil he so desperately longed for.

Despite the long road Dallas knew still lay ahead, he almost cried with relief.

Seeing the heavy ache pass over him, Cassie bit her bottom lip to suppress an impulsive need to push for a truth she knew hurt Dal like hell for its capacity to disarm him. Sucking up her pride, burying a desperate need to know what was shackling him this evening, Cassie simply leaned over, nuzzled her nose into the sweet, coveted hollow of his neck, sighed, and whispered, "It's okay. I'm here."

Pressing her to him, Dallas' shoulders shook. He buried his face in Cassie's hair so the bickering two in the front seat wouldn't notice his weakness, and he could not answer back.

Chapter Twelve

*T*he night before Dallas left for the gigs he promised Phil he'd do was the night he took the guitar over to the Montana on the bay side of the large park.

Ry wasn't there. He'd taken Caroline up on her invitation to spend time with her and Des at their quaint Lunenburg, Nova Scotia summer home. On the agenda were water skiing, speedboat riding and a trip to some ubiquitous water park. Heaven, to an eight year old.

Levi and his family had pulled out just before Ry left. The boys parted with promises to stay in touch, tucking the shared memory of a great week together into the far corners of their minds for cherished retrieval some day down the road. Their friendship was like a summer fling—the boys lived in the moment, in the intensity of the now. Levi's easy friendship would be missed.

Dallas delivered the guitar via the dusty old truck. He had no interest in drawing attention to himself by walking the small case up the busy treed road toward the bay side of the campground. The way he saw it, if he went walking with a guitar dangling from his fingers it might tweak someone's mind. That someone might be a country music fan…that someone might sense a curious familiarity…

Rounding the last curve leading to Cassie's premium site overlooking the Darnley Basin, Dallas had to talk his heart rate into slowing down. Taking a deep breath and counting to ten, he eased the old truck to a crunching halt next to Cassie's mammoth new Ford and wondered, while he twisted the key backward in the ignition, just which of the two things on his mind would upset Cassie more. Would it be the gift for Ry or would it be the news he'd withheld but had no choice now but to divulge—that he was leaving the next day for a temporary work commitment. What was really driving him around the bend was the deceitful secrecy surrounding both the origin and value of the guitar, and the true nature of his work.

It was late afternoon. After a day at the beach he had walked back to his tent, grabbed his things, and wandered up to the public men's room to shower. Cassie, after promising to meet Dal at her camper later for dinner, had biked up to the Montana to her personal shower.

Dallas was nervous. With the departure of Ry, Caroline and Phil, and a quiet day at the beach goofing around in the water, and light, shared touches while he and Cassie dozed in the sun, suddenly desire was crippling and the opportunity to satiate it was a wide open door.

Reaching for the guitar in the back of the truck, Dallas' cheeks colored. The schoolboy reaction surprised him; after all, he was a seasoned veteran in the ranks of sleeping with women. He was recalling the tender afternoon. The sweetest part of it was also the most painful.

He and Cassie were lying on the beach on a large handmade quilt Cassie was using as a beach blanket. They'd both just been in for a swim (and pees in the ocean, after Dal's two beers and Cassie's coolers) and were sun-drunk and sleepy. Something about that post-swim sun tanning state was deliriously pleasant. Fed by a light in Cassie's eyes that Dallas quizzically thought shone brighter with Ry's absence—maybe because her son's presence increased her worries about the quality of care she provided him—Dallas had extended a finger and drawn it down Cassie's skin, on her shoulder. They were lying on their sides facing each other, far enough away from other beachgoers on this hot day that nobody but themselves could read the heat that instantly shot up through their bodies at Dal's sizzling touch. His fingertip was a searing ember pulled from the remnants of last night's blazing campfire.

Drawing the smoldering stroke down Cassie's elegant body, Dallas held her gaze. Brazenly, he slipped the finger under the thin neck strap of the aqua-blue halter bikini she was wearing. He didn't dip away from her half-lidded, trusting emerald eyes until he couldn't stand it; then, making a little grunting sound, he let his eyes drop to the strap, to where it joined the small bit of fabric covering the breast he ached to set free, that he ached to touch, to place his mouth over so he could give the nipple a little tease with his tongue.

Cassie's chest started to rise and fall faster. Lost in this new man, watching him study her, tantalize her, she latched her eyes into Dal's so she could soak up his response to her body. Lifting a hand to place delicate fingers over his stronger ones, Cassie arched her back toward him and inched closer. Something in his eyes gave way; they dimmed, the pale blues glowing first, heated, then fading like falling stars to end in a desperate, penetrating yearning.

Frowning slightly, nervous, certain Cassie was telling him to stop when he didn't want to, Dallas started to pull his finger away, but she arched her back even more, half-closed her eyes, parted her lips, and pressed his whole hand onto her body so that the heel of his palm almost—but not quite— covered her sun-warmed left breast.

"Cassie," Dallas whispered at the time, the sweetness of her name a dusky wish on his quickening breath, "I would never hurt you. You know that, right?"

In answer, Cassie let her eyes more fully capture the blatant desire in his, and she pushed his hand down to fully cover her breast. Softly, he kneaded her, their bodies close enough together that they were in their own private paradise. Almost purring with need and want, Cassie grasped Dal's fingers and brought them to her lips, ducking her head so no curious onlookers could see her kiss the callused fingers that left hot trails of want on her skin, or watch her push the fingers deep into her mouth so she could suck softly on them, closing her eyes demurely now, because it seemed wanton, to her, to need and desire a man this much.

"Uhh," was the sound that escaped Dallas' lips, unbidden and from some primal part of his body as if it were his need and not his brain responding to that wet place where Cassie placed his fingers, where she tongued him while she sucked.

Dallas let her tease the hell outta him for a minute, but even the memory of the recent cold swim in the freezing Atlantic was not enough to quell the rising passion in his groin, so Dallas said her name again, softly this time, and removed his fingers from that perfect mouth, from those sweet lips, and from those now half-lidded, longing eyes.

"Baby," he said, wiping a wet thumb across the perfect lips. "I'll go there with you. Tonight, if you're ready—"

"I'm ready," she cut him off. "Please, Dal."

It took him a few moments to say anything more, so desperate was the ache in the innocent captivating jade eyes blinking up at him. Dallas wasn't sure if Cassie even realized it, but she was moving her hips now, slowly, toward him. Barely distinguishable to an outsider not paying attention, she was telegraphing desire to Dallas in a way he'd seen before, but not often, because the women he used to be with were ones he always took quickly without time to enjoy such sensuous foreplay—this long extended game of touch and retreat that he and Cassie started playing the day they met.

Now, at Cassie's campsite, all showered and clean, the sand between his toes washed away, the desire was excruciating. Recalling the painful but incredibly enticing afternoon, Dallas stepped into the Montana with the guitar for Ry in his hand, armed with the truth that Cassie wanted him. Hell, that was no secret. But Dallas couldn't help but entertain doubts. Cassie seemed ready, in a lot of ways, but she was a single mother with a weighty world of grief tucked into her soul and buried in her heart. Sure, there were strong feelings between the two, but Dallas was leaving tomorrow, and there was this guitar gift and how she would take it to consider...

Dallas needn't have worried. Cassie was slicing tomatoes for a salad when he filled her doorway, ruggedly handsome in a T-shirt and jeans and the usual boots, his hair still damp from his shower and not, at the moment, tucked under the grungy Jays cap.

Laying her knife on the counter of the small kitchen island, Cassie swallowed and blinked at Dal standing there in front of her, so uncertain, so unsure, so...scared. It was everything she had in her not to tiptoe over to him and take him in her arms there and then.

She went for humor instead, but her voice was a little higher-pitched than she liked, and just a wee bit squeaky. Glossing one hand over her sleek blonde ponytail and wiping the other on the soft brushed cotton mid-thigh sundress she had changed into after her shower—with a halter neckline like the bikini, Dallas couldn't help but note—she said, with a smile, "Did you leave your guitar out overnight?"

"What?" he blinked back at her, fighting the urge to toss the guitar case on the nearby sofa and take her right there, on the kitchen floor.

She gestured toward the guitar. "Small. It rained overnight. I thought maybe you shrunk it."

"Oh." Forcing a laugh, Dallas held up the case. Even to Cassie's inexperienced eye, it was still quite obviously shiny and new. "For Ry." Sucking in a breath, Dallas prepared for battle. "Cassie, he needs to practice. And even when he can strum on mine, it's too big for him. Ry needs one that's easier to wrap his fingers around."

"Wrap his fingers around," Cassie echoed, eyes widening with unrestrained pleasure at what that might mean for her later. And…for Dal. "Mmmm," she added, unaware that she'd uttered her obvious delight aloud.

"Cassie," Dallas warned, eyes narrowing. "You're okay with this? With me bringing this guitar to Ry?"

Sense took over. Shifting her weight onto her other foot, Cassie nodded. "I'm not surprised. I have to admit, I love how patient you are when you are teaching him. Sometimes I feel like the two of you don't even know I'm around. He's learned a lot."

"He's a good student, Cassie. Ry's talented, but more than that, he's interested. Your kid's got the gift of music." Glancing around for an out-of-the-way place to set the guitar down, Dallas decided that the living room floor would be best, away from the door. The instrument would wait for Ry's return over by the entertainment unit.

Looking up after setting it down, he couldn't help but notice that Cassie's husband's photograph was no longer on display. Freezing momentarily, he wondered whether Ry had taken it with him to Lunenburg.

Sidling up behind him, Cassie wrapped both arms around his waist and followed his eye line to the space where Eddie used to be. "He's still here," she murmured into the newly coveted hollow of Dal's fine, tanned neck. His damp hair smelled so fresh, so clean, so…new. "He's just resting for a while."

"Oh." Speechless for the second time in a few short minutes, Dallas wheeled slowly around in Cassie's arms. Lifting her chin, he searched her eyes. This was something. This meant a lot. "That scares the hell out of me," he whispered.

She shook her head slowly from side to side. The way she was looking at him now, all solemn and serious, frightened Dallas even more. Breathing in slowly, counting again, he tried to settle his nerves. Handling this woman… being with this woman…not being truthful was wrong. He knew it on every base level of his entire being. Those naïve, innocent eyes trusting him, loving him…he knew the tenderness she was loving him with now would be replaced by a hard, steely look once she realized who he really was, what his lifestyle was like—the women, the overzealous fans, the falsities, the mistrust…

And then there was the music.

"Look, Dal," Cassie sighed, thinking she could read what he was thinking. "I appreciate the gift for Ry, I really do. He'll love it. But at the end of the summer we'll give it back, okay? When we're back in Halifax I will buy him a guitar. If he even still wants to play. You know what summer's like, what kids are like…last week with Levi it was basketball and next week he'll figure he's on the fast track to the NHL. And it's not like you can afford a gift that precious, let's face it."

"I can afford it," Dallas managed in a quieter tone than he had planned. It came out sounding unsure, as if maybe he couldn't quite make next week's beer allowance now that he'd bought the guitar.

"Maybe what I am trying to say is that he'll never have a career in music. Especially, um," Cassie let her hands drift down to his elbows and followed the movement with her eyes, so she didn't see the hurt in Dallas' baby blues when she finished her sentence. "Especially with the kind of redneck tunes you play."

He recovered well, albeit the defense was still subdued, almost pouty. "You never know, Cassie."

"Look, babe, um…Dal…" Cassie forced herself to meet his eyes again, and the wounded look staring back at her almost crumpled her as easily as she hoped his touch would ignite her skin later on. "It's just that…I mean… I'm sorry if your own dreams haven't come true, honey. Playing a string of raunchy clubs and all, but…don't put your lost dreams on my kid, okay?

That's all I'm saying. We—Ry and me—learned a long time ago not to go after impossible dreams."

"No, sweetheart," he breathed back to her, almost physically recoiling. "I don't buy that. I see the way you look at those sandcastles we build, like they're filled with possibility. You want to let yourself dream, you're just afraid to. Dreams can come true." At the same time, Dallas chided himself. Because sometimes, lately, it seemed his music dream had become a nightmare. The only dream worth hanging onto now seemed to be this petite, beautiful woman in his arms.

"So I dream, Dal, but it doesn't mean I expect those dreams to come true. I've learned to take life one day at a time. One breath at a time."

"And the music? Why do you hate my music so much?"

She stuttered out a response. "Country music? It's low and rustic, Dal. It all sounds the same and the lyrics are all, like…" Backing away from him, she reached up and absently scratched a mosquito bite on her neck. "Like, my dog and my wife are on the back of my pickup truck, and my father's gonna run away with my wife, and I have a shotgun up my ass." With a self-satisfied smirk, Cassie crossed her arms and twinkled her eyes at him. "Wouldn't you say?"

Her smile faded quickly when she realized Dal's expression hadn't changed. If anything, the sorrow he was emitting in her general direction was deepening.

"Oh, shit, Dal. I'm sorry." Cassie swiped a nervous hand back over her ponytail. "That was thoughtless of me. You make your living singing about other people's heartaches. And, um," she sighed sadly, "maybe your own, I suppose."

Rallying, he straightened. A little of the sadness left his eyes, but only because Dallas had to bring Cassie down a bit more today. First, though, he said, "You talk about what you've learned. What life has taught you. The baggage you carry."

Apprehensive, Cassie tilted her head to better listen. Something in Dal's eyes begged her undivided attention.

He didn't waver. "Cassie, I've learned that I am tired—very tired—of people thinking I am something I am not. In some strange way I find it refreshing to know that you see me for who I am. Less than perfect. Just a man who sings sad songs."

"What are you running from, Dal?" The question was asked carefully, the man it was asked to once again in Cassie's arms, albeit her small hands were hooked on his belt now, at his waist. Weirdly, Cassie figured her tiny hold on him would keep him from bolting.

"It's not like that," he told her. "I'm not exactly running. Not the way you are."

The delicate, proud chin lifted. Cassie's velvety eyes flashed. "I'm not running. At least I've accepted who I am and what I need."

Countering, Dal shot back, "Have you?"

Instantly, Cassie deflated. But she retained her hold on the wide brown leather belt that somehow, instinctively, she knew held this incredible man together every bit as much as did the worn leather boots and the rusted old truck.

"Let's not fight," she whispered into his hurt, moist eyes. "John Lennon. Do you ever listen to his kind of music, Dal? Make love, not war. Let's make love."

Sweet Jesus. Dallas almost lost it then and there. Something hard gave in his soul at the way Cassie so simply suggested having sex. He reacted the way he'd told himself he would not. It was nothing to scoop her light yoga body up in his arms and carry her past the tiny kitchen up the few stairs, past the shower, and into the bedroom.

"You sure?" he asked her softly, laying her on her back on the bed and crawling over her, remaining in a half crouched position on all fours, tenting her with his body.

Closing her eyes, Cassie took a deep breath. *Is this real? Is this happening?* The musky, fresh scent of him—a heady mix of leather and shampoo and soap and sweat intermingling with the sensation and feel of Dal's muscled body on the hot day—was intoxicating. Cassie wanted to bring him inside her, to clench her body around his; she was desperate to belong to him the way she felt he belonged to her. In her mind she was his and he was hers, plain and simple. There was no doubt right now, here. Still, a niggling thought fought its way up to her brain. It screamed, *maybe it's just a summer thing, a physical thing.* Cassie pushed it away.

"I've never been more sure of anything, baby," she said in a low murmur that had the power on its own to make Dallas moan, mostly for the tender way Cassie called him *baby* as if she would, from this moment on, care for him the way a mother is supposed to care for a child.

Dallas felt childlike, despite his size and power over her, mostly because he lost power over himself when he was with Cassie, and when he simply thought about her. There were truths that still had to come out, starting with—

Inhaling for courage, he started them down a necessary path. "Cassie, if we do this, I want you to know..." He moved a wisp of hair off her cheek, following up the loving movement by placing his lips on her soft skin. Unsure, tentative, he pulled away, and raised his body up.

Moaning, Cassie tried to pull his mouth down to hers, but froze at Dal's next words.

"Cassie, I have to go away for a little while. Tomorrow."

"What? Why?" Staring up at him, she sucked in a breath and held it.

"For work," Dallas admitted, a touch of sorrow in the two dreaded words. "To work. I can't get out of it, I tried."

"Is that why your friend Phil was here?"

He nodded. "Yes. Phil takes care of my schedule for me. We've been friends for a very long time. He booked me into a few—uh, shows—ages ago. Before I took this leave of absence I keep telling myself I'm on. I have to honor my commitments. I've already cancelled a few but I can't get out of these."

"But—"

Spying the panic in those emerald eyes, noting that the sparkle was fading—like jewels falling into the murky ocean, spiraling downward—Dallas soothed Cassie with a gentle kiss on her forehead. "Sweetheart, I'll be back. I'll only be gone a week. I just didn't want to...you know...us..." Glancing around the room, he relaxed when he looked back at her, when he saw the tiny shine revert back to the eyes he loved. "What?" He, too, smiled. Just a little.

"I'm going to sleep in your tent every night while you're gone."

"Why?" Dallas chuckled.

"So I can call you in the middle of the night and hold the phone up to the ocean. So the waves can rock you to sleep. So you'll know what you're missing and so you'll come back."

"You talk about music? Now, *that's* music, baby girl." A few more soft kisses landed on Cassie's cheeks, but before Dallas gave in completely and surrendered to those perfect pink lips, he whispered, "And that's a sound I hope to hear for the rest of my life. With you alongside, if you'll have me."

"Dal, I've got news for you," Cassie breathed as his kisses intensified, as he settled lower onto her body, slipped a hand inside her halter, and moaned at the feel of a breast under his lips, and soon her nipple under his tongue. "I'm already aching to feel you inside me."

He melted.

Continuing, she reached for his belt. "You don't have to promise me life."

Too overcome to answer, afraid to frighten her away, Dallas let the comment slide for now. He helped her with his belt, and slipped her hand inside his jeans himself so he could feel her react to him. Tightening her hand against him, she slid it up and down and brushed a slender finger against the tip of his penis, her breath growing ragged at how wet he already was—for her.

Shortly, Cassie heard herself begging Dal to touch her, at least touch her, *there*. He seemed nervous to go there at first, to let go, but when Cassie pushed his jeans down over his hips and raised her own hips to pull her dress up to her waist, all that remained between them was a lacey pair of white panties.

"Please," she begged him, pushing her body up against him. "Please, Dal."

That word...that simple word...*please*...but first, one peek into her eyes to be sure she meant it, just to be sure...

There it was—love, trust, faith. Assurance that all was well between them, that this was okay.

Condoms...Dallas had a condom tucked away in his pocket. *My history...the women...* Not that he wanted to stop, but sense and reason won out. Fishing for it, Dal dropped it on the bed beside them while he reached up and yanked at the tie on Cassie's halter dress. It loosened, and he decided he wanted nothing between them, no soft cotton sundress, no lacey panties, not his T-shirt or jeans, either. Cassie was thinking the same thing. She let him pull her dress up over her head while she, delirious with desire, grasped his T-shirt at the hem and hauled it up over his head.

"Oh my God, I wanted to touch you at the beach, Dal, so many times...

149

I wanted to run my hands over you, over all of you…I couldn't stand it. I can't stand it."

His answer was a moan, a deep one, a gruff male kind of one. Dal's hands were on her breasts now, both of them, massaging her while his hips gyrated against her panties, while he tongued her nipples one at a time and sucked and played. In one swift movement he shoved the jeans and boxers all the way down, and cursed the damn cowboy boots he'd once again—as always—forgotten to take off at the trailer's door. He had to leverage himself up onto his knees to manage them. Inside, Cassie laughed, but outside all she could do was gasp and beg.

"Please, Dal, please," and this time when his hands and mouth came back to her breasts she grabbed his fingers in hers and pressed them down on top of her, in that intimate area that, when he cupped his hand fully over her, promised a kind of salvation both she and Dallas had often longed for, one that came with love and wasn't meant for pleasures of the flesh alone.

He had yet to really curse in her esteemed company, but now Dal couldn't help himself. "Oh fuck, Cassie," he murmured, moving the heel of his hand over her, over that part of her he'd dreamed about touching, about pressing his lips to. "You're so wet, baby girl. Is that for me? Can I go there? Can I see?"

"Yes," she rasped, thrusting herself hard into his hand while he played.

Taking her panties down, quickly, in haste, Dallas thought he might lose his dignity then and there. He decided he wasn't going inside without a taste, so he went there first, a finger, two fingers, his mouth, his tongue…

Writhing underneath this beautiful man, this patient, kind, loving man she trusted instinctively with her son, her life, her soul, Cassie cried out. And she could care less if the entire campground heard her, so desperate was she for some kind of release that being loved by him had earned.

Vaguely she heard the *rrrripp* of the condom. It was distant, muzzy; Cassie was hitting a supreme high, riding unrelenting hot waves of pleasure, twisting her head from side to side and grabbing at his hair, pushing his lips down onto her so she could finish. When she hit the almighty high that Dal instinctively knew was her ultimate high, he licked and tongued and fingered a few seconds longer so she could ride the wave. Yet he, too, craved release, so he moved up her body and replaced his probing fingers with his swollen penis.

There were other ways he wanted to take her. Cassie seemed comfortable with her body. Dallas ached to try other positions with her, but even if she was willing now, he was too overcome and in need to pull out and try again. Instead, he wrapped her in his arms, held that fragile body while she writhed and cried out underneath him, and he let go with a deeply satisfying cry.

This lovemaking was ten times ten thousand times more than ever before, for him. This coupling was above and beyond; it was more intimate, perfect and real than any coupling with any woman that came before it, and Dallas had had his share over the years of perfect bodies and adventurous women. This woman, this elegant, sad blonde goddess sobbing with pleasure in his arms, the one Dallas desired and held so dear as to whisper, for the very first time to her, "I love you,"—she sobbed and breathed the cherished words back to him—was the woman Dallas was, without a doubt, certain he would love for all time.

Unlike the others, Cassie was delicate and gentle, and carried an innocence that curtained a strength Dallas had been surprised to find in a woman this scarred from loss. She had courage, enough at least to face the things that scared her the most—she could sit in front of fire, for instance, and watch miniature flames like the ones that killed her husband destroy splits of wood as they once destroyed flesh and bone.

She could admit her wrongdoings, her weaknesses.

And she saw him for who he was—a man who sang songs that sometimes made people cry.

Holding her as they came down off their lovemaking, Dallas murmured in her small ear yet again. "I love you, Cassie." Pressing her to his body, he held her dear and wished to hell he could catch the flu so the trip to the States the next day could be cancelled.

He almost got what he wished for. Mid-morning the next day he drove back to his tent in the old truck so he could pack for his trip. Later he biked back up to see Cassie, to share some lunch and a last bit of blissful lovemaking before the inevitable parting. Cruising back down to his campsite on his bicycle after a somber, tearful post-noon farewell, he hit the asphalt in a spray of curses. A little redheaded girl on a pink bike had suddenly swerved sideways and pedaled right in front of Dallas. Startled, he had no choice but to veer away at the last second. Landing on his right wrist, he spent the flight to Nashville wincing in pain, cradling his hurt arm against his chest.

Eventually Dallas had to face Phil. He did it with a subdued gaze. "I can't play guitar," he muttered, half hoping it would be enough to get him out of the week's contracts. He could still taste Cassie's sweetness...

The curses Dallas loosed when he fell were nothing. Phil turned the air a nasty shade of blue that made Dallas cringe. Dal's old buddy finally got it together, grimaced, snuck his artist in the back entrance of a busy hospital, and put him on the stage anyway. A substitute guitarist was only too happy to show off Dallas' skilled, showy riffs.

In Prince Edward Island, Cassie pressed her iPhone to her ear, teased Dallas mercilessly about the damaged hand, and waited for him to come back to her.

Chapter Thirteen

"How's the hand?" Letting the door to Dallas' hotel suite slam behind him, Phil moved into the room with a couple of takeout coffees held high on a recyclable tray. "You're the talk of the festival."

Absently running his left hand over the tension bandage wrapped around the offending wrist, Dallas cringed. "The world has bigger problems than my inability to play guitar." Half reclining, Dallas was leaning back on a plush contemporary lime green sofa that was situated parallel to a large glass window. Booted feet up on an ottoman, one ankle crossed over the other, Dallas was studying the Nashville skyline when Phil came in, reflecting on the fact that it felt like a whole other world, another dimension even, compared to gentle, almost naïve Prince Edward Island. "It's so damn hot here. I need me an ocean," he grumped. "Preferably one with a few easy waves and a sandy beach."

"Let's not forget a pretty blonde in a tiny bikini."

"Mmmpphh." Dallas grunted, sighed, and leaned further back into the comfortable cushions.

Ripping back the tab on the coffee and handing it over to Dallas, Phil retrieved a paper cup for himself before sitting back and settling into a large chair kitty corner to his artist. "You haven't told her."

"What should I say? Oh by the way, Cassie, I make a living playing music you think is beneath you. I've got legions of female fans who'll do anything to get my attention, hell, I've slept with a shit ton of them, and my life is not my own. Privacy is not a thing. I live in a prison of my own making." Taking a sip of the hot beverage he was holding in his good left hand, Dallas continued to

153

stare out at the heat rising from the streets below. A low haze had settled over the city. Inside, he and Phil were relaxing in air-conditioned comfort, but the concert stage would be sticky hot. Just thinking about it made Dallas ache for the cool sea breeze of his island paradise, never mind the caring hands and tender kisses of a woman who liked him for who she thought he was.

"There are a lot of perks to your life, Dallas. I'm glad you're so clearly grateful for the hard work it took to get you here."

Dallas looked over at his manager and friend. "Phil," he stated blankly, "I'm not discounting the perks. I'm grateful for the good stuff. I just wish they didn't come with the bad. It's that old adage, you know? Be careful what you wish for. You just might get it." He took a sip of the steaming coffee and sighed again.

"Stop doing that." Phil frowned.

"What?"

"That heavy sighing thing. You need to chill out and get through these two shows. Cassie's an adult. She might surprise you. In the meantime, you've got bigger problems."

I can't imagine, Dallas thought. Part of him wished he'd come clean with Cassie from the start because the longer they knew each other, the deeper they had become embroiled. And the harder it got to consider coming clean with her, as if their sand piles on the beach were growing taller with each passing day. *The higher you go, the harder you fall,* Dallas considered. "Bigger problems?" he echoed Phil. "What, my hand?"

A hard look from Phil at least partly answered the question for him. "Like I said, the hand is front page news. Sulk about your career all you want, big boy, but there are fans in town that expected to see you riff on that guitar with both guns blazing. Some people actually appreciate that God-given talent of yours, even if you don't."

Dallas was too done-in to fight. He let the issue swift off to some far corner of the room, raised his coffee toward Phil, and said, "And? I know there's more. You might as well spill it."

"Deborah wants you to join her on stage for your duet."

"Well. That's not happening."" Dallas took a second to sip his coffee and consider what it would mean to join his ex-girl behind the microphone. Not that it would mean anything to him if he did. As far as he was concerned, that social climbing two-timer was no longer someone who had the power to really affect him.

"Call it a goodbye song."

"How well do you know Deborah, Phil? I could say a hundred goodbyes to her, she's like a wall of polished ice, none of them would stick. Bullshit, that ballad is. It's not a goodbye song, hell, it's likely a whole new hello. She's got ulterior motives."

"That ice thing? Consider your last goodbye stuck. She's moved on, Dal. Deborah's engaged."

"What?" That got Dallas' attention. "Oh. That was fast." *Why's this hurt? I don't care about Deborah, not like that…not like…Cassie.* A twinge in his heart caught him by surprise. Phil noticed.

Sitting forward, Phil tapped the bottom of his cup on his good friend's knee. He spoke quietly, with sincere care and concern Dallas was glad to find in his buddy. "Look, Dallas. Deborah was a good thing for you for a while. At least musically, you and she were suited. Look, she hurt you. You're only human, Dallas."

A small harrumph made its way out of Dallas' throat and into the space facing the distant wall, where Dallas turned his head so Phil couldn't see that he was partly right.

Phil continued. "Say your goodbyes to her and let her go. On stage, with music. Climb over that wall so you can move forward."

Turning back to Phil, Dallas tried to read the man's thoughts. Out loud he said, "And Cassie?"

A lengthy pause followed. Phil scratched thoughtfully at his chin with a thumb and forefinger. He filled part of the quiet calm by staring at a fingerprint on the glass window. In the end, he pointed to it.

"See that print, Dal?"

Grunt. Dallas fixed his eyes on what he knew was the key to some kind of example Phil was showing him. Phil liked to do that, to illustrate his points with visuals. Dallas had often teased him about it, said he should have gone into directing films instead of bossing country singers around.

"That print is you. You get what I'm saying, Dallas?" A serious stare made its way to Dallas' narrowing eyes. "You've left your mark, that's what I'm saying. On the country music world and on the wider world at large. Like it or not now, you and Deborah were a thing, a thing that people romanticized to pretty up their own ordinary little lives. Deborah messed it up and so she's moved on. You've moved on. But that fingerprint the two of you left is set in stone. A part of you will always be Deborah and Dallas. Always."

Shifting in his seat, Phil set down his coffee cup and faced Dallas more straight on. "Dal," he continued, shaking a finger in his friend's face, "if you bring that hurt little widow into your crazy life, you could destroy her. By the same token, I get that walking away from her could in some way destroy you. I just have to be honest here. I don't see how your two worlds can mesh. You belong with a Deborah, someone larger than life whose got balls the world can't destroy. Cassie is sweet, I like her. But she's not Dallas White material."

Dallas moved to speak but Phil silenced him with a staunch air palm to the face. If he had the energy, Dallas would have grabbed the obnoxious hand and given it a good hard twist, but today he could barely muster up the energy to talk back to Phil. He sent the guy a vicious glare instead.

Phil said, "I know what you're going to say. But don't bother, Dal. Face facts. You're not Cassie material, either. You no more fit into her world than she fits in yours."

Stunned, Dallas just stared at the man he considered his good friend. After a moment in which Phil sat back confidently, his coffee back in his hands like the self-satisfied shmuck Dallas suddenly saw peek through the usually genial guy he trusted with his career—and thus his life—Dallas mustered up some fight. "I fit just fine in her world, Phil. I did all right. Nobody bothered me."

"Speaking of adages, Dallas, here's another one—you chose to be a country star. You can't go back."

"I went back." Biting off the words, Dallas added, "We were good together."

"You weren't you, Dallas. Don't you see? That puny little island was nothing more than an illusion!"

Things were about to escalate into a nasty fight when an abrupt knock on the door sent Dallas' next biting words skidding to a sudden halt. Phil took advantage of the knock and jumped up. Escaped, even. He was trembling; it was never easy to manage Dallas when he was in this kind of pouty, sour mood.

Dallas was quaking in his boots. The truths Phil unleashed on him had been hiding all along like spiders waiting to pounce, swept into little creases like underneath the big air mattress he'd finally gone and bought that first week on the east coast to keep his bones from creaking so much when he rose in the early fog of damp island mornings. They were sneaking out, those uncomfortable truths; they were pesky little buggers just waiting to hijack him at a time like this when he had some distance and thus some perspective.

Taking his feet off the ottoman one at a time, Dallas groaned, set the coffee cup on the end table at his side, and buried his face in his good elbow. "I'm gonna be sick," he moaned.

"Not feeling well, Dallas?" A familiar set of feet bounced into the room behind him on red pointed toe cowboy boots that, Dallas knew, were intricately embroidered from the toes to the tops. He knew because he had given them to their wearer. The sound of them on the hotel room floor startled and disarmed him, but not as much as the familiar sing-song voice, which made him swallow bitterly and clench his jaw before he stood and swung around to face the woman he'd once thought he might make his for life.

Locking his eyes on her now, sweeping his gaze over the tight denims and low cut top, Dallas wondered what the hell he ever saw in her. *Deborah. Deborah and Dallas.* "Thinking with my balls, that's what I was doing," he chided himself. She had a body that wouldn't quit, all curvy and wild. He blanched at the thought of once thinking he'd spend his life with such a reckless, selfish soul. Prince Edward Island was suddenly reversed in his mind. Suddenly his perspective shifted. Tilting his head as the thought struck him, Dallas realized that this woman in front of him was not the real world. She represented everything false and untrue, everything devoid of real meaning, like material things and wealth. Fame. Back in P.E.I. was a woman who had little wealth, and what she did have she earned by working hard and by enduring incredible loss. Cassie had her issues, she needed nurturing and love to help her manage devastating grief, but she was willing to try, to get

157

help, to lean on Dallas, to let him help her. Deborah hadn't leaned on him. She'd just crawled over him and left him in the dust, his soul exposed and his heart bitter.

The object of his scorn stood before him now, her weight on one foot, her arms crossed. "Do I get a hug or are you just going to stand there and fire invisible bullets at me?"

He found his voice, which emerged scratchy, as raw as his damaged spirit the day he found her in bed with a fellow singer Dallas once considered a friend. "I've got nothing to say to you."

"Oh, come on, Dallas. Don't give me that lonely bullshit. You leave a gal alone in the cow pile, she's gonna find another turd to play with."

His eyebrows shot up into curious curves. "I hear you're marrying the turd."

Stuttering back, "You care?" Deborah ran a finger nervously over the top button of her western top. Intentionally or not, she exposed a part of the breast Dallas used to run his lips over on those crazy post-show all-nighters that, even now, brought a tingle to his groin.

"Nope," he retorted quickly, wondering why his heart gave a little twist when the word emerged all lonesome and unsure. Looking past her so he wouldn't dive back into those come-hither eyes that were his undoing in the first place, he crunched on a lip.

Phil raised a hand to wave goodbye. A moment later, the door announced his parting with a loud slam.

Dallas struggled for control. Looking back at his ex, he said, "I hope you're happy, Deborah. Truthfully, what you did was the best thing for us, for me. I wouldn't have left if I wasn't given a damn good push."

Her eyes brightened with moisture, which unnerved Dallas. He muttered to himself, *get a grip. She's playing you. Those are crocodile tears in those deceitful, philandering eyes.*

"Dallas…" Sure enough, the voice that made millions with slow melodies and poignant lyrics was soft and sweet, the voice of the Deborah that had sucked Dallas in back at some ubiquitous awards show he didn't even remember for its heightened gaiety and false love. He fisted his good hand and waited. She stepped forward and gingerly touched his bad wrist, holding it in her small palm like a mother bird tenderly caring for her baby. "I'm sorry that I hurt you. But you practically pushed me out the door, honey."

"Don't call me that," he growled. Yet Dallas was powerless to back away. His skin prickled at the memory of loving…well, of wanting to love…her. Somebody. And of being loved in return.

Cassie flashed before him again, all innocent and sweet and tender and real. A vision of her in a wispy mini-skirt floated by; the skirt flaring in the island breeze when she bent to pick up rare sea glass during a beach walk with Dallas and Ry. In the vision she was treating him to a cherished smile that lit up her wounded emerald eyes. The setting sun outlined Cassie's silky blonde hair like a halo, with just a tinge of sun-kist orange. Ry, too, was in the vision, his surfer hair emerging golden at the perfect end of a stunning incorruptible day they'd all spent on the beach, in and out of the water, practicing their sandcastle skills, almost a family—well, in some ways, already a family. Like puzzle pieces, they simply fit; they were ready-built, just waiting for someone to pluck them from obscurity and fit them into place.

Deborah was southern born and bred. She was a Georgia girl. The way she said *honey* made it drip like the thing itself, naturally sweet but thick and gooey so when you swiped your knife through it the knife got sticky and stuck. She lifted his sore hand and kissed the exposed fingers. "We can't go out all mad," she preened, letting her tongue play over the bruised knuckles as he tensed. "We're going to be seeing each other at shows, at industry events. We need to make up, Dallas."

"The duet," he growled, pulling his hand away before his body gave him up to her…to those soft mewls she was now making as she wrapped her arms around him and pressed her voluptuous curves against him. "I'll sing the duet with you, but not for us. For our fans. So they can let us go."

"Oh, but baby…" Gently, Deborah reached a hand down and stroked the outside of the black jeans Dallas'd struggled to raise over his hips with only one good wing. Increasing the pressure, she smiled against his broad chest when she got the reaction she was hoping for. "One last time, you and me. Okay?"

Oh, Jesus, Dallas groaned. It would be so easy. So many times it had been, in fact, with her and with countless others. But, Cassie…

It wasn't the physical thing so much with Cassie. It was more the way Dallas was able to relax around her, to feel needed and authentic in a way this world was not capable of delivering. It was also—he softened and pushed Deborah's hands off his body—a knowing, a simple knowing, that when Cassie's arms were around him, he was safe. Safe from the vultures waiting for him to screw up; safe from the nameless faces in the crowds at his shows who ached so badly for connection that it hurt; safe from his own disconnection and loneliness.

Cassie's arms around Dallas felt full. They felt like home.

Deborah's felt empty.

"Go, Deborah," Dallas urged. "Live your happy, selfish little life. But promise me one thing, okay?" *I'm not a monster,* he told himself. *Cassie makes me a better person.* Instantly he calmed as he realized he could let this woman go with light, and not accompanied by darkness and resentment. Dallas smiled. "Promise me you will always look for joy. Even if the days get tough and the only place you can find it is in your music. Okay?"

Confused, she half smiled up at him, then bent forward and brushed her lips against his, just once, lingering a little at the end. When she started to back up, Deborah left Dallas with awareness, spoken to him in her saccharine sweet Georgia lilt. "I don't know what's changed with you, hon. But I think I'm glad for you. You've got a peace about you, sweetheart." Sighing, she colored a wistful glance with a hesitant addendum. "I just wish it was me that was responsible for it. It's a woman, isn't it?"

Drawing his shoulders up, Dallas had to fight the strong emotion that charged over his body and snuck into his eyes. All those late nights with Deborah…trusting her and wanting her…wishing for more…there was a base layer to their relationship that had been good. And the music…the duet…there was a reason the fans cherished it. "She doesn't know who I am. That I sing." The truth emerged soaked with wanting, with fear. Despite an attempt to stay strong, Dallas' pale eyes started to float.

"Oh, honey." Deborah stopped moving and pondered him, this precious, adorable man so deeply loved by country music fans the world over. "That you sing? That you're a star, you mean?" And she left him with a sweet final parting gift that, even years later, would wash over Dallas with heartfelt love.

"Honey, you're a star with or without the music. Without the fans. You're the kindest man I know. She knows that, hon. If she really, truly, has your heart, she knows that about you. The rest can be figured out. Dallas?"

"Mmmm?" Astonished, humbled, Dallas had to knuckle a bit of moisture away from an eye before recovering and placing his good hand on a hip.

"Sweetheart, just so you know…she's one lucky woman."

Unable to respond with more than a nod, which sent Deborah to him for a tight, genuine hug, Dallas remained silent. He struggled to process this moment, this ending that, in so many ways, was also a beginning.

Deborah left with a last and final truth. "I'll always be here for you, honey. You ever need to talk, to sort things out, to…you know…understand why she's pissed at you some night, you call me, okay?" She waved a hand casually to accent the words that in some ways hurt, because it meant she was letting him go. "I can do that for you. I'm a girl, I know things."

He laughed then, and with a promise to meet her at the main stage sound check for her set, which was a few hours before his at the big festival, Dallas said goodbye.

Chapter Fourteen

*I*n Prince Edward Island, Cassie was sprawled out on her big bed, reading, breathing in the manly hint of Dallas' lingering aftershave, when the trailer started to gently rock.

"Remind me to take a more sheltered spot next summer," she mumbled, swinging over onto her knees and staring out of the big window at the Darnley Basin below the camper. "Oh, crap." Sitting back on her haunches, she dropped her paperback to her side and pondered what she saw.

Like a thick dense fog, an intimidating black thunderhead was rolling in over the water. Flanked on either side were more. Below each cloud, unforgiving gray curtains cascaded down to the water below, leaving a misty looking haze that, from Cassie's fairly nascent experience living this close to the water, was clearly rain.

She only hesitated for a second before hopping down the few steps to the kitchen area and yanking a raincoat and boots out of the shallow closet by the door. Grabbing her truck keys, she half ran down the few steps, jumping from the bottom one to land on the deck, hesitating there when her ears picked up a low, undulating roar. *Thunder.* In the distance, but moving her way. Darting a quick peek at the clouds, she cringed. "As long as there's no lightning," she breathed, and made a run for the truck just as the first few raindrops splattered on the deck.

Looking back at her camp as she fired up the Ford, Cassie decided there wasn't anything too desperately in need of protection at her own site. The barbecue was covered and the flowers had already been moved to the windscreen side of the deck, since there had been a fairly steady breeze all day.

But Dal's camp—just a tent and a new kitchen shelter she'd helped erect— would be vulnerable. His site was pretty much right on the cliff, fully exposed to nature's indiscriminate power.

Zipping up the slope toward the Lower Darnley Road, then crossing at the four way stop and easing through two security gates on the way, moving from the newer section of the campground to the older, treed area, Cassie gently depressed the accelerator and eased down the lane toward Dal's somewhat secluded site. Already his tent was struggling against the quick gusts. One corner tether had let go and was rustling loudly in protest.

"Damn." Sliding to a stop close enough to the tent so she could pitch some of the things Dal'd left behind into her roomy, dry truck, Cassie clutched the steering wheel and eyed the sky once again. Light from a nearby splinter of lightning filled the truck cab; she let out a mighty scream at the bejeesus crack of thunder that followed. It scared the crap out of her. "Wish you were here, Dal," she exclaimed loudly over the rain suddenly starting to pelt the cab with unforgiving force.

Placing a petite hand on the interior handle of the truck, she aimed wide eyes toward the ocean. Large waves were crashing against the beach, their lacey tops cresting angrily down over each other. Watching a power much bigger than herself go to war against itself, a weird feeling struck Cassie. Nature... well, she was an old soldier when nature turned on itself. Summoning up a strength she was well aware came from Dal's presence in her life, and with the love she would always feel from Eddie still surrounding her, Cassie depressed the handle and hopped out into the storm.

For Dallas, it felt odd taking the stage in the middle of Deborah's set. She was a remnant from another life, from another dimension.

The crowd went wild the second they saw their fave country star. On the grounds for the concert was the usual mix—young women baring their navels, some on hunky male shoulders; older folks grasping at memories of good times; humble singles sincerely in love with the music; thirty-somethings curious about Deborah and, by extension, Dallas, since the singers were an item not so long ago. But Dallas couldn't hear them, not really. They were there in his subconscious, but their raucous cheers were muted, as if wrapped in cotton. Deb's mouth was moving, but he couldn't make out what she was saying. The only thing that stood out, that made sense when he made his entrance, was the familiar crack of his boots on the stage, rooting him to the earth.

The boots…they had a power all their own; it echoed up his body like thunder, each step drawing him closer to Deborah—to the woman country fans wanted him to reconnect with. The bright stage lights overhead flashed around and above Deb like lightning, reminding Dallas that Deborah wasn't real. She was in a shell of sorts, one of her own making, aided by the powerful record label engine that supported her. Safe and protected, Deb was really just a caricature to the rambunctious, excited fans that reached for her when she leaned over the stage. She let them touch her. They brushed her arms, grasped at her fingers. Deb knew how to play the game, to give her fans just enough and leave them wanting more.

It saddened Dallas to see that—those anonymous hands in the crowd reaching out but unable to gain more than a surface level connection. Cassie floated across his mind.

Sweat trickled down Dallas' forehead and into his eyes, further obscuring the reality of a situation he wished was anything but real. *I should have told Cassie,* he thought, stopping a few feet away from his ex, idly grasping a microphone a stage tech thrust in his direction. He felt naked without his trusty guitar—Dallas was fully exposed, both to Deborah and to the world.

This is the thing, he told himself, staring out into the sea of anonymous faces. *Cassie knows the 'me' with no guitar, the Dallas she thinks just plays music for fun or in small redneck dives. She loves the man who sits patiently for hours with her eight-year-old son, carving castles out of piles of sand. She knows the guy who dreams away hot summer nights in a simple tent, who sometimes tips his head to the stars before tucking in, who breathes in the pungent sea air for its healing qualities. If she saw me on stage with Deborah—if Cassie knew the on-stage Dal—she would instantly discern the fear in my eyes. The falseness of this world.* Already she could read his soul that way, through a long, sweet look into his pale eyes. What she might not understand would be why he was trembling.

Standing in the glare of all who judged him for letting this voluptuous woman across from him go, for letting them—the fans—down, was excruciating. Dallas may as well have been a timid deer caught in the merciless glare of some careless, unconcerned hunters' headlights. For certain he felt like he was at the wrong end of a shotgun's cruel barrel.

Cassie…Dallas forced his thoughts back to Cassie…she was the healer in this uncomfortable equation. It was the thought of laying his lips on her wispy sea-breezed hair and of running a finger along her elegant, bronzed shoulders that settled Dal's rising anxiety, that slowly started to bring the sound back to his muted ears. Dallas' pretty east coast girl would understand that his true soul was buried by this on-stage circus storm; it had gone into hiding and put his body on autopilot. His real soul was alive and vital in the guy who was learning to grill a proper steak without burning it; in the beach bum frantically trying to knuckle shampoo and conditioner out of long, tangled, salt-water frizzed hair in the four minutes a quarter allotted him in Castle Beach's public men's room.

I should have told her about this me, the old me. I should have prepared her…

He and Deborah were on the cover of grocery store gossip rags. They were featured in TV entertainment shows, and in a plethora of online celebrity blogs. Cassie didn't follow those things, why would she? She had too much sense and self-respect to fuel her brain with fantasy lives. But someday she would clue in, it was inevitable, and when she did Dallas would have to do some serious back stepping to gently remind her that the man she held in her arms a few short nights ago was Dallas White the simple man, not Dallas White the superstar.

Dallas White the superstar was a persona he was shedding bit by bit. Starting with the guitar, apparently.

Something touched his hand. Deborah, snaking her long fingers in and around his as if she was afraid he was going to turn and walk away. Or float up into the lights and disappear forever.

The feel of her warm skin on his brought Dallas back to the stage. Sucking in a nervous breath, which surprised Phil, who was watching from the wing at stage left, Dallas faced her.

The sound came fully back.

It was overwhelming at first. Then some cell memory reminded Dallas that he was used to this, to this empty shell of a place, a place like the soulless Seattle stage where he'd found himself in a similar bizarre bulls-eye the night he took off.

Deborah was speaking into her mic—almost yelling, more accurately. "Dallas looks a little lost out here without his guitar, don't ya, honey?" Her searching eyes implored him to relax, to respond.

Numb, Dallas raised his sore right wrist. His attractive stage mate lifted the arm at the elbow and held it high so the crowd could see the tension bandage sticking out from underneath the long cuff of Dallas' brown leather jacket. Unsnapped, the cuff dragged over his bruised fingers as he stood uncomfortably, one ankle over on its side and a 'little boy lost' frown coloring the strong jaw and usually expressive eyes that now just looked sad and lonely.

"Think he can sing without his guitar to prop him up?" Every time Deborah said guitar it came out sounding like gee-tar, which finally urged a tiny smile from Dallas. He'd always gotten a kick out of her southern accent, which was, he figured, about the only authentic part of her. She played the part of a coquettish southern girl just fine, which gave her country singer image some serious credence. The crowds ate it up.

Now, they were begging for the ballad, their fists pumping the air with exuberant thrusts.

"Be careful down there," Dallas heard himself saying. Lowering his wrist, he yanked it away from his ex and gestured toward a young woman perched on her boyfriend's shoulders near the front of center stage. Clearly the young man was stoned and too lithe and thin-framed to be holding his buxom gal on his shoulders. The crowd was jostling for space near the front. It looked like the girl was going to topple any second now onto the burly shoulders of one of the security dudes positioned nearby with his back to the stage, arms straight, hands folded in front of his groin. Some old part of Dallas the superstar came back to him, pulled up from years of similar generic outdoor shows. He found himself grinning.

Visibly relaxing, Deborah signaled her lead guitar player to strum them in.

The girl in the audience lost her balance when her boyfriend stumbled.

Security did its job. Catching her, the black T-shirted dude positioned her safely on the ground.

Dallas didn't notice. The pretty intro to the famous ballad was carrying him away. Smiling at Deborah, whose cheeks pinked up at the new, soft warmth reappearing in the eyes of the man she loved, Dallas eased into the trusted safety of what he knew best—music.

Chapter Fifteen

"Oh shit, I really hope Dal's okay with this…" Inside Dallas' small tent, Cassie peered around at the interior with a semi-curious eye. Truth be told, she would have taken a closer look if she dared, but now was not the time. A roaring wind and pelting rain were enough incentive to hurry up and do what she'd come to do, which was rescue any personal items she thought might not survive should the tent come off its tethers and balloon up into the angry sky before sinking mercilessly into the Gulf.

"All right." Rubbing anxious fingers together, Cassie sent Dal a quiet prayer. "Forgive me." Water from the heavy rain was seeping in at the corners and dripping in rivers from the tarp overhead onto the grass at the sides of the tent. In a short matter of time the whole interior of Dal's summer refuge would be completely soaked.

A brilliant flash of light alerted Cassie to an incoming massive thunderclap. With a squeal Dallas would have found adorable and endearing, she leapt under the quilt on his air mattress and trembled in a fetal position. An ensuing scream did nothing to alert anyone of her fear—the thunder roaring in her ears seemed to split the sky in two. She swore the ground shook. Between rumbles, the shaking of the tent and its sinewy tough (but struggling) tethers added an eerie cacophony to the rescue mission, as if the universe itself was protesting Cassie's presence and questioning her right to be in Dallas' personal space.

It was a good twenty minutes before the worst of the lightning and thunder passed. And hail—soon there was hail too, small pellets that pelted down on Cassie's borrowed sanctuary with a force strong enough to bend the tent poles. Sneaking a peek out from underneath the heavenly quilt that smelled like the husky man she'd grown to respect and love, Cassie eyed the rest of Dal's things. There wasn't much to see. He'd finally bought a kitchen shelter that held his basic cooking things and a few coolers, so the tent mostly consisted of sleeping things. He'd taken a bag with him. The perimeter of the tent held only a few clothing items—beach type things, and a soft forest green hoodie Cassie loved on him, that showed off his muscular chest and ripped biceps. A stack of damp extra blankets meant for cool summer nights were stacked in a blue Rubbermaid container. A small battery-operated Coleman lamp sat by the head of the bed on a thick upturned tree trunk. Beside it, a shiny new flashlight waited patiently.

"My rustic man," Cassie smiled happily, the tension easing as the interval between the terrifying thunderclaps lengthened. "No electricity for you." The campsite had water service, but Cassie knew Dal shaved up the lane at the public washroom. For some reason she didn't quite understand, a cozy warmth settled in her heart at the image of a sleepy Dal trudging up the dirt lane with a shaving kit dangling from his hand. "He's all man," she breathed. "And he's all mine."

She was about to crawl over the foot of the bed and raise the zipper to the tent's entrance when her fingers touched something flat and hard. Glancing down, she was surprised to see a vinyl LP staring up at her. That was curious. Certainly there was no need for one here. Never mind the lack of electricity, there was also nothing to play a record on.

"Must be a favorite," she muttered, scooping it up for a closer look. "Huh," she questioned, noticing that the LP, a country artist's, was autographed. Feeling playful, exhilarated from the wild storm and from what she considered a necessary and pleasantly uninhibited view of the small micro-environment Dal was living in this summer, she considered the find an interesting clue to her mysterious new man's past. "Although I already know you love country," she grinned childishly, sitting back on her haunches with the LP balanced in both hands. "Silly boy. Classy guy that you are."

Holding the record out in front of her face, Cassie swiped a loose strand of wet hair off her cheek and pursed her lips. Knitting her eyebrows together, she stared at the LP cover. In one corner was the most curious scrawled autograph—above the artist's name, it simply read *I'm sorry.* In glittery gold marker. Squinting, Cassie was surprised to see that the brief message was actually written by the woman whose gorgeous eyes peered out from behind the body of a man; a man who was photographed with his back to the camera. Deborah was the singer's name. Cassie was no country music fan, but she recognized the woman as someone at the top of the country music ranks. She'd have to be living in a hole underground not to see, on the colorful covers of tabloids lining the grocery store aisles, the blatant sorrow of fans that claimed to be destroyed because Deborah Lacey and her fiancé Dallas White had split up at the beginning of the summer.

The man on the cover—apparently Dallas White, according to the album's graphics—begged closer scrutiny. Studying his back, a chill travelled up Cassie's body. "No way." She chided herself for even considering that the Dallas on the album cover, whose song was apparently featured on the vinyl inside, could in any way be her Dal. "Weird coincidence," she said to the lessening wind, to the gentler flapping of her man's tent. For one thing, the singer with his back to her was wearing a faded brown cowboy hat. Cassie had never seen Dal in anything other than the dirty old Jays baseball hat he wore like a crown. But the way he was standing with his hands on the woman Deborah's hips, his feet placed in a wide stance, ragged hems brushing the ground… a brown leather jacket…longish hair…

"Well," she decided. "This guy could be anyone." Indeed, there was nothing concrete about the man's image that would lead her to believe he could possibly be her Dal. But the name…Dal could be short for Dallas.

Her heart rate picking up, Cassie flipped the album over and studied the finer notes typed in black lettering at the bottom. Dallas White's management was listed as The Old Dirt Road Management. No mention of anyone named Phil. And Dal had told Cassie he and Phil were discussing business when Phil was around last week. She thought about doing an Internet search to see if there was a fedora-wearing Phil on The Old Dirt Road's roster. For a fleeting moment she also considered scouring the Internet for pics of Dallas White.

"I'm out of my mind," she determined in the end, resolving not to go there (intuition maybe, she realized much, much later, for fear of what she might find). "Dal is a second rate country singer. He likely picked this up in some sleazy bar or at some old flea market somewhere along the line." The signature mystified her, though. *I'm sorry?* Sorry for what, she wondered. Why would this Deborah woman write *I'm sorry* on an album cover that Dal had somehow gotten possession of? And the song, she noted as she pulled out the record itself, was only one particular tune. Instrumental on one side, a vocal duet on the other. Dallas and Deborah. Collectors' vinyl to accompany a digital release. That's all this was.

Still, Cassie felt sick. A slow nausea worked its way into her small frame and gnawed at her bones. Shuddering, she decided a bigger truth was unreal to even consider. No way could the man she knew as Dal be some famous country singer. Somebody would have recognized him. There were tons of country fans in P.E.I. Dallas White would not be spending his summer in a tent overlooking the beach in redneck Darnley. Heck, if a man that wealthy desired a beachy view, he'd be living it up in style in some expensive exotic resort in the Caribbean.

Before tossing the LP back on the bed, Cassie gave the guy on the cover one last peek. She moved forward and unzipped the tent. "Could be anyone," she mumbled again as she scanned the horizon, dismayed to see more thunderclouds. Wondering just how much Dal cherished the LP, since it was such an odd thing to find in his bare-bones camp, she scooped it up at the last second, rushed through the now gentle downpour and slid into her truck. A few more trips later for the sweaters and extra blankets, and then into the kitchen shelter (where she determined only a half-eaten loaf of bread and some forgotten bananas were worth preserving), she sat back in the big Ford and removed her ponytail elastic. Twisting her hair tightly, Cassie let the water seep out of it and onto her soaked sundress. Before she started up the big truck, she reached over to the passenger side to flip over the album so she couldn't see the image of the man in the cowboy hat with his big hands poised solidly on Deborah Lacey's sexy hips.

With a deep sigh, she turned away from the LP's concerning presence and fixed an uneasy glance out of the driver's side window. Dal's tent was bowed to the wind. Cassie couldn't help but intuitively feel that it was offering up some kind of humble apology on behalf of its owner, but for what, she really didn't know. One thing was certain—the right gust of wind would carry it away. All the tent needed was one harsh, wild, unrestrained blow.

Clearing her throat with a decidedly unfeminine grunt, Cassie inhaled for courage, fixed her gaze on the furious wipers frantically clearing the rain from her window, slipped the Ford into drive, and ran its big tires backward through the muck that was now Dal's campsite. With a shiver, a cold stare straight ahead, and some careful maneuvering to turn the big rig around in the small lane, she powered her way through the storm up to the sanctuary of the Montana.

It was magic, Dallas couldn't deny that.

Singing with Deborah on stage was simply magical. Part of the allure was the particular ballad they were singing, the one that had skyrocketed to the top of the charts—crossing over onto the pop charts, at that—in a few short weeks. And part of the magic, Dallas understood wryly as Deborah grasped his sore fingers to accept their applause, was the reminder of what he'd thought the song represented when they wrote it—love. A love that, Dallas now knew, was only real on some sort of peripheral level.

Leaving the stage after brushing his lips against Deborah's ear and whispering a sincere, "Good luck," Dallas raised the bandaged hand one last time to the over stimulated, energized crowd. They would greet him once again in an hour, when he would entertain them with a full set.

A wafting, rainbow-like energy encircled Dallas during the walk off stage out of the range of the powerful stage lights, but its optimistic trail dissipated like weak smoke when he sauntered into the wings. The old all-too-familiar emptiness grasped at him with loathsome, probing claws.

Waiting for him, Phil was paying enough attention to be concerned. A defeated looking Dallas approached. "Here, Dal," Phil grunted, tossing his artist a water bottle that Dallas deftly caught with his good hand. Phil allowed Dal to stride by. Trailing behind, he followed him off stage and out to the large RV Dallas was using as his backstage green room during the concert. "It's okay, buddy," he said when they were both inside. "It's over now. It was really somethin', by the way. That ballad'll buy you an island in the Caribbean before its run is over."

Eyeing him warily, Dallas dropped glumly down onto a comfy wing chair by a tinted window at the far end of the trailer. Using a foot to propel himself around, he stared out at a drunk straggler stumbling toward a row of green port-a-potties situated just outside the VIP gate. Nearby, security was escorting a twenty-something man in handcuffs toward a tent set up across the parking lot. Watching, Dallas frowned. Alcohol and flared tempers… another seedy side of his concerts. A young gal was tearfully following the trio, a female police officer's hand on her elbow, guiding her.

Dallas turned the chair back around and focused on his friend. Phil's comment was right on the mark. The ballad had been divine, although it looked like the young couple on their way to the RCMP tent sure as hell likely didn't notice. "It was okay," he said honestly. "Singing the ballad with her. It felt all right. Like it was okay to let her go that way. To let us go."

"You're breaking a lot of hearts, Dal." Ankles crossed, Phil was leaning against a wooden chair propped up by a dining table. Using a thumb and forefinger, he absently scratched his chin.

"Doesn't matter," Dallas stated hotly, holding the man's gaze. "It's over. We were done before we started. What I had with Deb is not what I want."

"I won't ask what you're not saying."

Groaning, Dallas dipped his chin and looked at the toes of his boots. He rubbed one against the other, annoyed that the movement did nothing to scratch an itch on the toes inside. "I have to try," he admitted. "With Cassie. She's the real deal, Phil. Her and Ry. I want them in my life." He didn't add *I need them in my life*. But he sure as hell was thinking it.

"They're an illusion, Dallas." Speaking cautiously, Phil added, "They're sunsets and sandcastles and summer dreams. They're not real."

"What's not real is standing on that stage, Phil. That's the illusion." Grumbling, Dallas vaulted up and headed for the refrigerator. As expected, it was stocked to the hilt with his beer of choice. He tossed a canned brew to Phil before struggling to open his own with the sore fingers.

"Give it here," Phil ordered, taking the beer and flipping back the tab for his friend.

Dallas made a *pffftt* sound, took the beer out of Phil's outstretched hand, and tipped it back for a healthy swig. "You think you're in sync with everyone," he said after a generous few gulps. "With the band, with thousands of fans. With Deb, and maybe we were, when we were singing. But then you walk off stage and what have you got? Nothing. And nobody. That's what." His voice softened. "I'm making a play for her, Phil. I have to at least try."

"Dallas…" Phil hadn't opened his own beer. With a small thud he'd set it on the table behind him before he flipped back the tab on Dal's brew. Now, he twisted halfway around to fully face his friend. "The ballad…out there…" Waving his arm to signify that he meant the craziness Dallas had just left behind, he said quietly, "You know it's already hit social media. YouTube. It's already been posted, buddy. We're living in a world of instant news."

"I know what you're thinking, Phil." Dallas pointed his cold beer at his friend. "But she doesn't have a clue. She won't be looking."

Phil's sudden silence was disconcerting. Tingles pricked their way up the back of Dallas' neck. The hairs on his arms stood up, and he bristled. His voice dropped to a tentative low grumble. "What the hell aren't you telling me, Phil?"

Shrugging, Phil tapped a finger against the table and stared at the unopened beer can. In the end he decided to just spit it out. "North Shore Music Festival wanted a statement, pal. So I gave 'em one." He nodded toward Dallas' bandaged hand.

"What? What the hell?" Raising the sore wrist, Dallas stared at Phil in confusion. "Tell me you didn't give me away. Tell me Castle Beach is still my…my…" He couldn't say the word *sanctuary*. He couldn't tell Phil what the Prince Edward Island paradise had come to mean to him—that it was a place of refuge, a place to heal, a place that nurtured and calmed his troubled soul.

Phil shuffled his feet and pushed at the beer can so it slid a few inches and left a wet, damp trail. He couldn't meet Dal's eyes. He dreaded what he would see there—fear. Fear of losing the little bit of security Dallas had gained, fear of losing…Cassie. "I emailed them a statement telling them you would not be playing guitar in Cavendish. I told them you hurt your hand in a bike accident." Holding up his fingers to represent quotes, Phil said the word 'bike' with enough emphasis to suggest that the meaning could be interpreted in more than one way.

Dallas clued in right away. "Ha. Well done, Phil. That's much more romantic and dangerous than saying some little kid swerved in front of me at a family campground." Tipping up the beer can, Dallas emptied a good half of it. His fingers were trembling. When Phil spoke again, Dallas left the can poised upward but he stopped drinking. When he lowered it, he swiped his good arm across his mouth to catch a few spilled droplets. Staring awkwardly at his buddy, he tried to come to terms with what the man was telling him. What it meant…what it could mean.

Phil was saying, "And I told them they could do a front page spread in the island papers. In Charlottetown and in Summerside—the Guardian and the Journal. So your fans would know what to expect."

"A…picture?" Dallas' voice was gruff. Afraid. "Did you send them a photo, Phil?" Both newspapers were featured prominently at the camp store at Castle Beach. Did Cassie buy them? No. For all Dallas knew, she read her hometown paper on her iPhone. A Halifax, Nova Scotia paper. Not an island one. But the chance of her not seeing the local papers when, for God's sake, she was simply buying a hot fudge sundae at the camp store, was slim. It was possible…she might not be in the store the day the story about him was published…but it was slim. Cassie liked her ice cream. And the papers were right there, for God's sake. On a stand in plain friggin' view.

"Front page?" he gasped, just to be sure.

"I'm sorry, bud. I thought…"

"You thought I would come back here and take up with Deborah again. That's what you thought."

Phil shrugged. "I hoped…that's all. This lady of yours from that magical place does not fit in your world, Dallas. How many times do I have to tell you this? Stop fooling yourself!"

"This is not—my—world!" Dallas shoved his beer can in Phil's chest and spat out the statement, which shocked the wiry man into a furor.

Phil grabbed the brim of his fedora and shoved it down hard before answering, "Bullshit! You'd be lost without music." His eyes sparked fire.

"I have music! In here," Dallas yelled, pointing back at himself and spilling his beer in the sudden movement. "It's in me. It doesn't have to be for anyone but me."

"Don't threaten me, Dallas."

Eyes widening, Dallas stuttered out his response. "You think I'll leave? Is that what you're scared of? No more big paychecks?"

"No! Damn it, Dallas, I just don't want you to get hurt *again*. That's all! I saw the way you were with her, with Cassie. You think I didn't notice your droopy starry-eyes when we went to dinner?"

"Again?" The thought of it floored Dallas. Yeah, it had hurt like hell when he found Deborah in bed with his friend, but on every level Dallas knew her misguided actions were no more than a ploy at the time. A cry for help in some ways, from a woman who was begging him to love her. Losing Cassie...well, that would be a whole other hurt on an entirely different level. Like...on a Grand Old Opry level. Deborah was some redneck honky-tonk in southern Georgia.

Losing Cassie would destroy Dallas.

"O-ohh," he managed with a stutter, and leaned back against the fridge. "All right. I get your point."

The tension gone like a clearing sky after a storm, Phil too, settled, leveraging his butt back against the wooden chair and swinging his beer up to finally flip back the tab and take a drink. "I'm sorry," he said with an amicable dip of the beer in Dallas' general direction. "I wasn't thinking when I told the papers they could run that picture on the front page."

"No worries," Dallas gulped. "Look, Phil," he rallied. "Gimme some time to myself, will you? I should...well..." Pulling his phone out of a pocket of the leather jacket, he held it up. "I should call her. Just in case."

Phil hesitated before answering. "I'm not sure that's such a good idea, Dal. You're on in less than an hour."

"Don't worry," Dallas assured him. "I've been a robot many times out there. I can be one again." The false bravery wasn't lost on Phil. Dallas' voice was the manager's specialty. There was a lingering fear there, and it showed up in a slight quaver.

"Uh-huh." Grimacing, Phil raised his beer, flipped around, and strolled across the small kitchen out of the trailer. He shoved the door closed behind him.

"Please be there," Dallas implored under his breath. He tapped on Cassie's name. "I need to hear your voice. I need that strength of yours." She had it; she had strength. For him, for Dallas. Just not always for herself...

The phone rang three times before Cassie's harried voice lit up the line.

At the far end of the RV, Dallas sank back into the comfortable chair and hung his head. He almost cried with relief.

"Cassie, I—"

Laughing, she cut him off. "It's storming like crazy here, Dal! Thunder and lightning. It comes and goes, but right now I can't even see the trailer next to me! And the Basin is a wall of haze. I can't see across to the other side. It's all foggy and ghostlike!" In the Montana, Cassie used two fingers to separate the living room blinds so she could see outside. True enough, the earlier calm must have been the eye of the storm. The malevolent chaos had started up again in royal fashion, eliciting terror at every insane clap of thunder.

"Cassie, I just have a few minutes…"

Something in his voice made its way past Cassie's fright. She sobered. "Dal, are you okay? You sound funny." The LP crossed her mind, but it seemed to Cassie that bringing it up over the phone would not be one of her more stellar ideas. It would wait. After all, the record was his personal property.

"I'm…fine. I'm just—"

Cassie screamed, cutting him off for the second time. Like a wave, ear-splitting thunder crested before fading into the distance. "I'm not so comfortable on the phone right now, Dal," she moaned. "Memories of my childhood, I guess. I've closed all the windows in here but I remember my mom saying not to be on the phone during an electrical storm. Is it the same with cell phones?"

So, you're not onto me yet, onto my…summer charade. Taking a deep breath, Dallas let it out slowly; it emerged in a relieved stream of barely contained nerves. Wisely, he chose to focus on Cassie's fear instead of on his. "You're really scared, Cassie?"

"Jesus, yes. I wish you were here, Dal. I'm about to pee my pants."

A small smile lit up his tired eyes. "Sweetheart," he started, loving her for her honesty, for her ability to ache for him over the phone instead of putting up a phony front about the scary storm, "Cassie, honey, wrap yourself up in your duvet and think about me and Ry. It'll pass."

"I went down to your site. I got some of your things, blankets and stuff. They were getting wet, Dal."

Tears were not far behind the admission, Dallas could tell. Cassie's words were swollen and fearful. "Be brave, sweet girl," he murmured.

"I'm trying," she almost wept. Another crash, another scream. This time a few sobs snuck through. "I'm really not a very brave person, Dal. I've got my rubber boots on and I'm all hunched up now in the middle of the trailer, on the floor. I've got your hoodie on, too. I hope that's okay."

A small chuckle made its way to her. Dallas was about to take the stage again, to do his own set in front of thousands of die-hard Dallas White fans, and he was wishing to hell he was in a camper in Prince Edward Island with his girl in his arms so he could console her during a thunderstorm. It seemed that as far as Cassie was concerned, his heart was growing softer and less bitter every day. Where she was concerned, his simple existence was pure, divine gold.

"Little girl, you wear my hoodie all you like," he said, smiling at the image of her buried in it, likely with the hood up over her head and scrunched tight over her face, maybe with just the little petite nose he loved peeking out. "Cassie, look, picture me there holding you. We'll make love during the next storm. You can scream all you want and the neighbors won't hear you, not one bit."

It worked. A laugh snuck past her frightened tears. "Promise?" she whispered.

Dallas' whole body ached for the sweet pleasure of holding her, with or without actually making love. He just wanted to be in her company, to watch her bend over a sandcastle that Ry was carving and molding into shape, or watch her brow—lit by a sparking campfire and a lowering pink sun—furrow in concentration as she poked a marshmallow onto the end of a roasting stick. "Cassie, I—"

Another thunderous clap, one more scream, a little less painful in Dallas' ear this time. Her anxious voice came through the line. "Dal, I hate to go but I really ought to. My mother…what she said about lightning…"

He chuckled again. Wiped a worried hand over his forehead. "Okay, sweetheart. Be safe. But honey…my past…I'm ready to talk, okay? When I get back, can we talk?"

"Yes, yeah, okay Dal. I'm glad."

"Um, anything you hear before then…or read…whatever…in one ear and out the other, Cassie. Okay? Promise me?"

"Hmmm? What?"

Dallas cringed. Cassie was obviously simply too distracted to compute the directive at this time. He balked at the futility of his—their—situation. After a soft *I love you* that he doubted she heard, he sighed from the depths of his booted toes and let her go.

Later, standing in the wing of the stage watching the sound guys do a final band check, for strength Dallas pictured holding Cassie in the lightning storm. Wrapped up in his hoodie, she'd be trembling from fright, but he'd keep her safe in his arms.

The first chords of the set's intro tune thundered in Dallas' ears. He didn't move. A squeeze on his arm got his attention; pulled him out of the deep longing to be breathing in fresh salt air at a seaside paradise instead of almost hyperventilating at the stifling, muggy summer heat here. Turning, he wasn't surprised to see Deborah at his side. It seemed natural to accept a generous hug from her; it was just something they'd always done before his shows.

"Break a leg, honey," she whispered.

Surprised at the moisture in her eyes, Dallas gave her an extra squeeze and found himself relieved and grateful for the embrace that, for once, felt sincere.

"Thanks," he murmured back, holding her aloft so he could send her a sad smile.

Reaching out, she cupped his chin and bent forward for a light kiss. "I wish," she breathed, "that you could be happy, Dallas. What I would give to see you smile. Really smile," she added with a half wink. Placing his hand over her chest, she added, "From your heart."

"I will be," he said. "I almost am, Deb. I swear. I'm close."

The crowd was growing more rambunctious, their excitement palpable in the sticky Nashville warmth. Dallas recalled the old days when he was starting out in the crazy country music game—when he used to look forward to taking the stage. When adrenaline rushed through his body and sent him out with both guns blazing. Now he just felt heavy, leaden. Today, singing was work. Today he ached to have a pretty Canadian woman by his side, the same way he felt Cassie would like to have him close by during the crazy summer storm.

The melody built, and it was time to move forward. Letting go of Deborah's hand, Dallas caught Phil's calm eye just before he moved onto the stage. He lost contact when a tech distracted him by thrusting a microphone into his good hand. The crowd went nuts the second they spotted Dallas, hollering their appreciation in a cacophony of accolades and praises.

The noise was deafening.

Like thunder.

Raising the mic to sing, feeling exposed and naked without his guitar, Dallas pictured what it would be like to have Cassie along for a big show like this one. *Afterward, after the final song ends with a satisfied twang, we would retreat to our hotel room, and lie on the big bed and make love all night, immune to the storms raging around us. Immune to storms like this one, with its frenzied people filled with false hopes all wanting things that don't matter, while, buried so deep inside they rarely acknowledge it, they long for things that do.*

He sang, imbuing an undertone of secret love in his lyrics meant specially for a frightened woman currently riding out a storm by huddling in the center of a camper. Desire passed over his lips and trembled in his body. Each song brought him one step closer to Cassie. Dallas got through the Nashville show with a determined resolve, each tune cemented by the burning need to tell her the truth, to hold her hands and explain his world to her—a world Dallas hoped he could help Cassie understand was not all about glamour and material success, and that instead was sometimes confusing and frightening, often leaving him feeling bereft and lonely.

When the big ole stage lights finally went out, Phil accompanied Dallas back to their hotel. They shared a quiet nightcap before promising to meet for breakfast in the morning. Finally, alone under the covers of his large bed, Dallas closed his eyes and drifted into a restless sleep, nudged there by the sweet promise of soon fading into peaceful slumber under starlit skies, his hand resting on the slender hip of his pretty Nova Scotia girl.

Chapter Sixteen

*I*t was inevitable. One storm ended and another began when Cassie saw the front-page article in one of the local papers. Her world didn't come crashing down the way Dallas feared it might, by a random glance at the camp store newspaper rack. Nope, in the end Cassie was alerted to Dal's deception by overhearing a chat on the beach.

Bored, missing Ry and Dal, she was on her knees testing her sandcastle building skills by dropping wet sand into tiny, pointed piles to create random trees. It was the day after Dallas' concert in Nashville, a travel day for him. While Cassie played in the sand, Dallas was flying by private jet—with Deborah, a last minute add-on passenger—to Louisville, Missouri for the second concert he promised Phil he would do on this trip.

Not that Cassie knew this. What she did know was that some of the sandcastle skills Ry and Dal practiced regularly had evidently morphed over to her, as did the disciplined way the boys went about practicing each particular technique. The trees were Cassie's third skill in an hour. In her heart she figured it'd be a nice surprise for her fellas if she joined in on their next castle-making session. These days, building sandcastles on the beach was making more sense to her.

"Just make 'em sturdy and don't push too hard," she said half in jest to a watching seagull as she reached over to an earlier built wall to straighten an edge. "Oh, poop." Frowning, she sat back and gave it a hopeless glare when it cracked under her fingers. "I hope that's not a sign." To her, the castles were Dal. They were never a thing between her and Eddie. He was a do-er, a beach walker, a stunt kite flyer, a kayaker. Eddie was always doing, doing, doing.

Sometimes, Cassie recalled now, considering Dal's proven patience with contained creative activities, Eddie was a kind of superman. Occasionally he was hard to keep up with. Sometimes he was downright exhausting.

"You, little castle," Cassie mused, leaning forward to remold the damaged wall, "will survive. I will build you one section at a time. I will plant one tree on you at a time."

Suddenly a name uttered on the breeze caught her attention. She paused, held her hands in forced, steady stillness over her sandy wall, and tuned in to a nearby conversation. She'd heard the name Dallas White. Tilting her head so she could hear better, since it was a name that had intrigued her since finding the LP in Dal's tent yesterday during the storm, she strained to listen. The day was blistering hot, 'a three-sunscreen day,' Cassie called it due to the multiple applications her pale skin required, especially when numerous brief dips to cool off in the Atlantic were necessary. Hot afternoons, especially on weekend days like today, meant that the beach was congested with colorful umbrellas and the tons of folks gathered under and around them. Dogs, babies, water toys—it was a joy to see everyone having fun hanging out together. But, truth be told, Cassie preferred a little space on the beach. Some sand to herself. Today, everyone was practically on top of each other.

Including the nearby folks now chatting about the upcoming North Shore Music Festival in nearby Cavendish.

"Is he still playing? Tell me he's still coming!" A young mom was practically quaking, one hand poised over a forgotten bag of barbecue chips balanced in the opposite hand.

An exasperated male voice cut in. "Chill, Skyla. Yes, your celebrity crush is still coming. He just won't be playing guitar."

"Why the hell not?"

The guy flipped his iPhone around and shoved it in his wife's face. "This is why not."

Watching, trying not to appear as if she was overtly eavesdropping, Cassie wished she could see the photo. A chill ran up her spine when the young woman's voice sent warning signals racing through Cassie's brain, flashing way too brightly, like yesterday's lightning, raw and frightening.

"His hand is messed uppppp!" Skyla, a pleasantly plump brunette, was downright wailing.

The caterwauling annoyed her husband, who took the phone back and read the rest of the iPhone article to himself until Skyla pissed him off further by kicking sand on him.

"Do you mind?" he growled.

Impatient, Cassie butted in. "Um, excuse me…?" Her heart was racing. "Are you talking about Dallas White? The country singer? Um…I'm sorry if I'm interrupting."

"It's fine." Skyla tossed the chip bag to her hubby and grabbed the phone from his pudgy, begrudging fingers. "And yes, we are. Jeff here scared the shit out of me. We only got tickets so we could see Dallas and Deborah."

"And…" Cassie hesitated. This was over-the-top weird. Reminding herself that she was nuts to even consider that Dal was Dallas, that the name and the country music and the LP and the damaged hand were all just some bizarre coincidence, she mustered up her courage—and curiosity—and pushed ahead. "And he hurt his hand…um, how?" Her voice emerged strangely high and pitchy. "Does it say how?"

"It says in a bike accident."

"An…um…a bike accident? Like, uh, a motorbike, right?"

Skyla squinted at the small screen. Munching casually on chips, her husband offered the bag to Cassie, who held up a hand as a 'no' with a small, absent smile. "It says here," Skyla read, "that Dallas White's manager Phil Lexington offered an explanation."

Phil…a wave of dizziness passed over Cassie. Sitting back, she grasped hopelessly at the sand and waited.

Skyla went on. "The bike skidded, Dallas reached out as it went over, he sprained his wrist and twisted some fingers. No other injuries were sustained in the accident, which Lexington considers a minor inconvenience more than anything, although he says his artist apologizes for letting down fans who were hoping to see him play as well as sing." She looked up at Cassie, wisdom and apparently a candid intimate knowledge of Dallas White giving her a superior, confident air as she spoke. "The man can really riff. It's sexy as hell. His guitar playing blows my mind."

"Not at the North Shore Festival, it won't," Jeff said with authority, shoving a handful of chips in his mouth. He grinned at Cassie as he munched. "Bike accident."

"So I hear." Swinging around so she could face the couple more head on, Cassie appealed to their friendly banter. "Does it say anything else about him? About, like, where he's touring now?"

"You're a fan? Do you have tix for the Festival?" Skyla was tickled to find a female friend she could swoon over Dallas with. If she had any idea that the object of her desire, and of many X-rated fantasies, had built sandcastles pretty much where she was sitting, she would have lost her shit then and there. But as it was, she was not in the know. Nor was Cassie fully…yet.

"Um, I don't, no. I'm not really into country music. But," Cassie waved at the iPhone, "I'd be living under a rock not to know about him. I've heard his name."

"You've likely heard the ballad too, then. It's been number one on both the country and pop charts for weeks."

"A duet with Deborah. Recorded before they broke up," Jeff piped up. "Pretty saccharine stuff, if you ask me. But Skyla likes it, so…" He winked at his lady.

Skyla sent him a wide smile. "Jeff lets me crank it in the car. He's good that way."

"Um…so when did they break up?" *Can't hurt to ask,* Cassie considered. Even though she was still certain there was no way…

"About six weeks ago. Deborah messed with his friend IN HIS BED. IN HIS HOTEL ROOM. Can you believe that? What a bitch. She broke his heart. Poor Dallas."

Leaning forward in his beach chair, Jeff pointed the chip bag at Cassie. "Secretly, Skyla's stoked. Her favorite country singer is supposedly single again. She'd toss me into the ocean for a chance at him. I'd be fish bait before you could call 9-1-1."

"I wouldn't be calling for help. I'd toss the phone over too," Skyla laughed outright.

Cassie couldn't bring herself to smile. "Um, can I see the photo of him? On your phone?"

"Sure." Wrinkling her brow, Skyla handed the phone over. "You might need to come under the umbrella. It might be hard to see in the daylight."

Ignoring her, Cassie shielded the screen with one hand. Her heart was thumping uncontrollably now, racing like a car on the Nascar circuit. The picture of Dallas White showed a hurt hand, all right, all bandaged up. But Cassie still couldn't accept that this was her beachy sandcastle man. Her son's guitar tutor. Not until she glanced up and saw, under the cowboy hat, the pale eyes she'd grown to trust and love, and the longish, layered hair that gave Dal the wild look that made her knees buckle. Problem was, there was more to the cover picture than just the man Cassie had surrendered her heart to. The article featured a thumbnail image. Squinting, widening it with her thumb and forefinger, already squeezing her eyes tightly shut so she wouldn't cry in front of these two strangers, Cassie opened them a moment later to see Dal—her Dal—in an intimate pose with his ex-fiancée. Nose to nose, Deborah's eyes were locked on him, and Dallas' were alight. According to the caption, the picture was taken at last night's concert.

"Oh, J-J-Jesus," Cassie stammered, to the surprise of Skyla and Jeff.

"What? Did I miss something? Are you okay?" Skyla reached for the phone that Cassie held out to her as Cassie stood on wobbly legs and started gathering her things.

Shaking her head, unable to speak, Cassie tried to smile a thank you at the couple, but it came out crooked. Grabbing her flip-flops, she turned to head toward the wooden ramp that led up to the campground, but as she did so she spotted the sandcastle bits she'd been molding earlier. With a great cry, she stomped her dreams to sandy mush before fixing her gaze back on Skyla. "You didn't tell me where he is now. Where is Dallas White now?"

Towering above Skyla, Cassie was obviously shaken. Rising, Skyla stared at her in silence.

Jeff answered instead. "He played in Nashville last night. He's on his way to Louisville for a show."

Guess I'll check my cellphone records. See where that call was from last night during the storm. "And when's...when's the North Shore Festival? The one in Cavendish?" Cassie managed. "It's soon, right?"

"Next weekend."

"And this Deborah singer will be there? Is she…is she with him now? At the Nashville and Louisville shows?"

"Hell, yeah. They did their duet last night. That's when this pic was taken. There are videos all over YouTube. People are thinking maybe they're getting back together. Lady…are you okay?"

"Not feeling so good," Cassie mumbled. "Too much sun."

"Drink some water and get some shade. Maybe we'll see you in Cavendish."

"Nope." She moved to go. "Like I said, I'm no country music fan. In fact," she rallied, waving a flip-flop at the two as she considered just how much alcohol she would need to get past this shock, "I fucking hate it. Too much damn heartbreak in it, you know?"

Tears did not slip down Cassie's tanned cheeks until she sat in front of her own computer back in the Montana, not even taking off her wet bathing suit and showering first like she usually did before surfing the net. She cried in silence, one big teardrop following another as she watched the man she knew as Dal sing a love ballad with his ex-fiancée, gazing into her eyes while Deborah held his bruised fingers, the fingers Cassie had let intimately touch and tease her, that brought her to the most amazing, beautiful climax here in Prince Edward Island—in this very camper—just a few short nights ago.

"It can't be. It can't be him." But it was. Cassie's Dal was Dallas White, often the object of entertainment biz gossip and speculation. Dal had been very cautious about his past. Cassie had prided herself on giving him the time and space to reveal his story on his own terms, but this was too much. *Obviously,* she considered, *he didn't want me to know. Caroline was right. I'm no more than a summer plaything. This whole thing, him living here…in a tent, for God's sake…hiding under a ball cap…it's just a game to him. Research, maybe, for some damn song.*

Deborah landed in Cassie's muddied brain and settled there. So the woman had broken Dal's heart. It made sense. He was here to hide. And now…now he was singing with the woman, likely getting back together with her for all Cassie knew. Cassie was no more than a toy.

As if to clear the cobwebs in her brain, Cassie shook her head. *It doesn't matter,* she scolded herself. *He's a big star. It's not like I'd have a chance with him anyway!*

Moaning, clutching her stomach, she clawed her way up to the Montana's small bathroom on her hands and knees. Retching into the toilet, Cassie let out a wail. This was too much to process. She wanted something to ease the pain, and she found it in an emergency stash of prescription Ativan. When Dallas called later that night, ten minutes after Ry and Caroline called and wondered why Cassie didn't answer, she was fast asleep in a world where Eddie was holding her hand. In her dreams she was sauntering down the beach with him, wading into a glorious sunset that eventually became a roaring fire. Eddie disappeared. Cassie screamed, then Dallas was there in the dream, reaching for her hand. The fire became stage lights. Cassie found herself the object of scorn amongst Dallas White concertgoers, who threw eggs at her and who chanted Deborah's name until Deborah herself appeared at Dallas' side and viciously laughed at Cassie for her naiveté.

Cassie rolled over once, onto a part of her pillow that was dry, while, settled in a nondescript random hotel suite in Louisville, Dallas fell asleep on an overstuffed couch and dreamed that he was plucking Ry from between waves again, but Ry became Cassie and he couldn't reach her. Cassie sank beneath the salty spray; Deborah was suddenly there, pulling Dallas back, holding him tightly against her sensuous, curvy body. Loving him, whispering soothing things he couldn't make out.

Dallas woke with a kink in his neck just as the sun peeked over the horizon. After checking his phone—no messages from Cassie—he dragged his weary body to bed. When Phil dropped in on him later he found his singer fully dressed, boots included, hugging a pillow, his blond hair masking a knowing fear.

Chapter Seventeen

"*H*ere, Cassie. Lemongrass tea."

Carefully accepting a scalding hot blue pottery mug from her sister, Cassie nodded a quiet thank you. She was sitting by the pool in the backyard of Caroline's summer home, a modern two story behemoth that Cassie relentlessly teased her about because, in her opinion, the place totally transcended the definition of cottage. It had every appliance and then some, including an expensive Italian built espresso machine that Cassie was certain neither Caroline nor Des had a clue how to work. Hence the tea.

"It'll calm your nerves," Caroline ascertained with an almost arrogant confidence. She eased down onto the end of Cassie's lounger and faced her. It was the only way Caroline figured Cassie would meet her eyes.

She was wrong. Cassie just stared at her mug and wrapped white fingers around it.

Suppressing the urge to lift the mug and put it to her sister's lips, as if the tea could instantly perk Cassie up the way water revitalized the often limp pink petunias at Caroline's front door, Caroline said, "Cas, look, at the very least he got you back into the dating world. I hope you got some good O's out of him."

"O's? For Heaven's sake, Caroline." Cassie hunkered deeper over her tea, her spine curving into a woebegone C. Beyond her sister's shoulder, a loud whoop was followed by a splash.

Straightening instantly, Caroline yelped and laughed. "He got me. I'm soaked. Ry's let loose this summer, Cassie. I've never seen him so relaxed and happy."

A steely look accompanied by downward slanted eyebrows landed on Caroline, threatening her with a more dominant enemy than Ry and cool pool water.

Caroline threw up her arms. "What? Oh. I suppose you figure Ry's doing better because he's been here with me for a bit. Well I've got news for you, Cas. Apart from worrying about you, which all young boys do where single mothers are concerned, he came to me quite animated and engaged in the world around him. I think you can thank Dal for that."

"Good," Cassie remarked sharply. "Let's just see how long the happy pill lasts."

Cassie had yet to take a drink of her soothing tea. Pursing her perfect lips, Caroline lifted a dainty finger and pushed the mug toward her moping sister. With a heavy sigh, Cassie reached toward a butter yellow and indigo blue glass mosaic table at her side and set the mug down. She'd jumped and spilled a few drops when Ry made his grand entrance into the pool, and decided she didn't need to chance more hot water spilling over her. The hot tears trickling down her cheeks like summer rain were plenty in that department.

Caroline shifted her butt on the comfortable chaise. Cassie tensed. Her sister was getting serious.

"Cassie, I saw your phone this morning when you were in the shower. When I left that cinnamon roll in your room."

Eyes narrowing, Cassie warned, "You better not have answered it if it rang."

"I see. He's called that many times, has he? Enough so that you think a call may have come in when you were showering?"

Sitting back against the poolside chaise, Cassie looked away. Her eyes caught Ry's slicked back swim-surf hair. He could have been Dal's son, not Eddie's, who was dark and more sturdily built than the soulful singer. Still, it raised Cassie's interest to note that Ry, when not weighed down by life, had Eddie's playful side. In the pool, he and a young neighbor he'd befriended were trying to stand on their child-sized body boards so they could jump off. The more times they fell off and went flailing into the water, the more determined they were to succeed. Cassie couldn't avoid a small smile when

Ry finally stood on his, albeit for the briefest of seconds. He celebrated his accomplishment with another loud whoop and a pumping fist.

"He's been calling," she admitted to Caroline, refocusing on the acute betrayal that made her suck in her gut with remembrance. "I just don't know what to say to him, Caroline."

"How about 'Hey Dal, what's up?'" Touching her sister's knee, Caroline treated Cassie to an empathetic smile instead of the bossy no-nonsense firm 'git-off-yer-butt-life's-meant-to-be-lived' face she gifted her with earlier. "Cassie, he's reaching out to you for a reason. Whatever it is—an apology, a goodbye, an explanation—the man has something to say to you. Regardless of the message, I think you'd feel better to hear it. You parted on good terms, right?"

A begrudging nod was Cassie's answer.

Caroline laid a warm hand on Cassie's wrist. "Then you're jumping to conclusions thinking of him as a sinking ship."

Like a yellow caution light at a busy intersection, the signed vinyl LP crossed Cassie's mind.

Caroline caught the look, which was somewhere between hope and despair. "What?" she asked simply.

"I always felt he was hiding something, Caroline. Or running from someone," Cassie admitted.

"That Deborah woman. He was supposed to marry her until…" Caroline let the ugly truth sink into the humid day. A light breeze came up once in a while, offering a modicum of relief, but not often enough. A swim would do the trick. Once the boys—and Cassie—were a little more settled, Caroline would take a dip. Des was away again. Caroline smiled. The day bloomed before her like a prized rose. Swim, drink, lunch at one of the trendy cafes downtown…a sister…no matter how gloomy, Cassie was a blessing to have around. Caroline adored her sisterly role. It was good to feel needed. It was a gift having the newly effervescent Ry bouncing around the house, injecting a sweet energy into the staid, formally decorated summer home. Now to help Cassie get over her blues…

Secretly, Caroline got a kick out of Dal's true identity. Inside, she was as bubbly as Ry, who had yet to know the truth about his sandcastle-building buddy. A famous singer? Interested in Caroline's sister? Apart from the raw hurt that Dal's secret unleashed on Cassie, Caroline was tickled pink. Dallas White had played at one of Des' big political fundraisers. A flush rose in Caroline's cheeks at the memory. She loved her husband, but there was something about flirting with a man and seeing attraction color his eyes, that was very—well, comforting—as a woman aged. She had thought she caught Dallas' eye that night, but only on a fun minor level. A game…that flirtation had been a game. Not much wonder there was some recognition when she first met Dal at the beach. It was the eyes she remembered. Dal's eyes were as pale as a full moon, and as soulful and wise as a man who'd lived many lives.

But Cassie? Cassie was a wounded baby bird. So was the Dallas White that Cassie had introduced Caroline to at the beach. Rethinking that, she decided that Dal was more like a lonely puppy—playful, in search of unconditional love, but filled rather sorrowfully with secrets that prevented him from getting what he wanted and needed. Remembering the obvious sadness in the man's quiet countenance, Caroline adjusted her thoughts to recall the warmth that replaced the sadness when he laid his beautiful, pensive eyes on her sister. And on Ry. More than once, Caroline had caught Dallas resting a thoughtful gaze on the two, as if he was sitting outside some transparent bubble just taking them in. His expression at those times had stopped Caroline in mid-sentence. The man was clearly smitten with the two of them. That particular day his lips were slightly parted and his eyes were searching, wondering. Dreaming, maybe…a little bit scared…

At the time, his little-boy-lost look had jarred and unnerved Caroline.

A warning. It was a warning that had breezed over her then, like today's light breathy fresh gusts, only more piqued and dangerous. Because at that point Dal was a roguish man living in a tent, keeping secrets that somehow tied in to his career as a musician, playing in what Caroline and Cassie figured were a string of seedy roadside bars. Mystery and intrigue surrounded him, but not really in a dangerous way. His secrets? *Well, you don't get to forty without some kind of baggage,* Caroline mused, studying the heartache on her sister's face now. Relationships, finances, life… They'd thought at the time that maybe Dal was hiding, sure, but his devotion to Cassie and Ry was clear. Caroline's overriding question when she realized with a start that her sister was smitten with him was whether he had anything positive to offer a single mother and her son besides romance and sex. A man had certain obligations when he hooked up with a woman, and those obligations deepened when a young boy was part of the package. Cassie was financially stable, but still… a seedy musician could easily take advantage of that, and use a kid to secure a 'home' or, at the very least, shelter for an upcoming frigid Canadian winter.

But now…well, if 'Dal from the beach' was actually 'Dallas the famous country star,' that concern no longer applied. The guy didn't need financial security from Cassie. He had that, in spades. What the heartbroken, jilted man really needed, was love.

Caroline's thoughts were crisscrossing her face like the soft yellow beams of a wandering searchlight. Wrinkling her eyebrows, Cassie watched her relax into some happy place. "What?" she asked pointedly.

Patting her sister's knee, Caroline said, "It's hot, Cas. Hot, hot, sweaty hot. Sticky, even. Let's swim. After, when you're cool and comfortable, you'll call this man of yours."

"He's not mine." The statement was a throaty growl. But Caroline knew her sister well. Underneath were raw worry and a healthy dose of belligerent hurt.

"You sure about that, Cassie?" Caroline glanced down at the mosaic table. Cassie's cellphone was vibrating, making a distinct smattering sound against the bits of yellow and blue glass. The caller ID read *Dal.*

Caroline waited only thirty seconds before she grabbed it and bolted to the far end of the pool. Crying out, Cassie jumped up on her knees but she didn't follow her bossy sibling. She did, however, tilt her head to listen.

"Hello, Cassie's answering service," came Caroline's singsong voice from beside a drooping row of large violet hydrangeas. "How can I help you?" Fingering a flower, she winked back at Cassie. A wide smile crossed her face. Groaning, Cassie rose from the chaise. She wandered over to a neatly coiled hose and flipped on the tap. Watering the hydrangeas seemed a good excuse to eavesdrop just a little bit closer, and if Caroline stepped out of line, well, she might just get a good watering of her own.

In Louisville, about to board the jet for Toronto to drop Phil off before heading back to Prince Edward Island, Dallas was pacing the tarmac with a hand on his hip. "Uh…Caroline?" he asked tentatively, worry knotting his heart. Her greeting seemed flip and chipper, so he exhaled slowly and tried to relax. If something had happened to Cassie, if she had sunk back into a depressed need to sleep, Caroline wouldn't be playing around with Cassie's phone. He knew the woman had the capacity to demand respect should she need it, from anyone. Even his superstar ass was not immune to being a target of her acerbic, clipped voice.

"Well, well, well," Caroline started, friendly enough, and not even remotely surprised at hearing Dal on the line. What did surprise her, at least a little, though, was the worry his husky voice was telegraphing from wherever in the world he was calling from. "If it isn't the traveling minstrel that's stolen my sister's heart. And broken it with lies and untruths, I might add."

Emitting a long, thoughtful *pfffttt,* Dallas bit his lip and stared at Phil, who was standing by the jet sending him his own version of worry—in his case, furrowed brows and crossed arms, one foot resting on the jet's bottom step. "So. She knows. And by the way, I never lied to her."

"Yes, she knows," Caroline admitted, frowning at Cassie, who was aiming the watering hose dangerously close to Caroline's hand on the phone. Caroline sidestepped a few feet away before she continued. "And no, you may not have lied, but you had ample opportunity to speak up and tell her who you really are, Dal. Or should I call you Dallas?" The last part was bit off rather cruelly, but in a false kind of way since, inside, Caroline was respectfully beaming.

Dallas ignored the question. He skipped to the main point. "Caroline, look, my life is complicated, okay? And the more I got to know Cassie, the more it killed me to think about bringing her into this craziness, okay?"

"Oh." Reality zipped across Caroline's face. Like the excess sand trimmed away from the P.E.I. sandcastles, her sunny countenance vanished, quickly and without mercy. Caroline glanced over at Cassie before she wheeled around on one bare foot and fixed a worried, angry gaze on a spider weaving a web on her high wooden fence.

Watching her, Cassie slumped and ached. The hose dripped more water on the pool deck than it did on the suffering hydrangeas.

"So you're calling to say goodbye," Caroline added, distinctly avoiding her sister's frightened stare. "I suppose that takes a certain reserve of guts. I wouldn't expect that level of concern from a star of your stature, Dallas. Should I get on my knees and thank you for your obvious kindness? Is that what you're accustomed to?"

Dal growled.

Caroline raised her head.

He spoke into an abbreviated silence. "Can I talk to her? Is she there?"

"She's here." Caroline waited. Cassie sucked in a breath and focused on a rivulet of water that was spewing from the hose and running over the deck.

"Put her on, Caroline. Please. I just need…I need…" Rubbing his forehead, Dallas couldn't finish.

"I'd almost think you really care about her. In another world though, right, Dallas?" Toeing the ground, Caroline sighed heavily. She'd had hope but now it seemed apparent that she would truly be left picking her sister up off the ground again. And Ry. Twisting at the waist to watch him play, she ached anew for the happy little boy splashing around her backyard pool.

Dallas summoned up some courage. "We need to talk. There are ways… Look, Caroline, I can protect her. And Ry. If she'll let me."

"Oh?" Caroline perked up. "But what about…Dal, the magazines, the blogs…they're all saying this Deborah woman broke your heart. That the ballad you sang together in Nashville and Louisville was your way of mending fences. She's on your level, right? In your world?" *God, I sound like I'm talking about a video game*, she sighed. *Not my sister's life.*

"Deborah did what she did because she didn't know any other way to reach me, Caroline. It hurt at the time, but let's just say that I've gained some perspective over the summer."

"So that's what living incognito at the beach was all about? Gaining perspective?" Caroline toed the water running from Cassie's hose, while Cassie remained quietly and frighteningly impassive.

"Yeah," Dallas jumped in hopefully. "Although Phil would say it was more like running away."

"Speaking of running." Caroline took the hose from her sister and dropped it onto the deck. She made her way to the outside faucet and twisted it counterclockwise to 'off.' "Summer on P.E.I. was that for Cassie, too," Caroline stated matter-of-factly. "More of a running away kind of thing." She watched Cassie make her dejected way back over to the chaise.

Dallas raised his eyebrows at the 'speaking of running' part, but he chose to bypass it. "Look, Caroline, I'm coming back," he said instead. "I'll be back tonight. Tell her, please, that I'm sorry. There just wasn't the right time to talk to her. It was kind of like if I said anything, our bubble would burst, you know? The magic."

A wistful smile at her despairing sister accompanied Caroline's solemn next thought. She continued her role as devil's advocate. "Maybe the magic was the sunsets and the ice cream and the place, Dal."

He cut in quickly. "No. No, I don't believe that. I mean, maybe the place conspired to help us recognize that we need each other, Caroline, but it was so much more than that. I need to talk to her in person, to explain."

A deep exhale preceded Caroline's, "Well, that could be tough. She spent most of today curled up in a ball by my pool."

"Nova Scotia? You're not at the campground?"

"She bolted, Dallas."

"Jesus, Caroline. Throw me a fucking ball here, will you?"

Trying not to sound surprised, Caroline softened. "You really care about her."

Dallas' throat thickened. Still, he managed a small, "Yeah. I do. I—I need her. And she needs me."

"I can't promise anything." Caroline ambled lightly over to her sister and sat on the end of the chaise.

"Just try. Let her digest all this. Look, I'll leave some tickets at the gate in Cavendish for you guys, for the North Shore Music Festival. How many? Will your husband come over? Kids?"

The hope in his voice relaxed Caroline further. She took Cassie's fingers in hers and squeezed. "Two. One for me and one for her. Des will be away, still, and Ry is too young to be around pot-smoking incorrigibles more interested in puking into garbage cans than in catching the music."

A wry laugh came through the line. "The truth emerges. The uptight Caroline has been to outdoor concerts."

"I've seen the seedy side to what it is you do. And don't get me started on your choice of musical genre." She smiled at her sister, whose shoulders noticeably sank at the reminder. Caroline held the phone out so Cassie could overhear more closely.

"Country's real, Caroline," he was saying. "It has its moments."

I bet, Cassie thought inwardly, the image of Deborah Lacey and Dal on the LP cover in her mind.

Caroline was having similar thoughts. "I'm not sure she's going to want to see those real moments live on stage, Dallas."

"The ballad? With Deb?" Dal sobered at what Cassie must be thinking. "It's okay. We've made our peace. Nothing's happening there. At least not on my side of the stage."

"You sure, honey?" Caroline asked cautiously. The politician's wife in her was sneaking out. *Step carefully,* she told herself as, next to her, Cassie visibly winced. "Because I don't think I can pick up pieces that big. Cassie's had her share of grief. If I can even get her there."

"Just bring her over. Let me worry about the rest."

"No promises, Dallas. I won't make a promise I can't guarantee I can keep."

Upon hearing that, Cassie woefully buried her head in her hands.

"I can accept that." Dallas' voice was infused with hope, which worried Caroline. Suddenly she felt sorry for him, for the hurts that—she knew because she'd looked into those sad eyes—were very real despite the man's fame, and perhaps were earned by it.

After they disconnected, Caroline absently tapped the phone against her thigh. Lifting one of Cassie's arms to give her wrist a squeeze, she smiled wanly at the piqued expression lining her sister's face with worry. "You up for some shopping, sis?" she asked. "Looks like we need to git us some turd kickers." Leaning closer, she winked conspiratorially. "In plain English, that'd be cowboy boots."

Shaking her head slowly from side to side, Cassie let her eyes widen. Her fear transmitted itself quite clearly over to Caroline. "N-nooo," she breathed. "I can't do country music."

"It's not about the music," Caroline grinned. "Sweetheart, it's about the man."

A tiny light flickered back on. Cassie licked her lips and sat up a little taller.

Raising her hand, Caroline touched a fingertip to the corner of one moist emerald eye. "Is that hope I see there, honey?"

"He's still Dal, right?" Cassie laid a palm over her sister's hand. "He's still the same guy I…" Biting her lip, she went silent.

"The same guy you fell in love with? Yes, Cassie. At least he sure sounded like the same lovesick guy. And I recall him saying just a few short moments ago that he needs you."

"I don't know, Caroline." The words *I'm sorry* scrawled in gold glittery ink across an LP cover darted through Cassie's mind. "What about Deborah?"

"Aw, you know these famous types. One bed to another." Caroline laughed with such infectious, robust amusement that even the boys in the water lit up.

"Lovely." Cassie hesitated, then added, "I'll think about it."

"You do that while I cool off with a swim." Standing, Caroline set the phone down on the mosaic table. She lifted a brightly striped sundress over her head. Underneath, her toned body showed off a petite aqua bikini that had earned her a lot of second looks on the beach in Prince Edward Island.

A couple of minutes later, Cassie slipped into the pool too, and swam over to her son. "Ry," she smiled nervously, gripping the edge of his body board, "how about you get on and I push you?"

He did, but Ry hugged his mother first. "Thanks, Mom. I'm glad you're feeling better."

"Me too," Cassie agreed. "Me too, Ry. I'm real glad."

She gave the board a gentle push after Ry made himself comfortable by straddling it and hanging on to the curved front edge. Soon Caroline had the young neighbor's board. Before long they were racing each other from one end to the other. It was almost a perfect day. The only person truly missed was Dal.

"Dallas," Cassie whispered, thinking about the man she loved, testing his full name on her lips. "I suppose I'm relieved that you're not on the run from the law. Or from a wife or family."

She took comfort in the fact that he still seemed interested in talking to her. Cassie would see her P.E.I. friend face-to-face soon. The biggest challenge would be to figure out how their two worlds could merge…

If, and when, they decided to try.

Chapter Eighteen

A sharp crack from inside Dallas' tent startled the industrious tan-breasted robin that was patiently poking at a worm in the lush grass underneath the picnic table. The angry snap was followed by three more cracks, the last generously accompanied by a few choice curse words. A determined *whoosh* later, and the robin scooted quickly away when the country singer emerged briskly through the flap of his tent into the great outdoors.

Clasped in the swollen fingers of Dallas' hurt hand was the cardboard LP cover Cassie had angrily tossed back on his quilt before hitting the road for her sister's place in Nova Scotia. In the other was the vinyl record itself or, well, what was left of it since it was now in pieces. In a deliberate move, Dallas dumped the jagged vinyl bits into a garbage bag in his mesh-walled kitchen shelter; shortly thereafter the album cover was heaved rather ungraciously onto a tented pile of kindling and wood-splits waiting in the campfire pit. A lit camp lighter—aimed like a pistol, its flame triggered by a worn, weary warrior—was mercilessly shoved into a ball of newspaper scrunched up underneath a corner of the kindling.

"Goodbye, Deborah," Dallas muttered to the flames. Sitting back on his haunches, he watched the fire take hold. Eddie crossed his mind. It was a weird feeling to see Deborah's image disappear into the smoke. In Dallas' mind, his ex needed to go away, and he needed to be the one to let go, even if it meant starting with a rather inglorious symbolic voodoo-inspired ceremonial burn. Picking up a long, thick stick, he heartlessly shoved the bit of her he could still see deeper into oblivion.

From up the sparse lane toward the wooden boardwalk leading to the main beach, Dallas was starting to hear a sporadic spattering of voices, accompanied by tire treads and the grating of plastic wagon wheels on dirt and gravel, and then on wood. The bright sun was arcing its way up high over the pristine Darnley Basin on the opposite side of the park. Today would be a hot island beach day, the relentless, sizzling, blazing heat kind that made outdoor eating of dripping ice cream cones an exercise in futility. The scorching white sand lining Prince Edward Island's entire north shore would soon be dotted with a maze of merry umbrellas. The cool Gulf would cheerfully welcome happy vacationers; judging by the increasing activity on the wooden ramp, some were already gracing its refreshing wavelets with paddleboards, kayaks and inflatable toys.

Dallas wasn't planning to join them. Not today; at least not via his usual lazy afternoon routine on such blistering hot days—swim, sunbathe, paddle and float, eat chips, drink beer, swim, suntan, float, suntan. A cool early morning dip was already in the books by this time (according to Dal's iPhone, which he had already checked a bunch of times, it was mid-morning now) and wrapped up with a restorative shower long before Deborah's cowgirl sex appeal disappeared into the unforgiving haze of sparks and smoke.

There was a healing peacefulness in Dallas' refreshing sunrise swim on the almost vacant beach earlier. The whispering waves had quietly beckoned him, the same way they called to a few other introspective folks too, with gently curling breakers and soft rippled *pooshes* sleepily exhaling their way to shore. The people on the beach at that early hour were, like Dallas, folks who understood—and needed—the simple meditative benefits of nature's restorative properties. Only a dog walker (today's token off-leash dog was some kind of border collie mutt with black spots on a white chest and a cute, perky white tip on its tail) and a jogger—an older, almost buzz-cutted gray-haired male likely running to some classic 70's music playlist, like maybe ACDC and Led Zeppelin tunes, Dallas considered with a wry grin as he watched the guy try to sing, breathe and jog at the same time—were cruising the sand when Dallas arced his palms together and plunged headfirst into the gentle surf. The water had warmed over the past few sultry weeks and was easier to dive recklessly into than in early July. Dallas cut through the gentle ripples with the grace and ease of an athlete, sinking into a quiet ecstasy as the water flowed around, under and over his lean, muscled body.

Over the summer he had discovered that swimming was an efficient and cathartic way to exercise, and today it seemed the universe agreed with him since the water was comfortably temperate. The barely-there waves facilitated an easy front crawl. As the sun rose higher over the ocean, the contented chug-chug-chug of distant fishing boats at work checking buoys and traps lulled Dallas into a hopeful harmony with the earth and the sea. Hungry seagulls swooped over the water, amazing Dallas at their ability to coast just over the surface, seeking breakfast, he figured. The water was relatively clear today, not all kelpy and seaweedy and murky like it usually was after a big wind. His feet touched on only a few football-sized sandstone rocks when he stood upright; huddled half-under and next to those were fist-sized crabs that occasionally abandoned their shelters and went out for scavenging scuttles across the ocean floor.

One cocky feller nipped at Dallas' toes, expressing its annoyance at his unwelcome invasion of its natural habitat. Dallas yelped, grinned at its audacity since he was many times larger than the crusty crustacean, then he wisely gave it a wide berth and launched himself above it with a quick dive and a strong stroke. Instead of cursing the crab 'this side of sideways' for its bold move, he chose not to disturb it or any of its bottom-dwelling mates. They lived life the same way he did; they were mere smoky images floating somewhere between earth and sky, solitary travellers that Dallas figured were not really connected to anyone or anything that really mattered.

Or maybe they aren't that way, disconnected like me, he later thought. *Maybe the crabs have buddies to scavenge with and mates to procreate with.* He hoped they did, because Dallas sure didn't feel linked to anyone or anything, which made for a lonely existence unless you counted the 'machine,' the good old country music star-making machine, that's all. When he was cutting through the ocean above the crabs, Dallas couldn't push away the niggling certainty that most of the time, he simply just felt alone.

Until petite, elegant, life-hardened Cassie and her soulful, sad, surfer-blonde son came so unexpectedly into his life.

She was coming back to the island today. Leaving her sister's gently nudging arms to head back to P.E.I.

Cassie would cruise over the indomitable Confederation Bridge later this afternoon. *She's leaving the womb,* Dallas thought now as he knelt in front of the flames. *She's in search of light, and she must believe she can find it here or she wouldn't be coming back.*

To him, the formidable bridge was a link to a sanctuary—a land-based one. But by piloting the big Ford onto Prince Edward Island's small rural roadways, Cassie would be taking an emotional risk, almost as if she were one degree removed from the curative golden canola fields and the rows upon rows of leafy green potato plants.

Still, Dallas was optimistic. He had to be. Picturesque red clay cliffs and dazzling ocean surrounded the island, which kind of made it feel like a nest— a safe, insulated place just like the nest above the men's washroom, the washroom where Dallas shaved every morning. That nest was perched oddly but contentedly on the small gray metal electrical box that sat above and beside the door to the washroom. For a while, two baby birds poked their heads up to greet him every morning—robins, likely, but now they were gone. He hoped and prayed they'd flown off to live rich and full lives, and that Cassie, too, would find it in herself to one day fly free with the joy of a happy and fulfilled life.

For now, though? Today? Well, Dallas barely dared hope that the emotional risk she would face the second her tires hit P.E.I. roads would be tempered with solace. Their island paradise would show them the way; Dallas had to believe that, because he sure as hell didn't know how Cassie would receive him without some kind of healing tie to the earth. And if she were even a little bit amenable to trying some kind of relationship with him, how would it work? How could it possibly work?

"It's not like I need the money," he told himself. "Or more awards. I can retire from music." But the nefarious thought chilled him. Despite his mixed feelings for the career choice that had set him on a surreal path to incredible success, Dallas couldn't fathom the thought of completely walking away. For one, music was and always would be a part of him. When he was on stage with Deborah in Nashville, a reminder of the energized reciprocal relationship between him as artist, and his fans, had come back to him. Silently, he thanked his ex for that. The magic was fleeting that night, but it was there. The unbearable loneliness assaulting him over the last few years was less acute, at least while he and Deb shared their hit ballad with the crowd.

"Because of you, Cassie," he sighed heavily. "Because I was seeing you while I was singing. That's why it felt better."

Grumbling at himself for sinking into a steadily growing despair while he tortured himself with scenarios that might play out later in the day, Dallas rose, wincing as his knees creaked. Grimacing at the knots in his joints, and cursing the interminable squats he'd done over the years that likely caused the creaking in the first place, he rubbed a knee and looked around his site. Over the summer his mark on the campsite had grown more complete. The tent had weather protection (to a point, he chuckled, remembering a particularly wet night a few weeks ago). He had a screened-in kitchen shelter, a pedal bike, a few coolers, a clothesline, camp chairs, and even two inflatable water rings with comfy backrests for days when the wind was down and he and Cassie could happily float about, holding hands and horsing around while they cooled off in the Gulf.

There was one other colorful bag that grabbed his attention now. A black and white striped durable zippered plastic bag was leaning with a casual nonchalance against one corner of the picnic table in the yellow-topped kitchen shelter, as if it was humbly asking him to notice it, to get it out into the light where its contents could work their magic.

"The sandcastle contest." Dallas had almost forgotten about it. He'd thought it meant something to Ry, and it had been meditative to spend hours honing his skills carving and molding piles of forgotten sand into miniature windows, doors, and once even a large angel with wings to guard a steep-roofed chapel. But Ry, according to Caroline's last text, was still on the fence about coming back over to P.E.I. with Cassie. She didn't say so, but Dallas instinctively knew the boy was unsure about being alone with his mother again. Did Ry know about Dallas' true identity? Dallas doubted it, but he wasn't sure. As far as the deep feelings between Ry's mother and the 'guitar-playing hobo' who lived in a small tent overlooking the beach, though, the kid had clued in, at least to a point. Ry's solemn eyes on their linked fingers and his curious, occasional half smiles cemented that hard fact.

There was something humbling about the sandcastle-building contest. Somehow it would punctuate the summer for Dallas. Castle Beach was famous for its sandcastles. Competitors would range from experienced carvers down to kids of all ages sporting multi-colored plastic shovels. He might be at the top of the country music world, but Dallas was a nobody in sandcastle world. He had nothing to prove, yet somehow that was the biggest attraction to participating in the competition. Would he compete alone if he had to? *Hell, yeah.* With or without Ry. With or without Cassie's usual comforting, watchful praise.

Dal's swim trunks, a new white pair with a blue water-wave motif at the lower hems, that tied in the front and almost reached his knees, were hanging from the line, drying next to a large blue Disney towel Cassie loaned him one day. She'd teased him when she handed it to him because Dallas had showed up on the beach with a small, plain, cream-colored face towel. *Not gonna dry much with that.* The light jibe had come with a cute wink.

"My towels are all in the wash," he'd said at the time, flushing with embarrassment, not realizing that Cassie found the pink that suddenly spotted his cheeks absolutely knee-melting adorable. The Disney towel was immediately his favorite. It and the castle building tools were the first things of Cassie's that had found a home at Dallas' campsite.

"All right," he rallied now, tossing aside his staggered thoughts and memories. "Work to do."

Glancing at his bike, which was leaning up against a tree at the rear of the small campsite, he decided against taking it. The truck was not an option, either. Dallas didn't need Cassie spotting the old rig, panicking, and motoring back up the small slope of the bay side never to see him again, and never dealing with their new reality. She may not see the bike if he placed it carefully against the outside of the windscreen by the Montana's deck, but Dallas decided the walk up from the main beach to the Darnley Basin side of the campground would do him good. At the very least it would hopefully settle his addled thoughts.

On the way, he dropped into the Castle Café to grab a coffee and a cinnamon roll. He gripped the coffee in his good hand and laid the plastic wrapped cinnamon bun on the white lid of the coffee cup, where it managed to stay without falling off. When he reached Cassie's deck he set them down on a small table and pulled out two sturdy deck chairs and their matching ottomans. Cassie had tucked the furniture against the windscreen for protection against the often blustery days. A large plastic storage trunk was cozied up to the trailer. Dallas opened the lid and retrieved the two patio cushions that he knew belonged on the chairs.

Settling into the newly cushioned chair nearest the camper's door, he propped his feet up on an ottoman and sipped on his coffee, alternating the sips with bites of the scrumptious plump cinnamon roll. As he ate he reflected on the fact that the Castle Café cinnamon rolls were rather famous. This did not in the least bit surprise him, since every bite of the warm dough elicited a satisfying *mmmm*. Silently he thanked the quiet woman behind the counter at the café. Her patient hand made the coveted rolls, which, due to popular demand, were almost always all gone by 9:30 in the morning.

In front of him on the Basin, a small two-man crew was navigating their long, narrow fishing boat with its large open back deck toward a set of mussel markers. Sighing with contentment at this easy way of life, feeling a small twinge of guilt at watching other men work hard for nowhere near the pay Dallas received for singing, he considered how blessed he really, truly was. It was a good life, his. Really it was. If not for the debilitating loneliness, it would be perfect. That perfection—and an ensuing eradication of the loneliness—would come via a woman who had gotten to know Dallas as Dal, who loved him despite thinking he was a down-on-his-luck roadside bar singer. Reflecting on that now, Dallas was humbled to think that it must have been a frightening reality for Cassie to consider, in truth.

Later, his snack and the tasty coffee consumed, Dallas puttered around Cassie's campsite. Making things seem normal was the least he thought he could do to welcome her back. He got busy rearranging the deck furniture to where he knew she best liked it. Grabbing the hose, he dutifully watered her baskets of flowers (hoping they'd perk up before she landed—they were awfully brown and sad looking, neglected and suffering in the heat, kinda like how Dallas felt at the campground without Cassie and Ry around). Trying to be patient but suffering at how slow the minutes seemed to be passing, he picked the dead brown bits off the flowers, then finally caved and opened up the Montana (the key was under a flowerpot—he'd once chided her for leaving it there where anyone could see her digging for it). Dallas opened each roof vent a little wider and let fresh air in through every window. As a last ditch attempt to stay busy and tidy up Cassie's site, he walked up the slope to a shed where he knew lawn equipment was stored for campers' use, retrieved a push lawn mower, hauled it back down the hill, and started mowing the lawn.

The oily old machine putt-putt-putted to a slow death before he got to the first corner.

"Damn it!" The rustic thing was out of gas. "Oh, for God's sake." The heat of the day was getting to him. Dallas wiped a sleeve across his forehead, propped both hands on his hips, and stared at the shed at the top of the slope. Shortly, he started back up the slope. He had the red plastic gas can in his hands before he realized it was chained to the shed. And the mower was...

"Jesus Christ!" Another walk down the slope. This one was more of a slow trudge on the stifling hot day. The air around Dallas was equally as overheated. Swearing was something he usually only did around his friends in the band and on the country music circuit. Somehow, Cassie was just too sweet to curse around. But she wasn't around at the moment...

The trailers Dallas passed were eerily empty. It seemed everyone was at the beach, except one small family who were barbecuing hot dogs and burgers. A large, rotund man waved at Dallas as he stalked by. He waved twice more when Dallas passed him on the uphill with the mower dragging behind, on the way up the slope, and again when Dallas cursed the air blue on his way back down the slope with a mower full of gas.

In late afternoon, Dallas sauntered back down to his campsite and changed into his trunks. The afternoon's ministrations to Cassie's site, and to his soul, had left him a sweaty mess. The 'time of mass exodus' at the beach, or 'the time of mass consumption,' as he teased Cassie, had passed, so there was less congestion, fewer umbrellas to navigate around. He took a cooling dip, showered in the public restrooms for the second time that day, changed into jeans, cowboy boots, a tight blue T-shirt with a small pocket over his heart, and wandered back toward Cassie's Montana. Stopping at the store on the way for sundries— orange juice, milk, potato salad, eggs, steak, veggies—he wandered down the bay side slope with two opaque gray plastic bags dangling from his good hand. Caroline had texted when Cassie left Lunenburg. Dallas had more time to kill. He made himself a meal at the Montana, then cleaned up after himself in the hopes that Cassie wouldn't throw a fit at his presence there.

"I don't think she will," he told himself with a spark of hope. "I'm still the same guy." He followed that thought with a quiet, "Damn it." The closer she was to landing back at Castle Beach, the closer Dallas was to breaking down completely.

Finishing his cleanup by hanging his dishtowel over the rack on the oven door to dry, he perched once again on the deck chair that, since he'd sat there so many times next to Cassie, somehow felt like his. Staring back out over the Basin, Dallas watched a fishing boat navigate the narrow channel toward safe harbor in nearby Malpeque, and realized Cassie had become an anchor for him. She was more than that, too. She was a light summer rain, a rainbow in the mist, a tether to the earth, a wise soul. Her touch was light and her calm presence was, simply, healing.

Reaching over to a small table to grab his phone, Dallas scrolled through the various pictures he'd taken over the summer. One stood out—it was one of their more recent sandcastles—almost perfect, in his opinion. The castle had become an entire walled village with intricate houses, trees in the front yards, a steepled church, gardens, and military parade grounds. Ry had even sculpted them a few animals, decorated the moat with damp, smelly seaweed, and lined the slightly arched bridge with white shell fragments.

Dallas texted the photo to Cassie.

Perhaps his bravado was fueled by the day's intimate work around her site, in the hope that the castle village would have the power to pull her back to him, to remind Cassie that Dallas was still the man she knew.

Dallas sank deeper into the deck chair, pushed away the thought of tomorrow's hectic, heady performance at the North Shore Music Festival, and he closed his eyes.

He fell into a light slumber just as a father and son stood near the cliff below him and urged a lime green bi-winged kite with a bright orange tail up, up, up into the air. The kite dipped and soared in the new light evening breeze coming off the water. Dallas' anxious spirit echoed its ups and downs.

Soon, Cassie navigated her shiny silver Ford truck onto the Confederation Bridge. Gripping the wheel with a growing fretfulness, she listened to a classical music station on the satellite radio, and begged her spirit to keep her afloat.

Chapter Nineteen

*D*allas was still hunched in the comfy chair on the deck in front of Cassie's Montana when the low rumble of her big silver Ford alerted him to her presence.

After cruising slowly down the small hill toward her camper, she was about to pull in and park when Dallas saw her brake the truck to a stop.

The first thing he noticed was her usual sleek ponytail, not beach-wild as usual, but instead freshly styled with hair products and a curling iron to give it a little upturn at the end.

He'd seen the ponytail first because she deliberately turned her face away from him.

Driving down the Lower Darnley Road toward Castle Beach Campground, Cassie had almost hit the panic button and turned back. Caroline had been honest in telling her that Dal was back at Castle Beach, but some part of Cassie had hoped that he would stop his little incognito undercover game and secure a Charlottetown hotel room, or even a private summer home somewhere instead. It wasn't so much that she was afraid of running into him. It was more of a general concern for his safety, should fans clue in to the true identity of the rogue who was hanging his hat in a vulnerable tent down near the end of Atlantic Drive.

Screwing up her courage, Cassie finally depressed the gas pedal and pulled in next to the Montana. The sandcastle text had helped. It was, as Dallas hoped, a reminder of shared sunsets and moonlight kisses and a growing, sincere love.

Leveraging himself upright, Dallas hesitated before making his way over to the big truck. Cassie was dwarfed inside, but he knew there was a tough core to the small woman behind the Ford's wheel. She could handle the truck. She could handle life. Cassie just needed the occasional mental health day to fortify her for the next leg on her journey.

And this leg would be a tough one.

He held up his iPhone. "Caroline texted me when you left Lunenburg. I figured with pee breaks and maybe a stop at Masstown Market outside Truro for those blueberry scones Ry told me rocked, that you'd be along about now." Peeking inside the front of the truck, he was almost surprised to find only a handbag, a paper coffee cup, and a tray from the Market. No Ry; no Caroline, either, although he already knew she wouldn't be along. He smiled at the five plastic-wrapped scones left on a Styrofoam tray, the sixth obviously long since consumed since only a few crumbs remained where it once sat.

Cassie considered him for a long time before she finally spoke, her voice emerging small and tired as she slipped down out of the Ford. "I'm alone, Dal. Uhhh, Dallas." Wrinkling her cute upturned nose as she slammed the door shut behind her, she let her eyes drift over him—over the boots, the jeans, the tight shirt—before raising both arms in question marks and summoning up some bravado. "I'd ask what I'm supposed to call you, but somehow the names that come to mind have shit-all to do with what's on your birth certificate."

"But they'd suit in one of those rundown bars you figured I played in, huh Cassie? Accompanied by a few well aimed beer bottles?"

Her glare was enough to shrink the little bit of confidence Dallas earlier told himself he had when he decided to meet her at the Montana. "Cassie… nothing's changed between us. I'm the same guy I've been all summer."

"You just play on bigger stages and sing songs everybody knows, huh? Oops, let me rephrase that. Songs the rednecks of the world know." Storming toward the Montana, Cassie dropped her empty coffee cup in the fire pit as she passed. Startled, she saw the makings of a campfire—paper on the bottom, kindling teepeed over it, a few larger split wood pieces on top. Her deck, too, was organized and welcoming. A gentle warmth tucked into her heart, but was quickly replaced with a nervous fear.

Dallas didn't notice her frightened look. All he detected was raised hackles on her back. Propping his hands up on his hips, he bit off a well-earned "Ouch" at the earlier redneck jibe.

She flipped around. "Dallas, Dal, whatever the hell your name is, I'll give you credit in that you told me straight up you would talk when you were ready. You were up front about that. But you said there was no woman—"

"There isn't," he interjected sharply.

"So this Deborah singer's what, CGI? A computer generated image? She's not real? Give me a break."

"Oh she's real, all right. And she's a damn handful. She's just not mine."

The hurt that Cassie saw back in the camp store on day one ripped across Dallas' usually pale eyes. This evening they were the color of the Darnley Basin, which was for all intents and purposes a serious deep kind of twilight blue. Interesting to note, too, was that his eyes had an unusual depth to them tonight. Mirrored with the indigo sky, they were sparked by streaks of lightning as Dal's temper flared.

Sensing that the pain she spied that first day was real, Cassie rocked back on her heels and eased up on him. "Babe, I get that this Deborah woman hurt you. Badly. I'm real sorry about that. Deny it if you want to, but she's still got power over you."

"I beg to differ." He raised his chin and jutted it out, just a bit.

Sighing, she tried to make him see what she saw, to understand one of the reasons she was afraid. "I see it every day, Dal. It's in the way you walk, the way you talk, and definitely in the way you sing."

"The way I sing?" he snorted. "My songs are not one woman, they're my whole life, Cassie, the same way Ry is your entire life. There might be heartache in my singing, but it's heartache that I forgot the second I got here and saw an endless ocean spread out before me like it was telling me anything's possible, that there's more out there for me than I can possibly know."

"So how is Ry my—"

"How is he your life? He wears your pain like a shroud, Cas. Molded to his small body, sealed tight so it won't crack. So he won't crack. And inside that pain, what he holds inside is you, and inside you is Eddie."

She had to struggle to speak. The setting sun spread out behind Cassie like cotton candy, lining the tranquil clouds with a broad pink wink to the end of another perfect Darnley day. The effect was startling and serene at the same time; it was peace and hope tainted with an almost eerie dignity. "And you?" she finally croaked out from between her suddenly constricted throat. "What else is inside your singing? From your perspective? Because I know what I hear."

"A life well lived, that's what." Dallas raised a thumb and two fingers to his chin and pawed nervously at his clean-shaven jaw. The lack of stubble threw him for a loop. Somehow it just felt wrong. Slippery, almost. In this heated discussion with Cassie, he needed something to hold on to.

It struck Cassie funny seeing him like this, like a different version of the man she knew. She decided to be frank, but glanced away and shifted her weight onto her other foot before she inhaled and jumped in deeper. "I know nothing about your career, Dal," she stated darkly. "I refused to look past the music videos I found on YouTube, which included a few of you and this Deborah woman lost in each other's eyes, by the way. Lovely to see those. They just made my day." Getting back on track, partly so she wouldn't lose it in front of him, she added, "So I don't know what route you took to get to the big time. All I know is that when you sing I hear a sadness that equals my own. It's in every word, in every syllable. In every heartsick note. And that's in the fast songs."

A low grunt alerted her to Dallas' take on the subject before he tossed out, "You must think I'm suicidal with the slow ones."

"I think nothing beyond the fact that I see before me a man who is a long way from dealing with the pain that got him those songs in the first place. I thought those tunes came from hard living. I didn't think the ones I heard you play this summer were the result of living in luxury. Oh, let me rephrase that. I meant to say a result of running from luxury and wealth, of giving it a good solid kick in the ass. As if you could care less that what got you there were the people who love your music."

This was impossible. Trying to explain his choices to the one woman Dallas was desperate to have understand him, was impossible. "You don't know a damn thing about my life, Cassie," he exclaimed wildly, throwing his hands up into the air. He stomped in a circle and gave her a look that she thought fit somewhere between frustration and puppy-dog hurt. "Is that what you think," he railed, "that I just turned around and walked away in some kind of diva move over what Deborah did to me?"

"Didn't you?" she fired back, emerald eyes blazing.

"It was a long time coming, Cassie. That's what you hear in my music, okay? Time. That's what you hear." Just like that, Dallas deflated. Like a used beach ball.

Swallowing, Cassie paused and took a moment to study the strong jaw line, the stubborn chin, the tensed biceps that she, even now, ached to run her fingers over. The verbal storm she'd considered spewing at him, and had practiced during the interminable drive from Lunenburg, ran amok through her mixed-up brain, but the twitch in Dal's fisted fingers and the vulnerable ache in his eyes made it hard to let loose in the fiery, angry manner she'd rehearsed. In the end Cassie just spit out her thoughts, but couched them with glistening eyes and downturned lips instead of with brutal, unremitting fury. "What I hear in what I've heard you sing is longing, Dallas," she said. "I don't know if I've ever heard any of the older songs that made you famous. I'm guessing if I do I'll be listening to songs about pickups and dirt roads."

"Don't forget the women in daisy dukes," he shot back. "Damn it, Cassie. Maybe if you listened to my albums you'd understand."

"I do understand, Dal," she countered, but with even less fire than her last blunt statement, although as the thoughts poured out her bell-peal voice became more of a dense, steady ring. "That's what I'm trying to tell you. I understand that you're hurting. That you were hurting when you got here. That maybe you've been hurting for a very long time, maybe even on the same level I hurt. Because of loneliness. Because of what loneliness can do to a person. And yes, I load it all on Ry, at least I used to. I'm trying to do better. I really am. But you hide, too. Maybe you hid behind Deborah for a while, I don't know. Maybe you still do, or at least behind that ballad that your fans rave about, that somehow makes them entitled to assuming the two of you belong together." A quick breath for strength, and she went on. Dallas trembled and cocked his head to be sure he didn't miss a single word being aimed at him from between the frustrated downturned lips he longed to taste. "But even more so, Dal, you load your music with it, don't you? And then you hide behind it. Behind music, behind your guitar, here on some random east coast beach where you seem to think a ratty old ball cap and a razor you only dig out every four or five days can somehow protect you from yourself."

"I don't hide behind my music, Cassie." Dallas was adamant. To get the point across, he took a step toward her. The action was enough to force Cassie to lock her eyes on him and really listen. "I need it the way the ocean needs salt," he declared hotly. "Like it's my best friend, the only thing that really gets me, you know? This is the thing about music, Cas. When Ry crashes he will have a place to go. He will have music to help him through whatever it is that sucks about his life. When people coming to my concerts are feeling lonely, I'm glad they can flip a switch, turn off the things that suck, and have music too." Lowering his voice, he begged her to understand. "You gotta cut me some slack, girl. Country music is the heart and soul of North America, the working man's music; it's raw and real and it helps to have someone sing about what hurts. You ought to listen to some, and let the hurt in instead of keeping it out. You ought to let yourself feel. Maybe that'd let you get what you had back."

Cassie blinked back the hot tears that threatened to reveal how she really felt right now, about how much hope she'd had back when he was simple old Dal instead of complicated new Dallas, and how that hope was somewhat gone now, carried away the way the tides carried off the seaweed piled on the beach in long lines that sometimes looked like snakes. The tremulous flickers that showed themselves between each blink laid bare the heart of Dal's deception. As much to protect herself as to hurt him back, she stammered, "I don't know if someone can find that kind of love twice in a lifetime, Dal. Pardon me. Dallas." His full name was bitten off with poison. Cassie couldn't find a single reserve of strength in herself to keep from spitting it out that way. She was quickly shrinking and starting to peek behind her to eye the Montana's door, but only so she could run inside her Castle Beach sanctuary and disappear. If she had a choice, one that wouldn't lead to new heartache, she'd much prefer to launch her body into the comfort of Dallas' embrace, but all she figured that would accomplish in the days to come would be more misery.

Dallas was more optimistic. "The castle," he exclaimed with a flash of hope. "With its sea glass windows and its pearl shell doors, and its sandy windblown nooks and crannies. With its stunning sunsets and murmuring waves and pebble strewn beach, perfect for strolling along holding hands. We have it, Cassie. You've already got it back. You're just scared to let yourself have it."

"You and I?" she asked, crumbling. "I don't know if I can be with a man who has the option to so easily fall into bed with any young thing who blinks at him. With a man who can afford to live a life of glamour and luxury but who ran away from it like a spoiled child. What we have is a summer fling. How can I be with a liar who, in all likelihood, will leave me in the dust?"

He went for her throat. "Like your husband did?"

She huffed but let the nasty comment slither itself under a rock. "Did you ever notice how much sunsets look like fire, Dal? The real bright orange ones? They can swallow a person up just as easily. With messed up expectations and stupid, useless dreams. If you look at them from behind, people walking into sunsets are all black."

In a hushed tone, Dallas whispered softly, "It's called a silhouette, Cassie, sweetheart. Silhouetted people walking into sunsets are things of beauty. Not fear. But you have to make the choice to look at them that way."

"Bullshit. You sound like you're writing a stupid country song."

"You sure know how to gut a guy, don't you, girl?" Backing away slowly, Dallas held her gaze. Cassie was starting to cry now, but Dallas was wise enough to discern that the tears weren't all just for him. He stopped moving when she spoke again, and knew that Eddie's shadow was right behind him.

"A summer fling, Dal," she wept, unable to gain the control she'd told herself she would have. "Our castles are all gone. The tide took them away. They lasted but moments."

"Ah," he answered wisely. "But weren't they perfect moments?"

Gasping for air like a fish out of water, Cassie angled in another direction. Reaching down, she gingerly picked up his sore wrist. It still hurt enough for him to wince when she moved it, but it was bare, no longer bandaged. It took her a few good swallows and a reminder of how angry she was at his deception before she could manage the words, but when she did, they emerged acerbic as hell. "Since we're talking about who's being the most truthful to themselves here, anything's a clue, is that it, Dal? You took off the wrap because you were afraid someone would put two and two together."

Harrumphing lightly, he looked away.

"Phil must be thrilled that you're back here in your redneck paradise."

"I keep my head down," he growled. "Nobody expects to see me here. I never get a second look."

Dropping the wrist, Cassie took two steps backward. "I guess we've got each other figured out real good, Dal. But what good will it do us?"

Raising his chin, Dallas unfisted his fingers. "I have money, Cassie. I can give you and Ry a real good life."

"Even if…" Sniffling, Cassie stopped moving and reached for the words to cover a betrayal this big. "Even if I thought I could switch gears and live with a celebrity of your stature, Dallas…if I thought I could do that, the travelling and the dinners and, well, let's be honest, even the country music… Babe, I don't think I could do the women. I don't think I could be with a man I'd have to share that way."

"I won't sleep around, Cassie. I'll be faithful. To you, I'll be true. Only to you."

A vehement shake of her head alerted him to the fact that he'd missed something. Cocking his head, Dallas listened closely as Cassie widened the already great divide between them with a few short words.

"Your fans, Dallas. Don't you get it? You're the dream every woman thinks will save her from being ordinary."

"Why not you?" The vehement question was low and husky, and accented with reclenched fists, the tenderness of one of Dallas' hands not even registering. It was eclipsed by the kind of desperation borne of impending loss. "Why can't you be that woman?"

She knew it. She'd known it from the moment she clued in to who Dal really was. Cassie was already crying, bearing the weight of maybe someday having to say goodbye to a man who could be an amazing addition to her and Ry's lives, if he wasn't who he was. "I want to be with you," she whispered. "I really, really want to be with you. But the thing about me, *Dallas*," she stressed his full name again, only with less poison this time, "is that I like being ordinary."

"I need you, Cassie," he tried. "I need you and Ry."

"We can't save you, babe. Any more than you can save us. We don't have that kind of power. We're barely hanging on ourselves, you know that, Dal, you know it." A last quick intake of breath, and Cassie added, "Go home, Dal. Leave this place and go back to your own sweet life."

"The contest…the sandcastle-building contest Ry and I practiced for…" It was a stretch, a rope Dallas was tossing, hoping she would grab it. One more day with her and Ry and maybe, just maybe, he could break that tough veneer Cassie wore like armor. He could prove to her that they could build a life together, not one built of sand, but one that was real and strong and secured on a foundation of love.

She burst his bubble. "Ry's not going to be here for the contest, Dal. Caroline's not bringing him over. I'm sorry. It's the morning after your concert, and let's face it, a big outdoor country music festival is no place for an eight-year-old boy."

"What?" Dallas fisted and unfisted his hands.

She was throwing back the lifeline, just a small fleeting bit. He grabbed it and hung on. It was small, but it was something.

"I'm coming to your show, Dallas," she reiterated with a huff and in different words. "I'll be there tomorrow, okay? No promises. But I'll go." The tears were drying up. Cassie almost smiled at the relief that crisscrossed Dallas' face like a rainbow.

"Why?" he pleaded, almost sinking to his knees in gratitude but needing to know all the same what it was that he had to hang on to. "Why bother, if you've already decided that the person I am isn't what you want?"

Hesitating, Cassie answered after a long, slow inhale that she released between pursed lips. "Because I know most of you, Dal. But I don't know the man on stage, the one who will have thirty thousand people at his show tomorrow night." The last bit was an almost desperate whisper. "In truth, I think maybe seeing you that way will make it easier to let you go."

"You like to go it alone," he stuttered. "Don't you, Cassie? With your ghost by your side."

She shrugged. "The thing about going it alone is that you can't disappoint anyone else. But honey…you already know that, don't you?"

"I won't be alone," he breathed while, at the same time, wondered what the hell she was doing with his heart. It felt about as wrung out as the white swimming trunks he'd hung on the line at his campsite twice that day. "You just told me you are coming."

"What? There'll be thirty thousand people there watching you sing, Dallas. How can one of me possibly sway the balance?"

"Listen to yourself, Cassie. You told me you understand me because I reveal my heart in my singing."

"Y-yes. I did. Something like that, at least."

"You get how fucking lonely I am. Me, Dallas White. Singer. Thirty thousand strangers, Cas. But…" He brightened, and his eyes lit up as he moved to wheel around and saunter away. "But tomorrow night, for once in my life I will not be lonely during my show. Because the woman I fell in love with on a Prince Edward Island beach is going to be there."

A pink flush flashed across the tops of Cassie's porcelain cheeks. "I won't know a single word. You know that, right? I'll stand out like a sore thumb. I don't even own a cowboy hat."

"Caroline told me you both bought boots."

"She made me."

"Forced them on your feet, did she? And then you left her in Nova Scotia. They're gonna be some cute on you."

"Oh, Lordy," she groaned and rolled her eyes before adding, "she just wanted an excuse to go shopping. Anyways, you said it, Dal. I like to go it alone."

Lifting his iPhone, he grinned and pointed at the bottom. "You know how to make the flashlight work on this thing, right? You'll need that."

Biting her bottom lip, Cassie cocked her head and asked, "Don't they have lights at those things?"

"You'll see," Dallas chuckled. Suddenly his heart felt full again. "Look, you have my number if you want to come backstage. The tix I left are VIP tix, so you'll have a few perks. But call me, okay? Or text, at least. I need to know you're going to be there. For sure. Cassie…please."

"Want me to jump on stage and hold your hand?" she teased. A frown preceded her next poor attempt at civility. "I thought Deborah would have that job."

"I'm not taking that bait, Cas," he warned. "I'm going now. See? Watch me. Watch me go." Whistling a light, airy tune, a traditional piece he picked up at some island Ceilidh, Dallas moseyed past the big Ford and started up the lane toward the gate that separated the new part of the campground from the old.

Dismayed, suddenly feeling very, very alone, Cassie watched him go. "Dallas White." She puffed up her cheeks and let out a long, slow exhale. "I knew your career in music would come between us. But I thought it would be the seedy roadside bar thing. Not in a million years did I think it would be because you can put a whole P.E.I. city in some farmer's field to watch you, and charge 165 bucks a ticket for the privilege."

Ahead, Dallas bent and scratched the ears of a bouncy Golden Labradoodle. He exchanged pleasantries with the owner before he continued his slow, casual amble up the slope. A few moments later, while Cassie was putting her things away with one hand and munching on a blueberry scone with the other, she heard the dog's owner flick on the radio in the big motorhome just above her Montana. Deborah and Dallas' ballad was playing—the one song of Dal's that Cassie immediately recognized. Wondering, with an unexpected small flicker of glee, if the dog's owner realized the man singing was the one who'd just scratched his dog's ears, Cassie fell backward onto her bed and found herself in a surprise giddy fit of laughter.

Chapter Twenty

*C*assie knew she was out of her league and way the heck out of her comfort zone before she even got to the festival grounds. Traffic on the two lane rural road into the National Park area known on Prince Edward Island as Cavendish was busy and congested. Tailgates to front bumpers, trucks and cars picked their way slowly toward the concert grounds.

It was a well-streamlined event. Cassie spotted a sign that read 'VIP parking.' When she turned right onto the gravel lane where she was supposed to park, a freckled twenty-something in an orange vest waved her down.

"Afternoon, Ma'am," he said amicably as she depressed the window button. "Can I see your parking pass, please?"

Cursing Dallas for forgetting that part of the equation (*likely never has to worry about such a mundane thing as parking,* she grumbled), she mumbled a quiet, "Sorry," and turned the truck around. Remembering a general lot she'd passed a ways back, she put her tail between her legs and nosed the big silver Ford into a spot there instead. Shuttle buses were doing regular pick-ups and drop-offs. Cassie joined a line-up and eventually got into a yellow school bus, which delivered her back to the concert grounds. By the time she made her way nervously to the small VIP box office just outside the gate, nerves were getting the better of her. Everyone else seemed to have someone to vent to, but the idea of listening to Caroline rant as she took charge, as she would, no doubt about that, was enough for Cassie to have chosen to leave her sister back in Nova Scotia with Ry. Second to eliminating that source of stress was the absolute certainty that in order to really process 'Dallas the star' on stage, Cassie wanted no distractions.

No nosey sister disrupting her thoughts and emotions with chitter-chatter or idle gossip.

At the box office, Cassie shifted her feet in the gravel. A light rain had dampened the heads of festivalgoers earlier in the day. Gratefully, she peered up at the sky to see patches of blue peeking through the soft gray clouds, and a few promising white puffs of cloud were drifting over the horizon on a north wind too, which was cool enough to dispel the heat from the occasional strong sun. The gravel was less dusty than it might have been had the day been hot and steamy, but the place still had a temporary, rustic feel. Almost a surprise to Cassie, it also had a festive air.

While waiting her turn at the box office, Cassie took a good look around. Clutching an orange camp chair in its canvas bag, and with one strap of a bulging knapsack over a shoulder, she was taken aback at how close the backstage section was to the VIP entrance. It was fenced in, but over the top of the metal barrier she could see trailers—big new ones like her own. No doubt Dallas was comfortably ensconced in one. No wonder he didn't blink an eye at the simple luxury of hers on that long ago day when rain forced Ry's guitar lesson indoors.

It was three o'clock. The first act of the day had taken the main stage, which was in front of the backstage area, at one-thirty. Now, music was everywhere. Already the guitars and redneck twang were an assault to Cassie's senses. It didn't help that the stage was facing away from the gates and sound was being projected in the opposite direction onto the large grounds, which made the music where Cassie was standing sound echoey and unnatural to her trained ears. As a performing arts theater administrator, she spent her career around smaller stages—avoiding most of the country acts that crossed her path—and so she had a solid understanding of the basics of projecting perfect sound. Immediately she straightened and decided she would mitigate the issue by finding as central a place as possible to watch Dallas' set.

"LCRS," she told herself. "Left-Center-Right-Surround," which translated to 'somewhere in the middle.' Best spot for perfect sound in the movie theater or at a concert. *Not much point in being here if I can't see and hear Dal at his best,* she figured.

That morning, Phil had called Cassie and offered to meet her and tour her around the site. He also promised her premium seats that he said were a step above the VIP seating. But something guarded in his voice turned Cassie off, as if Dallas had asked for the favor and Phil was only grudgingly complying. That and the simple need to process this surreal experience alone, which she knew Dallas understood, made her politely decline. Now, though, she wished Phil were around to help orient her to the grounds, if nothing else. Even better, it would have been nice to have Dallas by her side. With a sad twinge, Cassie was immediately reminded that there was not much possibility Dallas could ever experience a concert at her side this way. Hanging out incognito at a beach was one thing. Immersing one's celebrity self amongst thirty thousand fans was another ball game entirely.

A brusque voice jarred Cassie back to business. "Picking up or buying?"

"Uhhh…picking up. Um, VIP tix. Cassie Keough." *Brilliant,* she inwardly chided herself. *I'm at the damn VIP box office. That didn't sound bloody arrogant at all.*

"Cassie Keough," the woman repeated, fingering a list taped to the ledge in front of her. Hemming and hawing, which almost put Cassie's jarred nerves over the edge, she finally repeated Cassie's name with a triumphant pout and ripped a white band off of an attached bunch of similar strips. "Bracelet," she stated with a businesslike air as if she'd done this a thousand times already today, which she likely had, in fact. The woman held out the white band. "Arm?"

"Oh. Okay." Thrusting out her arm, Cassie let the attendant loosely fasten, around her slender wrist, the white bracelet that ID'd her as a VIP guest. "Um, where to?" she asked, pulling her arm back afterwards and uncertainly fingering the band.

"VIP gate's right there," the lady said, pointing to a lane clearly marked VIP. "Enjoy your day."

"Allrighty then. You too," Cassie mumbled. Sucking in a breath, she moved toward the entrance, wondering all the while whether Dallas was sitting in a trailer watching her.

The security staff working the gate was mostly women. One of them, a young, fit gal, watched Cassie approach. Underneath a black ball cap, the woman's eyes were dark and serious, but a flicker of kindheartedness crossing her tanned cheeks gave her true nature away. A tight black golf shirt that emphasized her small breasts matched the cap propped on her head. Cassie eyed it critically, and looked away the second she realized she was staring at the woman's boobs while she read the word emblazoned across the front in large gold letters—SECURITY.

"Stylish," Cassie decreed under her breath, disarmed and immediately chiding herself for doing 'that thing' she did when she was over-the-top nervous, which was putting others down based on how they were dressed. It only worked for a second to build herself up since she just felt worse about herself afterwards. The interesting thing was that this time the admonishment for her snappy chide came from Dal's voice in her head. It was accompanied by kind but loving disappointment in his eyes. The realization sent Cassie's gut reeling.

Almost as if she understood, the security gal swiped at her jet-black ponytail before smiling sympathetically and reaching for Cassie's knapsack. Setting it on a table at her side, she stuck her hand in and didn't even try not to appear smug when she removed an apple, a granola bar, and a bottle of water. Still, she was smiling when she looked back up at Cassie.

"No food allowed inside," she said kindly. "There are lots of vendors on the grounds."

Oh, for God's sake. Cassie hunkered up her petite shoulders. "Oh. Oops. I missed that part. I actually, um, just picked up my ticket. Uh, got my bracelet, I mean. I didn't know."

"Can I see your chair?"

Yeah, I've stashed a four-course meal in there. Take a good long look. Handing it to the security gal so the woman could thrust a hand inside that too, Cassie wondered whether she was looking for weapons or a hidden banana. The weapons part was a scary thought. *Dallas…on stage…so exposed…*

Overwhelmed with thoughts that frightened her, she pushed them away and tried to find a modicum of happiness to bring her through the tough day. Cringing, Cassie focused her annoyance on the food since it seemed a much safer place to direct her fears than on the man she loved possibly being the target of anyone's malicious actions.

"I don't eat red meat," she mumbled, feeling like she had to say something, anything, even if it came out kind of snotty sounding. Still, the comment was aimed at the ground. She wasn't about to engage in a full-blown argument with security, even though a part of her cringed at having to leave her apple and granola bar behind.

"There are lots of options." The friendly gal handed the chair and knapsack back to Cassie. "First time at the Festival?"

What was your first clue? "Yup. It is." Adjusting the knapsack over her shoulder, Cassie sighed and considered just pivoting around and going back home. She was close to tears, the whole thing felt so foreign. "I'm used to enclosed theaters with plush seats," she managed, finally looking up and meeting the kind eyes.

"And a glass of wine?" The woman winked. "I like your sundress. Looks cute with the boots."

For Pete's sake. Really? "Oh, um, I wasn't sure what to wear." With a sideways glance, Cassie noticed a horde of teen girls with plaid shirts tied above their navels, and worn cut-off denim shorts, make their way to the gate. All had pulled cowboy boots onto their feet, although one girl was wincing and carrying her boots, which looked brand spanking new. Cassie groaned and hoped her new ones would hold up. Behind the girls, two security officers were escorting two belligerent guys off the grounds, and an RCMP officer was engaged in a loud argument with a snotty thirty-something woman over her apparent refusal to dump a bottle of some obscure liquor she was drunkenly trying to bring onto the grounds.

"Those girls don't even have sweaters," the gal at security declared, nodding toward the group of girls before giving Cassie's bulging knapsack a look. "You're the smartest woman here."

Someone called her name then, loudly, and Cassie turned toward the voice. The woman from the box office was hurrying toward her on thick legs that looked sore with each lumbering step. Her T-shirt said *Volunteer,* which Cassie absently thought was kinda cool. Volunteering seemed like a good way to be involved in such a big show. The cool vibe disappeared presto-chango when she saw that the box office gal was holding out a snappy white cowboy hat with fringed edges, its band decorated with white twine.

"This was left for you, Miss." The volunteer gasped as she held it, rather proudly, out to Cassie. "By Dallas White's manager."

Cassie decidedly frowned at the hat. The woman stood in front of her for a few extended moments before giving the gift a push into Cassie's belly so she would have no choice but to accept it.

"Ummm…uhhh…hats are not really my thing." Nervous, Cassie lifted it anyway, and tested it on her shiny blonde hair.

The woman from security adjusted the hat so it tipped recklessly forward a tiny bit. "There. Looks better with the brim down in front. Now you're not only the smartest woman here, you're also invisible." She laughed, and Cassie let her lips turn up just a bit so she could smile along with her. "Dallas White's manager?" the gal added. "That's saying something. You might not want to tell anyone."

"It's not signed or anything," the box office volunteer announced knowingly. "No one will know the difference."

"Oh, Lord," Cassie breathed, but she grinned at the two women regardless, and headed onto the grounds as they watched her go, her new hat propped proudly on top of the elegant hairstyle she worked so hard to achieve this morning in her camper.

Twenty minutes later, after a brisk walking tour of the grounds—turned out she needed to purchase tokens in order to buy food, which she found out the hard way—she located the VIP area. People were flowing steadily into the site now, dropping their camp chairs and staking their claims. On the stage, a sound check was in full swing for the next band that, Cassie read in her program, was Ricky Skaggs and his band, Kentucky Thunder.

"Ricky Skaggs?" she wondered, because that was a classic country name she knew. Sipping on a strawberry-pineapple cooler that she hoped would settle her racing mind, she sank back into her camp chair and was held spellbound for the next hour by the older musician's flying fingers on an exquisite, beautiful mandolin.

"Whoa," she breathed as she studied his playing via close-ups on a huge monitor. "The man's unreal!" Already solidly impressed by the sheer talent of the bluegrass band, who were playing tunes that Skaggs introduced as 'the most pure form of country,' Cassie was completely blown away when a featured solo piece filled the air, reimagined by the band's stand-up bass player, a youngster who Cassie figured was not a day over twenty-five. There he was, settled in amongst some of the U.S.A.'s most talented and much older blue-grass musicians, all of whom were amassed from different American states, playing the earliest kind of country music as if he was born to it. The song was a waltz written by a bluegrass band in the 1950's. It was so beautiful, so divine, the young fellow's voice so sonically perfect, that during the second verse Cassie closed her eyes and raised her face to the heavens to soak it all in. It was humbling.

"Music is music, I suppose," she caught herself thinking afterwards as the boy stepped humbly forward to accept the raucous applause he so well deserved. When Ricky Skaggs started into the next song, a fast-paced pick-ing tune, Cassie reaffirmed her gratitude for the three jumbo-sized moni-tors placed behind and beside the performers, so she could hold her breath and continue to watch Skaggs' fingers fly over his strings. The hour flew by, and neither Dallas nor the need to pee even crossed her mind until Kentucky Thunder left the stage.

By the time Dallas was scheduled to play at nine-thirty, Cassie was waver-ing in her assessment of country music. Ricky Skaggs was a little off the beaten path in this contemporary venue, but his sheer musicianship would win over anyone who claimed to love music for, well, music. Some of the other performers had Cassie expectedly rolling her eyes, though. The first guy on after Kentucky Thunder was, for instance, sporting Converse Chucks on his feet, a hoodie on his torso, and a ball cap on his head. Cassie knit her eyebrows together and half smiled at his third tune—a well-known pop anthem Ry liked.

Deciding the guy and his band were more pop than country, she dug out her iPhone and snapped a pic for Ry.

Just as she was tucking the phone back into her knapsack, the small screen lit up. Cassie yanked it back out to spy a text from Dallas. Raising the phone up so she could see to read it, she had to laugh. It was simple. One word. *Well?*

The brevity of that one word, which Cassie knew was soaked through with a thousand unasked questions, tugged at her heart. *Is Ricky Skaggs as cool as he seems?* she typed back.

He's my hero, Dallas wrote. *I grew up on his tunes.*

"Well, I suppose that's something." Somewhat ashamed for judging

Dallas on his choice of music, she shoved the phone back in her knapsack and watched the show.

It seemed to take forever for the clock to tick its way to nine-thirty. The half-hour before Dal's appearance was energized with a half-dozen recorded snappy pop tunes that were designed, Cassie figured, to jazz up the crowd. She was okay with the tunes. They were catchy enough, and Ry would like them, but the coolest thing about them were that they got the thousands of people lined up in front of the stage singing. Suddenly the audience was not made up of parts—young and old, wealthy and middle-income, healthy and not so healthy, vigorous and lazy—suddenly everybody in the audience was *one*.

"I wonder, does Dal feel this?" Cassie thought, looking around. She was still snuggled into her camp chair, but realized she'd soon have to stand if she wanted to see Dallas from her place in the crowd. As the day wore on she had taken a few strolls during sound checks, one to get a tasty veggie wrap from a vendor, one to buy a fifty-fifty ticket (*why not*, she thought, deriding herself later for allowing herself to get caught up in the festive mood), and the second to get more nerve-calming coolers (which elicited more than one trip to the port-a-potties, which Cassie found kinda disgusting but manageable). At one point she stood in that premium LCRS center spot away from the stage near the sound booth where, she was right, the sound was perfect. The drums in particular amazed her. So clear and fresh, not muddled like you would almost expect in a field like this.

Now, she glanced at her phone. Dallas was due on soon. Should she wish him well?

Backstage, Dallas was almost quaking in his boots. Deborah was at his side, and he wished she'd just go away and leave him alone with his fears, with the expectations he tried to adjust for this show, which felt like the first of his career simply because Cassie was in the audience. His eyes lit up when a text came in at nine-twenty.

Am I supposed to say break a leg?

Good show is fine, he wrote back while Deborah wondered who was making the handsome man by her side smile.

Good show then, came Cassie's immediate text back.

Did you get something to eat? he asked.

Don't you have more important things to worry about right now?

He was standing in the wings, looking out. Searching for a white cowboy hat in the VIP section. *I do. But not what you think.*

"Ohhhh." Cassie's heart leapt. She waited. He sent her a photo. It was another of the sandcastles he and Ry had built. No words accompanied it.

Tears stung Cassie's eyes. All the photo did in this unreal place, in her perspective, was remind her that the man she loved was, for all intents and purposes, missing. The man she loved should be at her side. Suddenly she felt completely alone in that crowd of thousands. The lonely, claustrophobic sensation almost crippled her.

Her phone vibrated in her hand. She looked down. *Cassie…I need to know you're still here.*

The tears overflowed. They landed—*splat splat splat*—on the phone's screen. "I'm not alone," she whispered. Her body's quaking settled into a light tremble. "And neither are you, babe."

She texted back. *I'm here, Dal.* On a whim Cassie stood, whipped the phone up above and in front of her, opened the camera App, tapped on the icon that reversed the image, turned around so the stage was behind her, and snapped a selfie that showed where she was situated in the crowd. It only took a second to send it to Dallas.

He laughed outright when he saw it, a belly laugh that really got Deborah's curiosity going. She leaned over him, but he moved the phone away from her. Phil approached just as the stage manager raised his fingers to signal five minutes.

"She's wearing the hat," Dallas laughed to Phil. "She's here."

Is she, Phil mused. He couldn't help the feeling of sadness that passed over him. But what he wasn't privy to was the unseen current passing between Dallas and his summer love, despite the throngs of people and the seemingly insurmountable wall separating their two worlds. He was reassured, though, a few minutes later, when he tapped his artist on the shoulder and sent him to center stage smiling.

Chapter Twenty-one

*T*he next morning at the beach, Dallas jumped when a blue plastic shovel landed in the sand at his feet, startling him. Standing by his allotted section of competition sand on Castle Beach, hands on his hips, chewing on his bottom lip, his spirits were about as low as they could go. Near him on the beach he had caught the tail end of a conversation about his show at the North Shore Music Festival last night. Apparently the fans loved it. But he hadn't heard a word from Cassie. Not a *great,* or an *it sucked.* Not even an emoji half-smile or one with a tear.

He twisted around to see where the shovel came from. Dallas had to tip his face up to see above the brim of the usual ball cap.

Cassie, four feet away, was studying him, apprehensively wringing her fingers together in front of her stomach as she took in his decidedly un-super-starlike plaid shorts and blue T-shirt.

"Hey," Dallas murmured quietly, his pale blue eyes missing their usual warmth and light. Last night had been a loonngg and sleepless night.

"Hey," Cassie replied. The outer corners of her lips were turned slightly downward.

She was late.

The Castle Beach staff guy in charge of the contest, who was standing next to the judges—the tall weekly instructor and two of the campground's owners—lifted a megaphone to his lips and barked out orders. "Each team has until five to complete its sandcastle. That gives you seven hours. If you take breaks for lunch or to go to the restroom, or for a swim since it's gonna be a scorcher today, please ask one of the volunteers to watch over your masterpiece. As far as structure is concerned, anything goes. You will be judged on creativity and originality, with a little bit of skill tossed into the judging for good measure. Good luck, teams!"

Blowing sharply on a whistle to officially get the competition under-way, the guy moved off down the beach to ensure everyone was clear on the instructions. A happy roar lit up the beach. A flurry of activity energized the builders and the small crowd of cheery well-wishers who gathered to watch.

Neither Cassie nor Dallas moved. They remained still, not even toeing the sand to signify that their exposed nerves were getting the better of them.

Cassie finally shook her head slowly. She was wearing a bikini under a simple loose yellow sundress with a scoop neck. Landing mid-thigh, the dress lent her the air of a child, but her composure and words were about as adult as Dallas ever hoped to hear from her.

"The thing is, Dal, I'm having a hard time reconciling the man standing before me now with the one I saw on stage last night." Realizing what she said, she darted a look quickly from side to side to see if anyone heard and clued in, but Dallas didn't flinch. He decided that the only people who may have figured something was up between the two of them likely thought they were just debating strategy. Which in a way, they were. Just not sandcastle strategy.

"Sweetheart," he started softly. Raising a hand, he gestured toward his body. "This is me. This is the guy you know."

"I know that," Cassie returned with a frustrated stomp in the sand, try-ing not to cry for the umpteenth time since it'd hit her about two songs into his set last night that Dallas was too much for her. That his life was too much for her. "And this is the guy I love."

He melted. And waited, struggling to remain composed while what she wasn't saying bounced around his brain like a rubber bullet with no place to exit. His eyes gave him away. They, too, were melting; they were pools of rippled water like the ocean just behind him, but they were liquid hot and starting to drip like candle wax, whereas the ocean was cool and still. The only thing that was truly the same about his eyes and the ocean were the mysteries contained therein.

"I'll—I'll leave music," he stammered. Desperation edged his next words. "I don't want it without you, Cassie."

"Why me?" Running her hands through her hair after pointing to herself, Cassie started to break down. Dallas took a step toward her. She took a step back. People around them tiptoed quietly to watch the next team shovel great heaps of sand into a pile. "That's what I don't get," Cassie choked. "You could have anyone. You could have Deborah back."

"Because you get it, that's why," he whispered.

A strangled sound emerged from her throat. "I get what? Life? Life almost destroyed me, Dal. Sometimes it still does!"

"Yeah, girl, life!" he tried, aching to make her see, to help her understand. "That's what you get. And music. You get music too. I knew it the first time you and Ry showed up at my campsite on your bikes, that night when I was sitting on my picnic table playing guitar."

"We only heard you play for a few minutes that night, so why—"

"Because," he interjected, trying to inject a calm he didn't feel, "I was playing a song that was breaking my heart. And it was reflected in your eyes. That's why."

"All of your fans get that about you, Dallas. All of them." The words tumbled over each other. Cassie had held them in all night, but now she owed Dal something for the hard night he spent wondering, waiting. Worrying. She owed him honesty. "Last night was crazy," she told him. She fished her phone out of a pocket in her dress, held it up, and waved it at him. "That thing with the cellphone lights, and the flashing blue lights on the sunglasses, too, the glasses that the beverage company was handing out...everybody singing at once! Thirty thousand thrilled people elevated by your music, singing lyrics that you wrote, forgetting about the things they worry about every day!" Dropping the phone back in her pocket, she said in a softer tone, "It was surreal, Dallas. But babe...it's so damn big. Maybe it's too damn big for me! The way they look at you up there...the way you look under the lights, standing above everyone like you're some kind of god...maybe you're too much for me."

"That's funny," he said wryly, grabbing the end of the shovel because he needed to move, he needed to breathe, and staring at her in that cute sundress while she told him he was unreachable was suffocating him. "Because all this while I've been thinking you are too much for me. Too good for me."

"Ha. Really?" Cassie gave him a surprised half-assed smile. "I can't imagine why."

He shot her a look that landed somewhere between *that hurts* and *stop messin' with me.*

Twisting her fingers in front of her belly again, she went on. "You want to know something else that's funny?" Cassie swiped a bare wrist across her leaking eyes. "Eddie…loved country music. Isn't that funny?"

"Why?" Dallas murmured, focusing a heartsick gaze on her. "Why the hell is that funny, Cassie?"

"Because," she sniffed, "this was our beach. Our campground. This was where we made love for the first time, did I ever tell you that?"

"Like us," he acknowledged sadly. Always Eddie's ghost was standing over him, one-upping him.

"This was where Ry was conceived. And this was where we found peace when we needed it, because relationships take work, they're not just handed to you on a silver platter, you know."

"And?" Dallas' muscles were bursting at the pent-up need to dig, to start building the base for their castle, but he refrained from starting. The adrenaline coursing through his veins raced its way to nowhere. A nerve on his temple started to pulse.

"We used to fight about it," Cassie admitted. "The music. We never quite learned to respect each other, to find a 'middle ground kind of music' that worked for both of us. That's what we should have done."

Lifting the shovel, dropping its blade into the sand, then repeating the action, Dallas hardly dared breathe. "What are you saying, Cassie?" he managed, locking his eyes into hers.

"I'm saying maybe we start to build this castle, Dallas," she explained cautiously, shoring her heart up for what she feared would be hard days ahead and wondering why the hell she was even considering taking a chance on this confusing man. "And maybe somewhere along the line we'll find a middle ground. But…babe…" She shook her head as a wanton tear splashed into the sand. "I don't know if there is a middle ground for us. You know? Maybe we'll just be digging a bigger hole than the one we're already in."

Dallas' shoulders relaxed. His eyes were hard to see under the brim of the cap, but if Cassie could meet his gaze she would spy bits of light. Bits of hope. "What was it the guy who taught us to build sandcastles said?" he reminded her. "Don't push, or what you're building will crumble. Slide and swipe, he said. Take your time."

"And use lots of water." A low chuckle emerged from Cassie's throat, which was tight and sore at the effort to remain at least somewhat composed. She pointed to her eyes and wiped away the last few tears. "I don't know if that's a good thing, Dal. I'm not sure I can handle any more water."

"I only know one thing for sure," he whispered as he let go of the shovel handle and took her in his arms for a long, slow kiss. "And that's who I want to share the rest of my life with, Cassie. You're the only real thing out there. You're the only person who really sees me."

"And you, me," she answered fondly, drawing a finger slowly down his cheek and curling it through a strand of his blond hair. "But I just don't know how this is going to work. It's like you're two different people."

"No," he demanded, in a tone Cassie heeded for its quick, sharp intensity. "We'll take this one day at a time, Cassie. No worrying about the future. We'll figure it out."

They had a castle to build, and they needed to start now. Cassie hadn't practiced as much as Ry and Dal had, but all summer so far she'd been a careful observer. She pulled Dallas close to her and softly moaned at how damn good it felt to hold him and be held by him. Despite his cautionary admonishment, she couldn't help but wonder whether the romantic foundation they were considering building would be built on sandy dreams or on something sturdier.

Not on a stage, she sighed into his muscled chest. *We won't survive if we build our lives around a stage.* She pictured the concert last night and how it had briefly felt suffocating. At one point during Dallas' set she had made her way out of the VIP section and pushed her way into the heart of the general crowd to a spot directly in front of the stage. It took a ton of shoving and a lot of mumbled *excuse mes* and *sorrys* to get there but she eventually found a place to settle, earning only a few sore stepped on toes in the process. Watching Dallas from below like that felt like someone was pointing a big 'ole finger into her chest. She could swear she heard a loud booming voice thundering out the words, "He is above you. He is on a higher level than you. He will always be above you."

In that part of the crowd a catfight started between two young women who were drunk and elbowing each other for space to better see the man they paid a lot of money to worship. Cassie had to duck to the side to avoid getting an elbow to the chin. Pot smokers were everywhere too but Cassie didn't mind that so much. Inhaling clouds of the pungent weed only lifted her to someplace even deeper in her soul, to a place of connection that felt divine while Dallas sang his heart out, and which soothed as she cried openly during the soulful ballad with his ex-fiancée (she wasn't the only one, although her crying was for a different reason than everyone else).

The lights...Oh, the lights. So that was what Dal's vague comment about the iPhone light had been about. Like the rest of the crowd, she had held hers up last night and looked around to see thousands of similar lights beaming their love and respect toward the man who, bathed in spotlights and elevated above all of them, appeared Godlike and surreal.

A teenager near her had hooked an arm around Cassie's elbow while she sobbed during the ballad. "It's okay," the girl said at the time, misinterpreting Cassie's angst. "He's too good for her anyway."

"What?" Cassie had said back to her, confused.

"She broke his heart. We can't have that. We can't have someone like slutty Deborah L breaking our Dallas' heart. Can we?" It was spoken with a reverential, universal ownership. Dallas didn't belong to Deborah, and he didn't belong to Cassie. He was alone, a solitary, quiet figure staring out at a crowd from a place where he did belong, serving the people the way celebrities with talent serve people.

He's alone, Cassie had breathed. *Separate. Apart from any one person, but belonging to all. To everyone.*

Now, on the beach, as he held her and kissed her and loved her while everyone around them whistled and cheered, she caught herself ashamedly thinking a few final thoughts.

But that's Dallas.

And this is Dal.

And this is the man I love.

"I don't want to let you go," she said softly into the tender blue eyes lost so lovingly in hers.

"Then don't," he whispered back, tracing a tear stained cheek with his thumb. "Let me build you a castle."

She smiled, a rainbow after the storm.

Dallas let his hands slide down her arms before he let her go, before he could bring himself to look away.

Whistling happily as Cassie blushed shyly and knelt to pick up the blue plastic shovel, he dug his toes into the earth, grabbed the larger shovel, and started to build.

Chapter Twenty-two

"We lost, Ry. We suck." Dallas ruffled Ry's hair while the boy groaned.

"I guess I shoulda been here," Ry said in response, grabbing Dal's hand and giving it a friendly twist. "You guys need me."

"You got that right, kid." With his free arm, Dallas treated Ry to an affectionate shoulder hug.

Watching, Cassie's radar went on high alert. Ry wasn't letting go of Dallas' hand. "Oh, boy," she breathed. Not for the first time, it crossed her mind that taking a chance on her new man also meant subjecting her son to Dallas' high-profile adrenaline fueled life.

Dallas caught the concerned look and sent her a small smile. *We can do it*, he seemed to be saying. *We can protect him.*

Cassie wasn't quite as confident. A niggling feeling in her belly took hold. Intuition? She wasn't sure, but she didn't take the time to dwell on it. She and Dallas were just coming off a week spent almost entirely alone in each other's company. His hand was healing, which she was grateful for because he had put it to creative use during their lovemaking—at night, before the beach, after the beach, and it would have been *on* the beach if they could have found a secluded cove somewhere. As it was, they mostly stayed at the campground, which both Cassie and Dallas were increasingly thinking of as their own private heaven.

Last night, they talked about Eddie.

"I feel like he led me to you," Cassie told Dallas. She was absently running a finger down his chest. Tilting her head while she spoke, she paused her movement and rested the hand on his hip. "As if he knows we need each other."

Dallas' feelings were mixed. "I have to admit," he said slowly, tenderly wiping a loose wisp of hair off her cheek, "that I feel a little like I'm stealing Castle Beach from the two of you. I know it's your special place."

"Hold up there, music man," she teased, planting a delicate kiss in the cozy hollow of his neck, which she found intoxicatingly sweaty and more than a little salty from an earlier swim. The rush up from the beach to make love had ended in his tent this time. Its close proximity to the beach was proving useful after sun-soaked post-swim rests. "Eddie and I had a lot of special places. This campground was only one of them."

"Then we'll find some more of our own too," Dallas responded with a diabolical grin and a wink. "I passed a clover field the other day that looked inviting."

A gentle swat was Cassie's answer, accompanied by a sweet flush that crested her cheeks with pink. Leaning forward, Dallas brushed his lips by the corner of her eye. The light in the sparkling jade these days was humbling, eclipsed only by the realization that he, too, was adrift in the blissful days of new love. The best part of that, apart from the physical releases punctuating each coupling, was trust and simple connection. For too long Dallas felt like he was living life on the outside, full tilt forward, as if he could outrun the loneliness that followed him like a sad puppy on a leash.

Now, Ry was back in P.E.I. Under her breath more than once, Cassie caught herself talking to Eddie, chiding him for his devious spirit in bringing her and Dallas together in a way that brought Ry into the relationship from the get-go. No way would she have introduced Ry to Dallas for months, if they hadn't been drawn together from the start.

Near the end of August, both Cassie and Ry were sulking at the thought of having to move back to Halifax. School would be starting soon, and Cassie's sanctioned leave from work was drawing to a close.

"It'll be stressful when I get back," she grumbled knowingly to Dallas after dinner one night. They were sitting on a wooden bench inside the playground, spooning half-melted ice cream into their mouths while keeping an eye on Ry, who was gleefully dashing around playing color tag with some kids from Ottawa. "I've had a few calls already. Things are piling up." Cassie elbowed her seatmate playfully. "There's a country show booked in my theater for next spring. Some up and comers, I think, supported by Dean Brody as headliner. He lives in Nova Scotia, apparently."

"I heard that." Wiping a thumb across Cassie's mouth to swipe up some hot fudge on her top lip, Dallas stuck it in his mouth and sucked lightly, to her great embarrassment and delight.

"Is it bedtime yet?" she giggled.

"Soon, pretty girl," he told her, tucking an arm around her shoulders so she was squeezed rather tightly against him while he finished his ice cream. Her giggling grew louder. Cassie set the remainder of her sundae on the bench next to her and wrapped both arms around the waist of the man she'd come to love dearly. Encouraged by idyllic pink ribbon'd clouds that stretched out from the Basin up to the playground, and which covered them with beatific cotton comfort, Dallas sighed happily. The pure contentment oozing from his spirit was lined with peace and joy.

"You should come play a tune or two. At Dean Brody's show." Cassie's smile tickled Dallas' chest. He scooped up the last of his ice cream, set down the dish and hugged her to him. Her last phrase came out muffled. "Guest star or something."

"So," he grinned brazenly. "I wonder how Brody likes Nova Scotia."

"Toronto too much for you?" Inhaling the heady musky maleness of him through his T-shirt, Cassie peeked up from his chest.

"The opposite. It's not enough," he smiled, laying a cheek against the top of the silky blonde wild beach hair he had come to find so dear. "Not enough people I love there."

"Awww, Phil loves you," she retorted playfully, poking a finger in his chest.

"Phil loves the paycheck."

Relaxing her hold, Cassie sat up straighter to really look him over. Dallas' hair was shorter now—Cassie cut it for him in her trailer one night, scissors in one hand and a glass of wine suspended high in the other until he grabbed the wine from her and threatened to run into Charlottetown to have his hair cut professionally. The cut was meant to be a temporary measure so Dallas wouldn't have to wear the ball cap all the time to hide his true identity from what Cassie called his redneck fans. He'd have his regular stylist trim his hair up properly when he was back in Toronto.

"He cares about you, Dal," Cassie said quietly now. "Phil's your friend."

"Mmpphh." Dallas watched Ry high-five a new friend across the playground, on the deck of a large wooden pirate ship fixture. "Nobody's really your friend in the music business," he griped. "They either want your money or to be able to say they know you, or there're other artists climbing over you to get to the top."

"Will you see Deborah in Toronto?" Letting go of him, Cassie reached for the soupy mess of ice cream at her side. She focused on it while she waited for his answer.

"I will," Dallas admitted. "We've got some gigs lined up. But Cas, let's not do that thing where we hash out old relationships, okay? Or worry about what they do or don't mean to us now. And let's try to find a way to spend time together. Distance won't do us any favors."

"I think we've both learned that the hard way, haven't we, Dal?" The emerald eyes Dallas loved were small, afraid.

"What I've learned is that I miss you when I go down to my campsite to get clean clothes. I can't say how that makes me feel about you going back to Halifax and me going back to Toronto."

"How about this?" Eyeing her plastic spoon, Cassie blushed.

"What?" Leaning forward, Dallas rested his forearms on his thighs and looked back at her on the bench. "You're awfully cute when you get that look on your face, by the way."

"What look?" Cassie finished the last bit of her ice cream and started scraping the edge of the white plastic spoon around the bowl. Holding it up to him, she smiled and licked the spoon off. "Gotta get every last bit," she explained.

"Uhhhh…" He eyed her adorable pink tongue.

"Soon," she laughed. "Bedtime's soon. The sun is setting."

"Thank God."

"Serious, now." Straightening, Cassie spoke thoughtfully, continuing her earlier proposition. "How about for September you go back to TO and sort out your schedule. Do what you need to do in order to get organized, give Phil a bonus to rearrange some dates, or whatever. Fly east to us on Fridays if you can. The campground closes October 1st. We'll be here every weekend in September."

"Tent might get chilly…"

"Goofball." Seemingly of its own volition, the spoon flicked Dallas in the arm. He grabbed it from her. "The Montana's got a heater."

"Deal," Dallas agreed. "If you can promise I won't freeze, I'll help you pack up and get that thing back to Halifax."

"Rrrrrr," she teased. "You'll look damn good behind the wheel of my big truck, music man. I always feel silly driving it."

For the second time in a few short moments, Dallas was rendered speechless. He had yet to admit the full nature of his wealth to Cassie. Lined up in the garage at home in Toronto were a number of vehicles. Not just new vehicles, either. Dallas owned some classic vintage cars, and two small antique airplanes. His favorite was a Tiger Moth, a World War I biplane. Dallas didn't fly it—no one did—but one of these days he planned to get it restored and up into the air. Just…the last little while he'd kinda lost the desire. Now the skies were suddenly a deeper blue, and beckoning him again. *Life* was bluer and beckoning again.

"I'd—I'd be happy to drive that big wreck of yours," he stuttered, then relaxed and reminded himself to have faith in her. Grasping Cassie's hand, he gave it a little pressure and gazed serenely into her beautiful, trusting eyes.

She frowned. "Um…I know you're not a real redneck. Can you actually tow that trailer? I can get the campground to store it for me."

"Ouch!" Slamming a palm into his chest, Dallas sat back and feigned being hurt. "I think you just mortally wounded me."

She went white. Realizing what he'd said, Dallas gasped. "No. That's not what I meant, Cassie, you know it's not…"

"I'm just teasing," she croaked. "You told me you grew up on a ranch. And I've seen that fancy clothesline you rigged up between two trees. I know you're capable of more than just looking good on stage and belting out songs with three chords." A spot of color worked its way back into her cheeks.

"Don't forget the tarp. That thing was a bitch to tether."

"Speaking of forgetting, don't forget the blue-tick hound. For your next song, I mean. Every second country song has a blue-tick hound in it."

"Cuz it sounds cool," Dallas grinned. "Say it out loud with a sullen bite to it. Try it now. Blue-tick hound." He laughed.

"Ah," Cassie prodded, giving him a jab in the ribs. "Can you say that in bed tonight? Whisper it in my ear."

"Honey, I will say whatever the heck you want in bed."

It was Cassie's turn to be rendered mute. It was all she could do not to climb onto Dallas' lap and start kissing him now.

The sultry moment was broken when Ry rushed over and leaned on his mom's lap. "Mom, are we having a campfire tonight? Because if we are I wanna invite Jack and his sister over. And guess what? Jack takes piano lessons. But he hates piano. He wants to learn guitar. I told him maybe, um..." He looked at Dallas.

"Your mom can ask Jack's parents if he can come over," Dallas said with a wary look at Cassie. "If it's okay with them, you and I can show Jack a few chords. How's that sound, Ry?"

"The whole neighborhood'll be over," Cassie sighed as Ry high-fived Dallas and ran back to his new friend. "In Halifax, I mean, when they find out who my new man is."

"Only the rednecks, right? Maybe we'll find out where Dean Brody lives and how he's getting along. We'll move next door." Dallas tucked an arm around Cassie's shoulders again and leaned back against the high slatted fence that protected the playground and kept the campground kids safely enclosed.

"In the meantime, Dal, as long as Ry is here at Castle Beach I think we need to find a way to keep him from introducing you to too many people. Someone's bound to recognize you."

"They won't." Dallas drew a finger through the shorter locks that, in many ways, liberated him. A weight was lifted when the long snippets of his blond hair landed on the floor of the Montana at his feet. "They don't expect me to be here, Cassie. Nobody's got me on their radar."

"Well, no songs tonight, at least. Your voice has this husky, sensual quality that—"

"Oh, we're back to that, are we?" A deep pearl blue settled into Dallas' eyes.

Cassie shivered with delight. "I really hope Jack and his sister have an early curfew." She leaned into him. "Then you can sing all the songs you like."

He chuckled before answering. "Everyone's on summer holiday. Do any of these kids have curfews?" Dallas waved a hand around the playground. Nearby, two children who couldn't be more than two or three were fighting at the bottom of a yellow slide as, above, the sunset deepened into garlands of grapefruit pink and the sky sighed into its magical end-of-day blue-black.

"Then we'll give Ry a bedtime. How's that, singer-man?"

His grin was enough of a response. They settled back to watch Ry play for a few more minutes before they eased up off the bench to join him and his new friends for a few rounds of color tag.

Later, a crackling campfire sparked its way into their memories as one of the best of the summer. Dallas and Ry played their guitars until Jack's parents joined them for s'mores and happy chatter. After the kids went to bed, Dallas led Cassie up to the Montana's small bedroom, and they sank into each other's bodies the way new lovers do, with reckless abandon and never-ending kisses.

It was a perfect night that ended the way perfect nights do. Cassie and Dallas pushed away the thought of summer coming to a close. The idea of their island sanctuary winding down and prepping for fall was untenable. Soon everything would change, and real life, with its ups and downs and hurts and challenges, would start anew.

Chapter Twenty-three

*I*t was okay at first. The weekend travelling was tiresome, especially given the late nights in each other's comforting arms, which were more than just sex. Cassie and Dallas had a lot to learn about each other. Late night chats perched on the Montana's king bed became exploratory in more ways than one, and soon their relationship, which really began with soulful looks in a camp store, was cemented on shared secrets and long-buried hurts that somehow seemed less painful when they were brought out into the light of trust and love.

At the end of September, closing up the Montana for the winter had the dual effect of adding a new layer to a blooming love—an elevated chapter of new things to come, per se—as well as creating a nervous apprehension that the magic of Castle Beach might not carry over to the reality of day-to-day life. Using fingers and plastic knives to nudge tiny homes and villages out of sandy beaches and taking hand-in-hand strolls around sandstone rocks were magical in themselves, but they happened in an illusory place where the setting sun had the power to add colorful textures and dreamlike bliss to a simple day. Now, the real world awaited—one where jobs and schedules and the daily grind would take precedence over cuddles and lovemaking under a carpet of stars during an enchanting, surreal Darnley summer.

Cassie's heart did a double-take the day Dallas traded in his flip-flops and plaid shorts for worn brown boots and jeans, and replaced his ball cap with a cowboy hat before sliding in behind the wheel of the silver Ford to tow the big trailer back to Halifax.

The man was her summer lover, no doubt about that. Dallas took her fingers and brushed his lips against them before turning right and making his way slowly up the lane to the Lower Darnley Road. But there was a newness about him now. When it came to important manly pursuits like winterizing the trailer with antifreeze and pulling the thing off its summer lot next to the Basin, sweet, sexy, spoiled superstar Dallas turned out to be as focused and capable as the 'guy next door.' Peering intently in the rearview and side mirrors while he drove, he took on a serious countenance as he studied the weight of the trailer and how well it adjusted to being towed.

Driving toward the Confederation Bridge, Cassie pondered that over the summer she had also discovered that with him there was always music of sorts. Dallas' very essence was soaked up in music. He even found it in the day-to-day rhythms of life by the shore, like in the chickadees and robins telling stories over wispy branches as the sun broke over the horizon, or in the salt-sea spray that washed over the sand in a low, peaceful flow. When he worked on his sandcastles or barbecued or dried the dishes, Dallas hummed—happy melodies usually, and Cassie never asked but she always wondered if he was going over his current hits or whether new tunes were taking hold in his busy, creative mind.

Heading south, they passed fields of ripe soybeans, the wispy stalks now rough to the touch and brown with age so the entire fields were waves of russet beauty. Potatoes, too, were not the verdant, leafy wonders they were earlier in the summer—island farmers had sprayed the crops to put a halt to the growing process, so the potato skins wouldn't be too thick. The tops of the plants were decaying and lifeless now, which jarred Cassie as they passed. Even though this was the expected cycle of the agricultural season, this definitive and final end to the growing period was hard to bear—cruel even, as if the island itself had an end-of-summer expiry date that said the fairylike spell was over.

Leaving the simple day-to-day living of Castle Beach, their home under expansive skies nestled in the bosom of nature, was painful; it had been in the Eddie days too. But a surprise awaited Cassie and Dallas, and it gave the difficult day new hope. With Ry in the backseat of the big silver truck, his sunburnt nose stuck in a video game on Cassie's iPad, they made their exit from the blessed Darnley beachside paradise in a light sun shower and were sent on their way to new beginnings via the wondrous, mystical appearance of a dazzling rainbow. It was a surprise spied by Dallas via the rearview mirror. When he alerted Cassie to its presence, he wound his fingers around hers, so she let the sadness of leaving Castle Beach go, relaxed her shoulders, smiled, and eased her tired body back into the passenger seat of the big Ford.

All the way back to Halifax she was soothed by the easy creak-creak-creaking of the trailer moving over bumps and rolling along the highway with the grace and elegance of an eagle, piloted by the capable hands of a man whose love she did not expect to find on Prince Edward Island's north shore, and whose simple presence next to her during the three hour drive seemed to be a divinely orchestrated gift.

Halifax was a harbor city marred by the age-old tragedy of an exploded munitions ship during the First World War. The fiery inferno killed thousands on that fateful day and reduced much of the city to ashes, as if some unseen giant laid an arm over the place, wrinkled up a lip in a diabolical grin, and heartlessly swiped the arm sideways.

Like Cassie and Dallas, the city was a survivor, bent on thriving despite its losses, bent on carrying on the way the salt-sea air did, in fits and spurts and in dreams and hopes as the ocean breeze saw fit. Cassie's historic home in the south end was snuggled into the fabric of the city the same way Halifax's history was a part of her tragic makeup. The house survived the 1917 explosion—its occupants did not, since they were on the waterfront that awful day proudly showing visiting family members the seafaring busy-ness of their hometown harbor. Maybe it was that knowledge that got Cassie out of bed on the tougher days—that she and the house owed each other something, that they needed each other's strength to carry on, and each other's shelter and tender loving care to let tragedy go, and to simply exist.

To Cassie, Halifax was the little red squares in the center of the larger squares that made up the log cabin quilt on her guest room bed. Those squares represented the hearth fires of yore—kitchen fires that were kept burning twenty-four-seven. They were lights that gave her hope. The historic city was a place that screamed 'start over,' where folks from the more rural parts of the oft-downtrodden east coast maritime provinces travelled when they needed work, where people went when they were in need of a change.

Maritime culture was bigger than life in Halifax. Traditional and contemporary music, art, walks along the boardwalk that often ended with a peek inside the Maritime Museum of the Atlantic to lay wondering eyes on the wooden deck chairs found floating in the icy waters after the ill-fated Titanic sank; that was the fabric of Halifax. She was a living, breathing fighter, a bustling city with a haughty attitude that said, "I dare you." In the next breath she whispered, "Welcome."

But most of all, Halifax was a place where Cassie belonged, a city where Eddie's spirit was rooted, where Ry first made his squalling appearance into the world and where meaningful work gave Cassie purpose. Introducing Dallas to Halifax would make him a part of all that—of the things that mattered, the things that didn't, and the things that should.

In many ways for the already fidgety Dallas, Halifax would be a test.

Despite the sadness of leaving their summer refuge behind, stepping inside Cassie's house turned out to be a coming home, for Cassie and Ry, obviously, because the heritage house was their compass—it was their permanent nest. But it was a homecoming for Dallas as well—especially for him—because to him, home was where love was, and his Toronto mansion was no more than an empty cave. It echoed its artifice and loneliness from the north wall to the south wall, and everywhere in between.

Wisely, Cassie stood back and let Dallas wander through her cozy home without her for the first time, although Ry was at his side the entire time, respectfully quiet as if he understood the gravity of allowing another man into his father's domain, even if it was only Eddie's spiritual essence and not his physical body that populated the place in the last six years. Humbled, Dallas did okay until he spied Cassie and Eddie's wedding photo on her dresser. He'd expected to come upon some of Eddie's things, so the photo wasn't mind-numbing cruel to stumble upon. Instead, it spoke to Cassie's capacity to deeply love a man. Knowing what he meant to her only served to remind Dallas of just how privileged he was to be the man to break through her tough façade, to be deserving of her love. At the same time, the responsibility to love her right, to love Ry right, was daunting.

It almost seemed that Ry could read his mind. Cassie had stepped up behind them. As she watched, Ry took Dal's hand and gave it a little shake. Dallas, standing at the entrance to Cassie's bedroom, looked down at him.

"Dal, my dad is glad you're here. He's real glad," Ry told him, his eyes serious and steady.

"Oh. And you know that how?" Dallas was grinning just slightly, enough to counter the wet sheen that crossed his eyes as he peered down at Eddie's child. He wondered if Ry had some kind of intuitive connection with Eddie's ghost, which he had to admit was more than a little unsettling.

"Because," Ry smiled widely, squeezing Dallas' hand. "He was worried about my mother. He didn't like her being alone so much."

"Ah." Dallas couldn't speak. Glancing over at Cassie, who had lifted a hand to her mouth and was anxiously pinching her bottom lip with her thumb and forefinger, he raised his chin and smiled. Intuition had nothing to do with Ry's comment. Both Dallas and Cassie knew this; they knew Ry well enough to discern that the person who was really glad to have Dallas take the reins was, well, Ry. Pulling the boy to him, Dallas whispered a hushed *I'll do my best* to Eddie. A moment later, Cassie joined the family hug. From over Dallas' shoulder Eddie watched, frozen in time on the day he married Cassie, when life was new and filled with promise.

Later, Cassie tucked the photo away.

Dallas stayed in the city for part of the week. The first of Cassie's 'people' besides Caroline to meet him was her staff when he toured the theater. The day he left, with a sad smile and a promise to see her the following weekend, she was accosted with questions. It was the first concrete—but not surprising—clue Cassie had that her new love truly belonged to the world at large, and not just to her.

"What about Deborah?" This was from Marla, a young Irish raven-haired communications officer hired to market the theater. Impertinent, brusque, efficient, tailored in dress and speech, she was of the uber-confident generation that feared nothing. Marla was the kind of gal that walked down the beach looking for someone who was drinking beer so she could ask to use that person's bottle opener on her non-twist-off-cap cooler bottle.

Outside of the theater, Cassie would be found hiding in Marla's shadow. Running the theater was an exception for Cassie, although Marla's scrupulous

Indigo-blue eyes were set on the prize—Cassie's job. Thankfully for Cassie, theater admin tasks utilized her pre-Eddie persona—the one part of her that splintered off and stayed strong when all else fell to pieces.

Crossing her arms when she put Cassie to the test, Marla leaned her full weight—ninety-eight pounds soaking wet, not counting new Nine West heels—against Cassie's office door frame. She didn't have the social filter not to add, "Deborah's the love of his life. Everybody knows that."

Under her breath, Cassie seethed. *Marla, do you actually believe all the garbage you read on social media?* She made a new point of checking on what the young woman wrote about the theater and its artists before anything was posted online. "They ended their relationship in June," was all she managed to say out loud, however. Sometimes she had to remind herself that she was Marla's superior. The girl's Irish boldness could be intimidating when she wanted it to be, and now was no exception.

Marla didn't give up. "They were supposed to get married," she complained. Standing in the doorway of Cassie's office, looking down at Cassie who, in her plump leather chair, felt somewhat dwarfed in the direct line of the girl's glare, she added, "All the best celebrity blogs said they set a date and everything!"

Cassie sat back and folded her arms in imitation—or was the movement a silent snipe, she wondered inwardly—before she retorted sharply, "You don't strike me as a country music fan, Marla." A quick scan of the girl's tight black skirt and matching tailored jacket over a breast-busting white blouse sealed the supposition.

"So describe country music fans, Cassie." Irritated, Marla bit off, "You might want to learn a little more about what you're getting into before you go digging your Christian LeBoutin heels into Dallas White. Can't see you sitting through half a tune without rolling your eyes, much less an entire show. At least Deborah understood his music." Turning to storm away, evidently heartbroken, Marla was clearly sulking when she whipped around one last time and haughtily declared, "How can you even suggest that you love the man if you don't give a hoot about his soul? His music is his soul, Cassie. Dallas White is famous for bleeding all over the stage. And his ballad with Deborah crossed over to the pop charts, by the way. Debuted at the top of the charts and stayed at number one for weeks on end. But you classical music types have your pretentious little heads buried so far up Beethoven's ass that you wouldn't lower yourselves enough to have a clue about that now, would you?"

And with that final stamp on the betrayal that Marla and the rest of Dallas' fans were about to take on as their own when Cassie's relationship with Dallas became known, Marla swept away in a shower of lilac perfume, her movements marked by arrogant clicks of her new shoes on the hardwood floor.

"Oh, boy," Cassie exhaled, lifting a hand to her mouth and running two fingers over the top lip. "Someone needs to do her research." And she wasn't talking about Marla.

That night after helping Ry with his homework, Cassie got on the phone to Caroline. The next evening she felt prepared enough to jump on a three-way Skype meeting with Dallas and Phil.

"I need to know how this is going to work," she said.

By midnight, a schedule was ironed out. Cassie would join Dallas at certain industry events (her stomach cringed at the thought of all the insincere small talk she'd have to indulge in. Yeesh. Local business events were hard enough to stomach). Some of these would be fundraisers, some were dinners, some were on-stage appearances and some were full-out concerts. All would involve a certain spattering of backstage wanderings—hopefully, Cassie calmed herself, with a glass (or three) of Pinot Grigio in hand.

"Into the breach," she said to herself when she signed off the Skype call that night.

And into the breach she went.

Initially, despite the usual wide-eyed surprise that most of Dallas' acquaintances tried to cover up (usually kindly but not always graciously), Cassie and Dallas got along well. He held her hand and squeezed it when he felt she needed reassurance, and he never left her floundering on her own like Phil did when Dallas left Cassie's side and headed to the stage.

"They've all got their own issues, trust me," Dallas told Cassie one day when Cassie remarked how seamless the whole transition into Dal's life as his romantic partner seemed to be going. "These people are all me-me-me. Two seconds and they're over us."

It was the gossip columnists and the bloggers that set the wheels turning counter-clockwise, and it was nosey Marla of all people, from Cassie's office, that got them there.

Marla got a call from a celebrity blogger one day, a half-hour after Cassie left the office in a hurry, bounding out of the door to head to the airport to meet Dallas' private jet for a trip to L.A. Brimming with jealousy, Marla was only too happy to answer questions.

"Eddie? Oh, Cassie's *husband*. Yes, he died in that fire in Alberta. Led nine other guys to their deaths, too. Tragic. No, he wasn't from Alberta. Nova Scotia sent firefighters out west to help. Was it because he wasn't experienced in fighting forest fires? No, um, I..."

With a nervous twist of her updo clip, Marla sneered, shrugged in a nonchalant sort of way, and went for Cassie's throat. "Well, Eddie was a reckless kind of guy. What do I mean by that? He liked his toys, let me put it that way. Four-by-fours, motorbikes, Sea-doos...I think he even had a sailboat for a few years. He only cared about himself, about having fun. He was selfish and he used others to prop himself up, to get promotions at work, that kind of thing. What do I mean? Do your research. He was a trained firefighter. Ask yourself why he would get himself and his team caught in a hopeless situation like the one that killed them. He should have known better. That's what I'm saying."

With or without Dallas, Eddie was Cassie's soul. One reason her relationship with Dallas was working so well was because Dal got that about her, that she once loved a man with an intensity that, six years later, still sometimes crippled her. That she was capable of that kind of love. Eddie—for Cassie— was what music was to Dallas. He fed her spirit before Dallas came along; his memory was what often kept her going. He, like Dallas' slow tunes, was the part of her that bled.

But for Ry, Eddie was his dad. Eddie was a superhero Ry could only conjure up deep in dreams at night or in tellings to his schoolmates that left him trembling with loss for a father he would never truly know.

The day the first media story broke, it was Ry who got wind of it first.

One crisp autumn morning when the leaves littered the ground in crimson glory, their trees bared to the bitter breeze above them, a kid grabbed Ry's shoulder and flipped him around to face him. Ry staggered back with a bloody nose before he even had an inkling of what was coming, and definitely before he had a chance to defend himself. They were on the playground at school, it was recess, and a full five minutes of accusations and lies passed before a teacher got wind of what was going on and broke in between the two. Ry didn't fight back. Stupefied, all the strength he could muster was to hold his forearms in front of him like a shield and gape in confused, bewildered silence at the bully who attacked him.

"He's a liar," the kid, stocky Ernie Lawless (*appropriate name*, Ry thought since the boy was the school's most famous bully) maintained to the angry teacher, hunching up his shoulders to make himself look tougher than Ry knew him to really be. "He said he was a hero. My dad says the papers are saying he's the one who killed them!"

"Who?" the teacher asked, clearly puzzled as to whom they were even talking about. "Who was a hero?"

"Ry's dad, that's who! But he wasn't. Ry's a liar! My dad says they were just covering up the truth, that's what. But now everybody knows."

A slow, silent tear trickled its way down Ry's cheek. Mixing with the blood from his nose, it worked its way toward his mouth. Swiping a knuckled fist across it was the only way Ry could figure to stop the bleeding. Oddly, afterwards he caught himself staring at the smear on his hand and wondering how he could get it off before his mom found out.

After she got the news about Ry's messed-up school day, and the 'why' of it, Cassie spent a few good hours on her knees vomiting off and on into the toilet in Dallas' L.A. suite. It was Sunday before she heard, two days after the playground attack. Figuring rightly that hearing about it wouldn't do Cassie any good, Caroline had staunchly avoided putting Ry on the phone all weekend.

"Birthday party," Cassie moaned to Dallas, who rushed in a few hours later, grabbed the softest, most plush bath towel he could find, and gently lifted Cassie's small frame so he could place the towel under her knees to cushion her from the hard, mirror-shiny tile. "And hockey practice. The day at the Discovery Center made him too tired, he's sleeping. She used every excuse she could find not to put him on the phone with me."

Dallas panicked. He'd found out from a band member yesterday, a guy who trolled social media the way big game hunters troll for places to hunt—always looking for the next big thing. Like Caroline, Dallas had kept the news from Cassie as long as he could, even going so far as to commission Phil into staying silent. But tonight on the red carpet, some unscrupulous asshole of a reporter had asked Cassie point blank how her husband died. And followed that heartless question with an all-knowing, "Is it true he's now being posthumously charged with murder?"

Hence the vomiting for the last few hours. Cassie retched again while Dallas ministered to her. He had nothing to say. She was pissed enough at him tonight for not being accessible to her—starting before the show, before he had to go on stage, before she was expected to sit through it. (She didn't—after the reporter accosted her, she feigned a headache and dashed back to the limo in the care of an assistant while Phil dragged Dallas away, threatening a lawsuit if he broke his contract to perform). All Dallas could muster post-show now was a weak apology while he dabbed Cassie's brow with a cool washcloth.

Seething, knowing in her heart that Dallas' musical appearances were beyond his control, Cassie shoved his hand away. When the latest bout of retching stopped she sat back on her haunches and sobbed. "I had decided I could handle it," she moaned. "You, I mean. Us. I knew it wouldn't be easy on Ry. But I never considered they would attack Eddie." His name was uttered with reverence; with the expectation that Dallas would understand how low the reporter had stooped.

Speechless, Dallas raised his arms and sat back against the closed door. *How can I tell her that the way this works is like a ferris wheel that goes faster and faster and faster until someone goes flying off? How can I tell her that this is only the beginning?*

"Dallas…" Cassie was crying openly now. "My husband has been gone for six years. How can they attack a man who is not even here to defend himself? How can they destroy a boy this way? I know Eddie wasn't perfect."

"You can't call a man a hero, Cassie, and then wonder why his myth disintegrates so fast when the truth comes out."

She shook her head. "I never thought of him as a hero. I knew the truth, Dal. I always knew the truth. He could be reckless. But it was usually for the greater good, at least in his mind it was!"

Dallas' response was a solemn, heartbroken whisper. "I'm not talking about you, sweetheart. I'm talking about them. The people who make this stuff up. Who pump it out to the world."

A light came on. It blinked on as surely as the power button on the camera that caught Cassie's astonished reaction earlier on the red carpet at the awful accusation, at the tarnishing of Eddie's long gone spirit for his young son to discover. "You're talking about you. About what they say about you."

"I see it all around me, Cassie. It's one of the reasons I needed your magical beach. That hero talk destroyed me too. I disintegrated when I realized the truth of who I was. Of who I am. That I'm not the god the world makes me out to be."

Cassie peered up at him from behind long, damp lashes. "Us, Dal. It's going to destroy us."

"No. You know why? Because we won't let it." He reached for her hand.

"He's eight years old, Dal. Ry's just a boy."

Grasping her fingers, Dallas appealed to Cassie's sense of logic. "Don't hit the panic button, Cassie. We've got a good thing going here. You and me, we're a good thing. Our castle, remember? This is our castle."

"Castles aren't real, Dal. They're illusions, every bit as much as walking on stage is an illusion for you. You said it yourself. In the end we're all just alone. They can attack me all they want. They can even attack Eddie if they want to go that low, and it seems they do, the vultures." A sob interrupted her little speech, but Cassie steeled her nerves and marched on. "But they cannot attack my son. This, whatever we have…it can't destroy my son. Do you see? Our castle didn't win, in the end."

The first real twinge of panic skittered across Dallas' worried face like a skater skidding to a stop. Shards of ice flew in every direction, covering their idyllic paradise with the same bone chilling frost that would soon permeate Castle Beach. "Our castle was never about winning," he said carefully. "It was about building something good and true, and continuously working at it to make it better. If you were to put them all together, they were a whole ton of castles, strung together along the beach like beacons. Like hope. Each and every one we built gave me hope. That I would be okay. That everything would be okay."

Cassie tossed her arms out to the sides. "And then what happened to the castles, Dal? Hmmm? Each and every one? The tide swooped in and carried them away. It picked at them bit by bit until there was nothing left but memories of what we built."

Dallas stood, but made no effort to help Cassie up off the shiny floor. She stared at her newly pedicured toenails as he spoke. False. It was all false, this world Dallas lived in. It was vicious and mean, and as fake and cruel as the paint on her nails, shiny at first until it got beat up on the rocks and grit of everyday life.

He turned in a circle before he spoke. "You know what your problem is, Cassie? You give up too soon. That's your problem. One little thing puts a dent in your equilibrium, and you bury your head under the covers and forget about all the good. You're a hider. You hide."

Gripping the edge of the toilet bowl, Cassie rose and faced him. "Yes," she whispered harshly. "I hide. I'm good at it, I know. I've had six years of practice. But Dallas?" She emphasized his full name. "At least I know what's most important."

Faltering, he hesitated before answering. But adrenaline and fear were getting the most of Dallas. "This was never a contest between your son and myself, Cassie. Don't make it out to be."

"My son," she whispered. "*My* son."

He took it as Cassie taking possession of Ry again.

She meant it as a hurt response to the way he referred to Ry—*your* son.

But neither had the wherewithal to get past the new pain to sort out what Ry meant to both of them and to Dallas in particular.

A knock at the door jarred Cassie and Dallas away from the futility of the situation and back to action. Phil floated in on a managerial wave of heightened suspense. He was waving something in the air.

Paper, which he handed to Cassie, not bothering to note the greenish hue of her small features.

"A ticket," she breathed, afraid to look at either Phil or at Dallas.

"I thought you'd want to head home right away, Cassie," Phil said, his air of authority breezing past Dallas and landing on the woman Phil felt distracted Dallas from where he ought to be, on the stage or writing or recording, whatever, just anyplace but with her.

Snatching the paper from her hands, Dallas held it up in front of Phil's face. "What the hell is this?"

"You need to do Dallas, Dallas. You have a show there tomorrow, remember? And another in Houston on Tuesday?"

"I need to be with Cassie. And even if she decides she needs some time alone with Ry, she sure as hell ain't flying on some damn commercial flight!"

"I'm fine," Cassie interjected, anxious to water down these new sparks before they erupted into full-blown fireworks. "I've flown commercial a thousand times."

"Not when your face was all over the news," Dallas decreed. "Not when you're bound to be recognized."

"Ha!" she laughed, a bit wickedly, he thought. Pushing past him and rushing into the bedroom, Cassie grabbed a baseball cap from a side pocket on his large duffel bag. "I'll just borrow this ragged old thing. If I'm lucky there might even be some Prince Edward Island sand on there to bring back some of those precious memories that are trying to hold us together." She dropped the cap to her thigh and tapped it with a rhythm that echoed her beating heart, which was fast and suddenly energized. "Dal?" she added as her eyes flamed. "Maybe I'll surprise you. Maybe I learned something from you through all of our castle building and destroying, and rebuilding. Maybe I am stronger than you think. Maybe when it comes to my kid I can be stronger now."

Melting, he reached for her but Cassie was losing the battle with her emotions, despite the tough statement about strength. She yanked her arm out of his reach.

Behind them Phil gloated and ordered Cassie a cab.

Chapter Twenty-four

"They're saying Eddie just wanted the adrenaline rush." Caroline wrinkled the gossip magazine she was reading as if the sudden movement could rearrange the hostile words typed in black ink on the page. "The glory. That he didn't like how the country looked at us east coasters like we were all no-gooders who exist on cycles of employment insurance. He wanted to make a statement. They say he wanted to be famous."

"Fame. Ha." A low chortle escaped Cassie's throat. She slammed her chef's knife into a tomato, which bled seeds and watery red juice all over her wooden cutting board. "You can take fame and shove it up Eddie's ass. And Dallas' too, while you're at it."

"Cassie," Caroline chided, nodding toward the door. They were at Caroline and Des' home in Halifax, since Cassie's one-and-a-half story south end heritage house was currently under siege by the media. Caroline's big house was a modern affair, classy and elegant, like the madam of the house herself. Ry was peeking around a door frame by the kitchen, as silent as he used to be in the old days when he used to watch his mother self-combust. The only difference these days was that Cassie seemed to have some serious fight in her, whereas before she was always quick to crumple into a ball and check out for a day or so.

Twisting around, Ry went back to the den where he had access to his uncle's Nintendo Wii, Des' chosen stress reliever. Soon the women in the kitchen heard the intro music of a video game start up.

Cassie stared at the empty space where he was standing a moment earlier. "His teacher says he won't participate in school. Not even in gym or in music class. He used to be so proud of what he could play on the guitar."

"He'll pick it up again someday, Cassie. Next time he sees Dallas—"

"There's not going to be a next time." Slam went the knife.

Cringing, Caroline dropped her magazine down on the counter she was leaning against and reached for a plastic container full of mesclun greens so she could give them a whirl through the salad spinner. "Easy, girl," she warned. Dropping the greens into one half of her double sink, Caroline levered the faucet and ran some cool water over them. "Des is looking into law suits. Defamation of Eddie's character, that kind of thing."

"Just what we need. A long trial and our heads dragged through the news day after day after day."

Cornering right, Caroline swished the greens around and heartily avoided glancing at her sister. "Have you talked to Dallas? He must be devastated. He's got a soft heart, Cassie."

"No. Nope."

Flipping around, Caroline fixed a hand on her hip. Her fingers were dripping, but she ignored the cool water. Like tears, drops fell on the robust ceramic floor. Ignored, they sat there and waited for someone to care enough to mop them up. "You might want to consider that man's feelings, hon." The words were spoken with an edge garnered from three days of Caroline watching her sister sulk and pout like a tiger on the prowl for prey. Low throaty growls were even occasionally heard as Cassie moped around the place looking in dark corners for who-knows-what to settle her racing mind and anxious heart.

"I'm considering him, all right. I'm considering what a rollercoaster knowing him has been. And how bad it can get. They're calling me a gold digger, Car. I didn't have a sweet clue who he was when I met him, I thought he was some goddamned travelling minstrel, yet they're calling me a gold digger." *Slam.* Now a cucumber was feeling the brunt of Cassie's anger.

Later that night, long after dinner was consumed and cleaned up—very little of it eaten by Cassie and Ry—Cassie succumbed to her longing and took a call from Dallas. As Caroline had months before, she answered the phone since Cassie didn't appear to want to pick it up. Cassie couldn't say no when the phone was shoved into her hands, connecting her to a man she now had to admit she loved with a fervor and passion that hurt. It connected her to a man she deeply missed and whom, unlike Eddie, she reminded her-self as she lifted the phone to her ear, was still on the planet.

She stepped quietly up the stairs to speak to him in private. Left behind, Ry snuggled under his aunt's arm and buried his face in Caroline's warmth and comfort.

The first thing Cassie clued into was that Dallas had been drinking. Sinking down onto Caroline's guest room bed, she leaned forward in some hopeless attempt at getting her breathing under control, making the wise choice not to bring the drinking up off the top. In their months together, all Dallas drank around her was a few beers, usually. But tonight he was slurring his words, just enough to give his hurts—and where he buried them—away.

"Cas…" Dallas started, from the deeply cushioned wing chair he'd dropped into before he called. "I'm tired. I need to go on stage. But I have something to say to you."

She cut in. "Ry hasn't spoken, Dal. Hardly a word since that kid attacked him at school. Did you know that?"

A frustrated *rrrrrrr* followed a wounded silence. Unable to keep an edge from his voice, Dallas said, slowly so as to get the weary liquor-infused words out, "How…could I know that? This is… the first time…you've taken my goddamned call."

"Dallas…" She bit her tongue, navigated into new territory, then started anew. "Dallas, you're a ghost. You're a ghost every bit as much as Eddie is a ghost. Up there on stage surrounded by lights coming at you in every direc-tion, you're this filmy, untouchable entity. I can't touch you there. Nobody can. The same way I can't touch Eddie. And yet…and yet…everybody around me keeps trying. They think by writing about you or by talking about you, about both of you, that somehow they can touch you. But they can't."

"Yes, Cassie…they can. They can't…hurt Eddie anymore, Cassie. But they can still hurt me. Especially…when I'm on stage. That's the core of it… that's where it starts."

"Bullshit. You're hiding up there. Do you get that, that you're hiding? Every bit as much as I hide when I pull the covers over my head? Every time you go out onto that stage you're ducking and hiding. It's your place to run to, to escape to."

"It's my job, Cas. It's what I do." He sounded completely done in. Cassie was just about to picture him in some swanky hotel room with his feet up on an ottoman—booted, of course, and maybe his belt was loosened and an elbow was resting on an armrest—when she heard a sound that alerted her to a new location. She had to switch her mind's eye to some backstage dressing room. Cassie was new to the whole high-level music scene, but already the happy buzz and clink of bottles coming to her now over the phone was familiar. It was the sound of partiers after a show.

She wrinkled her nose. "What time is it there, Dal?"

He caught on. "We haven't…done the show yet, Cas. We're…just getting wound up. Band's…gittin' pumped."

Dallas was in Houston. Maybe more inebriated than Cassie originally thought. Alarm peppered her brain, which fired into some weird hybrid offensive/defensive mix. Taking a breath, she dove in. "You been drinkin', Dal."

"Oh. Yep, well, just a bit of the old black rum. Thassall." In Houston, Dallas lifted an arm and Deborah climbed onto his lap. He tried to put a finger to his lips to signal to her to be quiet, but the movement propelled the phone out of his slippery grasp and sent it flying. It landed between his thigh and the seat cushion.

She went fishing for it.

He groaned, and Cassie listened while Deborah chided him. "Now Dallas, rest up. Let me have that thing." A moment later she spoke into the phone. "Hello, Cassie."

Cassie was rendered mute. Deborah continued while Dallas tried to keep his eyes open. She spoke in a low tone, but both Dallas and Cassie heard and computed every word. "He's in trouble tonight, Cassie. We're on in less than an hour and your man can't keep his eyes open. It's not all liquor, either, if that's what you're thinking."

"Weed? He's been smoking? Or something worse?" *Alarm…*

"No, honey. Have you ever known Dallas to light up?"

"Oh, um…he's not sleeping, then."

"Is that a surprise? I suppose you're drifting off into dreamland every night like a baby."

"Every night." Cassie sighed sarcastically, rested her elbow on her thigh and buried her forehead in her hand. "Like clockwork."

"He talked to me, you know." Deborah saw Dallas' eyes flick open. She held his worried gaze. "He told me that you don't like his music."

"I never really...I like some of it." Cassie swallowed.

"You know what I think? I think you're a pretentious bitch. He deserves better."

"Lovely." *I'm gonna be sick.*

In Houston Dallas grunted, narrowed his eyes, and reached for the phone. But since it appeared there were two phones in his vision, or maybe even three, he failed miserably and chewed on his lip instead.

Deborah continued. "He said your husband liked country music. And you loved him."

Cassie blinked and raised her head. "He did. Eddie was a redneck."

A low chortle came over the line from Texas. "Aren't we all, honey?" The sugary Georgia accent didn't have a hint of liquor in its saccharine sweet tone. "But you've never given country a chance. Not even with this Eddie you apparently loved so much that you hid his reckless butt from the world."

"What happened in Alberta is not really known, Deborah. And it has nothing to do with me, anyway."

"I realize that, honey. And I don't think this whole 'dragging your long gone husband through the dirt' thing is really what has you running away from my sweet Dallas here. My sweet broken-hearted man."

Cassie gulped.

"You're hiding behind your little boy and behind the power this business has to destroy people, but what you're really afraid of is losing Dallas the same way you lost Eddie. You're afraid you're not enough for him. You weren't strong enough for Eddie—you're still not, Dallas says—so how can you be strong enough for a man with the fame and power Dallas has?"

"It's true, Deborah." Cassie was losing it now. Someone was finally voicing all those thoughts that Cassie pushed away time and time again, because she wanted him—Dallas—so badly. Someone finally had the courage to call her on it. "He's a ghost too. I just told him that. On stage he's already a goddamned ghost. All those lights...like he's in Heaven. Unreachable."

"Like your husband."

"Like Eddie. Yes."

"He's reachable on stage, Cassie. I think you've seen him sing enough to know that now."

"I don't know." Cassie swallowed. "He didn't used to think he was. He used to think he was alone up there." *Until I came along. And made him vulnerable.*

"I heard what he said to you just now. But I'm not talking about the power to hurt him when he's on stage." Deborah softened on Dallas' lap as he blinked his eyes shut again and quietly listened. "All those people, honey. He said you understood that, that all those people get his music. So I think he's reachable. In a good way. There's a reciprocal relationship there, between us singers and our audiences. Otherwise why would we bother? The problem, honey, is that he feels lost, like he's being pulled in too many directions. And that the one person whose opinion really matters and who could truly give him the anchor he needs is the one person who is too damn selfish to see him for who he really is. And that, girlfriend, is a man who is drawn to his power the same way your husband was drawn to his."

"And we know what happened to Eddie, Deborah. Where his reckless power maybe took him. Don't we? That's what's happening, and it's hurting more than just Dallas. It's hurting my son."

"Dallas is not Eddie, Cassie. Dallas is not a reckless man, he's just a man who, above and beyond all, is in love with a woman. It's that simple. But love is a two way street. You're the only audience he cares about. You're the reciprocal relationship that really matters."

"Deborah…sometimes I think it's a sign. Seeing him up there in all those lights…like he's surrounded by all this glory, by this glow…"

"Pshaw. If you're going to say it's a sign and he's in Heaven, let me pooh-pooh that nonsense right now. The only Heaven this man is in on stage is the one where the music elevates him to some special place in his soul. Get that nonsense out of your head right now."

Despite herself, Cassie laughed. It was actually a relief to hear Deborah tell it like it is.

"You still love him, Deborah?"

259

In Houston, Deborah smiled fondly at Dallas. She bent and softly kissed his cheek. "You bet, honey," she sighed. "But I've long ago learned that men who love other women are not worth the effort it takes to skin a cat. But let me add one thing…"

"What's that?" Even through the phone, Deborah could hear Cassie smiling.

"I love him enough to want to see him happy. And if you can't make him happy, then I'd rather you step aside and let someone else try." She frowned at Dallas, who blinked on eye open and shot her a terrified look. "Not that he's ready for anyone else yet. Might be a while," she admitted, and half smiled at the forlorn eyes peeking sleepily up at her. "We have bigger problems now, anyway. Phil's gonna fire half his band for gittin' Dallas drunk before a show."

"Can you put him back on the phone, Deborah? And…thanks, by the way."

"You got it, honey. Incidentally, though, before I go, I can help you with that gossip stuff. So you don't need to think you're not strong enough for him, to deal with the downside of his fame, I mean. Most of us learn the hard way how to deal with it. But it's only the tough ones who survive. And Cassie… somehow I think you're one of the tough ones, even if you don't always see that in yourself."

"Thanks." Mumbling, Cassie's heart was full. How strange that the person who knew her the least…somehow knew her the best.

Deborah handed the phone back to Dallas, who tried to open his eyes and focus on the bell-peal voice he loved and missed.

"If I was there I'd kick your drunken ass to Alaska and back," Cassie whispered to him, in a much tender tone than she started their conversation with. "Go take a cold shower, redneck singer-man. Music man of mine. We'll talk next week, okay?"

His eyes lit up, followed by a quiet smile. "Next summer," he told her, mustering up some strength, "we'll build ourselves a real sweet castle, Cassie. We'll get Ry in on it. And we'll win that contest."

"Somehow," she sighed, "I think we've already won, Dal." She brightened. "Did you know that when castles were still being lived in, the people in them listened to baroque music?"

He frowned. "I don't even think I know what that is."

"Come to the symphony at my theater next weekend and find out." She was giggling when Phil grabbed the phone out of his star's hand and spoke abruptly to her.

"I suppose I should be grateful you got a smile out of him," he snarled, giving Dallas a righteous glare at the same time. Relief washed over Phil, as if someone had blissfully and peacefully sprinkled him with gold dust straight from Heaven. For a few serious moments tonight, he had rehearsed a difficult conversation with the venue, part of which was 'yeah, well, I can kick Dallas' butt from here to Highwater, but it ain't gonna translate to a good show.' Nope, the only thing Phil knew that could possibly put Dallas in a good enough mood to do his usual knock 'em dead set was the power held by the feminine voice on the other end of this phone. Despite the relief, it kinda pissed Phil off.

"I'm hitting 'end,' Cassie," he snapped ungraciously, and punched the iPhone's red 'hang-up' icon before she had a chance to protest.

Dallas had lightened up, *Thank God for that,* Phil muttered under his breath, but there was one other thing that, in Phil's experience, his artist needed in order to get sobered up enough not to trip all over the cables stretched here, there and everywhere on the stage. Grabbing Dallas' leather jacket at the shoulder, he clenched a bunch of it in a fist and hauled the singer to his feet.

Stumbling, Dallas protested. "Easy there, big fella." The room spun.

Catching Phil's eye, Deborah grabbed Dallas' opposite elbow and helped propel him to a large washroom at the back of the green room space.

Dragging his feet on the way there, Dallas asked Phil what baroque music was like. "I've heard of it…I just can't identify it," he slurred lightly.

Phil harrumphed. In his opinion, his singer had no business thinking about any music other than country at the present moment. "There's not much chance you can even identify your own tunes right now, Dal," he bit off. "Get in the bloody shower. You've got twenty minutes to sober up."

Deborah yanked off her ex's jacket and dropped it on the floor. It puddled around Dallas' feet and lay there forgotten until Phil, knowing it was part of tonight's on-stage wardrobe, grudgingly kicked the jacket back so it wouldn't get stepped on.

Curling up a forefinger and hooking it toward her body, Deborah grinned viciously at Dallas. "Gimme your boot, honey. And if you have a mind, don't stop there. I miss those abs."

Raising his arms, Dallas backed away, narrowly missing his leather jacket and almost tripping as he moved. Phil let a few expletives fly, most of them aimed in Dallas' direction. A few leaked their way over to Deborah, who ignored him by tossing her hair and rolling her heavily mascara'd eyes.

It took the two of them to get Dallas in the shower, but it wasn't the cold water that gave him the push he would need to get through his set. It was the sweet voice of an elegant, jade-eyed woman telling him to come to her theater next weekend, and the soothing promise of future moonlit nights holding her in his arms.

Ry and Caroline were whispering conspiratorially when Cassie came back downstairs. Caroline tapped on her iPad and beamed up at Cassie, who narrowed her eyebrows and looked at her son. Ry seemed brighter, somehow. As if a load was lifted off his small shoulders.

Caroline winked. "Bedtime, methinks," she smirked at her nephew, who slipped off the couch and took his mother's hand.

"What?" Cassie asked the two of them, thinking somehow that they were up to no good. Certainly Caroline had the look she used to get when the girls were kids and she'd ripped off half of Cassie's hard-earned Halloween box chocolate bars.

"Later," Caroline answered, jumping up and grabbing Ry's small body for a backward hug. "I love you, kid."

"I love you back, Aunt Caroline," Ry smiled openly before looking up at his mom. "I love you too, Mom."

Surprised, Cassie's eyes widened. "I love you too, Ry. Now come on," she demanded. "Let's Google us some sandcastles. I don't know about you, but I need some inspiration for next summer."

"I saw one the other day that was a dinosaur. Maybe we should make us some stuff besides sandcastles next summer."

"Maybe we should," Cassie sighed, dreaming already of poking her toes into the warm summer sand of Castle Beach.

At the very same moment in Houston, as icy water ran over his body Dallas leaned against the tiled wall, closed his eyes, and did the same.

Chapter Twenty-five

"This is my dad."

Clutched in Ry's hands was the framed photo of his father in working fireman's clothes, complete with the battered helmet that Ry knew was the crowning glory, the reason the kids in his fourth grade class exuded a hallo'd *ahhhhh* all at the same time.

"He was a fireman, and he died six years ago while fighting a forest fire in Alberta."

In the back of the classroom, seated on a kid-sized chair, Cassie brushed a loose wasp of hair behind her ear and leaned both forearms on the desktop in front of her. Next to her, Dallas got a little attention when he shifted his chair closer to Cassie and it made a big *scrunchhh* across the floor.

"Oops," Dallas whispered. All the kids turned to look at him. The teacher was already focused on him. For Mrs. Stewart it was hard to look away, despite the fact that one of her quieter students had shoved fear aside to stand in front of his classmates and talk about his deceased father.

Cassie giggled and let Dallas twine his fingers through hers. If the classroom had been a high school, Mrs. Stewart would have separated the two with a shake of her head and a low *cluck-cluck-cluck*. Thankfully, Ry didn't notice. If he had, he would have pumped a fist in the air and cheered, anyway. There was light and happiness in their home when things were good between Dallas and his mom. When Dallas was actually around, which was happening more and more often these days, the house was downright glowing with fireworks and a golden-hued white light.

"Lately, some people have been thinking maybe my dad was reckless and that he made a decision that cost him and nine other firefighters their lives. Nobody really knows what happened but let me tell you what I learned. The wind shifted and they got caught. It sucks because I miss my dad every day but sometimes I feel like he is close to me and that really helps."

Dallas switched arms. He used his left hand to hold Cassie's and lifted his right arm to wrap around her shoulders. She was swiping at a tear now, but it was more from pride for her son's brave move than it was sadness anymore. Strangely enough, it was Deborah who inspired the bold 'show and tell' in the first place. Glancing around to the perimeter of the room, which was lined with reporters and bloggers, Cassie smiled warmly and caught Ry's eye.

"It starts at home," Deborah had told them. "Get control of the media so they don't control you. Take action, be first if you can, but if you can't be first, put the thing in reverse and act like you were."

Ry sent his mom a rainbow smile before he inhaled deeply and continued. "What you really need to know about my dad is that he was a lot of fun. He made everyone around him laugh, especially my mom and me. I don't have a lot of memories of my dad because I was only two when he passed away, but what I do remember is laughing. A lot."

Dallas bent his head to Cassie and closed his eyes. He'd learned from the get-go that Eddie would be a tough act to follow but somehow, today, it was okay. Being included in this very personal telling was like exchanging a scarred white flag of truce for a big ole welcome mat.

Setting down his dad's photo, upright on its small stand so everyone could look into Eddie's eyes and see how bright and happy they were, Ry reached for the second. This one was more ceremonial—it was the one from their living room. In it, Ry's dad was formally dressed.

"The other thing about my dad is that he really believed in service. Not just at work, but at home and in his neighborhood too. He did a lot of extra things for people, like shovel their driveways and mow their lawns. But mostly he did a lot for my mom and me. My mom says he took real good care of us."

Cassie sniffled but held her head up high. Caroline and Des were on her right. Caroline gave her a little squeeze around the shoulders, over Dallas' comforting arm. Des straightened proudly.

"The other thing my mom says is that my dad really knew what it meant to play." Ry looked surprised when the adults in the room tittered, but it wasn't a judgmental laugh. It was more of a 'we're in this with you' kind of laugh. Clearing his throat, Ry continued. "He knew that it was important to really live your life the best way you can, meaning have fun when you can because, I guess, he understood that life can be short." He looked at his mom. "I guess because he knew that sometimes firefighters can die. So he made sure he always had fun even when, mom says, sometimes it was hard to keep up with him."

Setting the photo down next to its mate so everyone could see the different facets of his dad at work, Ry grabbed a third. A family picture. The classroom went still as he struggled to talk about the family he barely recalled. He lost the struggle and appealed to his mom for help, but Cassie, and Caroline next to her, were both fighting their own battles to stay composed.

Des eyed Dallas. Both men were well accustomed to being on the public stage, but Des knew this moment belonged to Dallas. Dallas was astute and gracious enough to wait until Des gave him a nod before he kissed Cassie lightly on the top of her head and rose to stride up the short aisle to Ry.

At the front of the classroom, he took the picture from Ry and held it up high as shutters clicked furiously around the sides of the small room.

"This is a family," Dallas started, raising an arm and laying it around Ry's shoulders. "This is love. This is the most precious thing a man can have. Not money, not wealth, not fame." He paused when Ry's skinny arms went around his waist. The boy buried his face in Dallas' side. "And certainly not some kind of battle-won glory. This is what is most important about Eddie. He was a man who knew what he had—a beautiful woman," Dallas sent love on some invisible draft direct from his heart to Cassie's, who forced a final tear away and sent him love right back, "and an amazing kid." He grinned down at Ry and widened his smile for Caroline and Des in the back. "And I think he had a pretty awesome sister-in-law and brother-in-law too."

"My dad and Aunt Caroline argued a lot, Mom said," Ry offered, raising his head from Dal's leather jacket. A wholesome laugh filled the room. Caroline groaned and swatted her sister playfully.

Dallas' laugh was infectious. Propping up the family photo next to the others, he hugged Ry with a generous, authentic love. "You can say what you want about Eddie. Make your own speculations. But I gotta tell you. Ultimately he was a father and a husband, a good father and a good husband, from what I hear. And that makes him a hero to me."

"And to me," Ry whispered hopefully, his eyes wide, beaming up at the man who made his mom smile again.

Dallas caught Cassie's eyes. His laughter eased off into a gentle kind of warmth. Silently he pictured another woman, one who surprised him in the end by putting his needs ahead of her own. *Thank you, Deborah,* he murmured to himself. *Thank you for loving me enough to give me this.*

In Honolulu, wearing white on a sun-kissed beach, Deborah was marrying Dallas' friend Cole while the 'show and tell' was happening in Nova Scotia. Her gaze landed on an endless ocean and the kind of constant waves that suggested life was bigger than she understood. Raising her face to the sun as the gentle breeze sent a misty salt spray onto the beach, a wave of peace and genuine love passed through her spirit.

She turned to Cole, smiled when she thought of Dallas feeling a similar healing vibe in last summer's Prince Edward Island paradise, and whispered, "I do."

Chapter Twenty-six

Cassie bent to her ankle and adjusted her shoe. At the same time she cursed under her breath, but straightened and planted a smile on her lips when a graying board member sauntered past with his designer-clad wife on his arm.

In simple dark heels just a pinch too new, an inky black hip-hugging leather skirt, and a tailored white blouse unbuttoned at the top to reveal a lacy white camisole underneath, Cassie was rushing around her theater's lobby helping the front-of-house manager seat a wheelchair patron and his companion while Dallas and Ry stepped into the semi-darkness of the venue itself and found their seats with the aid of a volunteer. Momentarily Cassie joined them, dropping into a seat next to Ry with a relieved and audible exhale. She was unable to hide the quick blush that sparkled across her cheeks at the sight of Dallas next to her son. The country singer was taking this night seriously, it appeared, which Cassie found sweetly humbling. He'd skipped the usual casual leather jacket and jeans and was, for this little theater anyway, rather formally attired in a dark suit, complete with shiny square-toed shoes. Ry was dressed in similar fashion. Both had ties fastened at the necks, which was plainly obvious since both were tugging at the suffocating knots.

With a mischievous glint, Cassie leaned behind Ry to speak to Dallas. "This isn't Carnegie Hall." She gave his tie a pull. "But just so you know, you're absolutely precious. Both of you."

Her eyes telegraphed a promising postscript that Dallas read to mean *can't wait to undo that tie and put it to use.* Lifting her fingers now, he kissed them, held them against his cheek, and simply radiated joy.

Between them, Ry was bouncing. His school 'show and tell' had won the day for all of them and, especially, for his father. Press was now citing Eddie as a family man who craved adventure rather than a reckless man with a death wish.

Cassie was happy too. Besides the sheer joy of having Dallas at her side, the imperious Marla was now working in a dark basement office marketing the city's electric utility. Work for Cassie was now, for the most part, a peaceful, happy place.

The theater went to half-light. Thirty seconds later the lights were completely off, soaking the patrons in a comfortable darkness. The curtain rose with a light *shufffftt*.

"You sure you're ready for this?" Cassie whispered across Ry to Dallas.

He was twisting the symphony's program around and around in his fingers, looking more nervous than Cassie thought he ought to be, given that he was well accustomed to concert settings and formal events.

"Sure," he responded, rifling long fingers through his lengthening hair. "Baroque, right? I was singing this stuff when I was a kid on the ranch."

"While you rode broncs and wrassled snakes with your bare hands, right?"

"Poisonous ones. When I was six." He winked at Ry, who covered his face and groaned.

Cassie took Ry's hand just as the first strains of a violin brought them to their senses about a half second before a full-on giggling fit would have overtaken all three. A few minutes into the first piece, which floated up and around them like feathers on a summer breeze, she looked over at Dallas to find him completely overtaken by the music. Misty-eyed, his lips were parted; it was hard to tell if he was even breathing.

I knew you'd love it, Cassie thought, gazing in awe at the strong jaw, close-shaved for tonight, and the gentle peace and love—combined with a strange case of nerves, apparently, which she wondered about—exuding from his strong body.

He disappeared at intermission, though. Literally. Just after she asked him what he thought of the symphony, Dallas excused himself to take a leak. Before he left Cassie and Ry, he winked at Ry and nervously brushed his lips against Cassie's cheek. "See you in a bit," he murmured before wheeling around on his shiny dress shoes and striding away.

Narrowing her eyes at him, Cassie looked down at her son when she felt small fingers take hers. "He seem nervous to you?" she asked Ry.

Ry was bouncing. He shook his head. "Nope. He's fine, Mom. Dal likes the symphony."

"Good." Ruffling his layered hair with her free hand, Cassie added, "Because I'll never be a country fan, so at least we have half the battle beat."

"So you'll never come to my shows?" Ry was so serious that Cassie had to stammer out a well-intended response.

"Um, well, of course, Ry. But there's a whole world of music out there. You don't have to play country just because Dal does. Look at him here tonight, he's expanding his musical horizons."

"You ever think you need to expand your musical horizons, Mom?"

Cassie was at a loss for words. Finally she gave him a quick peck on the cheek and said, "How'd you get so wise, Ry?"

Ten minutes later she was starting to worry when everyone was back in his or her seat and Ry was tugging at her fingers. Dallas wasn't in sight.

"Do you think he left?" she asked Caroline, who had appeared at her side with two glasses of Pinot Grigio during intermission.

"Of course not. Maybe he ate something bad and he's stuck in the bathroom. He'll be along when he's ready."

"C'mon, Mom. They'll be starting."

True enough, the house manager was nervously eyeing Cassie.

"Go ahead," Cassie sighed to her anxious employee. "Start the second half." To Caroline she muttered, "I guess I was too hasty in thinking a country redneck would have any appreciation for real music."

Behind her back, Caroline and Ry high-fived.

Inside, back in their seats, a low hum started in the theater when an announcer from Halifax's country music station strode onto the stage in cowboy boots and a cowboy hat. A microphone in his hand, he waved happily at the surprised crowd.

Cassie almost bolted, but Ry grabbed her wrist and held fast. "Wait, Mom," he demanded, his eyes dazzling in the soft light bleeding onto them from center stage. "Just wait."

Behind the unexpected emcee, all of the symphony instrumentalists were seated. Cassie couldn't help but note that they were more animated than usual, and were sending secret smiles across to each other. Even the more sedate violinists were vibrating, it seemed.

With a repeated downward motion of his palm and a happy, "How are y'all tonight?" the country station emcee settled the buzz that had started with his out-of-the-blue arrival on stage.

The house quieted to wait in nervous anticipation; the few rustles that gave away the more impatient by-the-book patrons quickly receded when the guy spoke again.

"As a favor to my good friend, the symphony's conductor, Maestro Carmen, I was asked to introduce the next musical selection to all of you." Like a cresting wave, the audience's shared curiosity rumbled and faded out. The guy in the cowboy hat continued. "A friend of mine has a point he wants to make to a friend of his. Inspired by heavy metal band Metallica's regular gig with the San Francisco symphony, my buddy has something to say. With music. About music. Please welcome to the stage country superstar Dallas White."

Cassie gasped. "He's hijacking the concert?" Ry slipped his hand down to her fingers and squeezed them so hard she had to pull her hand away to readjust their shared grip. "What's this about, Ry?" she demanded, apprehensive and anxious as she watched Dallas, still in his formal attire but partially covered by his usual Gibson guitar, take the stage with a wry grin and flushed cheeks. "Huh. So that's why he was nervous. Caroline know about this?" Almost frantic, she darted a glance around the theater, bewildered at the amusement she spied on the faces of most—but not all—of the symphony regulars.

"Ssshhhh, Mom! Be quiet and listen!" Yanking his hand out of her grip, Ry stretched himself up higher so he could better see his friend on stage.

"Sneaky little buggers," Cassie mumbled, smiling now, her gaze locked on the sexy man she planned to lecture later in her moonlit bedroom. Using his tie to make a point, perhaps.

The usually refined audience was roaring now, at least a few of the ladies were, revealing their familiarity with the country music scene as well as perhaps clearly communicating their versatile tastes in music—or maybe even their true musical preferences.

Dallas lifted nervous fingers to his unusually smooth jaw, blushed openly (and adorably, Cassie thought, pinking up) at some of the whistles filling the theater, settled into a chair in between the flutes and violinists, and grinned happily at a stage tech who adjusted his vocal and guitar mics.

He nodded at the conductor, who raised his baton, paused, and lowered it with poise, dignity and grace.

The musicians came to life. Cassie would have groaned and ducked her head, but from the very first note she was completely transfixed. There in the middle of her beloved symphony orchestra was her country singer man, cozied up to the flutists, playing a love ballad with a purist country flare, and nesting it comfortably into the full wide range of classical instruments. He tapped a foot lightly against the stage floor as he played; closing his eyes, Dallas lost himself in the music. Cassie saw him smile from someplace deep within as the music took hold. Somehow she intuitively knew that this concert was as much for him as it was for her. He was making a point, no doubt about that, but her singer-man was also reconnecting with his music—his soul—the same way he was bringing her fully and completely into his circle.

Into his heart.

"Oh God, I love that man," Cassie whispered to Ry, who couldn't make out exactly what she said, but who knew by the deeply seated awe in his mother's eyes that she was desperately in love with their summer sandcastle mate.

When the ballad reached its height and the violins floated off into perfect, sweet oblivion, Cassie wept. She closed her eyes, but only for a moment. Never was a piece of music so spiritual, so soulful, so perfect, than at that moment, performed by a symphony, but anchored by a man.

Dallas stood when it was over, although it took him a minute to gather his senses first. The entitled, almost aristocratic audience rose, their discerning tastes and stereotypical views of country music thrown quite aptly by the wayside, into the backs of their classy Audis and polished Beamers.

He took a bow before he spoke, maneuvering his guitar via its strap to his back as he moved. When his voice emerged, husky and emotional, Dallas' words were for everyone, but directed at Cassie.

"I get that you may not like my style of music, but it's the only way I know how to express myself sonically. I grew up on a working ranch to the sounds of country music on the radio in my home. It's a link to my mom and dad—my dad's thing was bluegrass, my mom's was Conway Twitty and Loretta Lynn. I rebelled and cut my teeth on different kinds of classics—The Beatles, The Stones, ACDC, Metallica. I normally don't admit this, but as a kid I even liked the Backstreet Boys."

The audience tittered. Most were 'all in' by this point, although the grayer set had no clue who the Backstreet Boys were.

"After a while," Dallas continued, "after, like, twenty years of playing on some of the world's biggest stages, I stopped caring. My tunes became business. And so my lyrics and music became formula, devoid of personal meaning for me. They were just songs designed to sell."

He took a look around the stage, at the musicians seated around and behind him. Waving an arm he said, "These people live and breathe music for the sake of music. I know it's a job for them, for you," he added directly to them, "but I also know you love what you do. At least I hope you still do. I became a pawn in a very big game and I have to tell you, it got to the point where I was so disconnected from myself, from my soul, that I got lost. And I got lonely."

Picking out Cassie and Ry in the semi-dark theater, he smiled. "Until one day I met a gal who very succinctly told me that country music had no heart. She may have said it in different words, but the meaning was clear. What I realized was that she wasn't hearing the music, I mean *really* hearing the music. But then again…what I was playing, and what I know some other artists are still playing, was music meant to sell. It wasn't always music from the heart. So maybe there wasn't much to hear, at least not in my tunes. Tonight was about finding that again, that heart. The soul that music is meant to convey in the first place. And I don't think it's something that you can box or classify or segregate. I think many people are not stuck on one genre or style, even though they have their preferences based on life experiences or whatever. I think music should be played for the sake of pure enjoyment, disregarding a labeling of genre, to reveal emotions, or truths, whatever. I think music is universal. Genre-less. I think we proved that tonight."

"Encore!" someone in the audience yelled. Cassie laughed quietly and shook her head in wonder. She recognized Caroline's voice and wondered what the sophisticates who voted for Des thought of Caroline now.

The audience took up the chant. And soon Dallas played them one more tune, a song about building sandcastles on the beach and about recognizing the work it takes to build relationships on solid foundations. He even had a line about slushies made up of different colors that, he explained when he introduced the song, represented the plethora of emotions that come with new love.

At home later in Cassie's big bed after a particularly exhilarating lovemaking session, he held her close and murmured in her ear, "You were impressed. I know you were."

"You didn't say trucks and tailgates once," she rallied back. "And I didn't hear beer or whiskey either. Or daisy dukes. That impressed me. But I'm still waiting for blue-tick hound."

"Doing what?" he asked, wrinkling his eyebrows.

"Whatever it wants," she giggled.

"How about those strings?" Leaning forward, he playfully nipped the end of her nose with his teeth.

"Magical," she agreed, placing a soft kiss on the lips from whence the touching lyrics had emerged that evening.

"Magical indeed," he said, following the pronouncement up with the heavy emotion the night wrought, voiced in three powerful, tender words, "I love you."

"I know you do." She was almost arrogant in her knowing, in a playful, pride-filled sort of way.

"You do, right? You trust me now."

Touching a fingertip to his lips and running it down over his chin, she whispered, "I've always trusted you, Dallas. I think I was just scared to admit it to myself at first."

"I think the biggest thing we learned this past while was that we have to trust ourselves, Cassie." Dallas sobered. "Our souls. I know that, at least for me, I wasn't fully accepting who I really am. And that closed the door for me when it came to letting someone else in. I didn't fully accept myself until you accepted me."

"I accepted a hobo on the beach." Laughing, she swatted his hand away when he groaned and tickled her. "A travelling minstrel, then," she teased between cries of "Stoppp tickling meee!"

"No," he admonished, tossing an eye roll in for good measure. "You accepted a musician. Period. And a man."

"A sweet man," she smiled into his chest when he finally stopped torturing her. "The man I love." Letting her gaze drift back up to meet his eyes, she added, "And I had to accept who I am."

"A woman who loved and lost," he sighed.

"No," she breathed, her soft jade eyes liquid in the pale moonlight. "I mean, that's a part of me, but no. First and foremost I am a woman who is a mother and," she blossomed into a sad smile, "a woman capable of loving a man again. How blessed am I? To experience such deep love twice?"

"How blessed am I?" Dallas whispered. Pulling her close, he tenderly wiped back a loose strand of the golden hair he'd come to cherish. "Two for the price of one."

Down the hall, Ry was sound asleep with his father watching over him. Happy and content, Eddie was peering out from a picture frame, from a time not really all that long ago in the greater scheme of things.

On the opposite nightstand stood a photo taken over the summer of another man who loved Ry and Cassie, who watched over them now with steadfast love and an easygoing, contented warmth. The three of them were in the photo; standing prominently in front of their tanned bodies was a newly built sandcastle, formed with the patient fingers of a man who thought he was lost, a woman who was hiding from loss, and a child who needed to be found.

Chapter Twenty-seven

The next summer

*C*FCY 95.1 was on low volume in Cassie's Montana when her ears perked up. Maren Morris' tune *My Church* had Cassie tapping a foot and singing, much to Ry's embarrassment. He ducked into the living room and closed the accordion door separating the kitchen from his Castle Beach bedroom as, outside, truck wheels crunching on gravel slowed outside the camper, which was parked in its usual spot overlooking the pristine, sparkly Darnley Basin.

Under an immense perfect night summer sky dotted with hopeful pinpricks of light, Cassie stepped outside to meet Dallas. Folding her petite frame into his warm embrace, she giggled when they both sighed at the same time. Looking up at him, she treated him to a playful smile and said, "Some show. Who needs the gym? Just go to a country music festival and dance your calories away. I had three coolers and one beer. Phil sent us home with your driver. He's grudgingly having someone drive my truck home tomorrow."

"Good thing," Dal grinned, leaning forward to brush his lips against her forehead. "Did Ry like it?"

"Are you kidding? The kid's one of you. But he growled at my singing. Apparently I'm not very musical."

Dallas chuckled. "I'm just impressed that you know my lyrics. Was he okay, then?"

"Every word," she laughed before addressing his query. "He was more than okay. Phil had us seated in the special viewing area. We almost had our own private section. Although," she winked and smacked her lips, "we did sneak out for pizza and those deep-fried cookie things. Let me just say yum."

"And the show?" He smiled expectantly as she led him to an outdoor cooler and reached in for a beer. Taking the can from her, Dallas flipped the tab back before taking a long pull and offering it back to Cassie.

To his raised eyebrows and happy smirk, she slurped it up in a rather non-ladylike way. "Well, I've learned that country music, contrary to popular belief by those who do not cherish it the way we do," she emphasized the *we*, "is not about the fishing, the hunting, or the beer…it's mostly about living a simple life and," she added, "it's about cherishing the ordinary moments that make up that life. Even the sad ones— moments, I mean." She sobered. "Dallas, at one point I looked around and the audience was completely bathed in light. I've never seen so many happy people in one place at one time."

"As long as that includes you, baby," he said in his deep 'God I love this woman' voice.

"It did. It included me. Dal…can I ask you something?"

"Ask away, sweetheart."

"Is it still lonely up there? On those big stages? Is it still business to you?"

"The thing about the business side of what I do," he answered honestly as they eased down onto a chaise together so they could watch the stars twinkle magic into their hearts, "is that eventually I get to be off work and snuggle up with you. So the answer to your question is yes, sometimes it's still lonely, but I like my music better these days and that helps. The concerts you come to help. The seedy side is still there, Cas. It's not going away. But the good stuff eclipses the bad. I'm very grateful for what the universe has gifted me."

"Abundance."

"Abundance in love. The rest I don't care so much about. Phil just about shot me when I started my Foundation."

"Buying musical instruments for schools is a valuable gift, Dallas. You're planting some very special seeds in many kids' hearts." Snuggling up against his chest, Cassie sighed and closed her eyes. The contentment was almost overwhelming. Simply loving him, and being loved by him, was humbling.

"Don't you mean I'm giving them a good place to hide?" Dallas' voice was quiet as he contemplated that simple truth. He'd done it many times—hidden behind his music. Since forever, really.

Cassie's small voice tickled his chest as she spoke. "I think maybe that's not such a bad thing," she answered. "Nobody's life is perfect. Sometimes we all need to do a little hiding."

"Until someone comes along and helps us move forward again, huh Cassie?" Tipping back the can, Dallas let the smooth beer slide down his throat. It tasted about as perfect as beer ever got, out here under the stars with Cassie in his arms, and Ry safe and happy in the Montana behind them.

"Thank God," she retorted. He handed the can to her. "I'd still be buried in dreamland if it weren't for you. Um, Dallas?"

"And I'd be camping my way around the world feeling sorry for myself." The beer came back to him, and he finished it off with two great gulps followed by a satisfied burp. "What, Cas?"

She elbowed him. "Redneck. Thanks for that. Tomorrow's supposed to be a nice day. What do you say we build ourselves a sandcastle?"

"Can I wear my Jays cap?"

A hearty laugh echoed over the Darnley Basin. "Everyone knows you're here now, Dallas."

"Yep, I know," he acknowledged. "But I've learned that they won't bother me."

"You might have to sign a few autographs."

"Not tomorrow. The rest of the rednecks on Prince Edward Island this week will be in Cavendish drooling over Blake Shelton."

"You'll be safe, then," she agreed. "I'll build the church."

"I'll do the walls."

"Ry can decorate the moat."

"I'll make us a village store."

"I'm not sure castles had village stores, Dal."

"This one will. It's ours. It can be whatever we want it to be, sweet girl."

Loving the sound of that, Cassie nuzzled her nose deeper into his chest. "Um, Dal?"

"Mmmm?"

"How about we don't build a castle this time. How about we build something else?"

"Like what?"

She shrugged. "I don't know. Maybe a...cat. Or a dog like that one we saw last summer. A puppy."

"Out of sand?" Trying to picture that, and form the implications of how to build a puppy out of sand in his mind, Dallas wrinkled his eyebrows together. The effect was breathtakingly adorable.

"Sure." Reaching up to turn his face toward her, Cassie glowed and brushed her lips over his mouth. "We've already got the perfect castle. Ummm..."

"And?" Smiling, Dallas leaned his forehead against hers. "I sense an 'and.'"

"I say we start filling it up. I'm not getting any younger here."

Dallas couldn't answer. He had the cutest expression, all joyous and happy. In the glow of a perfect moon his eyes were misty-bright, and his life, complete.

Cassie snuggled deeper into him and the two fell asleep to the low hum of country music wafting sweetly from the Montana's radio out of an open window behind them.

Chapter Twenty-eight

Six weeks later, a small boy's hands angled sand out of a compression at the base of a sand sculpture. "Like this," he said to his mother, who crouched next to him and peered closely at his gentle movements. "You need to just move the sand away so you can give it some definition, the guy said."

"Definition, huh? Like this?" Cassie started moving sand away from the base of their creation.

Ry sat back. "Yep. That's it." He wiped guitar-string callused fingers on his damp swim trunks and looked up at Dallas who, on the other side of Cassie, was forming a flipper out of sand. "It's perfect," Ry announced to the small crowd of fans standing around watching the three build their third sand sculpture in as many days.

Unfolding his knees and rising, Dallas nodded in agreement. He raised his hand and Ry high-fived it. Cassie stood, too, and wrapped an arm around her man's waist, which was comfortably hot from the sun and somewhat salty in texture from his earlier swim.

"How come there are two baby sea turtles?" Ry asked, crinkling his nose as he glanced down at a mom and dad sea turtle, and two smaller ones flipping along behind. "I thought it was supposed to be us. Our family."

Cassie reached for him and pulled him close. A gold wedding band on her left hand caught the sun and glistened in its warmth. "It *is* our family," she said in a voice that Ry knew to take seriously. It meant she was telling him something important.

He took a quick step back and looked at her. By the time his gaze shifted to a nervous Dallas, who was shuffling his feet and grinning like a school-boy, Ry caught on.

"It is us?" he asked Dallas, unsure.

Dallas pulled Cassie to him and opened up an arm so Ry could climb under. They would go to the store to get slushies and ice cream later. And this time when Ry filled up his slushie cup with a bit of this and a bit of that—lime, strawberry, orange, grape—the old sadness in his eyes would be replaced with sheer joy.

Music is like that, Dallas thought. *It's every color, all mixed in to make its own special flavor.*

Life is this, Cassie thought. *Ordinary moments made special by allowing yourself to really live them. In every way.*

Ry smiled. "It's perfect," he said, voicing what all three of them were thinking. "It's just perfect."

Climbing in under Dallas' raised arm and wrapping his own boy-sized arm around his mother, Ry closed his eyes, inhaled slowly, and started to hum a happy tune.

The end.

Thank you!

If you liked this book, please take a few moments to leave a review on Amazon or Goodreads, and consider sharing your thoughts on social media. Self-published authors like myself count on your support to help us continue our writing journeys!

Have a wonderful day ☺

Susan

Join the *Drifters* family by signing up at **www.susanrodgersauthor.com**. As a welcome gift, I'll send you a free bonus/deleted chapter from book one of the *Drifters* series, *A Song For Josh*. Happy reading!

www.susanrodgersauthor.com

Facebook: search **Susan Rodgers, Writer** and **StillTheWatermovie**

Twitter: **@srbluemountain**

Instagram: **SusanDrifters**

Pinterest: **Susan Rodgers**

email: **fatcat@pei.sympatico.ca**

About the Author

Susan Rodgers' first novel *A Certain Kind of Freedom* was a Finalist in the Writers' Federation of Nova Scotia Atlantic Writing Awards for unpublished manuscripts. Her short story from the novel of the same name, published in two anthologies, has received rave reviews, as have the Drifters novels, Susan's all-time favourite books to write.

Owner/Operator of Bluemountain Entertainment, Susan is a 'Diploma With Honours' graduate of Vancouver Film School. She produces mostly documentary style client films and short dramas with plans to one day shoot a Feature Drama based on the novel Atlantic Blue.

Formerly a Museum Curator, in winter Susan lives with her partner Steve and her striped cat Oliver (Lucy Maud Montgomery once said the only good cat is a striped cat) in Summerside, Prince Edward Island, Canada. In summer, she hides in a small trailer in Darnley, P.E.I., where she writes novels, paddles kayaks, and crafts sandcastles on the beach. She makes frequent trips to Vancouver to visit her son Christopher, where she enjoys life in the hippie city while listening to great music and sipping on good espresso.

Books by Susan Rodgers

Dallas White series:

Castles In The Sand

Drifters series:

A Song For Josh

Promises

No Greater Love

Riptide

Whispers of Home

And Then There Was Silence

Let the Music Cry

If I Could Sing You Home

After the Rain

Into the Blue

A Sacred Peace

Watch Over Me

The Light In Me

When The West Wind Moves

Listen To The River

Feature Screenplays:

The Story of Jack & Emma

Still the Water

Beautiful Jane

They Were Dreamers (adapted)

Short Stories:

S12

A Certain Kind of Freedom

A Gentle Peace

www.ingramcontent.com/pod-product-compliance
Lightning Source LLC
Chambersburg PA
CBHW060605030726
47498CB00005B/1546